THE SPAWN OF SPIRACY

THE
SPAWN OF
SPIRACY

JESSE NOLAN BAILEY

THE SPAWN OF SPIRACY

Copyright © 2021 by Jesse Nolan Bailey

Printed in the United States of America

First Printing, 2021

ISBN: 978-1-7343616-7-4

For more information, visit:
www.jessenolanbailey.com

THE FIVE
TRIBES

SASSERE

EKREWAI

Osho Island

Destruum
Settlement

HELDRETKA

Editshi
Temple

The Sachem's
Fortress

Twister
Coven

IRAULI

Vekuuy
City

VEKUUY

2021

THE STORY THUS FAR

As accounted in Book 1, *The Jealousy of Jalice*

As a child, **Jalice** and her friends discovered something sinister in the forest—a massive structure of black metal nestled at the bottom of a giant crater. The children dubbed it the **Black House**, and Jalice was brave enough to enter it. Inside, she stumbled across a monstrous creature that was trapped in a cage.

It called itself Dardajah.

The creature asked her to free it from its bondage. In exchange, it would give her whatever she most desired. Unbeknownst to Jalice, the creature was a **dokojin**—a malicious entity from the astral **Apparition Realm**.

After witnessing her very own brother, **Kerothan**, bestow a kiss upon the boy she'd intended to court, Jalice took the dokojin up on its offer. She wanted the unchallenged affection of this boy, **Hydrim**. Jealousy over the kiss she'd witnessed had blinded her.

A deal was struck. The dokojin gave Jalice a poison to give to Hydrim, which would manipulate the boy's mind such that he'd become obsessed only with Jalice. In return for its help, the dokojin demanded permission to enter Hydrim's body so it could leave the Black House caging it.

Too naive and selfish to realize that this deal would cost her everything, Jalice agreed.

Dardajah entered Hydrim's poisoned body, and thus began a new era of chaos and violence. With an unhealthy obsession over Jalice and with a dokojin possessing him, Hydrim declared himself the **Sachem** of the Unified Tribes. His tribe, the **Ikaul**, enslaved their neighbors, the **Vekuuv**. Jalice permitted these atrocities to occur and lived a lavish life as the Sachem's chieftess.

***

Decades passed. Finally, two women of the enslaved Vekuuv decided that this wickedness could not go unpunished. **Annilasia** (Jalice's childhood friend) and **Delilee** (Jalice's cousin, appointed decoy, and friend) hatched a plan to end the Sachem's reign. One night, Annilasia kidnapped Jalice and whisked her away from the Sachem's Fortress. Meanwhile, Delilee remained behind to pose as the chieftess by means of a lethal potion that made her appear identical to Jalice.

The goal: spy on the Sachem and find out what purpose the mysterious **Decayer device** served.

It was a risky plan, but Annilasia trusted that Delilee would discover something they could use to overthrow the Sachem. As she dragged Jalice away from Hydrim, she slowly came to realize that Jalice didn't remember anything about the Black House. The chieftess didn't even comprehend the atrocities her husband had committed against their own tribe, the Vekuuv.

Annilasia couldn't let this go. She needed Jalice to remember, and convinced herself that perhaps Jalice's hidden memories of the Black House might offer clues to taking down the Sachem. This hunch would pay off, but not without a steep price. She made a bargain with an **aethertwister**—those who use glass wands to wield the astral energy known as aether—in order to gain access to Jalice's memories. The method of access: a drug-based journey from the physical Realm into the Apparition Realm.

But this intrusive method proved destructive. Though Jalice began to regain her memories, she was assailed by an endless stream of flashbacks that splintered her sense of reality. If not treated, this ailment would eventually drive her mad and kill her.

Desperate to return Jalice to health and get answers about the Black House, Annilasia consulted with a **mirajin**—an ethereal entity native to the Apparition Realm. The mirajin, **Elothel**, relayed that Jalice must return to the Black House, as her most vital memories were tied to that place. Only there could the mirajin alleviate Jalice's suffering. So, with the begrudging help of a wilderman, **Mygo**, and his chymist companion, Vowt, Annilasia escorted Jalice to the mysterious Black House.

Along the way, Annilasia caught the unfortunate attention of her own dokojin—a cruel and malicious entity called **Inzerious**. Slowly, this parasitic entity ate away at Annilasia's sanity, even marring her skin with wounds that scarred over time. As if this wasn't enough to deal with, the journey to the Black House meant braving a forest infested with **flayers**—chimeric beasts of unknown origin—that proved difficult to slay.

Meanwhile, at the Sachem's Fortress, Delilee played her part as the stand-in chieftess. Although she failed to procure information on the Decayer device, she was present when the Sachem proclaimed his plan to reunite the aether Realms with the physical world, which would only bring more chaos and violence. Soon after this announcement, she was kidnapped by a rebellious tribe known as the Vekaul—an amalgam of individuals from the Ikaul and Vekuuv tribes bent on resisting the Sachem. Their leaders, Geshar and Yetu, tasked Delilee with locating the Stone of Elation that they believed the Sachem had hidden within the Fortress. They feared that the Sachem planned to use the Stone to meld the Realms, a plan they vowed to stop.

Feeling as if she had no choice lest her cover be destroyed by these unpredictable rebels, Delilee agreed. She found the Stone, but before she could make off with it, the Sachem caught her in the act. Her identity as an imposter provoked the Sachem's fury, which ended with Delilee fatally disfigured. Desperate to locate Jalice, Hydrim translated to the Apparition Realm in order to search Delilee's mind and, in the process, obliterated her memories. This rash decision left him far too vulnerable. Dardajah, the dokojin inside him, took this opportunity to hijack control.

Dardajah finally had what it wanted: control over a physical body.

But the dokojin feared its plans were compromised. It feared that somehow Jalice knew of the Decayer device and its capabilities, and that she had left to go and destroy it. After tracking her down, it discovered she was headed to the Black House. There, it met her in its projected, translated form with the intention of ending her.

It was this confrontation that finally moved Jalice to accept responsibility for the pain and violence she'd seeded the world with. She recognized that jealousy had driven her to make a selfish decision that had turned Hydrim into a monster that enslaved her tribe.

This internal confession was not enough to banish Dardajah though. The dokojin taunted her, spewing vile claims. It alleged that Jalice's brother, Kerothan, had died years ago by the hands of Hydrim. It informed her of Delilee's demise too—of how her cousin had failed as an imposter and died for such treason. These assertions were too much for Jalice. Had the mirajin, Elothel, not come to her rescue, she would have succumbed to the torture of this souldrain.

Having banished Dardajah—and therefore Hydrim—through a portal vortex, Elothel reunited Jalice with the others. It was then that Jalice confronted Annilasia about Delilee's death and made clear that she blamed Annilasia and her schemes for Delilee's fate. Convinced that Jalice would no longer aid in overthrowing the Sachem, Annilasia departed, still secretly harboring the dokojin parasite, Inzerious.

Jalice nearly gave in to despair, overwhelmed by guilt and shame over her childhood decisions regarding Hydrim and Dardajah. Elothel, however, offered her some hopeful news.

Her brother, Kerothan, may yet be alive. Not only this, but there was a chance that Hydrim could be saved from his fate with the dokojin. But this could only be accomplished by addressing the three ailments plaguing the Sachem:

The *disease* of the mind that kept Hydrim obsessed with Jalice.

The *curse* that was created when Jalice made a deal with Dardajah, thereby giving the dokojin claim over Hydrim's body.

And finally, the *possession* itself. Only a powerful amount of aether could force the dokojin out of Hydrim now.

Difficult though it would be, Jalice clutched at this hope of saving Hydrim. Taking Elothel's claims to heart, she knew that this quest must start with her finding her brother.

His forgiveness might just break the curse.

CHAPTER 1

The Geibor Trench carved the earth like a giant bite mark. A mile or so deep, and concealed amid the miasma of thick fog that engulfed the land preceding it, the abrupt plunge often surprised unsuspecting travelers—perished souls whose bodies would never be found. The jagged cliffs of obsidian rock offered no mercy, shredding the bodies of its victims as they plummeted to their deaths. Those foolish enough to roam the area, either by some ill fate of local residency or stationed there by higher authority, heard all too often the unnerving cries of sheer terror that would swiftly silence as quickly as they'd struck the air.

For miles, the only way to traverse this devouring pit was a lone stone bridge that stretched across the mile-wide gap. Yet this promise of safe passage mocked those who wished to use it. Just as the Trench had been forged by the wands of aethertwisters during the time of the Purge, the bridge too had been raised by their glass wands. Furthermore, those who had created it were the same who controlled its passage. Commissioned by the Sachem as a means of containing the Delirium, the Trench marked the border between Ikaul and its neighboring territory, Heidretka. From the day of its construction onward, the Ikaul had controlled who came and went between the two tribes—and very few were deemed worthy of doing so.

Jalice, when faced with the daunting task of crossing into Heidretka, had known the bridge was an impossible option. Too many Ikaul warriors had crowded the mouth of its arches. Other measures had needed to be taken, the result of which now had her traversing the plunge and trekking across the Trench's depths.

Jalice's gaze traveled skyward, following the length of the bridge's pillars. Far above them, the faint outline of the bridge's underside peeked through the fog. Risking only a brief glance, she looked back down at the ground to ensure her footing. The floor of the Trench rippled with an endless maze of desiccation cracks. Interspersing this terrain were formations akin to stalagmites that promised to impale any clumsy soul with poor footing.

The crunch of boots and shoes against the obsidian dirt marked the only interruption to an otherwise tense silence. Though accompanied by others, Jalice hadn't uttered a word since they'd started the climb down the cliffside. Neither had anyone else, as instructed by their guide. Noise beckoned unwanted attention. If they were caught, their chances of survival thinned—illegal passage into Heidretka was grounds for execution by decree of the Sachem—and they already faced disheartening odds.

Behind her, Elothel kept a close proximity. More than once, the mirajin had offered a steadying touch as Jalice maneuvered the uneven and upraised terrain. If she happened to lose balance and fall back, fae was certain to catch her. Faer only condition to this arrangement was a careful distance from their other companions.

Several strides ahead, these other members moved between the rocks and crevices with a steadier confidence. The pair of fraternal twins kept close to each other. Both brother and sister wore matching attire, outfitted with ponchos of geometric patterns and dully colored undergarments. Skin ink betrayed their Ikaul origins. Elothel had offered up a theory that they were aethertwisters attempting to infiltrate Heidretka, thus the mirajin's demand for distance from the pair.

Leading the strange group was a Heidretka native, clearly signified by the dozens of metal ring and stone piercings decorating his face. Introduced as Elishmael, the man of olive complexion had spoken mostly in affirming or rebutting grunts unless the conversation demanded otherwise. As payment for the guide's help, Jalice had hefted over quite a bit of coin—accumulated when she'd sold her entire feather collection to an Ikaul trader—but had been unable to secure passage without conflicting company such as the twins. It'd been an even greater shock when Elishmael had thrust counterfeit wands upon her and Elothel and suggested they play the part; no one but twisters attempted to leave Ikaul these days. Elishmael had explained in blunt terms what the twins would do to them if they suspected Jalice and Elothel weren't fellow twisters. The forgery wands were incredibly rudimentary though, and if the twins got too curious, the ruse would quickly collapse.

As had been the case during their previous travels together, Elothel remained bundled in layers upon layers of tunics, scarves, and a large cloak that wrapped around the entirety of the tangle of clothes. A pair of goggles, complete with reflective lenses of black glass, obscured the mirajin's eyes. From head to toe, fae left no exposure of skin.

In a similar, if less excessive, fashion, Jalice wore a comfortable assortment of undergarments overlaid by a single, overhead tailcoat of grey linen. Maroon thread laced the coat's seams, while the inside was insulated with wool. A charcoal head scarf wrapped over her head, concealing her ginger hair and most of her face. Her oceanic eyes peered out from the obscurative headpiece. Upon her disappearance from the Ikaul Fortress months ago, the Sachem had ordered his warriors to hunt her down and bring her home. Though the Sachem was now missing—after Elothel banished him through a portal vortex—his orders would stand. She couldn't afford to flaunt her identity in the open, and the frigid temperatures of Wither Season provided ample excuse to hide under endless layers of clothing.

Her eyes trailed past the others and into the fog. The journey across the Trench so far had offered no clue as to how close they'd managed to come to the other side. A wave of relief washed over her when she saw a giant wall coalesce in the fog not far ahead. By some miracle of Sahruum, they'd reached the opposite cliffside without incident.

As if to threaten this, a boulder rocketed down from farther up the slope. The group grew still. The boulder struck the ground, the sound echoing around them. Jalice held her breath. Silence ensued. Or was it silent? She couldn't tell over the blood pounding in her head. Her gaze darted between the others and the cliffside, watching for any signs of movement.

Sahruum, keep us hidden. Keep us safe.

A constrained sigh left her when Elishmael eventually broke his rigid posture and motioned at them to resume their trek. His steps, however, betrayed a heightened sense of caution. The twins seemed more alert as well. Jalice shivered when they both unveiled their glass wands from under their capote capes.

It took a second to hit her. The wands. If the twins had them out, it'd look strange if she and Elothel didn't. She turned and pushed a hand into the folds of her tunic. Her fingers wrapped around the forgery and she yanked it out into the open air. She caught Elothel's attention and gestured with the wand. The mirajin groaned but followed her lead and withdrew faer own. Jalice turned forward again and looked to see if the twins had noticed their moment of oversight. Fortunately, the pair appeared more focused on a potential ambush ahead than on Jalice or Elothel.

No other interruptions occurred during the approach to the cliffside. Upon arriving, Elishmael turned to face the group.

"Welcome to the glorious territory of Heidretka," he said dryly. "We're nearly finished with our joyous caravan, but don't let your guard down. This border is highly patrolled by my kin. They don't like outsiders coming into their land these days any more than the Ikaul do. Many of my trips have ended with everyone but me dead."

"Seems suspicious. How come only you survive?" the male twin asked darkly, his raspy voice indicative of a smoking habit.

"There are reasons, aetherbator," Elishmael sneered. "But trust me, those reasons won't work for you. Keep your wands in your pockets and your mouths sewn shut. If we come across anyone, you're escaped Vekuuv slaves, got it?"

Jalice's throat tightened as she thought through the new ramifications of their ruse. If she and Elothel continued to handle forgery wands, and they were for some reason cornered by Heidretka, they'd be falsely implicated as twisters. Yet if she and Elothel ditched the wands, and the twins noticed, it wouldn't end much better.

She glanced at Elothel, but within earshot and in clear view of the others, the two were unable to discuss a plan. The mirajin hadn't spoken since their arrival at the Trench. With a unique voice of masculine and feminine synthesis, speaking at all within mixed company would certainly betray faer identity.

As such, Jalice had done all of the negotiating with Elishmael. "Lucky for us, we don't have to climb all the way up," said their guide. "There's a cave about two-thirds of the way up with a more gradual incline to the surface." After exchanging a look of disdain at having to stow their wands, the twins scrambled after Elishmael, who had already initiated the climb up the cliffside. Jalice counted it as a blessing that she wouldn't have to worry about the twins and their wands for a time.

The fog persisted as they ascended, again obscuring their forward progress. Oddly, this helped Jalice stave off the certain panic that vertigo would have induced. For all her brain could figure, the ground lay only a few feet below the limits of her vision rather than the true span of a fatal plunge should her fingers or feet slip.

Her shoulders burned with veins of fire while sweat threatened to loosen her grip. Exhaustion from days of travel over unforgiving terrain pulsed in every muscle. After a while, her arms trembled with the urge to slacken.

Don't you let go. You've come too far to die from a clumsy fall.

No sooner had she scolded herself than a strong, firm grip hauled her up. She yelped, unprepared for the sudden shift in weight and sensation. The grip released her, and she collapsed onto flat ground. Behind her, the guide assisted Elothel with the same wordless yank, and the mirajin came to rest beside her. Jalice looked up to survey the dark cavern that Elishmael had dragged her into.

"Not going to lie, I thought for sure you two would fall before we made it up," Elishmael muttered as he stood over them. He shook his head when Jalice stared up at him blankly, and turned to the twins, who stood a few feet off facing the cave's darkness. "This is where we part ways. The cave forks quite a bit. Just keep to the right till you're up top."

"You're not coming with us?" Jalice gasped. Her breath soaked into the folds of her headscarf. The air up here was thin, and her lungs were struggling to acclimate.

"I stay alive because I don't linger," Elishmael grunted. "And I don't stay where I'm not wanted." He took a step past Jalice, who shot her hand out to grasp his leg. The man froze and glowered down at her.

"You can't leave us with them," Jalice whispered. Her gaze flickered to the twins, then back to Elishmael.

The man stared at her without a hint of empathy. Offering no words of comfort, he moved away with heavy strides, freeing himself from her hold. Jalice watched over her shoulder as Elishmael sank to the ground before crawling down the lip of the cave's entrance. He disappeared over the edge.

Jalice turned forward again to watch the twisters. She tensed. The male twin scowled at her with stark blue eyes that evoked in Jalice the sensation of being submersed in a lake of ice. Trapped, with no way to breathe.

"Shall we go, Tishir?" the male twin spoke. His words were clipped as if he despised breaking the air with such inconsequential questions as the one he'd uttered.

His sister didn't turn or indicate acknowledgement. She continued to stare into the cave, her back to the others. The slightest tensing of her limbs alerted Jalice to the attack. Tishir screamed, but this sound broke off abruptly. A sudden and horrific combustion blew the twister apart as if she were a delicate bubble cursed with an inevitable burst.

The woman's flesh and innards splattered the ground with a violent smack. Before Jalice could react, Tishir's brother drove his arms through the air in quick strokes. A halo of aether rippled from the tip of his retrieved wand, but the energy itself proved impossible to glimpse. Invisible to the eye, aether could only be seen in terms of its effects on the world around it. Dirt swirled in the air, roused by an unexpected wind, and several cave columns ruptured with loud cracks.

A shout echoed farther in the cave.

Jalice shielded her eyes from the dirt cloud just as Elothel's hands gripped her. The mirajin dragged her a few feet away from the unfolding chaos.

"Get behind those cave formations!" fae shouted. "Don't let—"

The words vanished within the deafening shriek of the other twister. A loud pop ended the male twin's cry of agony, followed by the same brief sound of heavy rain striking the earth. Jalice turned in an attempt to witness the man's fate, but a sharp whistle pierced the air and pain burst through her abdomen.

Her entire body tensed. Jalice sank to her knees before crudely collapsing fully to the ground. More shouting erupted, but for some reason, it was muffled. She reached with shaking hands towards the source of her pain. Her fingers ran along a thin reed protruding from her stomach.

Not a reed. An arrow.

She whimpered and craned her neck forward to glimpse the arrow jutting through the folds of her tunic. A large stain of blood was fanning out from the puncture wound. Jalice let out a choked wail as her head sank back. She stared up at the cave ceiling, not truly seeing it. The pain commanded her focus.

A veiled face came into view. Jalice gasped and clutched at Elothel's garb, but the mirajin pressed her arms down and shushed her. Black spectacles reflected Jalice's pathetically strained expression back at her.

Stars, I can't even handle an arrow, and we've only begun this journey.

"Don't move," Elothel stated. Still crouched by her side, fae turned to face the cave's tunnel and stretched faer arms across the ground. With unfathomable speed, Elothel brought faer arms up through the air towards each other while faer fingers twitched with precise movements.

Due to the pain, Jalice wasn't certain if the arc of shimmering orbs around Elothel—vague and translucent in texture—were real. She squinted as her body clenched against a spasm that rolled out from the wound. She thought she witnessed Elothel tracing a finger across the orbs. A wave of the same translucent energy burst from the formation. As quickly as they had appeared, the orbs vanished.

Elothel crawled back to her. "I've set up a shield. Their arrows can't reach us now."

The words blurred together and sank in her ears. Rather swiftly, the black film of the cave's surface melded with a new darkness that subverted all thought and sense of being.

The pain, the noise, the fear—all bled away.

CHAPTER 2

The torpor lifted slowly. Jalice peeled open her eyes, blinking against hues of yellow and orange. A strange crackling noise filled the air. She attempted to move but immediately froze after a sharp wince. Pain webbed across her abdomen and chest.

"You shouldn't move," a firm voice said in a harsh tone. "You'll reopen the wound."

Jalice's vision focused. The glob of yellow colors fleshed out into flames on a torch, and this in turn explained the source of the strange crackling sound. She eyed the enclosed area around her—a small chamber that was vacant save for a sole rug, the cot on which she lay, and a weathered cabinet. A chair in the corner hosted the only other figure in the room.

The stranger's tone and build, as well as their stiff posture, suggested a masculine identity. Tan leather armor fit across the chest and arms, while clay-colored cloth decorated his shoulders like a shortened capote. The same color traveled to his bunched-up trousers, which dove into a set of dark boots. Very little of his face showed where he peered out from a headscarf designed to cover the sides and front portions of the head. A cut-out section on top permitted a nest of brown feathers, angled backwards, to crop out from his scalp. It gave him the appearance of a nighthawk watching her as if she were prey. A sheathed sword hung at his waist.

This was a warrior sitting before her. But with no exposed skin to rove, Jalice was left to worry over which tribe he hailed from.

"Who are you?" she wheezed. A sharp inhale followed. She hadn't expected the stab of pain in her lower chest when speaking. She managed to force a few additional words out. "Where am I?"

The stranger eyed her silently for a long moment. Eager to escape his study, she looked down towards her stomach. Blankets swaddled her legs, but only a tan bandeau served to cover her upper torso. Farther down, bandages wrapped tightly around her abdomen. She saw no blood, but the pain confirmed some sort of injury. That seemed familiar, but she couldn't be sure.

"You're lucky," the man finally said. His voice carried a weight to it, not quite heavy with age or ailment, but with brooding. If she were to guess, she'd peg him as middle-aged, like herself. "My archers don't typically miss—and we don't typically take prisoners. That arrow was meant for your heart."

Jalice balked. "Prisoner?" She winced again and snapped her mouth shut as her thoughts slipped about like eels. "Why can't I think right?"

The man dodged her question and responded with his own. "Why did you cross the border?"

Jalice grasped clumsily at her own words. "I . . . We were . . ."

"Why were you traveling with aethertwisters?"

"I'm not . . ." She inhaled deeply. "I'm not a twister."

"Obviously. Otherwise that arrowhead would have sent your innards across that cave like it did the others."

Jalice squinted at the man. "Who . . . are you?"

"You traveled with a mirajin. What is your relation to faem?"

Jalice gasped, the reaction earning her another pang of pain. She unclenched the muscles in her chest. "Where is Elothel? Did you harm faem?"

"Answer me!"

Jalice startled at the man's stern command and stared with wide eyes back at him.

"I am obliged to allow you nothing," the man stated. "You have trespassed into a land that is not your own. A land that does not want you. You will answer my questions, and I suggest you do so without preamble or incessant questioning of your own. The decision over your fate depends on your responses."

Jalice swallowed. "I seek refuge in Heidretka. Nothing more."

"You claim innocent passage into a land that borders the Unified Tribes?"

Jalice glared in response to his sarcastic tone. "I bear no insidious threat to this land or its people."

"And yet you fail to supply proof of your proclaimed innocence."

Jalice tensed. "These days only a fool would claim unquestionable innocence."

Silence. Discerning eyes studied her. This time, she did not look away.

"As I said, we don't normally take prisoners," said the man. The dead are not subjected to my questions. Perhaps you wish to join that tradition."

Jalice swallowed and licked her lips. Her mouth opened, and the words came slowly. "I came here looking for someone. I mean them no harm. In fact, I came to seek their . . . forgiveness." She faltered over the last word.

"A dangerous risk for such a bland reason," the man grumbled. "You cross illegally into a land to assuage your guilt?" The man stood and squared his shoulders. His eyes bore down on her. "I guarantee that whoever it is you seek would rather you keep it."

Jalice gaped at him. Anger replaced caution. "You have no idea who I am. How dare you make snap judgments against someone whom you injured without apology?"

A grated chuckle passed through the scarf. "I know exactly who you are, Jalice, Tecalica of the Unified Tribes." He spat out her name and title with obvious contempt.

Jalice stiffened, and her stomach clenched in a painful knot. He knew her somehow. Perhaps it was the red hair, perhaps he knew her face; regardless, she didn't have the energy to deny her identity. She closed her eyes as nausea overtook her.

"By declaration of the Council of Clanheads, you are hereby a prisoner of the Heidretka tribe," he stated. "As Tecalica of the Unified Tribes, you will face trial for your crimes against the land, against the people, and against Sahruum."

Her eyes snapped open and fell on the man again. This she couldn't ignore, and the words sobered her for a brief, vivid moment. "A . . . trial?"

The man continued on without sympathy for her disorientation. "You are to be taken to the Teftiki Valley for the trial. It's been decided, though, that the journey will wait until you're healed enough to travel." He turned towards the door to leave.

"You accuse me of crimes and declare me a prisoner," said Jalice. "But you don't have the honor to reveal who you are."

"As I said," the man growled, "I owe you nothing." As if that concluded all discussion and debate, he exited the room, slamming the door on his way out.

CHAPTER 3

Kerothan swore under his breath. Heat boiled his blood despite the frigid cold prevailing through the corridor. His eyes caught briefly on the two men standing against the wall opposite the door he'd just slammed. He saw the questions in their eyes, the concern etched across their faces, but he ignored all this. His boots thudded on the stone floor as he marched down the corridor.

Part of him hoped they wouldn't follow. Another part of him wished they would.

Or at least he wished Ophim would.

Kerothan listened for their footsteps. But as he turned the corner into another hallway, no sound came to indicate either of them had bothered to rush after him. A pang of disappointment pinched him, quickly swallowed by the wave of fury that had spurred his retreat.

It was her. He'd spoken to a ghost. Yet there she'd lain, as petulant and delusional as he remembered her.

Jalice. His sister.

The name skulked about in his head, teasing at a flood of memories barely held at bay. He allowed his anger to burn away this threat. He didn't have to dwell on buried memories today any more than he had in recent years. Nothing about her return changed his life. He was still Kerothan of the Begalia Clan. Still a warrior of the glass sword. Still safe, and no longer a lost, orphaned child.

But the fact of her presence still burrowed beneath his skin. By the time he reached his quarters and heard the click of the bolt as he locked his door from outside intrusion, the lie he'd been trying to tell himself had shattered.

This changes everything. My damn sister is here, all the way from Vekuuv and with a mirajin at that.

Kerothan tore off the headscarf and feather cap, unveiling his signature red hair and an array of metallic rings embedded in his facial skin. He flung the headgear to the ground, removed his belt and sword, and began pacing the room. Adrenaline urged him to take action, to do something—anything—to remedy the circumstances. He wanted her gone. He never wanted to see her impish face again. He wanted her thrown into a dungeon cell and left there to rot.

But he couldn't do that. Higher powers would decide her fate. So, with no way to channel his distress, he paced, and paced some more. Tears swelled in his eyes, and he came to a halt.

What in dying stars has got you emotional?

Yet the tears persisted, making him stiffen. He knew if he lifted his hands to banish them, they'd fall. If he blinked, they'd fall. Any acknowledgment would end in a torrent of emotion, now held back only by his wavering resolve. His hands trembled. He could barely see. Flashes of memory erupted in his mind. Harsh scenes, disconnected and sporadic.

His mother and father shrieking as flames engulfed them.

Hydrim towering over him where he cowered on the ground, waiting for the death blow.

Jalice ignoring him with blatant disregard as, bruised and bloody, he begged her to flee with him and away from the Sachem.

Kerothan's hands clenched while his every muscle quivered. The tears had yet to fall. He wouldn't cry.

A knock at the door broke his focus. He inhaled a shaky breath before clearing his throat.

"Go away," he shouted, though he was grateful for the distraction. Tears no longer crowded his eyes.

The knock came again, light and tentative.

Ophim.

He strode over to the door and lifted his hand to the bolt, then hesitated. His hands hovered over the lock.

"It's me," came Ophim's muffled voice when Kerothan still hadn't answered.

If he let Ophim in, it would mean talking about Jalice. Ophim would think him vulnerable and weak. That wasn't something he wanted.

But wouldn't not *answering look just as weak?*

Kerothan swallowed, straightened his shoulders, and unbolted the door. He opened it enough to glimpse Ophim's thick frame, then retreated back into the room before the other man could see his face. He feared his eyes might yet betray him, still glossy and tinged red at the edges.

He heard Ophim enter—the man's impressive bulk made stealth impossible—followed by the click of the door shutting again. Kerothan waited for his guest to speak first.

"You left rather quickly."

The voice carried a gentleness that some thought strange from a man armored with iron muscles and a bull's frame. To Kerothan, it suited the man, whose heart seemed proportioned to his physique. Kerothan didn't answer, hearing the unspoken question in those words. *Are you alright?*

How was he to answer that?

"Does she know now?" the larger man pressed.

Kerothan kept his back to Ophim and moved to the nearby dresser that boasted a half-filled bottle of brandy. He went to pour the drink.

"I don't think that's a good idea."

Kerothan huffed and broke his silence. "If there were ever a time to drink, it's now."

"You don't drink," Ophim pointed out softly, and his boots scuffed the floorboards as he slowly made his way over to Kerothan. He drew up beside him, gentling the cup out of Kerothan's hand.

Kerothan stared down at the brandy, unable to meet Ophim's gaze. He wouldn't let him see the pain coursing beneath his skin. He didn't move away though. This closeness with Ophim seemed to be quelling his turmoil.

Perhaps Ophim would reach out with his hand to comfort Kerothan. Would it be too much to wish that? Kerothan convinced himself that a friendly embrace would be enough to banish the pain and fear. If anyone could do that for him, it was the man standing at his side.

As if reading his thoughts, Ophim brought a hand to Kerothan's shoulder, fingers flexing ever so slightly in a gesture of care. He used the grip to push Kerothan to face him.

"You should talk about what you're feeling," Ophim said, voice low and tender. "I sense a great deal of turmoil from you, and you shouldn't keep that pent up."

Kerothan averted his gaze and glanced absently out at the room. Ophim's voice alone chipped at his stubborn resolve, and the hand on his shoulder threatened to crumble Kerothan's fake stoicism. "There's nothing to speak of," he grumbled.

Ophim's grip gently pressed him towards the bed. *Towards the bed.* To what lengths might Ophim go to comfort him?

"Sit. At the very least, tell me what was said between you two." Ophim pulled up the sole chair in the room, faced it towards the bed at Kerothan, and sat down in it.

Kerothan inhaled, closed his eyes, and sighed. He pushed away the disappointment of Ophim's lost touch on his shoulder. "There's not much to tell."

"Does she know who you are?"

Kerothan shook his head. "I don't think so."

"And you're sure it's her?"

Kerothan snorted. "Unfortunately, yes."

Ophim leaned forward. "And what did you say to her? Why is she here?" As Kerothan beheld Ophim, he wondered if the wood holding the man would buckle. Ophim filled out the chair and no doubt challenged its sturdiness. A set of timber-thick legs squeezed past the confines of the side armrests, and his torso strained as if locked in a tiny cage. Even still, Ophim sank back into the chair with an easy confidence, a calm that rendered others like Kerothan envious. The world seemed to favor Ophim, perhaps in reward for the gentle spirit he offered to counteract his intimidating bulk.

"It doesn't matter why she's here. She's an enemy. She's the wife of the Sachem for shite's sake. That archer should have aimed higher and ended her on the spot." Kerothan heard the callous tone in his own remark and suppressed a flinch at what Ophim would make of it. He lowered his head in preparation for a rebuke that never came.

"Maybe she's running away from him," said Ophim. "She came without warriors after all and with a mirajin instead. That'd be rather strange for someone acting with ill will."

"Maybe she kidnapped the mirajin. Maybe this mirajin isn't on our side."

"I don't think that's the case," Ophim stated, unfazed by Kerothan's outlandish theories. "Did she say nothing that revealed her motives for crossing the Trench?"

In his silence, Kerothan felt Ophim's eyes on him and finally lifted his head to stare back. As expected, he was met with an intense wave of empathy pouring from the other man's gaze, but Kerothan deflected this emotion. Ophim wouldn't see him shed a single tear.

As the light from the window poured over Ophim and reflected off the bald dome of his head, Kerothan studied his face. Tiny metal rings lined the side hidden from the light's touch. Still, the golden hue of the metal glowed against Ophim's tan skin. A prominent choker, bossed with amber studs, clung to his neck, but Kerothan tried not to concentrate on this piece of jewelry and the connotations that surrounded it lest he succumb to further envy. Already he found himself in his typical pattern of wishing he could be like Ophim. If the world bent to Kerothan's will as it bowed before Ophim, then life wouldn't be nearly as difficult. Instead, Kerothan had to wrestle and conquer to have a chance at life's pleasures.

"Maybe she's come to finish what she started," Kerothan muttered. "To ruin my life even more until she's satisfied with my despair." He meant these words, and when pity swelled in Ophim's eyes, Kerothan turned away. "Don't look at me like that."

Ophim sighed. "Forget your shame. You weren't expecting to see your long-forgotten sister at your doorstep, and your past with her hasn't miraculously vanished into the void. You keep pushing that pain down, it'll eat you alive. In the end, if you're lucky, you'll only be hurting yourself, but more likely, you'll also end up hurting those around you when those emotions boil to the point of eruption."

Kerothan knew he meant well. But Ophim knew nothing about which he spoke. Jalice had taken everything, *everything* Kerothan had held dear, and tossed it away. He'd nearly died because of her. So many *had* died in the wake of her delirious decision to betray her tribe, her parents.

Him. Her own star-blazing brother.

He'd worked hard to callous the bleeding wounds of his heart, and now they threatened to blister once more. The despondency as he'd fled his homeland, uncertain if he would ever see it again. The fear of whether he was sick with the Delirium like his parents. And then the awful realization that came later, when the Heidretka had proven to him that the Delirium was all a ruse—that the mind sickness had been caused by the Sachem when he'd altered the locations and vibrations of the Stones of Elation that resided in Vekuuv and Ikaul. This alteration had radicalized the minds of the Ikaul while poisoning the minds of the Vekuuv. It had all been a ploy for power, and so many of Kerothan's kin had died because of it.

Unaware of his inner plight, Ophim continued. "Perhaps it is the fate of Sahruum that she has traveled so far and happened to cross while you were stationed here—"

Kerothan exploded to his feet, facing Ophim full on. "By dying stars it's fate! Sahruum has smoked a field of hopper's weed if this is supposed to be fate. And if it is, she's *fated* to execution."

"You still mean to take her east? To the Teftiki Valley?"

"By every aching bone in this body, I am," Kerothan snapped. He saw the shock in Ophim's expression and jabbed a finger in the air at him. "Don't pretend to know what should be done with her."

Ophim's face hardened, his eyes fit to melt Kerothan's still pointing finger. "And are you as certain of how I'm to be treated?"

The reprimand wormed its way past Kerothan's fury, and his head and arm dropped in shame. The tears finally fell, and he choked down a sob. He heard Ophim spring up from the chair and rush over to him. The same strong hand as before gently pressed into his shoulder. A light pressure there forced him to face Ophim, who this time brought him into a tight embrace. Still, Kerothan struggled against his emotions. He inhaled sharply, pressing down the sobs that ripped through his chest, and moved out of the embrace. This wasn't how he wanted to be with Ophim. Not like this. He blinked furiously to clear his eyes. It was impossible to hide the tears that had fallen, but he was determined not to release any others.

His eyes shifted to Ophim's face. The embrace may have ended, but the other man still sat close to him. Kerothan smelled the leather of his armor mixed with the tang of a laborious day's sweat. In the moment of a breath, he took in the details of Ophim's face—the curve of his cheeks, the groomed stubble of a beard framing his round face, and a set of earth-tinted eyes that boasted a paradoxically tender strength.

A reluctant hope lifted in Ophim's eyes, and for one heart-pounding moment, Kerothan almost dipped his face in to press their lips together. A second longer, and he would have done it.

But whatever daydream Ophim had spoken with his eyes vanished in the next instant. He stood up quickly from the bed to put a few steps between them. Clearly flustered, he searched for somewhere else to land his eyes and cleared his throat. "I'm sorry."

Heat broke out over Kerothan's face, and he grunted. "I know not what you refer to."

"I shouldn't have . . ." Ophim trailed off, collecting his thoughts. "I only meant to offer genuine comfort. Or, by which I mean, no more comfort than would be"—he coughed—"comfortable."

Kerothan held his tongue. To deny further would only be offensive to Ophim. They both knew what that brief moment had held—a temptation of spectacular betrayal, given their positions. "I wish things could be different," he said quietly. He lifted his eyes to Ophim, wishing he wasn't the source of the regret swimming in the man's eyes.

"They could be," Ophim whispered, as if speaking such a thing might be a betrayal in and of itself. "But you've told me what your choice was before."

Kerothan heard the subtext in that statement, one that questioned if things might now be different. A war waged inside of him, and he almost blurted out that he had indeed changed his mind. That things *were* different, and that the lost connection of moments earlier could now be traced in full. But silence haunted his tongue. He knew nothing had changed. The conditions he'd need to agree to for such wild fantasies were beyond his willingness.

The door opened, and Ophim turned towards it. Kerothan paled.

Cephus stood in the doorframe, eyes flitting between the two men. The immediate suspicion in his eyes evolved to a knowing confirmation. Something else crossed his face—perhaps jealousy, though the older man hid his emotions well.

Kerothan fought off an instinctive disdain. Cephus had an uncanny ability to appear out of nowhere anytime Kerothan and Ophim found a private moment. Yet for all his frustrations with the older man, Kerothan couldn't blame him. Not without being a hypocrite at least. Cephus and Ophim were joined together in something akin to marriage. *Lebonds*, as the Heidretka tribe called it. *Husbands*, or at least that was the closest translation and definition.

Ophim cleared his throat, voice pitching with suppressed shame as he spoke. "Is something the matter?"

Cephus continued to eye them with a look that reminded Kerothan of an owl. His unruly white hair didn't help the matter, what with its stubborn tufts sprouting like an unkempt nest. Nor did the neck-length beard that evoked a sense of eclipsed age. A foot or so taller than either Kerothan or Ophim, and quite thin when standing near Ophim, Cephus observed them with eyes that sat high in the air, much like a bird perched in the trees.

"We've been summoned to council," said Cephus. "Suit up. I've been told we leave after."

Kerothan's curiosity piqued. "Have we found the twister camp at last?"

Cephus regarded him with a guarded look. "Something has been discovered, yes. But the details remain unshared. I'm sure this council will reveal more. Let's not waste time."

Ophim was already striding towards the door, and Kerothan watched him with the hope he'd be granted one final glance. No such fortune came. Instead, Ophim watched Cephus as he passed, probably panged by remorse or guilt, before sliding past the door and out of sight.

Kerothan moved his stare to Cephus, unwilling to let the older man intimidate him. Like Ophim and Kerothan, a line of metal rings ran down the side of Cephus's face. But it was the metal choker around his neck, identical to Ophim's, that taunted Kerothan. He wished he could tear it off his clanhead's neck and put it on himself. He fantasized for a moment about what he and Ophim would be if only he wore the lebond choker rather than Cephus.

"You aren't required to respond to this summoning," Cephus stated. "Your circumstances are highly unusual, and thus excuse you from your normal duties."

Kerothan squinted. "By whose command does this come? I didn't ask to be pitied."

Cephus lifted his chin. "As your clanhead, this decision is mine. No need to get defensive. Additionally, the matter of your sister requires further deliberation, which the other clanheads intend to discuss with you in my absence."

Kerothan turned away to gather up his belt and sword. "Tarnished stars. That traitor being pampered in the lower halls isn't my sister. My family is all dead."

"Regardless of how you perceive your blood kin, your connection to her isn't something we can ignore."

Kerothan clipped his belt on, adjusting his tunic underneath it. "I'm not staying behind. Not if it's got anything to do with the twisters. We'll need every sword."

When he looked up, Cephus offered an apathetic shrug that indicated he no longer cared to press the issue. The two crossed through the Temple's halls without further exchange, though Kerothan's mind churned. His thoughts tumbled—one moment fussing over Jalice's presence while in the next replaying his moment with Ophim.

He wondered how much Cephus had heard outside the door. Part of him hoped his clanhead had heard everything; let him know exactly what had passed between his own lebond and Kerothan. Another part of Kerothan wanted that affection to remain a secret—an intimate and private delicacy of which Cephus could enjoy not a crumb. Regardless, as he marched in step with his clanhead, Kerothan grew more and more frustrated at Cephus's silence on the matter, as if the older man was confident nothing of substance would ever occur there. Perhaps more enraging was the strong possibility that nothing ever *would* occur between Ophim and Kerothan.

Which, if he was being honest, was his own star-blazing fault.

CHAPTER 4

Giant glass windows lined the towering walls of the Editshi Temple's meditation chamber. In days long gone, the elongated space served as a gathering place for masses of templites dedicated to translating to the aether Realms. Now, an emptiness pervaded the Temple, rendering the chamber silent and haunting. As Kerothan passed through the double doors that led inside, he was struck by how forsaken the Temple had truly become. Those who now resided within its elegance were mostly warriors; only a few templites remained. With the threat of invasion from the Unified Tribes, the previous tenants had fled farther east to safer environs.

Daylight poured in through the amber windows, illuminating the cluster of armed warriors in a warm yellow. The light glimmered off the golden and silver jewelry decorating the clannites, mostly metal rings embedded in the skin, some of which were connected with chains of similar composition. A few stragglers in the crowd stood out against this Heidretka warrior majority—Ikaul defects, denoted by their body ink, and a few liberated Vekuuv with aggressive designs painted across their skin.

At the center of the crowd's circle stood the other clanheads, and with Cephus's arrival, all twelve were now present. An opening formed to permit Kerothan and Cephus access to these renowned leaders. Clanhead Tesritt gave the pair a respectful nod before performing her assigned ritual on Cephus while Kerothan waited his turn. When Tesritt gave a dismissive nod to Cephus, he went to join the line of other clanheads. In his absence, Kerothan stepped forward, extended his hand, and recited the familiar motto for the ritual.

"All the sons, all the daughters, all those born as neither, join in Sahruum's domain."

Tesritt took his hand and pricked it with a silvery needle. A glob of blood formed on his finger.

"May the waste never claim you," said Tesritt, and she nodded just as she had with Cephus.

Kerothan turned and went to join the crowd now that he'd passed the test. Had he been a twister, the needle would have ended him in a spray of exploded flesh and blood. This method had earned its place in Heidretka as a sure way to prove one's allegiance, at least so far as not being an aethertwister. As such, everyone carried a needle for this purpose, and if someone doubted another's identity, they'd prick them for good measure. The ritual performed by Tesritt was more a formality in these mass gatherings, but more than once, it had proven essential in cleaning out infiltrators. Twisters lurked everywhere, and the Heidretka couldn't be too careful.

Kerothan made sure to stay at the front of the crowd's inner circle. If the clanheads intended to protest his inclusion on this new quest, he wanted to be able to step forward quickly and make his case.

Damn Jalice to Dardajah's maw. She will not have me left out of this.

He found Ophim standing in the inner circle as well and came up beside him. If any emotion remained from the earlier exchange, it no longer showed on Ophim's face. He nodded stoically to Kerothan before returning his attention to the clanheads.

The low murmur of the warriors died when a weathered voice from the center spoke. Attention turned to Clanhead Orithmor, the eldest of the clanheads. Thin, stringy white hair sprouted from his head, and he boasted a long, grey beard that spiraled down to his upper chest. Wrinkles beset his face, and he eyed the crowd from a set of squinted eyes. Unlike the other clanheads, who wore leather armor and tightly fitted clothes, he donned a brown cloak of heavy material to keep his frail body warm. His days of travel and adventure were far behind him, and he remained here at the Temple during raids and skirmishes. When he spoke, his voice dipped at times, as if it couldn't quite bear the weight of words anymore.

"We are on borrowed time, and we can't afford to waste it with preambles. If you haven't heard already, there has been a discovery near the northern caverns, a few miles from here and past our blockade. Scouts reported twister sightings this morning." Orithmor paused and pursed his lips while he gave a quick glance towards his fellow clanheads. A strange look crossed his face, as if he hesitated to utter his next words. "One of the scouts reported something quite disturbing inside the caverns. The twisters gather at the site of active forbidden tech."

Alarmed murmurs erupted, and the crowd stirred. Kerothan shared a confused look with Ophim before they returned their attention to Orithmor, who raised his hands to quiet the clannite warriors.

"We don't know what it does or where it came from," said Orithmor. "Those answers will come in time. For now, we know that the twisters have utilized it in some manner and that they must be stopped."

"Could it be what's causing the Endless Sleep?" someone called out from the crowd.

Murmurs rose to life again. Orithmor's eyes narrowed even more, and he pursed his lips as he let his audience settle into silence once more. "There is no proof of that, but anything is possible," he said. "The sickness that has befallen our brethren could certainly be traced to these filthy twisters, and to this device."

"Perhaps one of the templites should go on your raid."

Everyone fell silent at the unexpected voice, and a path split through the warriors to make way for the newcomer. Kerothan spotted the Temple's priestess, Rejiett, gliding towards the clanheads. Her face remained hidden beneath a generous hood of silk. Her unblemished white cloak trailed behind her, fluttering as if caught in a nonexistent wind. She stopped in front of the clanheads and beheld them a moment before speaking again. Her voice lifted like a dove taking flight.

"It is only fitting that those more familiar with the ancient artifacts be the ones to examine this device."

Clanhead Tesritt stepped forward, needle at the ready, and waited for Rejiett to present her hand. The two stood in silence for a moment, and a growing tension gripped Kerothan's chest. Surely Rejiett wasn't refusing the needle? This crowd would find a way to burst her open, twister or not.

"Is that really necessary?" Rejiett asked in a mirthful tone teetering towards mockery. "I've proven myself on numerous occasions."

"And on those occasions, you were not a twister," said Orithmor. "Anyone can become a twister at any point in their lives. We are the only ones who stand between the free tribes and the evil that threatens to overtake them. We cannot afford to be infested with that same evil within our own ranks."

Rejiett laughed, no longer hiding her unspoken ridicule. "You are a paranoid group, aren't you? Fine, then." She lifted her hand to Tesritt, who glared at the priestess before looking down at the uncalloused hand offered.

The needle broke skin, and Tesritt's shoulders seemed to sag. Kerothan cringed at the idea that perhaps Tesritt had wanted something more to happen. He watched the clanhead return to her ranks, and though he couldn't see Rejiett's face from where he stood, he could feel the vindication radiating from the priestess and certainly hear it in her voice when she spoke again.

"Now that we have that out of the way, I'll repeat my request. Let one of us templites go with your warriors to the site of this twister base. We can determine the purpose of this ancient technology."

Orithmor shook his head, scowling at her. "It will be unsafe for a templite. Our own warriors will be at dangerously high risk, and they are trained for combat."

"Even so, should we not destroy whatever we find at the twister base?" Cephus interjected. "Our weapons won't need to understand it."

"I advise against that," said Rejiett. "It could be catastrophic to improperly defuse such complex machinery. You could end up causing more harm than whatever damage it is currently inflicting."

"Sounds like you're advising we keep the twister's schemes in play," claimed Tesritt.

Rejiett sighed. "Don't be so brash. Listen to the only person standing here who knows how forbidden machinery functions. Sometimes, it takes a wicked knowledge to stop a wicked thing."

Orithmor continued to eye her warily. "You speak wisdom with a flare of deceit, priestess. Be it far from me to advise in a field not my own, but I daresay that you should spend time cleansing your wisdom of its nefarious threads." His chest rose before he released a heavy exhale. "It would, indeed, be rash to swing swords at a foe of unknown origin. We commit to not razing the site, but you must allow us to secure it before the templites are permitted to examine the device."

Rejiett stood silent for a moment. Kerothan shifted his weight between his feet, wishing the priestess would simply agree with Orithmor and dispel the tension in the air.

"So be it." She turned and glided again through the crowd, who parted quickly for her. She seemed unaffected by the mass of glares directed at her, or perhaps she didn't notice them, hidden as she was within the confines of that unstained hood and with her head bowed.

Upon her exit, the tension slackened some, though the mood of the gathering had soured. Perhaps sensing this, Orithmor dismissed his audience with a final statement. "Time is of the essence. Gather yourselves. Departure will occur within the hour." His instruction sent the clannites into an organized frenzy as they scrambled towards the doors leading out of the chamber. Before Kerothan could follow, Orithmor addressed him. "Kerothan of the Begalia Clan. Your clanheads wish to speak with you."

Irritation shot through Kerothan as he watched his comrades leave. Soon the chamber's frazzled energy dissipated with the last of the clannites. Remaining were the twelve clanheads, their gazes now fixed on him.

"We understand that you've met with the prisoner per our request," said Orithmor.

Kerothan gave a slow nod, reluctant to speak before they absolutely demanded it of him. He didn't want this conversation, and he intended to make them aware of this.

"Is she indeed your sister, Jalice of the Vekuuv?"

Kerothan gave another clipped nod. He saw irritation and confusion edge into the clanheads as his silence persisted.

"Did you confirm her purpose in crossing our borders?"

He sighed, finally forced to speak. "Her motivations remain unclear. She offered some shite excuse of seeking out someone for forgiveness. Nothing she said aligned with her past behavior or her affiliation with the Sachem. It's a charade."

Eyebrows rose, and a few of the clanheads frowned at him. "Your tone indicates you don't deem her trustworthy," said Orithmor.

"I don't see why she should be trusted. She's a traitor. She's condoned the deaths of thousands. Anything she says should be dismissed as fabrication and deceit. More than likely, she's here to infiltrate our ranks, much like the twisters. She's spent years in league with the Sachem."

Orithmor studied him for a moment. "Do you agree, then, with our decision to have her brought to the Teftiki Valley to face trial?"

Kerothan nodded. "She needs to answer for her crimes."

"I sense an impatience in you, Kerothan," Cephus stated.

Heat flooded his face. Kerothan refused to look at his clanhead but said, "I don't wish to hold up my clan from departing on the raid."

Orithmor cocked his head. "Do you think it wise to participate in this raid when, no doubt, your emotions might cloud your judgement in the heat of battle?"

"I have no emotions invested in the traitor," Kerothan stated. His tone had taken on more aggression than he'd intended, and he softened his next words. "Nothing has changed. I've known Jalice to be a traitor for many years now, and her arrival here has confirmed my convictions. Her fate is sealed, and I have a duty to this Temple and this land to keep at bay the evil attempting to breach these borders, blood or not."

Orithmor waited. Kerothan maintained a stern gaze with the clanhead. He couldn't afford to have the clanheads witness any reason to keep him at the Temple like a child while his brethren confronted the twisters. Finally, Orithmor nodded and said, "Be on your way, then. Depart with the others, and bring Sahruum's justice to our enemies. May the waste never claim you."

Kerothan offered only a stiff nod before about-facing to march out of the chamber. A waste of time, but at least it was over. No more trouble with Jalice. She would face judgement miles away, and he didn't care what that would entail. As long as it meant never seeing her again.

Now, time to slay some filthy twisters.

CHAPTER 5

Heat emanated from the walls of the cavern. Sweat poured over Kerothan's forehead, and he wished he'd left his thick wool cloak behind. What comfort it'd offered from the frigid air that assailed him while journeying across the barren terrain of black rock didn't seem worth it now. Torchlight glistened off the film of sweat coating his fellow warriors. It was too late to discard the cloaks now though, and they'd need them again upon resurfacing. His tunic and scarf clung to his skin. He wiped at his forehead. The sweat's salt burned, and he blinked to try to drive it from his eyes.

Stagnant pools of pinkish water pocked the passageway, and the warriors cautiously stepped around these with steady feet. It'd been years since anyone had accidently interacted with the unforgiving liquid, but the warnings of its effects resurfaced with each sighting. The water's acidic properties guaranteed flesh-eating burns and a swift demise.

Kerothan crept through the tunnels, shifting into odd angles to maneuver through the cavern. If the twisters truly were hiding within, they had made no attempt to make the cavern easier to traverse. He heard some of the other warriors grumble as much under their breaths, even voicing concerns that nothing waited for them as they continued to descend.

Perhaps they had the wrong caves. The cavern's eerie quiet lent credence to this possibility. Aside from the scraping of their boots on ground or the occasional scuffle as a warrior slipped on wet stone, the space remained devoid of sound. Over this absence of noise, darkness reigned. For every dozen or so men, a torchbearer had been assigned, offering a few feet of murky vision. Yet Kerothan wondered when the flames would flicker out. The utter darkness of the place seemed wont to swallow the light. If the twisters truly did reside in these depths, it was a wonder that they did so without a clearly lit exit.

Most of the journey forced the warriors into tight formations. More than once Kerothan fought down panic as the walls pressed in around him and his armor scraped rock as he squeezed through. Some of his fellow warriors weren't so calm, and a few actually whimpered when they became lodged in crevices and had to be yanked out by their comrades. Kerothan chalked up his own retained sanity to watching Ophim, who was managing to remain collected and composed.

After hours of this torture, the passage flattened out. As each broke through the tunnel into a vast open space, a collective sigh of relief passed from one warrior to the next. A few murmurs of praise to Sahruum commenced.

Kerothan's hair stood on end. Relief melted into caution. He took one of the torches from another warrior and lifted it to get a sense of their surroundings. His eyes caught on unnatural patterns carved into the walls and ground. He slowly edged forward.

Sigils. Hundreds of sigils.

Kerothan rushed back to the throng of warriors congregating near the tunnel they'd crawled out from. He unsheathed his sword as he approached Cephus. The motion drew the attention of the others, who reacted by quickly glancing about and brandishing their own glass blades. Forged of the same element as that of the twister wands, the blades sparkled in the torchlight.

"We need to get out of here," Kerothan murmured to Cephus. "There are sigils everywhere."

Cephus frowned and peered past him into the open space. "Then that means they were here. We're following the right trail."

"Maybe, but it seems odd," said Kerothan, studying the darkness of the chamber. "Did they leave? Did they know we were coming?"

Cephus took the torch from Kerothan and wandered farther in. He bent to examine some of the markings. Kerothan came up behind him, staring into the darkness that stretched on beyond them. The other warriors pressed forward as well, the torchbearers illuminating more of the chamber.

"None of this implies they've abandoned the caves," Cephus stated. "If anything, it proves they're in here somewhere."

"That's what I'm worried about," Kerothan muttered. "I'm worried they're still here. Waiting."

A few yards off, one of the torchbearers halted and craned his arm into the air to hold the torch higher.

Kerothan gasped. "What in the deep void is that?"

Everyone in the chamber grew still and followed his gaze. At the center of the chamber rose a giant pillar of stone, revealing that the ground they occupied was akin to a moat. The pillar flattened out at the top, several feet above their heads, and on this dais was what looked like a massive metal flower. An orb core was suspended in the air, held up only by a set of metal bars connected to the stone pillar. Sprouting out of the giant orb were cylindrical petals that jutted out in every direction like quills on a porcupine.

"Is that the machinery?" someone asked.

The sweat congregating on Kerothan's skin brought a shiver across him. He looked back at the tunnel that they'd exited. A growing tension snapped inside him. "We need to go," he stated, bestowing upon Cephus an urgent look. "This is a trap."

"We don't know—" Cephus began, but Kerothan cut him off.

"Go back to the tunnel!" Kerothan shouted as he caught Ophim by the arm and attempted to drag him back.

It was too late. There was a grinding sound, and in the dim light, Kerothan saw a webbed gate appear out of the tunnel's ceiling and slowly drive down. He sprinted and dove under it, and Ophim followed suit. Cephus, abandoning his torch, managed to crawl through seconds before the gate plunged into open sockets in the ground. The three were sealed off from their fellow warriors, who were darting about the chamber in a growing panic.

Elsewhere, the sound of similar gates scratched the air as they fell into place. Alarmed shouts erupted. Cephus gripped the metal bars and shook them before trying to push them back up, but either by weight or some sort of locking mechanism, it refused to budge. The other clannites rushed up to them in a chorus of shouts and panicked voices.

"We need to find another way in," Ophim told them. "Someone hand us a torch." Through the open slats, a lit torch was passed to him.

"Look for other ways out," Cephus commanded.

"There were a few other openings, but they're sealed up now," someone shouted back.

"Keep looking for others," said Cephus. "Don't give up. There may be entries higher in the walls. We're going to see if we can find one."

With that, the clanhead pushed past Kerothan and Ophim and led them back the way they'd traveled. The trio scanned every crevice they passed, and finally Ophim spotted one that looked wide enough to try.

As he crawled onto his belly and followed Ophim, Kerothan fought against a mounting sense of panic. The gates left no doubt that a trap had been sprung. He didn't think it likely that this trap ended only with the warriors secured inside a pit. Something far more sinister seemed imminent.

Ahead, Ophim broke free of the shaft and scurried out of the way. Kerothan saw flickers of light beyond him. Hope sparked, and when he poked his head out, he saw the same chamber as before, his fellow clannites' torches scattered at a lower angle below. He wedged himself from the shaft onto a narrow ledge that overlooked the pit trapping his comrades. As he pushed himself up with his hands, he noticed how smooth the ground was here.

Too smooth. Unnaturally so. His eyes scanned past Ophim, who stood beside him, and he noticed the ledge snaked off into the darkness along the cavern wall, while part of it forked off into a bridge that led to the spiked machinery.

As Cephus came out of the tunnel and rose up to stand at Kerothan's side, he shouted down to the clannites to ask for a status on their findings. Below, the warriors were scattered, each trying various methods of escape. Some were attempting to climb the walls, which were worn smooth aside from the sigils engraved in them, while others followed the torchbearers in search of other, more promising methods.

A roar shook the ground. Kerothan gripped Ophim to steady himself. The sigils of the room illuminated in a brilliant red like a spreading fire, revealing the entire chamber to be marked from the ceiling down to every stalagmite. The warriors shouted in surprise and shielded their eyes from the blinding display.

Kerothan picked up the sound of rushing water. Seconds later, rivers charged through the gated tunnels at the ground level of the pit. Panicked cries below shifted to high-pitched shrieks of pain. Torches were snuffed as they tumbled into the waters, leaving the sigils as the only source of light.

And in it, Kerothan could see the unmistakable pink of the flood.

The screams twisted into unbearably tortured wails. Warriors, emboldened and jaded by years of battle, screeched as acidic water swept around their legs. Many fell against the torrent of water, and their bodies tumbled about in the churning liquid even as their skin peeled and dissolved.

Kerothan stared on in horror. His whole body shook with adrenaline. Beside him, Ophim wept. Cephus didn't move, didn't speak, as they watched their comrades kick and flail against the onslaught. Most had been killed by the initial tidal wave. Those who survived long enough to have their legs eaten flailed against the bodies bobbing in the waters, slapping up splashes of acid that burrowed into their chests, their arms, their faces. Within only a few short breaths, all screams stopped as the last few succumbed to their wounds or slipped fully beneath the water.

The last remains of the clannites fizzed in the water, now only odd humps floating as they dissolved. The red light from the sigils slowly dimmed. A sizzling filled the chamber as the acid continued to feast, followed swiftly by a thunderous boom and another brilliant flash of light. The sigils burst with their vivid red again, pulsating this time as if the energy contained within them thumped with a heartbeat. Screams filled the chamber as though the souls of the deceased warriors had been yanked back from the aether Realms to haunt the Terrestrial. Their cries pitched, shrill and endless, no longer constrained by the limits of physical lungs.

Kerothan covered his ears. The sound tore its way inside him, clawing at bones and thoughts and senses, and he begged in silent pleas for it to stop. Whatever torment these souls were trapped in, he couldn't bear it with them. He needed the noise to cease.

The screams reached a level beyond what his ears could perceive, yet their torment remained. He trembled as the agony of the warriors shook the chamber, their imperceptible voices stealing the air. He inhaled, shuddering when he failed to breath out. He gulped in another inhale and moved his hands to his chest.

Just breathe. Stop thinking and just breathe.

As sudden as the nightmarish scene had unfolded, it ended. The air collapsed into a final silence, and the nauseating pain of the perished left Kerothan. He gasped, unable to maintain any sense of bravado, and fell forward onto hands and knees, muscles quivering. A soft sound filtered through his own heavy breathing. It took Kerothan a moment to identify it as Ophim's sobs.

"What in Dardajah's spit was that?" Kerothan coughed out. Hands fumbled across his face before one pressed tightly against his mouth. Prepared to struggle, he slackened when he heard Cephus's whispered command to be quiet. Seconds ticked by in silence. If any water remained on the chamber floor, it no longer ate at anything; the sigils no longer pulsed with intense lighting, instead offering only dim illumination. Kerothan waited for the scuffle of boots or any other indication they weren't alone. Perhaps there were survivors.

A voice from farther inside the chamber's vast darkness broke the silence. "She was right. They found us. We should shut this perimeter point down."

Kerothan peered past Ophim, who also stared in the direction of the voice. Just as the sigil light vanished, he glimpsed a trio of cloaked figures emerge from the darkness, traversing the same ledge that held him. The cavern's darkness hid these newcomers, but their voices carried. Kerothan's heart pounded in his chest as he considered the possibility they would collide unknowingly with him and his companions, but then the three voices veered off, and he realized they had taken the bridge over to the spiked machine.

"If we turn the Fence Post off, it limits the scope of Spiracy's lair. It was never decided that this Post should be turned off."

"But if we don't, we risk it being found again—and tampered with."

A third voice, much quieter and yet firmer, joined the conversation. "We can't have that. Turn it off. They'll understand our reasoning. The Fence's perimeter can work without this one; it just needs to be recalibrated."

Kerothan felt a tap on his shoulder, and warm breath pressed into his ear.

"There's only a few of them," Cephus murmured. "Three by my count. If we keep them cornered—"

One of the voices cried out. "Someone's here!"

Kerothan saw three thin lines of light breach the darkness like suspended star-streaks in the night sky. He'd seen enough wands—the way aether glimmered when caged within them—to know what came next. He ducked down just as the cavern wall behind him erupted with shrapnel. He shielded the back of his head with his hands, wincing as rock cut his knuckles.

Movement to his right told him Ophim had survived the attack, and in the faint lighting, he saw Ophim's figure charge down the pathway and onto the bridge towards the three twisters. The man's sword flashed out, and when more aether charged at him, the glass blade absorbed the energy and took on a light of its own. Ophim swung it down at the first twister in his path before they could escape. With the bridge offering no room to dodge the attack, the blade struck true. The twister's flesh spat out in all directions from the sudden combustion, most of it falling into the acidic moat below.

Kerothan heard Cephus shouting behind him, but he couldn't register what it was his clanhead was saying. He sprang up from his crouch and, wasting no more time in shock though still taking care with his footing, leapt across the arched bridge. The other twisters, fleeing from Ophim, were edging along the platform encircling the machine. Kerothan took the opposite route of this path so as to cut them off. The decision brought him face to face with one of the twisters.

Aether charged towards Kerothan, and a wave of vibrations tickled his skin even as the glass blade of his sword illuminated like a star with the absorbed energy. He roared as he dove at his attacker and swung his weapon. He caught sight of their face beneath the hood of their cloak and reveled in the fear there. They knew their death was coming with the justice of his blade.

Kerothan pictured it seconds before it would occur. The twister's filthy essence would pour out of torn skin, burst innards, and spraying blood. Their body would never be found, fated for the same acidic water that had eaten his kin.

The blade missed.

He paused in the aftermath of the downswing, staring at the ground where the twister had stood. He heard the sounds of a struggle around the curve of the machine's platform, and when he rounded the corner within sight of the bridge, he realized what had happened. Ophim and Cephus had the twister pinned to the ground, the tip of their blades held to their opponent's neck.

"I had him," Kerothan snapped as he approached.

"We need one alive," said Cephus. "We know nothing about this place or what they're doing here. This one can give us answers."

Kerothan tried to push past them to get at the twister. "He deserves death." Cephus pushed him away and fixed him with a reproachful look while Ophim continued to keep the twister secured. "You're defending him?" he yelled. "He killed our kin!"

"And he will face justice for that," said Cephus. "But we'd be foolish not to take him captive for questioning." Kerothan tried to charge past, but with how narrow the platform was, he simply ran square into Cephus again. "Stand down, clannite," the clanhead commanded.

Kerothan's shoulders sagged as he caught his breath. He glared at Cephus even as the clanhead turned back to the twister on the ground. A fury brewed inside Kerothan, set to a ticking clock that would eventually run out. For now, he locked it away. Whatever anger he held towards Cephus would have to wait. Yet if Kerothan blamed anyone beyond the decrepit twisters for the lost lives, it certainly was Cephus. Kerothan had confided his suspicions about a trap. Cephus had ignored him.

Others had paid the price for that unwise decision.

"Did you hear how they screeched?"

Kerothan looked down at the twister, whose face was illuminated by the glow of Ophim's sword. A sneer contorted the man's face, and his eyes flickered between his three captors. A chuckle shook him.

"So many auras fed to our Spiracy. The succulent energy of fear and pain." The man's tongue darted out and licked his lips erratically. "Someday you'll scream too."

Kerothan clenched the hilt of his sword. Heat flooded his face, and the only reason he didn't shove Cephus aside and plunge his blade into the imbecile was because of the damned acid underneath them. A topple from here would mean more than a broken arm for his clanhead. As if summoned by the twister's mocking words, the nightmarish noises of his dying kin echoed in his head. Sounds of men screaming as their bodies disintegrated. Sounds of auras yanked into an unknown Realm after the torture of their flesh.

All because Cephus hadn't listened to him.

CHAPTER 6

The crypt beneath the coven smelled of mildew and rot.

Annilasia stood at the far end of the vast chamber, silent and alone. The place was frequented by other pupils on occasion, but she'd chosen an hour when they were sure to be busy elsewhere. Like them, she should have been preparing for her upcoming wand trial.

But finding the Sachem always came first in her list of priorities. The great leader of the Unified Tribes had eluded her, as he was no longer hidden away at his Fortress farther south, all thanks to a pesky mirajin named Elothel who had forced the Sachem through a vortex portal. Annilasia hadn't actually witnessed this event, and there was no telling where that portal had spat him back out. The last time she'd laid eyes on the Sachem had been years ago—before she'd betrayed her fellow tillishu warriors, back when she'd dutifully served him under the threat of death. That part of her life seemed like an eternity past, or the life of some other unfortunate Vekuuv slave. Had it not been for the skin ink on her arm that denoted her as such, she might have dwelled on such things far less.

Yet it was her past that had spurred her down this path of hunting down the Sachem. He would answer for his atrocities, and she'd ensure that judgement came by her hand. Wherever it was that he was hiding, she would find him, and once he was located, she planned to depart the Orphan Mountains and end him.

No more Sachem. No more tyranny.

Now, before her where she sat, three large mirrors stood upright against the crypt's rocky wall. The outer two were turned slightly towards each other, while the central piece directly faced Annilasia. She'd discovered the mirrors by accident while following Iveer one late evening. Her mentor had gone into the depths of the crypt at this same hour, when the pupils were

THE SPAWN OF SPIRACY

occupied with a preordained set of nightly rituals far off coven grounds. At first, Annilasia had supposed his trip would involve the other mentors, but as she followed him and time passed, she realized he'd come alone.

Like hers, Iveer's quest had led to the Three Mirrors. A web of giant tubes and intricate wires snaked across the ceiling downward, eventually plunging into the back of each giant rectangle of glass. The mystery of these mechanisms was of no interest to Annilasia. She knew it to be old technology from an ancient time prior to the Residuum Era, and was aware that the wires fused the mirrors to aether in some manner. Forbidden technology. Yet forbidden arts were a specialty of aethertwisters. It came as no surprise to her that the coven hosted such things as the Three Mirrors in their monastery within the Orphan Mountains.

She'd watched Iveer sink to the ground, cross his legs, and grow still. The slightest quiver disrupted the air of the crypt, and she recognized it as the energy of translation. She dared not follow the mentor into his trance, but she'd decided to return in her own time to learn what these odd antiques could offer.

And Dardajah's spit, did they offer.

Whether by some trick of the mind or a bend of time and space, the mirrors could summon just about anything into their reflections. Like looking through a window into any other part of the world, one could spy on the most secretive of schemes, the most reclusive of hermits. She could watch Mygo, that stars-awful grunt, take a piss from his bunker in the Ikaul Forest, or eavesdrop on her fellow twister peers as they whispered about her behind her back.

She could spy on the elusive Sachem of the Unified Tribes.

At least, that was her theory. She had yet to accomplish this. Prior trials on different individuals and locations had proven the mirrors' capabilities, yet the Sachem still eluded them. Some ward, no doubt, or an attribute of the dokojin that possessed the man she sought. She'd even tried that—summoning the all-powerful Dardajah, but that too had proven futile.

Perhaps today would be different. Today, she had a new spell to try.

Annilasia inhaled, then slowly breathed out through her nose. The foul odor of the crypt curled through her nostrils. She stared back at the harsh reflection currently staining the center mirror—her figure against the backdrop of the crypt. A permanent scowl wrinkled her face, and she stood with rigid posture under a swaddling of clothes meant to seal away the Wither cold. Smooth black hair crowned one side of her face; the other side was shaven down to her brown skin. Her time with the twisters had aged her. She saw it in the slight hunch of her shoulders, the lost spark of fury in her eyes. She'd seen too many horrors while under the schooling of the aethertwisters.

Before melancholy could set in, she sighed heavily, shook her hands as if to free them of some invisible spider web, and sank to the ground. Her charcoal tabard settled around her as it came to rest on her knees. Crossing her legs always ended with needleskin—she wasn't sure how an old croak like Iveer could stand it—so she knelt.

Her internal clock ticked to life. She had a slim window before someone was bound to breach the crypt for their own nefarious needs. She closed her eyes, and the twister mantra drove away all other thoughts. She focused on the words and their meanings.

There is no reality.

All things are, and all things are not.

The mind is all beginnings, and all ends.

The physical world—the Terrestrial Realm—was nothing more than a dream. It wasn't real any more than the aether Realms were real. For all things to be real, nothing could be real. Fantasies were a mere obstacle, a fool's excuse to abandon ambition.

All things began and ended in the mind.

Her mind.

A wave of vibrations drowned out the silence. Physical sensation shifted, replaced by a disconnection. A prickling crawled over her. The ground beneath her vanished, and a false sense of freefall tried to jolt her back to the Terrestrial. She resisted, pressing her mind further.

There is no reality.

The transition ended. Her emotions drifted around her, disconnected threads that she could tap into if she saw fit. The vibrations smoothed until they dissipated, and the prickles ceased.

She opened her eyes.

A desert of nothingness surrounded her. Void stretched in every direction, and the boundaries of the crypt's ceiling and walls were gone. Before her stood the Three Mirrors—the only material objects she'd intended to meet here in this place. Everything else—her body, the ground beneath her legs, the stench of rot—meant nothing to her. She knew enough about translation now to filter out those pesky details.

There'd been a time when shifting from one Realm to another—translating—had bothered her. Though she'd now mastered aspects of it—such as the journey between one vibrational frequency to another—the laws of the Apparition Realm still confounded her. Unlike in the physical world, the typical senses of the body weren't nearly as vivid here, though pain could most certainly register. She figured that this was due to the idea that pain was linked to the mind. If the mind perceived it as real, then it was to some extent.

That seemed to be the key to understanding it all—the Realms, translation, aether, twisting. The mind had to be convinced of reality. Whatever it believed, it made so.

Despite the confounding nature of the Apparition Realm, she made use of her limited knowledge, which included how to extract aether, just like the other pupils. For all its mysteries, there were at least a few constants in this Realm that she could always count on. Among those were the lifestone beside her and the lifechain of interlocked links that ran from the stone to her ankle. These objects were symbolic and didn't hold much constitution. If she were to run her hand over them, her form would pass right through as if they were smoke.

Regardless of their insubstantial natures, she knew the silvery sphere represented her existence in the Terrestrial Realm. Furthermore, the chain of miniscule links that ran from the stone to her ankle symbolized a tie to a physical body. The laws that these objects held and performed were still abstract in her mind, but that wouldn't impede her. Nothing seemed to affect them, and as long as that constant held, she wouldn't concern herself with their presence. At least not for her current task.

She focused on the mirrors, murky clouds swirling within their frames. It was time to find the Sachem.

Her thoughts homed in on that one goal. She'd find that bastard and drag him out of whatever hole he'd burrowed into. No one could escape the mirrors.

With that, she opened her mouth and began the ritual.

***

The faintest of movements stirred in the reflection of the first mirror.

Annilasia's eyes latched onto it, and she grew quiet, letting the words of the ritual die on her lips. She counted it a twisted miracle that she'd managed to conjure anything at all, much less something that would reveal itself to her. It was one thing to summon a human or location into the mirrors.

It was another to try and summon a dokojin.

A darkness deeper than night still filled the space around her, while an even bleaker void filled the mirrors. A presence at her back beckoned for her attention. So excited for her objective upon first arrival, she hadn't given it much notice. But it made itself known now, like a blood clot over time.

Inzerious. Her very own dokojin companion.

She didn't turn or acknowledge it. She knew what horror awaited. At least it was a caged horror. Observing it would only unnerve her, and it was the mirrors that needed her focus. As long as the phantom behind her remained silent and restrained, it would be nothing more than a pesky canine on a leash.

She scanned the edges of the center mirror. No more movement. Whatever had caught her eye before had either left or remained obscured within the mirror. Her heart jumped when something flashed in the glass on the left only to vanish beyond the edges of its frame.

Stillness again. Annilasia dared not flinch lest she banish this newcomer.

Time ticked on, and dismay wormed its way through her. Perhaps her anticipation had fueled nothing more than a hallucination. Iveer had cautioned that this ritual might not yield results. Its origins were primordial, nearly as ancient as the mirrors themselves. For all she knew, the ritual might be another forgery. Plus, Iveer hadn't known at the time that she intended to combine the ritual with the power of the Three Mirrors.

Her gaze twitched back to the center glass, convinced again of movement. *Don't blink. Whatever you do, don't blink.*

All doubt vanished, replaced by an instant dread that sickened her stomach. Her eyes fixated on a lower corner of the center mirror, where a crescent shape of pasty complexion was ascending like a moon. Only when a set of sunken black eyes peeked over the frame's edge, placed within the crescent's form, did she realize that what she was witnessing was the emergence of a head. The creature stared back at her and grew still. All she could see was the dome of its head and those unblinking eyes.

Eyes that swam with a ravenous energy akin to bloodlust.

Dying stars, don't blink. If I blink, I die.

As if to challenge this, a new motion twinkled in the third mirror. She resisted the urge to glance at it. An inexplicable knowledge told her that if she were to look away in the slightest, the dokojin that lurked in the center mirror would pounce. The entity remained ever so still in an attempt to trick her mind into accepting that it had always been there.

It had always been a part of the mirror.

She could look away.

It wasn't going to move. It was a part of the mirror—

Annilasia raised her hands. Words leapt from her lips, striking the air with a powerful force. Whatever was creeping in the third mirror responded with a blood-curdling screech, and spiked tendrils leaped out from that mirror's glass.

Her verbal command took. The glass of all three mirrors flickered, erasing the inner shadowy Realm and its inhabitants. She shuddered with relief, freed from her stare-down with the dokojin. Her reflection returned to the glass, and she faced her own figure once again. Only, it wasn't her physical body. Instead, a deep, endless black filled out her silhouette, a darkness set against a backdrop of deeper darkness, and within her silhouette soared dozens of orbs of light.

She was like a walking galaxy of stars. The term for this was aura. Of what she'd read in the ancient texts, it was akin to what her ancestors defined as her soul. The priesthood of her time theorized that auras were symbolic of the universal essence imbued in all humans. That is, the idea that the soul was made up of the same material as the distant stars and the very dirt of the world.

When she translated, her energy took on this astral form, just as the energy did of any human who translated from the physical world to the Apparition Realm. Always accompanying her aura were her lifestone and lifechain, which rested beside her.

All this was reflected in the mirrors.

So was the dokojin behind her.

She knew to expect this. Its presence sank into her like a knife, and despite her hatred of it, her gaze lingered on its reflection. Always with her. Even in the Terrestrial Realm, where the distractions of a physical body and a material world tempted her to forget her plight, she couldn't shake its ominous presence.

At least Inzerious no longer spoke. The dokojin didn't have much of a choice; Iveer had locked the dokojin in a cage that rendered it unable to whisper its dark musings into her mind. The visible restraints of this arrangement also comforted her. Iveer's handiwork bound the entity in a film of white web that hung off it in restless tendrils, making it so the dokojin hovered above the ground, a mere specter. Only vague impressions pressed into the webbed shroud, hinting at skeletal features meant to evoke terror. Before this entrapment, Inzerious had lurked about in a nasty, decayed form. Now its horrors were hidden.

Annilasia spotted the glint of her lifechain rising up to the dokojin's form. The dread from before returned tenfold. It didn't matter that Inzerious was caged. She couldn't shake it. Inzerious was always with her.

Always attached.

THE SPAWN OF SPIRACY

Her focus settled back on the mirrors themselves rather than what they reflected. She growled as the success of her attempt soured with its failure to produce the desired results. Five weeks. Relentless attempts that had yielded no results, and in one damn session she'd managed to lure out two unexpected dokojin—the creeper in the corner and the tentacled monster. But they weren't the dokojin she sought. She would have to try again.

Words whispered from her mouth. The air tightened, unsure what violent musings or language she'd uttered, and cowered away. She herself knew little about her incantation, only that it demanded to reveal the most powerful of dokojin. Perhaps this time she'd actually summon a glimpse of Dardajah.

The darkness in the mirrors shifted, hinting at a change of scenery despite their vacant oblivion. The mirrors stirred ever so subtly, a blend of greys and inks that shimmered enough to betray restlessness. She was getting somewhere.

Come on, you filthy bastard. Where in the forsaken abyss have you fled?

She muttered the words again, wringing them out like a wet cloth for all they were worth. The shadowy void gave way to emerald static. Annilasia stiffened and watched closely. In transient flashes, the static solidified before instantly disintegrating back into chaos. During those moments of clarity, a barren backdrop of an empty corridor appeared, a lone silhouette standing at its far end.

The bursts were too quick to make out more details. Annilasia leaned forward.

Did I summon it? Did I finally find Dardajah?

As seconds passed, and more bursts of clarity occurred amidst the static, she decided the newcomer too slender and humanoid to be Dardajah. Nevertheless, something about this new dokojin distressed her. Made her keep watching.

Movement occurred. The silhouette raised a spindly arm, pressing its hand to its mouth. A single finger erected to form a lone tower.

It shushed her.

A claw slammed across her shoulder, and the static-filled Realm in the mirror vanished.

Annilasia jerked her head back to find a cracked skull mere inches from her face, lathered in black ichor. Inzerious was free. No webbing covered its form. Sunken eyes, wide and unblinking, bore down on her. Images of flayed corpses stunned her thoughts while a suffocating sense of dread wafted off the dokojin and swam into her.

Its maw opened. Gashed lips peeled back to reveal chipped yellow teeth and a reptilian tongue covered in blisters. Warm, rotting breath struck her as blackened blood splashed from its gums onto her shoulder. A screech bubbled from the creature. The sound shook Annilasia, and the grotesque imagery assaulting her mind intensified. She saw bodies—faces frozen in terror and agony. Faces of people she knew—Iveer, her fellow pupils, the other mentors—screaming in a writhing mound of thrashing limbs.

Annilasia fell back and pushed with her hands to backpedal away. Her mind reeled. It shouldn't have been able to free itself. This wasn't possible.

The dokojin sprang at her. Its overwhelming mass pressed over her, and she got swamped in the ichor discharging from its bones.

"Time to sleep, Bloodspill."

It pushed into her, as if forcing itself against her would weld them together. Some of the black ichor dripped down, gluing onto her silhouette. She yelped, yanking at the sticky black liquid that connected her to the dokojin. Yet it clung to her form like amber trapping a mosquito. The dokojin began absorbing her. Her screams grew muffled as she squirmed against the ichor holding Inzerious's rickety bones together. A metamorphosis initiated, with Annilasia's struggles seeming to only accelerate the transformation. The two were becoming one, human meshing with aetherwaste. A chimera of human and dokojin forming.

"Just let this happen, Bloodspill," Inzerious hissed. "Give up control, you stupid bag of bones."

It was almost too late. She had to get out. Annilasia shifted her focus off the struggle for the briefest of moments. The mantra of the twisters sprang up to focus her.

There is no reality.

All things are, and all things are not.

The mind is all beginnings, and all ends.

The world shimmered, and an uncomfortable vibration joined the already agonizing shapeshift occurring between her and Inzerious. She'd permitted herself to dwell on the mantra for only a moment. But it'd been enough time for the dokojin to seize even more control. The translation ended, and Annilasia found herself back inside the crypt, where the dokojin slammed her physical body against the ground. The loud smack of her head striking the floor popped in the silence. Annilasia shrieked. Her limbs contorted and twisted like an insect flung on its back writhing in hope of turning over. Inzerious bucked, sending her limbs in defying angles that shot pain through her nerves.

"Give up, Bloodspill," it hollered. "Time to go to sleep!"

Darkness invaded Annilasia's vision. *Star flares, it's going to take over my body. I've lost control.* Just as the panic of defeat washed through her and the darkness threatened to overtake her vision entirely, a voice boomed through the crypt.

Inzerious howled, still wrestling to seize control of her body but now flinching with discomfort. The new voice continued, sounding off words in an unfamiliar language. The dokojin clicked and shrieked. Annilasia sensed her lips parting to permit the dokojin's noises to escape—odd animalistic grunts breaking out from her throat.

A weight lifted.

She inhaled sharply as the darkness around her vision fled, returning her eyesight. The struggle in her own body ceased as well. Her muscles melted with exhaustion. She lay on the floor, sweat soaking the folds of her clothes. A long, heavy breath crept out of her as she realized just how close she'd been to succumbing to full possession.

Inzerious had almost hijacked her body.

CHAPTER 7

"Foolish."

Annilasia flinched at the rebuke. She remained on the floor, not wanting to rise and face her unwelcome savior. Without warning, bile bubbled up her throat, giving her no time to fight it down. She instinctively turned her head to spew out black fluid mixed with chunks of undigested food. Sputtering a few times to get it all out, she slid her eyes up to the figure standing a few strides away.

"I suppose you enjoy seeing me like this," she murmured, glowering up at the elderly man.

Iveer stood poised with the massive sleeves of his cloak interlocked in front of him. His hood was drawn, casting him in the engrossing single shadow of the crypt. Despite this, she knew a sneer surely wrinkled his face.

"Not as enjoyable as some of our other sessions, but yes, watching you lose to a dokojin and spit up its ichor discharge..." The man released an eager, filthy moan.

Annilasia closed her eyes, revolted by Iveer's pleasure at her pain. She wiped the sleeve of her shirt across her mouth before leaning up at the waist. When she opened her eyes, her reflection met her, this time without the brilliant orbs within a dark silhouette. She was back in the Terrestrial Realm now—back in her physical body. In front of her, the three giant mirrors loomed, absent of any danger.

She stood, letting her tabard settle across the length of her figure. Dampness chilled her thigh—somehow some of the vomited ichor had ended up on her—and she cursed under her breath at the moist spot on her pants where the overhead tunic hadn't covered them.

Dardajah's fiery spit.

Unable to avoid the confrontation any longer, Annilasia turned to face Iveer with squared shoulders and pursed lips, clenching her jaw when Iveer

THE SPAWN OF SPIRACY

cocked an eyebrow. *Old bastard can eat my juicy ichor vomit.* "I suppose I'm in your debt for saving me," she said.

"How is it you managed to fray the cage I put on it?" Iveer demanded. "Inzerious should not have been loose."

"Your guess is as good as mine. I translated and saw it as you left it—all strung together with that slick webbing that makes it float like a bubble. I consulted the mirrors, and in the next moment, that damn parasite was all over me."

"Then whatever idiotic actions you performed while translated must have compromised my work. Don't do that again. I'm tired of keeping your stupid arse alive when said arse doesn't do much to pay me in return for such misplaced generosities."

Annilasia groaned and moved past Iveer. "Then stop saving me, old croak. I don't need your help."

"It will kill you, Annilasia."

She froze. His words had drained much of her stony disposition, but she maintained a resolved tone. "No, it won't."

"It will. What I just witnessed is proof of its obvious intent. But I didn't need to see that to know the dokojin's nature. It will kill you, and there is no escape."

A needle prick of fear stung her, but she banished it quickly and played it off. "Care to make any other bystander comments?"

Iveer clucked his tongue. "I didn't care to make such statements before. You came to me a scared little thing, begging to be released from that parasite's torture. But I didn't release you. Think about it. What did I do instead?"

Annilasia let go of her resistance to the man's absurd proclamation and decided instead to humor him. She flashed through the months of torturous training, the months of wondering if she'd rather die than sustain loss after loss under Iveer's mentorship, the months of worrying that Inzerious would tear her body limb from limb before she could learn to subdue it.

The journey to the Orphan Mountains had taken longer than she'd initially anticipated. If it hadn't been for Inzerious's constant maiming of her shoulder and back, she could have made the trek in half the time. It took her three months instead. By the time she stumbled upon the coven monastery, Annilasia had nearly given herself up to the dokojin's will. The coven's twisters proceeded to interrogate her, which only worsened her fraying sanity. Then Iveer arrived from some extended absence from the monastery. When he found out that Annilasia had brought with her Korcsha's spell book, he took a turn speaking with her. Eventually he learned of her dokojin parasite, which led to her release.

Broken would be a cruel understatement to describe her mental and physical state at that point. Madness had set in, and she couldn't keep delirium—perpetuated by Inzerious's cruelty—at bay. If it hadn't been for Iveer . . .

. . . then yes, she would have died.

But that was before. It was different now.

"You boxed the dokojin in a cage," she answered. "It can't threaten me anymore. No more scars, no more screaming. You showed me that it can be controlled."

"But did I release you from it?"

A chill rushed through Annilasia. She turned her neck slowly to regard the old mentor. "I thought you said I could get rid of it."

Iveer cocked his head, pretending to contemplate this. "Did I?"

No. I suppose you didn't. Dying, blindly streaking stars.

"I've asked you since day one to teach me how to get rid of this thing."

"And yet, I never promised I would. I've slowly been teaching you the foundations so that one day you could place your own restraints on Inzerious. Set aside the fact that you've hardly mastered any of those; the endgame is that it is a temporary fix to an inevitable fate."

"You choose to tell me this now," she said with a clipped tone. "Why today? Just in the mood to shatter some carefully nurtured hope?"

Iveer slowly turned his head in the direction of the mirrors before gazing back to her. "You're wasting your time. Time that could be better spent learning to harness aether in a more reliable way. You can't keep relying on your parasitic friend to keep fueling you with it."

"I'm not," she snapped. "It's caged, remember? I'm using my own aether—"

"No, you're not," he interrupted. "What a foolish belief. It doesn't matter if the dokojin is silent or still. It is connected to you. Connected to your lifestone. Anytime you interact with aether, you're interacting with Inzerious. Your aetherwielding is fueled far more from Inzerious than it is from you."

"Who cares then?" Annilasia challenged. "If it's going to kill me, might as well take advantage of it before then."

"Because you're only advancing that doom." Spit shot out with Iveer's invigorated words as he lunged forward to bridge the gap between them. He leered at her face. "You have no idea what awaits you. You think it's a quick and painless way to go? This dokojin means to steal your body before it ends you. Days, months, years will pass with you stuck inside a pit of your own soul while it dances around in your bones and flesh. You'll feel every abominable thing it does to your body, all while you go mad. By the time you *do* perish, you'll have long forgotten what it means to be human—what it means to even be *you*."

Annilasia avoided his eyes, staring straight ahead. She wouldn't let him glimpse the slightest indication that his words had frightened her. She swallowed, steadying her voice. "What do you care? One less pupil to teach."

Iveer curled his lips to bare his teeth as he took a few shuffling steps back. "Insolent child. I don't care about your life. You could trip and crack your head and rot in a ditch, and I wouldn't bat an eye. But with you gone, what do you think your parasitic friend will do? If your demise happens anywhere near this coven, you'll leave us with an unleashed dokojin to prey on one of us."

"So, what's your point exactly?" she asked. "If you're so afraid of where I'm going to die, then why not banish me off coven grounds? Why keep teaching me?"

"Are you so daft that you've not yet pieced it together? Every time you interact with aether, it is a wild energy that is further imbued with chaos because of your parasite. Inzerious perverts your aetherwielding with wicked intent, and it shows. But this could be quelled. If you could focus your aether into a conduit, like a wand, then there's less chance of the dokojin's wild aether slipping in with your own and therefore toxifying the land needlessly. There's not enough pure aether as it is."

"That sounds like a dampening effect. A less powerful outcome. Why not use the power that comes with that chaos? I could be more powerful than you and your pointy glass stick."

"Because, as I said, you advance your own doom. Make no mistake, you will die at the hands of the dokojin. But you can control how fast that fate descends upon you. Continue to meddle with unpredictable, tainted aether, and you accelerate that process. Learn to focus it, to cleanse it, through a wand, and you might live as long as the rest of us before the dokojin overtakes you."

And with that, Iveer moved past Annilasia to ascend the stairs.

Annilasia remained paralyzed in place long after Iveer had left. Her mind latched onto the pronouncement of doom, unable to dismiss it as an overdramatic scolding from her mentor. She balled her hands into fists, squeezing them until her fingernails dug into her skin.

He's wrong. Inzerious won't kill me. I won't let it.

"Bloodspill . . ."

A shiver ran down her spine. No other words crept through her mind, and she wondered if she'd imagined it. Inzerious was caged again. It couldn't hurt her.

For now.

CHAPTER 8

A biting wind tore across the summit upon which the wand trial would commence. The ascension to it came and went in silent endurance as each mentor and pupil made their way up. Annilasia avoided eye contact with the other pupils. For three months, she'd lived amongst the coven inhabitants but kept to herself whenever possible. Her reclusive habits had earned her no friends, which was just as well. The others saw her as an isolated basket case, a prejudice built on what they'd witnessed upon her arrival—a lost, deranged woman riddled with scars and clothed in rags. When she'd emerged from the dungeons with Iveer, the other pupils shunned her. She hadn't minded this. There were no allies to be had amongst these filthy twisters. She wasn't one of them. Her reason for remaining at the coven was her own.

To infiltrate, to learn, and to eventually betray.

But first, she would take her knowledge of twisting to the doorstep of the Sachem and slay him with the very aether he'd tainted. Until then—and she still had much to learn—she'd play the part of the lonely pupil with no friends and a secretive past.

She squinted through the wind at the figures far ahead of her. No one waited behind with her despite the fact that they were all very aware of her physical impediment. Long before her journey to the Orphan Mountains, she'd earned a leg injury during a standoff with a group of particularly nasty monsters. A lucky swipe, a hooked claw into her lower leg, and now she was blessed with a constant limp. Annilasia knew a bit of aethertwisting might do away with the hindrance, but the cost didn't seem worth it. Twisting always came back to bite. She found ways to justify it during her training or when she was tracking down clues to the Sachem's whereabouts. But when it came to her own skin and bones, the idea unnerved her. She could still walk well enough without having to worry about that.

She startled at a voice behind her.

"Quite a cold one today, eh?"

Annilasia had thought everyone had passed her already. She looked over at the young man, who waited patiently behind her. His hood covered his head, and a blue scarf veiled all of his face except his eyes. The wind yanked at his cloak, threatening with harsh tugs to break the clasp that held it in place around his neck.

Drifter. The apothecary apprentice. She remembered his name only because he'd once offered to find a remedy for her limp, which she'd declined. She'd learned early on not to trust the other pupils. Many were more likely to backstab than extend genuine aid. No nobles among twisters.

"Just step by already," she shouted through the wind. "You know I'm not going up as fast as you can."

"Want some company?" he asked. "Wind's a bit strong. Don't want you knocked off the side with no one to catch you."

Annilasia scowled at him. "I've managed quite well for months at the coven. I think I can ascend a staircase with a little breeze."

She couldn't see his expression, but his eyes twitched a little at her harsh tone. He gave a clipped nod and moved past her without another word. Annilasia's curses, some directed at him, were drowned out by the wind.

At the top, the mentors told the pupils to disrobe down to their innermost undergarments. Annilasia bit her tongue to keep from unleashing a torrent of expletives as she stripped to a measly loincloth and bandeau. Her muscles clenched and her teeth clattered. The howling wind besieged her with a plague of shivers.

She kept her gloves on though. For it wasn't the wind or the cold that distressed her, nor the near-nakedness she now boasted for her peers and teachers. Removing the layers of cloth was equivalent to removing one's armor amidst a war zone. Twisters were vulnerable to nature's earth elements such as metal or stone. A mere prick from a sword's blade would combust a twister like a popping bubble. The vulnerability came from spending too much time in nonphysical Realms and interacting too much with aether, an element unnatural to the Terrestrial. As their auras acclimated more and more to an existence separated from the body, their physical shells took on a paradoxical sensitivity to surfaces in the physical Realm.

The reaction was almost as if the body was rejecting its own world in favor of the aether Realms. Or perhaps it was the mind that was rejecting the body, having grown fond of those other Realms and no longer caring for the material world. This sensitivity to physical elements was why Annilasia no longer carried a blade, something once as inherent to her as her own limbs. The twisters had stripped her of such crude weapons, but it hadn't taken long for her to adjust once she'd started her apprenticeship at the coven.

Annilasia eyed the other students warily and then the mentors too. If there were any infiltrators amongst them, this would be the time to strike—when all it would take to end each of them was the nick of a blade. If she herself had not converted, this would have been her moment as a tillishu to strike. But time had assimilated her to their way of existence—had made her susceptible to their weaknesses.

There were a little over a dozen students gathered on the square tiles of the summit. Each stood on a symbol carved underfoot. Annilasia knew the calligraphy and interconnected lines as the Primordial Oral, the written language of the dokojin. It was an incomplete and crude manner of communication, one set with the impossible task of conveying the violence and gravity of such barbaric entities.

Iveer strode into the center of the square, pacing across the engravings while his cloak traced the ground. "Of the throngs of pupils who have foolishly thrown themselves at this coven's steps, you are the very few who have advanced, and survived, to this point."

His eyes swept across each of the shivering students, pausing briefly on Annilasia. She swore the man's glare deepened on her.

"You have studied, suffered, with desperate ambition to arrive here. Aether has until this point been your master, twisting and molding you into its tool. Now you will turn the tables and enslave aether to your will. You will bend it, trap it, and use it to whatever ends you see fit. This can only be done with the conduit of a glass wand."

At this, the mentors broke their formed line to approach each of their mentees. Iveer strode towards Annilasia with stoicism etched into his face. He extended his arms towards her, and she reached out to take his gift. The glass wand fell into her gloved palm. She stared at it as Iveer turned and went back to reform rank with the other mentors. The velvet glass was like frozen blood solidified in the unforgiving temperatures of the mountains. She turned it with her fingers, feeling the jagged edges that ran across its length.

Glass was one of the very rare elements that naturally translated from one Realm to the next with ease. It was also one of the only elements within which aether could be collected in the Apparition Realm. Its natural transparency removed mental barriers that otherwise kept aether from infusing physical objects. As it was, not many ethereal objects could facilitate transference between Realms either. Such objects did not so easily acclimate to the Terrestrial Realm.

This made glass wands a coveted commodity.

Up until this point, the mentors had lent their glass wands to the pupils during lessons and demonstrations. Outside of these, though, the pupils were devoted to topics and studies that did not require aethertwisting. This trial would prove their worth at earning such a powerful tool.

Annilasia curled her fingers around the wand. This would be hers if she passed this trial. She would be an aethertwister. She flinched at the thought. Aether*wielder*. She'd be an aether*wielder*, not a twister. Deep down, she knew there wasn't a difference anymore. But for her own sanity, she clung to the archaic contrast. She wouldn't ever consider herself a twister like the rest of these filth. Her skills with aether, learned here at the coven, were a means to an end. They did not define her. She would strive to wield aether only with pious intent—to avoid creating more aetherwaste. At least, as much as her goals allowed. But in the end, even if she needed to twist aether to defeat the Sachem, the good accomplished would outweigh whatever consequences occurred.

Iveer paused before delivering the final lines of his ceremonial speech. "Go into the Apparition Realm. Collect aether into these glass wands you've been gifted. Return."

With that, his arm rose up, then flashed in a downward slash. A ripple of wind-like energy erupted from the needle point of his wand that now peeked out from within his sleeve. In response, a low grumble crescendoed to a roar, and the entire summit began to quake.

Annilasia glanced down at her feet as the ground shifted. The dokojin symbols on which she stood revealed themselves to be built-in switch mechanisms, which clicked as they slid beneath the stone tiles to expose holes underneath them. A gust of vapor shot up from these openings and assaulted her eyes and nose. She recognized the hopper weed smell. Her eyes and nostrils burned, though these sensations quickly shifted as translation overtook her.

A sickening vibration fizzled across her skin, and her head swam. She expected the Apparition Realm to shimmer into existence. She waited for the vibrations to cease.

Instead, the vibrations intensified. A strange disconnect occurred where she could feel her body but no longer see or sense her surroundings. She screamed, but her voice didn't register as sound. She felt the air in her lungs as it pushed out, felt the scratch in her throat from the scream. The vibrations tore at her, eels feasting on a stunned fish. Whether it was her body or her aura that they feasted on, she couldn't tell. Pain could be traced to both. She cowered away from the stinging vibrations that nipped at her.

Light blinked into existence as tiny particles of grey and black. She searched amongst this sea of static for anything familiar as the eels elicited more pain. She still couldn't hear her own screams.

The static light blended together like splotches of paint in water. White streaks became reflections of light; black morphed into one massive shadow that pressed in on these reflections. Her screams finally broke through to her ears, but vibrations continued to assail her even as their fervor diminished.

She grew quiet. A low hum peaked before leveling out.

What in black stars and infernal glory is this place?

Annilasia glanced down at her ankle, relieved when she saw the familiar lifechain and the stone to which it connected. She'd made it to the Apparition Realm. Yet this comfort refused to settle inside her. As she studied her odd surroundings, she wondered if she'd somehow managed to cross into a different aether Realm. It'd be absurd to assume anything on the level of the Ethereal, but other Realms certainly existed. They just weren't as easy to reach as the Apparition.

Confirmation came when she studied her own details. Her body didn't bear the shadowy complexion characteristic of the Apparition. No orbs or lights swirled within her form. She removed her gloves and beheld her physical hands. Skin, wrapped across muscle and bone.

Panic rose in her throat. She pressed her hands together, going so far as to dig one set of fingernails into the opposite palm. Pain blossomed at the point of impact, and one nail managed to break skin. A splatter of blood formed around the opening. Only it wasn't red. Despite the poor lighting, she could see there was no catch of color. The blotch was black, with tiny reflections of light bouncing off of it.

Annilasia twisted around as she remembered Inzerious. If she was physical, what did that mean for the dokojin? A mere glimpse over her shoulder at the specter, blanketed in the tendrils of web, was enough to assure her of its captivity, so she turned away with no desire to behold the dokojin for long. Whatever strange laws this Realm held, the dokojin's cage remained.

The light that beamed onto several points in the room's center had no source. It simply bounced between edges and curves, creating the glob of shadow that dominated the chamber. If there was a ceiling, the light refused to flesh it out for her. For all she knew, it could be a few feet above her head or miles up.

Where the light reflected brightest, thin tubes crawled over rock formations like a massive spider. They erupted out of a single source point and shot out in every direction. Annilasia traced those that were coming towards her and found that they ran beneath her feet. After replacing her gloves, she bent down and ran her fingers across the tubes, reminded of refined rubber rather than something organic.

An awful moan bled up from some depth and reverberated around her. The sound plunged deep into Annilasia, surfacing her panic. She sprang up and searched the splotches of light.

"Who's there?" she asked, her voice croaking.

Another moan answered—a slithering sound of suffering that sent her stumbling a few steps backwards. She teetered on the uneven surface of the tubes. Silence followed. Her initial deduction was that someone was hurt—the noise sounded too tortured to be a threat—but another part of her held tight to a paralyzing fear. Something else tainted the noise. A danger she couldn't detect in full.

When the moan sounded again, she forced herself to move. Whatever was making that sound, it wasn't moving. Maybe it was indeed someone injured and in need of help. Her legs marched a path perpendicular to the illuminated center of the room.

A few steps in, she froze.

What had previously looked like stone formations now bore more distinctive shapes. A body lay across a slab of stone. Though several yards away, she could make out its frailty—its skin and bones soiled and sagging. It let out a deep moan, the same as before. The sound sickened her, and thoughts of silencing it by whatever means shot through her head.

Then she noticed the standing figure. Needle-sharp panic prickled across her skin.

Tall and elegant, a wraith of terrifying beauty levitated a few inches off the ground. Long, glistening strands of hair that shifted from light to dark pooled across its shoulders like a frozen waterfall. Eyes of murky darkness, set within a perfectly proportioned face, peered back at Annilasia. For all its perfections, the arms were too long and too thin, its face too angular and pointed, its lips too refined. The darkness of the room clutched at the edges of this figure, or perhaps the wraith wore a cloak made of shadows. The difference remained irrelevant.

Dread overwhelmed Annilasia. She'd seen this entity before. In the Three Mirrors. She'd watched it shush her mere moments before Inzerious had broken loose.

Her eyes caught on something that glittered in the light near the figure. A thread of silvery links ran from its hands down into the shadows.

Annilasia gasped and jerked her head down to her ankle. Her lifechain. With growing panic, she tracked the length of it—and it went in the direction of the wraith.

Only mirajin and dokojin could see and interact with a person's lifechain and stone.

This was no mirajin.

The dokojin's semblance of humanity, its feminine beauty and allure, only accentuated its alien appearance. Every curve of its unblemished skin triggered treacherous horror in its beholder. Annilasia trembled at the slight curl of its lips, coated in raven black ink. The wraith opened its mouth, but rather than the air rupturing with its own voice, it was the figure lying on the stone dais that emitted sound. The frail individual stretched their mouth open and unleashed a tortured moan. When the wraith sealed its lips once more, the moan ended, and the person on the slab snapped their mouth shut.

To demonstrate the horror once more, the dokojin ever so slightly parted its lips. Its victim unhinged their jaw, and the horrid sound scratched the air once more. Both snapped their mouths shut in unison.

Then the dokojin finally spoke.

"You keep muffling your friend, Skinflake. My kind should never be silenced."

The voice caressed Annilasia with a yawning seduction. The words rolled out like clouds of perfume to sweeten the distance between them. Even so, she experienced a vivid panic when the dokojin yanked on her lifechain. There was a sharp tug on her ankle. She braced for some unfathomable effect to ensue.

Pain. Fear. Anything.

But it wasn't her that the dokojin targeted. From behind her, a growl thudded into her ears.

"Stupid, stupid, Bloodspill."

A whimper bubbled up from her chest. She wouldn't turn around. She didn't want to see. But she knew that voice. She knew the nickname her parasite had given her.

Inzerious was free again.

Her mind raced. She remembered the wand in her hand. Her arm shot up, and she pointed the glass tip at the wraith by the stone slab. She searched around for aether and willed it to enter the glass. But the wraith was faster. It brought one of its hands up, its elbow bent, and coiled the fingers into a tight fist. Her wand shattered in her hands. A cackle broke out from Inzerious at her back.

Vibrations erupted across her. She cried out at the unexpected transition and fell to the ground. She saw the edges of Inzerious form above her. Its cracked skull grinned down at her, and a glob of black ichor dripped off its chin and fell across her eyes, turning everything black.

The vibrations tore at her, and she believed her aura would be ruined. One final screech tore out as translation rushed her back to the physical Realm.

CHAPTER 9

Annilasia sputtered and spit up ichor as spasms shook her. A dull throb seized her head. She rolled over towards the summit and away from the mountain clouds hugging the cliffside. It took her a moment to realize she was no longer screaming and that the shrill noises were from one of the other pupils. The scene that unfolded before her now overpowered the trauma from moments earlier.

All of her peers were strewn about the ground, much like herself, as if they'd fallen over in a deep trance. Of those she could see clearly, none moved or stirred. Her focus caught on four mentors who were gathered around one of these collapsed figures; only, this pupil wasn't motionless like the others.

This girl writhed like a cretaceon on its back.

The mentors struggled to help. One moment the girl would roll her shoulders and grow limp only to thrash violently in the span of an eyeblink. Her limbs struck at the air with uncoordinated swings. It reminded Annilasia of a doll on strings, only the strings were invisible and whoever was pulling them wanted this doll to rip itself apart. Annilasia flinched when one arm, unconcerned with the damage this would bring, slammed down on the ground. A loud crack mixed with an unnerving squish. Blood stained the stone tile.

The pupil never stopped her tormented sounds. When the lungs, exhausted and marred, gave out from shrieking, the noises dipped into low moans. This never lasted long. The screams would return, a sound that burrowed into Annilasia as a sickening dread. These were the sounds of a soul that didn't understand where the pain was coming from. Only that it would never end until they were dead.

Annilasia scrambled onto her feet and started to move towards the commotion, then froze. For a moment, the pupil defied the grips of the mentors and did something impossible.

The girl's body hovered above the ground.

It lasted mere seconds. The mentors heaved their weight upon the distressed pupil to drop her back down to the stone tiles. Aether suddenly erupted from the chaotic mess. The four mentors soared back in different directions, none managing to retrieve their wands in time. They tumbled to the far ends of the summit, a few nearly crashing over the sides and through the clouds.

The pupil, still screeching, shot up in one fluid motion to a standing position, as if something had heaved her up by the chest. The girl's head vibrated as screams and curses spat from her mouth. Her frantic hands clawed across her chest and arms, leaving deep streaks of blood where fingernails carved into the skin. Annilasia flinched again when the girl's hands finally found her own face. A finger plunged into an eyeball socket, excavating it. Blood erupted across the pupil's cheeks and lips.

Annilasia risked a quick glance at the mentors. They'd recovered, but to her shock, none of them moved to help again. Iveer wore a grave, defeated expression. When she looked back to the pupil, more self-inflicted damage riddled the girl's body. Blood lathered most of what Annilasia could see of her. Then there was a loud pop, and the girl's back exploded, propelling blood out with violent force.

The end happened quickly. Her arms shot out in opposite directions and tore off from her torso to slap the ground. Unbalanced, the girl teetered as one leg swung up towards the sky before driving down into the ground with a horrible crack. The aftershock of this impact ran up the girl's body and split her apart from the chest through her head.

The screams died.

Silence, aside from the merciless wind. No one moved.

Annilasia stared at what was left of the pupil. Blood bathed the vicinity around the corpse. When she mustered the will to look over at Iveer, her jaw clenched. A strange, unjustified expression of solemn knowing hung on his face as he stared back at Annilasia. As if this event should somehow mean something significant to her. They stood there for a moment. Her staring at

Iveer, Iveer staring at her. The other mentors didn't move either, unwilling to deal with the aftermath of their failed efforts.

One of the other pupils gasped and shot awake, looking around frantically before relaxing at the familiar scene, only to startle again upon observing the nearby carnage. The young man—Drifter, Annilasia realized—scrambled to his feet, hesitated, and then took tentative steps towards the dismembered body. In his hand was a glass wand, and it gleamed with a restless light.

It was then that Annilasia remembered the point of the trial. She looked down at her hands. The gloves remained, though her right was shredded across the palm. Her gaze fell to the ground where she spotted the shards of her wand at her feet.

Her encounter with the dokojin flooded her mind.

"I see no wand."

She stiffened at Iveer's sudden presence at her side. To avoid him witnessing her startlement, she went about dressing herself again to escape the biting cold. Her muscles spasmed with the endless shivers rippling through her.

"I'm not surprised," Iveer continued. "You've wasted your time here, sneaking around and using half-baked rituals for your misplaced endeavors. Your peers have spent that time training and preparing for this."

"What in damnation just happened?" she asked. Out of the corner of her eye, she could see a mass of red, but she refused to look back at the desecrated remains of the dead pupil.

"You mean Feliss? She must have stumbled across a dokojin. An aggressively nasty one at that."

"Dokojin don't do that," Annilasia stated as she fixed Iveer with a stern look. "You and I both know that."

"If you're basing that assumption on your intimate relation with your own personal dokojin, that would be a stupid thing to do."

"Answer me straight, Iveer," she hissed. "What just happened?"

"A dokojin tried to hijack Feliss's body," Iveer said with monotonous indifference. "The girl was no match and wasn't in control for most of what we witnessed. But the dokojin was impatient. It wanted control, it got control, and then it didn't know what to do beyond that. Worse, the brain could not keep up with the dokojin's manic thoughts and instincts. The rash transition from an Apparition existence to one inside a physical body was too much, too fast."

"Wait," Annilasia interjected. "You're saying a dokojin possessed her. But we already know what that looks like." She kept her voice hushed, side-glancing at the others on the summit to see they weren't listening. "Inzerious hasn't acted that erratic."

"Inzerious is patient."

Annilasia scoffed. "Sahruum's ass it is."

"Inzerious restrains itself. Your dokojin is quite wise for its kind. If it hadn't shown restraint, you wouldn't be alive." Iveer paused and leaned in, lips inches from her ear. "But make no mistake. Inzerious intends this very end for you after it is finished with your shell of a body. And without a wand to channel your own aether, it will conquer you before Wither's end."

Dread washed over her as she instinctively looked over to the maimed body still haunting the summit. That would be her fate. Blood and a violent, self-inflicted demise.

Iveer looked down. "What exactly *did* happen, Annilasia? Before the episode with Feliss, we heard you cry out and then witnessed your wand shatter. I was in the process of dragging you back to the Terrestrial Realm when I was interrupted by Feliss. You were ... whispering something unintelligible."

She stirred from her haunted stare, grateful for the distraction as she turned back to him. Her gaze followed his to the shards of her wand. She recalled the nightmare that had transpired in the dim-colored Realm.

"Inzerious is free."

Iveer shot her a dark look. "That isn't possible."

"I don't think I went to the Apparition Realm," she said, scrambling over her words with growing panic. "I translated somewhere else. There was no color, but that wasn't my doing. This place was different. The vibrations were stronger. The translation there and back nearly tore me apart."

"Slow down, you're blabbering."

She fixed him with a harsh gaze. "Listen to me. I encountered another dokojin. It held my lifechain, and it somehow freed Inzerious again."

Iveer scowled at her. "Again? You've met this dokojin before?"

"It—" Dying stars, she hadn't wanted to tell him all that'd occurred when she'd used the Three Mirrors. It was likely he could somehow bar her from using them again. But if Inzerious was free, and that—that—she glanced again at Feliss's remains—*that* was her immediate fate? She needed to be forthright. "It appeared in the Three Mirrors. That's how Inzerious was free the other night."

The scowl marring Iveer's face grew deeper. "I suppose a dokojin could undo my cage on Inzerious . . ." He pondered this for a moment. "But if your dokojin is free, why isn't it hijacking you, like poor Feliss over there?"

"I don't know. I don't care. I just need you to translate and cage it again."

Iveer grew quiet and closed his eyes. Annilasia could feel the slight vibrations that buzzed off him as he translated. She envied his ability to do so with such ease. It took her complete silence and mantras to reach a state conducive to natural translation.

His eyes snapped open. He frowned at her.

"Inzerious isn't there. Your dokojin is gone."

CHAPTER 10

Iveer and Annilasia retreated from the summit, leaving the other mentors and pupils to finish the final hours of the wand trial. Twilight fell across the barren trees as the pair returned to the coven dwellings. A clearing marked by stone tiles, much like those of the summit but absent of engravings, preceded a cluster of giant pineoaks, the branches of which hosted a tiered system of huts. Connected by several sets of spiraling stairs, these served as the quarters and study spaces of the monastery. The crypt lay directly beneath them but was unviewable and inaccessible from this location; its entrance was a mile or so off in the forest.

The journey from the summit back to the coven was spent in relative silence. Iveer couldn't be bothered to answer Annilasia's panicked questions; he simply frowned deeper every time she pestered him about Inzerious. She eventually gave up and concentrated on warming her body instead. She couldn't shake the wave of chills seizing her, even after she'd fully reclothed. She broke this silence when they were finally in his quarters. Her words dragged out between long breaths, a result of the long climb up the spiral staircase. It'd been a struggle to keep up with him.

"Get . . . to talking. Where . . . is Inzerious?"

She couldn't quite believe it. It didn't seem possible. Yet she hadn't had the concentration or energy to try and translate again on the summit. The unsavory temperatures, the gathered audience, and the morbid backdrop had made that challenging. For now, she was taking Iveer's word that the dokojin was gone, though she still had no details on what exactly he'd seen.

Iveer's eyes crawled over to meet hers, and a scowl wrinkled his forehead. He sank lazily into a tired cushioned chair. Threads unraveled at the base of it, and frayed plumes sprouted from it like it was a wild bird's nest. Unlike the worn status of his chair, Iveer's features found a tempered balance between seasoned and youthful. Though past his prime, the greys infiltrating his black hair congregated neatly at his temples in an arguably fashionable highlight. A well-trimmed goatee accentuated his age, but the steel in his eyes and a lack of wrinkles kept him from looking weathered. Annilasia had rarely seen him wear anything other than robes, and so wasn't sure how kempt his body was, but nothing in his posture or strides suggested weakness. Still, there was something about her mentor that always unnerved her. Perhaps it was the mere fact of his pursuits in aethertwisting. But his vile personality and sadistic methods in teaching meant there was probably something more.

Because of this, she found it tiring to look for long at him, so she instead let her eyes rove about the room as she all but collapsed into a less comfortable wooden seat. For such small quarters, it was furnished in an efficient manner that elevated the space. Books found their placement on dark wooden shelves, occasionally accompanied by oddities like jars of floating animal heads or by contraptions belonging to the pre-Residuum world. Annilasia's eyes always found the massive book with which she was well-acquainted.

It was part of what had brought her to the coven, though only a very small part. A twister had told her to deliver it to Iveer. Many times she'd thought of tossing the book aside and abandoning the task. But her need to be free of Inzerious had kept her on the path to the coven, and consequently, she'd fulfilled her agreement to hand the book over to Iveer.

The mentor had been displeased to find pages torn from it and was furious when he discovered that a particular artifact—a card—was missing from within the book's binding. Annilasia was to blame for both, but she'd kept quiet. No need to compromise herself, especially since she'd already used up the card.

"I don't know where your friend is, Annilasia" said Iveer. "I translated, expecting to cage your pesky parasite, and found nothing but your entranced aura."

"So, there was no offshoot from my lifechain? It's just gone?"

He cocked his head. "You know I can't see your lifechain. Only you could confirm that. But my inability to perceive Inzerious has me wondering. Perhaps it's gone off somewhere as a result of this new liberation you witnessed."

Annilasia tried to process this even as she sputtered out her confusion. "Gone off? Can we call it back? I can't have this thing wandering off only to return when I'm not prepared."

Iveer shrugged, taking this far more casually than she appreciated. "I don't know what's possible. I don't know what's truly happened." He leaned forward as if remembering something. "You said you went to a different Realm?"

Annilasia nodded. "It wasn't the Apparition Realm. I had some physical form there, but it had to have been an aether Realm because I could see Inzerious. I could see my lifestone and lifechain. There was no color, and I could make out only vague details." She paused to swallow as she recalled the moaning figure. "There were wires everywhere, running up to some sort of slab stone that held a person on it. They were in pain."

"You mentioned another dokojin. Was that it?"

"No. The dokojin was separate from whoever lay on the slab. The two seemed joined though. Like the dokojin could elicit pain in the victim." Her eyes widened. "Do you think that other dokojin did this?"

"You claimed it set Inzerious free, so it's possible that your dokojin's vanishing is its work as well. Did it give you its name? What did this other dokojin appear like? Do you feel like you were connected to it in some manner?"

Annilasia blinked as she tried to keep up with Iveer's questions. "It wasn't like Inzerious at all. It mimicked a human type of beauty. A frightening allure, like a flower with knives instead of petals. I wanted to stare and look away all at once. It was tall, slender. Had hair that couldn't decide if it was light or dark. And no, I don't think I was connected to it. It touched my lifechain, but it never wore it like Inzerious does." She'd been watching Iveer stiffen as she talked, and she recognized the look of knowing in his eyes. "What do you know?"

"Your description fits that of a dokojin I know well. She—forgive me, gender tends to be ascribed to this one, due to its attributes—she belongs to the twisters."

Annilasia's eyes narrowed. "Belongs? That's an odd way of putting that. What in dying stars are you getting at? Also, I think it goes without saying that relegating a gender to a dokojin is an insult to anyone who identifies under that label. That's disgusting."

"We made *her*," Iveer stated, emphasizing the pronoun with a defiant tone meant to dismiss Annilasia's judgement. "We call *her* Spiracy."

Annilasia shot out of the chair, her voice rising to an alarmed shout. "That isn't possible. Humans don't *make* dokojin. Dokojin evolve."

"And so did this one . . . at the hands of twisters. And the Realm you got caught up in is her lair. Her home." He paused and watched Annilasia struggle to accept his explanation. "Sit down. You're going to want to hear this, and it takes some explaining." After a moment of stubborn refusal, Annilasia sank back into the chair with a glare. Satisfied by her willingness, though begrudging, to comply, Iveer continued.

"Spiracy is an infant as far as dokojin go, but she is more powerful than you might imagine. The Realm you went to is where we've grown her. It's not within the Apparition Realm, but rather a dream Realm. I'm sure you know full well from your studies that countless Realms exist. We typically refer to the Three Realms—the Terrestrial, Apparition, and Ethereal—but there are many others."

Annilasia shot up her hand to interrupt. "A dream Realm? Those come and go with each passing night. They exist only so long as the sleeper is dreaming that particular dream." She closed her eyes as her mind worked and failed to piece it together. "Was I dreaming on the summit? Was she *in* my dreams?"

"No. You were in someone else's."

Her eyes snapped open. "How in the void and shite did I end up in someone else's dream?"

"That's a bit hard to explain. So pay attention."

He slipped the glove off his right hand. Turning to the cabinet at his back, he retrieved a jar of greenish liquid that sloshed around as he faced forward again in the chair. He placed the jar on the table and then screwed off the top. A crisp odor filled the room, and Annilasia scrunched up her nose. She opened her mouth to complain, but Iveer's hand shot up, so she said nothing. Iveer withdrew a stick from a nearby cabinet and held it up for her.

"Do you know what this is?"

She scoffed at him upon observing the hollow circle at one end of the stick. "Are you going to blow bubbles at me?"

"Good, so you know what it is." He dipped the bubble stick into the liquid, bouncing it a few times to thoroughly lather it before withdrawing it once more. The liquid dripped across his hand and onto the desk, but he showed no signs of irritation at this.

Iveer brought pursed lips to the circular portion of the stick, where the liquid bridged across it in a thin film, and blew out a stretched puff of air. The liquid bent under the pressure until it bloomed into a bubble that was anchored around the rim of the circle.

"So glad you can make a damn bubble, Iveer. Can we get back to—"

"Listen closely. See this bubble? Pretend it's a Realm. It exists there, fragile like a dream, ready to burst. That is the Realm you went to. But . . ." He trailed off and slowly rotated the stick so the bubble's arch faced him. Once again, he pursed his lips and blew, this time with less force. The bubble buckled and retreated from the new pressure, eventually pushing through the stick's circle to blossom through to the opposite side.

". . . the Realm isn't always in the same place."

"You've lost me."

"It's a crude demonstration, but I need you to keep it in mind as I explain this complexity to your tiny mind. Spiracy exists in a dream that is sustained by a dreamer, just as you've postulated. But unlike a normal sleeper, the dreamer never wakes. They dream this Realm for Spiracy, and they keep dreaming it until they die. Not only that, but there are actually two dreamers sustaining this Realm."

He brought his hands up to the stick and traced his fingers around the circular rim on the side without the bubble dome. "One dreamer here . . ." He popped the bubble before tracing his finger along the other side. "One dreamer here."

He held up the stick and looked through the circle at Annilasia. "One shared dream. And what I meant before is that Spiracy's Realm isn't always here at the monastery. That's why you've never before gotten caught in it. Remember the bubble. The Realm is usually with the other dreamer, at a different location from here." He pointed to the stick's circle. "It was on the other side of the stick."

Annilasia stared at him with mouth agape. It took her a moment to find the words that could encapsulate what her mind was screaming.

"What a bunch of shite."

Iveer glowered at her. "Don't be like that, Annilasia." He dropped the bubble stick inside the open jar before putting his glove back on.

"So, your incubated baby dokojin set my star-humping parasite loose. Is that what you're saying? I accidentally stumbled across your insane experiment Realm, and that's why we can't find my damn dokojin now?" She threw her hands up. "Why am I the only one who got stuck there? Why didn't the other pupils?"

"A curious mystery," Iveer mumbled. "One I don't have an answer to. Her Realm wasn't even supposed to be at the coven today, much less during a wand trial. And it's only accessible by dreaming. Perhaps the hopper's weed you inhaled was too much for you, and it swept you into sleep."

Annilasia stood up and paced what little space wasn't occupied within Iveer's quarters. "You've gone mad, Iveer. You can't control a dokojin. Why in blazes have the twisters gone and done this?"

"Spiracy will conquer Dardajah. That dokojin inside the Sachem is far too dangerous to have set loose on the world. We needed something to combat it."

Annilasia balked at him. "I think it goes without saying, a newborn doesn't stand a chance against something as primordial as Dardajah."

"Spiracy learns quickly, and she strategizes," said Iveer. "Much wiser than its primitive ancestry. She will annihilate Dardajah."

"So, your logic was to create a dokojin powerful enough to take on Dardajah, the very foe that none of us is able to defeat? Wouldn't that just make your dokojin a worse foe to fight after it has destroyed Dardajah?"

"Unlike Dardajah, Spiracy is under our control," Iveer emphasized. "And we have ensured there are ways for us to dispel her once she's accomplished her task."

Annilasia locked her hands together across the back of her neck as she paced. Regardless of Iveer's hollow assurance, Spiracy was yet another dokojin to worry about. She pushed away the anxiety of another danger on the horizon and returned her focus to her own problems. Back to her own dokojin parasite.

"Forget Spiracy. There has to be a way to get rid of Inzerious before it returns from . . . wherever," she said. "If it is still attached via my lifechain, then now is the time to break that attachment. It can't be impossible to sever a lifechain."

"You're talking about altering something that shouldn't be tampered with. To sever it, as you propose, would be severing your tether to your body. A kind of reverse astral suicide. But it's not a matter we need to argue about, as it's not possible. If it were possible, then people would have been prone to unfortunate accidents back when the Realms were melded as one. Accidents that would have permanently separated their auras from their bodies."

"I'm not trying to sever my lifechain. I want to snip off a vine that's growing from it."

Iveer shrugged. "The principle is still the same. It's not an object that we can alter. Its translucent quality is evidence enough of that."

"And yet mirajin and dokojin can interact with them," she murmured while deep in thought.

"Have you ever wondered why that is?"

Annilasia squinted down at him. "What do you mean by that? They come from that Realm. The lifechain and lifestone exist in the Apparition Realm, so it makes sense that entities from there can pick them up and . . ." She trailed off, her eyes widening. "Are you saying I should get a dokojin to do this for me? Or even a mirajin?"

"A dokojin would see no benefit without a cost to you," said Iveer. "Not to mention it's dokojin that have you in this bind to begin with. As for mirajin, we both know they aren't keen on us twisters. Sure, you could ask one, but you risk the mirajin stripping you of your power. That isn't what you want." He leaned back in the chair and waved a hand at her. "And that isn't quite what I meant by my question. Let me rephrase. Do you know what aether is?" Annilasia bristled, unsure if she should be offended. "I'm at an aether-twister coven. So yes, I know aether."

Iveer cocked an eyebrow. "A person can pick up a sword and wave it around, and still not know that the blade is made of steel. Aether is as complex as the air around you. Air isn't always clean, it isn't always breathable, and it isn't always in the same state. There are degrees of differentiation—both in air and in aether. Mirajin are the most concentrated, purest form of aether."

Annilasia inhaled. The two stared at each other for a moment as she tried to grapple with his implication.

"It's quite a poor reflection on my mentorship that you haven't figured that out yet in your time here at the coven. At least tell me you can quote the Cryptogram Pieces, stanza five."

Annilasia blushed and clenched her jaw. She wracked her mind for the proverb, saying it slowly so as not to misquote it.

The body is of dust, and it rots when it stops.
From the stars did we come, and the sea spat us out.
The aura is of aether, and sheds what it wants not.
From the dispel of emotions, aether gathers and clots."

Iveer smirked. "Word for word. I'll spare us both a lecture you don't honestly care about, and instead skip to the part you'll latch onto. That last line: 'From the dispel of emotions, aether gathers and clots.' It's talking about mirajin and dokojin. Those entities evolve from our emotions, our deeds, our intentions. When we die, our aura passes through the Apparition Realm, where it sheds the unnecessary burden of emotions and memories. Then we move on to higher vibrations. But those discarded abstractions gather and collect, until a day when this amassed type of aether takes on a sentience of its own. A mirajin, if it's pure aether. A dokojin, if it's instead aetherwaste."

When Annilasia said nothing and could only gape at him in utter shock, he sighed. "All that to say, it makes sense that entities made entirely of aether are able to interact with elements of their home aether Realms. Like the lifechains and lifestones."

"None of this helps me," she muttered. "It all raises more questions than answers about the aether Realms."

"Answers you'd have already found in our library if you'd taken the time to study," Iveer retorted.

Annilasia was silent as she mulled over the new revelations. Her lifechain—the one Inzerious clung to—was of the aether Realms, where everything was made of aether to some degree. Mirajin and dokojin were made of aether, both a result of discarded emotions.

Her mind made a startling connection.

Glass wands held aether. Twisters controlled wands.

"Could mirajin aether cut through the lifechain?"

Iveer frowned at her. "That's a mystery that even our library has no answer to. And you'd be hard pressed to find a mirajin willing to give up that amount of aether for any purpose."

"But do you think that it could be done?"

Iveer hesitated. "You'd need a wand to contain the aether. You don't have a wand."

Annilasia opened her mouth, but then caught herself before she spoke. Her lips sealed again. To ask a twister to lend their wand was of the highest atrocities condemned in the coven creed. As invested as Iveer seemed in her current plight, she knew he was merely curious about her pain. He would never hand over his wand to her, not unless she earned it, like at the trial. A trial she'd failed at. To ask such a favor now would only bring out some unfathomable punishment—perhaps even banishment.

Iveer broke the silence. "Perhaps the fate I've warned you of is upon you, Annilasia. Best prepare for that. For now, I suppose it is a waiting game for your pesky friend to return. As we wait, it's best if we lock you away. You will pose a threat to us should Inzerious succeed in hijacking your body."

Annilasia quivered, her hands balled into fists. This man didn't care at all. She could roll over and die, or explode into a million pieces when

Inzerious hijacked her body, and Iveer wouldn't bat an eye. To him, she was an experiment with an inevitable expiration.

"You're caging me?"

Iveer didn't blink, just stared up at her with a blank expression. "Better than ending you right here on the spot." He lifted his arm and let his wand slip out of his sleeve into his gloved hand. The tip pointed up at Annilasia.

"Your apprenticeship at the coven is at an end."

CHAPTER 11

Jalice didn't belong here.

The monochrome world around her left her disorientated, causing a foggy distillation of emotion. Almost as if none of what she was seeing or feeling was real. All she knew for certain was that she shouldn't have been here, and that she had no memory of ever arriving. She simply became aware here.

Though she was having difficulty focusing on any one memory from her past, an unnerving recognition grew inside her with each step she took across the dark metallic tiles that lined the floor. She knew this place. The twisting, endless corridor, made entirely of obsidian tiles that were too smooth and absent of markings, was all too familiar. Despite this, she couldn't place it. As if she'd visited it, only to forget that it ever existed until her return now.

Jalice halted, breath catching in her chest. A presence followed her. She turned ever so slightly to glance back. Down the stretch of hall, at an abrupt bend that took the path in a different direction, a sharp silhouette broke the otherwise natural dimness that reigned. Distinctly humanoid, the figure stood still only long enough for her acknowledgement. It sprang forward with powerful strides. Linear streaks of light lined the ceiling in a constant glow, and slowly this everlight revealed the details of her stalker as they approached.

Jalice gasped and clutched at her chest. Air wheezed through her constricting throat.

It was Hydrim. He'd found her.

She turned and ran. A voice of chilling familiarity called after her.

"Come back, my Tecalica. Have you not missed your Sachem?"

What started off as Hydrim's voice devolved into something guttural and inhuman—a screech of clamoring voices forced to speak as one in an unholy unity. By the time the last words punctured the air, an ancient wickedness pervaded around Jalice, feeding off her terror. She glanced back mid-stride and stumbled over her steps at the sight she beheld. It was no longer Hydrim that chased her.

It was Dardajah.

The bipedal dokojin charged at an erratic pace. Hunched over and constrained by the dimensions of the corridor, it pressed its giant wings into its body like a sleeping bat while its spiked horns dragged across the ceiling tiles, even as it careened towards her. Despite the black and white that dominated this place, or perhaps due to her foreknowledge of this monstrosity, its warped and decaying skin glistened, as though it'd been mutilated by fire.

Upon making eye contact with her, the dokojin unlatched its jaw in a shrill cry of ravenous anticipation. Teeth gnashed together feverishly. Jalice screamed and turned back to focus on her steps. She couldn't afford to stumble or falter. One misstep would seal her fate.

Her gaze, jolted by her sprint, happened to glimpse a strange apparition ahead. Her pounding heart skipped a beat, and the dreaded stumble broke her stride. She fell to her knees but kept looking ahead to confirm her flounder had been warranted.

At the far end of the corridor—a stretch of distance Jalice had failed to close—a new, lone figure stood shrouded in the everlight that streamed down from the ceiling.

Another dokojin.

She'd experienced too many of the damned entities not to recognize another. Unlike Dardajah, though, who maintained an overwhelming stature of horror that siphoned a victim's courage and bravado, this newcomer wielded an arsenal of uncannily terrifying features. An eerie yet elegant spray of hair draped past the shoulders and upper chest, blinking from light to dark hues. Grey skin glistened as if coated in a translucent creme, while a set of black, cavernous eyes gleamed with a similar iridescence.

It wore a human face, a feature that disturbed Jalice more than anything else. Its humanity continued on in its seductively smooth skin and hypnotizing curves. A cloak of blinding light ensconced it, serving as its only form of covering. Where the cloak joined at the neck, it plunged into a deep gap at the chest, exposing the inner crescents of breasts at the edges of its seams.

Its beauty wasn't real. Jalice knew that. But she couldn't look away.

This dokojin was nothing like the one that chased her. Dardajah had a way of drowning its victims in floods of violence. But this dokojin staring back at Jalice exacted an elegant distortion, one antithetical to Dardajah's disfigurement.

A sickening, moist warmth pressed into her back. Dardajah was upon her. Jalice opened her mouth to scream one last time. Time shifted around her, and in the span it took for her panicked air to breach her lips, the dokojin ahead of her had moved.

A pale, slender arm lifted out from the blinding cloak and floated up towards its face. The fingers, their tips like sharpened knives, curved into a fist that hovered for a mere second in front of its sealed mouth. Then one finger spiked in a fluid motion too seamless to reproduce. The dokojin's lips, previously sealed like a cursed chamber door keeping at bay all forms of wickedness, parted with such clean precision it seemed almost fake, a mockery of natural human behavior.

A shushed breath seeped through ebony teeth and curled past the vertical finger.

A razor-sharp rebuke to silence Jalice in her moment of death.

The scream that had evolved in Jalice's lungs, and had ascended in earnest through her chest, lodged in her throat like unchewed meat. All air refused passage, eradicating her ability to breath.

Dardajah collapsed upon her in a violent gnashing of teeth.

Vibrations erupted, tearing at her aura.

* * *

Jalice's eyes snapped open. She couldn't breathe.

Her limbs flailed as she convulsed, muscles rigid and clenched. She clutched at her throat. Someone hovered above her, and they uttered soothing words that did nothing to release the exhalation caught in her chest.

Where was the eerily beautiful dokojin? Where was Dardajah? "Take this," the voice said. It was deep, but unthreatening.

Though her lungs burned, her mind focused, trying to reorient her.

I'm in the Temple. I'm not with Dardajah. I'm in the Temple, awaiting trial.

"Hold this over your mouth," the masculine-voiced stranger repeated with intensity.

Jalice grasped for the proffered item. She pressed it against her face, nestling the odd cup across her mouth. Smoke barreled through the contraption and into her lungs. She sputtered, but a firm hand guided the mouthpiece back to her face.

"Breathe in deeply," the man instructed. "Breathe in, breathe out. Breathe in, breathe out . . ."

The man's rhythmic words eventually overrode Jalice's instincts, and she managed to wheeze in the smoke and then blow it out without coughing. The smoke exited through a slender tube that connected the mouthpiece to an oblong base, from which it bloomed into the air.

"That's it," the man encouraged. "Keep at it. Breathe in, breathe out."

Jalice repeated the process, inhaling the smoke into her lungs and then blowing it out through the tube. Her breathing slowly returned to normal. Relief and exhaustion replaced her waking panic. Her arm sank to her side, and the man retrieved the tube from her grip.

"I was afraid you'd succumb to suffocation," said the man. "The barra-bubak helped."

No longer fighting hyperventilation, Jalice noticed the man's thick accent. His golden eyes channeled a gentle, if enraptured, concern. This man was a stranger, yet she knew instantly that he was someone she could trust. Whatever his allegiances or motivations, he truly wished her no harm. Her willingness to accept this with little evidence startled her, but she didn't have the energy to fight or question the inclination.

Thick locs sprouted from his head, cresting at varying heights and melding with his brown skin. Baggy clothes draped his torso and legs, making it difficult to estimate his build. What little she could discern suggested a person who had spent much time on his feet but did little in the way of manual labor. A fit yet slender frame.

Jalice sat up some but winced. The pain pressed her down in the cot again, and she moaned.

"Don't move too much," the man instructed. "Your wound is far from healed."

"Who are you?" she asked.

The man gave a gentle nod. "Xiekaro. And you are . . . ?"

Jalice squinted, ignoring the invitation to share her name. "Where did the other man go? The one who threatened me."

A reluctance twitched at Xiekaro's smile. "He's . . . away. You get a break from that moody mess of a grump."

Her eyes widened, and she fixed Xiekaro with an expression of obvious desperation. "Can you get me out of here? He's going to have me executed. I need to escape before he returns."

Xiekaro rolled his head and winced. "That I cannot do."

Jalice frowned. "You're my guard, aren't you? He's charged you with keeping me in place."

Xiekaro spread out his hands, gaze drifting about the room. "Not quite. More of a healer than anything."

Jalice leaned forward. "I'll pay you."

Snickering, Xiekaro met her eyes again, his own prancing with a timid lightheartedness that carried into his words. "Afraid a few extra coins clinking in my pocket isn't in my future. Not much use for it here."

Jalice slumped back into the cot with a defeated sigh. "Everywhere requires coin. What makes this place so different? Where are we exactly?"

Xiekaro cocked his head with a teasing quizzical expression. "He didn't give you a tour?"

"You're a fine stooge," Jalice groaned. "Listen to me. That man you said is away? He's keeping me captive against my will. This is serious."

"Only as serious as you make it," Xiekaro retorted with a raised eyebrow.

Jalice huffed and clutched at the blankets to keep from lashing out. "You're infuriating!"

Xiekaro held up his hands, his playfulness sobering. "No need to get all ruffled. I was just trying to lighten the air you're so desperate to sour." He stood, walked to the sole dresser in the room, and placed the barrabubak atop it.

Now at a distance, she observed the tool that had helped ease away her hyperventilation—a thin tower with a fat bowl at its base where the smoke was meant to congregate. Open-ended cylinders drove out of this bowl to release the smoke; two of these were capped, while the other was fitted with a long, flimsy hose that coiled like a snake before ending at the mouthpiece she'd used. A second skinnier tube—the one she had breathed out through—connected at the bottom of the device, where she could see the tiny holes at the base that had let her exhalations sift into the air.

"What was that you gave me?" Jalice asked. "I'm not familiar with that contraption."

"Not surprising. Barrabubaks are rarely seen outside of their native homeland."

"And where is that?"

Xiekaro leisurely made his way back to the chair at her bedside. "The distant Indiligo Islands."

Jalice's eyes widened. She associated only one other item with that legendary place—a ring that her husband had given her many years ago. A ring she'd since tossed into the wilderness in a flimsy gesture of her disavowal of the same man who'd gifted it to her. A wave of nostalgia churned a sickening sensation in her stomach that bubbled up, but she quickly suppressed it.

"You're making that up," she said.

Xiekaro's brow furrowed, but his grin persisted. "Not a kind thing to accuse someone of, especially regarding a place so dear to their heart."

Realization dawned, and her eyes glazed over in awe. "Your accent . . . I couldn't place it before. It's very similar to the Sassere Tribe's, but it doesn't quite fit their speech pattern."

Xiekaro chuckled. "I'm not a damn ruby gem. You don't have to gawk like that."

Jalice blinked as her cheeks flushed. "Sorry. I just . . ." She shook her head. "The Unified Tribes hasn't received trade or shipments from there in so long.

It's easy to slip into the belief that such a place never existed."

Xiekaro's gaze faltered, drifting to the ground. "Rest assured, despite the Sachem's claims, my homeland and my people are very much real."

Jalice blushed harder, her muscles now rigid. "I—I didn't mean." She clenched her jaw. Why was she about to apologize? This banter and chatting had been a distraction. She'd wasted valuable time. "I traveled here with a friend. Where is he?"

"He?" Xiekaro, not hiding his disapproval of her earlier comment, continued to avoid eye contact. "Don't you mean *fae*? We're quite aware of your companion's mirajin identity."

"What did you do with faem?" she demanded. "If you hurt Elothel—"

"Peace," Xiekaro interjected. "We have not harmed your friend." He paused, and Jalice realized he was debating whether to add his next statement. "But I'm afraid fae isn't available for you to converse with."

"What does that mean?" demanded Jalice, her voice strained.

Xiekaro finally looked back at her. Seeing her anxiety, his eyes softened and his tone melted. "Be at peace, Jalice. Your friend wasn't harmed. But fae has entered a . . . coma of sorts. Or I suppose it's more of a trance." He noticed the flash of uncertainty and fear crossing her face, and rushed on. "There are other mirajin here. You're inside a Temple. When you and Elothel arrived, fae met the other mirajin who reside here, and together . . ." He trailed his hands through the air while searching for the right words. "They initiated some sort of ritual. And in this ritual, they've become unresponsive to the outside world."

"Why didn't anyone stop them?" Jalice asked with despair.

Xiekaro responded with a skeptical look. "You thought a group of mirajin could be stopped by mere humans?"

Her muscles slackened and she fell away from Xiekaro into the blankets. "I'm doomed," she whispered.

"Doomed is quite the dire conclusion," Xiekaro offered, the teasing tone returning to his voice. "Never had my company found so repugnant."

Jalice groaned, unable to decide which was worse: her current guard's humor and unwillingness to sympathize with her misfortune, or the man who had so fiercely interrogated her before vanishing.

"I want to see Elothel," she said sternly.

Xiekaro pursed his lips and sucked in a hesitant breath. "I was told to keep you in here. Besides, you shouldn't be up and walking in your state."

"I'll manage," Jalice seethed between clenched teeth. Fire raged across her stomach, but she forced herself up. Part of her despised Xiekaro's instinctive assistance when he bounded out of the chair to lend his sturdy weight for her to lean against, but she took his offer without much choice. Her legs wobbled beneath her even as she pressed her weight into the man's flexed arm.

With no concept of how far they'd need to travel, the journey sapped Jalice's resolve to see Elothel with each passing step. Sharp knives cut across her stomach as her muscles shifted, making her pace excruciatingly slow. When they finally reached their destination, sweat drenched her clothes and bandages, and her breath fluttered shakily.

"We've arrived," Xiekaro said, a strange reverence in his tone.

Jalice broke out of her pained daze and lifted her eyes. They stood in the doorway of a chamber. No more than a dozen or so strides from the room's walls, the floor dipped inward in a descending sequence of joined steps, forming three nestled squares that ended in a flat empty space. At each corner of this area, a sword was embedded in a hollowed-out slit in the ground that swallowed most of the blade. Of the four, only one glowed with a shimmering light.

A brilliant illumination surged at the center of the room, originating from between four silhouettes. The figures, sitting cross-legged on the floor and facing one another in a circle, remained utterly still. Their skin flowed with veins of multi-colored rivers that surged with pulsations of light and buzzed at a subtle vibrational frequency. None of them moved to acknowledge Jalice's or Xiekaro's presence.

Jalice stared in awe, unable to speak for a time. Finally, she asked, "Who are they? What is this place?"

"The swords are made of glass. When the Temple warriors accumulate too much aether in their blades from blocking twisters' attacks during skirmishes, they bring the blades here to have the energy discharged by the mirajin. But now, because they're in this trance, the mirajin are unavailable to do that." He paused, letting this information settle, then gestured towards the sitting figures. "Elothel is among them."

Without thinking, Jalice cried out her companion's name. She half expected Xiekaro to reprimand her for the outburst, but he did not. But neither did she receive a response from any of the mirajin. She tried calling Elothel again, disheartened when she received the same outcome.

"We're not sure if they can hear us," Xiekaro explained as if anticipating her next question. "They've been in that trance, emanating that energy and light, since you arrived—and they have not responded to any external noise or interruption."

"They've obviously translated," she said. "Has anyone done the same to try and reach them?"

"That has indeed been attempted. But we know only that they're within the Apparition Realm. No one knows to where in that Realm they have fled." Xiekaro turned to look at her. "Elothel explained only that connecting with the other mirajin would restore the depleted aether that Elothel has lost over the years and allow the mirajin to search for others of their kind. Fae stated it would be necessary before what is to come."

Jalice fell silent. Nausea overtook her, and the world suddenly spun. Xiekaro snatched her as she dipped into a half-conscious collapse towards the floor.

"We need to get you back to bed."

His words gargled in her ears, distant and slurred. Her vision crept with shadows. One thought repeated in her stricken mind.

I'm doomed.

CHAPTER 12

The trek back to Jalice's quarters brought with it far more pain. She winced as she hobbled forward, clutching at her abdomen. Xiekaro tensed, and his muscles flexed as he supported her weight.

Jalice gave a curt gesture with the hand that wasn't clutching onto him—a pitiful attempt to refuse his aid, especially as she was leaning into him fully. She expected a sly remark, or at the very least some hollow query regarding her safety. But neither came. Smart man.

When she grew tired of looking pathetic, she slowly shifted her body weight off him and back onto her own legs. The pain eased as she stilled but was ever at the edges, waiting to pounce with the slightest movement. She took this moment of relative reprieve to study her surroundings.

They stood in the center of a large corridor flanked by giant glass windows and gilded doors. Light poured across the carpeted floor, though it shone a muted grey due to the blanket of clouds in the sky. She stared at the outside world, soaking it in. Her quarters—or dungeon, as she knew it to be—had no window. This would be all she would get for a time as she healed. Yet the view wasn't much—just cliffs and ridges of black stone and darkened dirt, similar to the terrain of the Geibor Trench.

Her gaze flickered back to the empty corridor. She marveled at its grandeur—at how architecture of the Temple's majesty existed in such a secluded environment. Nothing of its magnitude stood within Vekuuv or Ikaul, not even the Sachem's towers and Fortress. Neither of the Temples within either tribe was of much comparison to this one.

Her appreciation descended into disquiet. The silence that surrounded them struck her, and she watched for any others who might be coming and going through the numerous doors that interrupted the inner wall.

"Where is everyone?"

"In other parts of the Temple. Trust me, we aren't alone here."

Jalice shook her head. "No, this isn't right. The place is too big, too empty. A waste of space if all its corridors aren't meant to host a crowd."

"A fair observation. Editshi Temple was once a hub for priestly academia. Those who wished to study under the mirajin came here to learn the secrets of translation and of the aether Realms. But alas, the last two decades have witnessed a mass exodus due to the threats at the border. Most academics have either left to train elsewhere or have defected to the twisters."

"Where did the loyal ones go?" she asked.

Xiekaro shrugged. "The templite apprentices went farther east, I suppose. As for their teachers, not many mirajin are left after the Sachem's decree for their eradication. Tillishu assassins traveled across the borders to kill them. The ones you saw earlier are all that remain to our knowledge."

Jalice looked up at him in confusion. "This seems like a strange choice for their home. Why stay so close to the dangers of the border? Why not flee east with their apprentices?"

Xiekaro broke their gaze to stare out the windows. "That's not something we have the privilege of discussing freely."

"Because I'm your prisoner."

Xiekaro didn't respond, but he looked down at her and smiled. "A prisoner only to circumstance. I have a feeling that if you weren't wounded, you'd be more than a match for me."

Her eyes narrowed. "You're not like the man who interrogated me. You have no sword. Your clothes are rather pedestrian, if a bit foreign. Why are you here?"

"Because this is my home. It has been for a while."

"You're a templite?"

"Of sorts. I specialize in healing. My practices have undergone a major shift towards more terrestrial approaches ever since the Realms split, which made using aether a less balanced exchange than it used to be. Leaves too much aetherwaste if not done precisely. I certainly came here to become a priest, but I never ascended the ranks due to the chaos of the Sachem." He held up his hands and wiggled his fingers. "See? Only one ring."

Jalice beheld the sole piece of jewelry on the man's right hand: a silver band with a bright red gem. It looked oddly familiar, yet she couldn't recall having ever met a priest. Then again, her memories were far from reliable. Some, when called, surfaced in vivid detail while others remained murky or fractured—a frustrating side effect after the liberation of her memories at the Black House. It seemed that some had simply decayed beyond the point of recollection, whereas those she'd recovered pestered her like waking nightmares. Often the flashbacks would steal her mind away and commandeer her body. She'd react and speak back to her hallucinations, and only Elothel had the skills to quell these episodes. She worried what might happen without faem present. Someone might get hurt when she slipped into her next flashback.

Xiekaro noticed her far-off expression. "Let's get you back to your room. You need rest. You've pushed yourself hard. With that gash in your gut, I think your body will be thankful for the bed once we get there."

Jalice wanted to argue, but she knew he was right. Her body swayed at the thought of having to move again, but she leaned into Xiekaro and they made their way down the rest of the corridor. They'd traveled only half its length when an unexpected voice at their backs called out.

"Xiekaro, what is this?"

Xiekaro shifted against Jalice to crane his head over his shoulder, inevitably moving her as he did. Wincing, she turned to glimpse the owner of the voice, and her breath caught.

Three figures trotted down the length of the corridor towards them. She quickly recognized the armor and scarves of the man who had interrogated her; the same attire was donned by the two well-built men flanking him. Unlike before, though, her interrogator no longer hid his face. Red hair, bushy and thick, swelled across the top of his head, and the same reddish hue bled into the trimmed facial hair across his face—all accentuated by firm brown eyes that glared at her with the same rage she'd seen in them before.

A thousand jolts of lightning sputtered in her head. The face that stared back at her, aged and far too weathered, no longer matched the features she knew, yet it was him.

Kerothan.

His appearance—the sweat that glistened on his forehead, the sheathed sword his belt brandished—mocked her frail memory of him. The boy she remembered had hated the demands of manual exertion and the sword's silent yearning for violence. The ring piercings in his cheeks, nose, and ears came as an entirely separate shock; they were a cultural custom of Heidretka, to which Kerothan did not belong.

He was *Vekuuv*, just as she was.

Yet undeniable similarities to the brother she knew remained. The red hair, the hesitation that constantly swirled behind his eyes, the posture that commanded a ready defense despite a lack of threat. His voice had deepened, but she heard Kerothan in it. Judgement traced its finely tuned edges, troubled with a disapproving tone.

"What happened?" Xiekaro asked in alarm, and Jalice realized the three warriors' disheveled state. Grime and dark streaks of blood marked their faces and armor.

"Nothing that should be discussed in front of her," Kerothan growled.

One of the men at Kerothan's back came forward to step in front of him. Much taller, and by far the eldest amongst them, the man looked to Xiekaro with a somber expression. "It was an ambush. We lost many of our kin. But it was not without small victories. We go now to discuss all this with the other clanheads." His gaze flickered to Jalice, then back to Xiekaro. "Take her back to her room and stay there with her."

"Kerothan."

All eyes fell on Jalice as the name left her lips, haunting the air like the ghost of her brother.

For so long, she'd thought him dead. Even Elothel's revelation—that Kerothan survived the Delirium and the Purge, and that he'd fled to Heidretka—had never settled in her heart as a reality. It'd been over twenty years since she'd seen him. Those last days now roared to the forefront of her mind—her betrayal, and every thread of memory tied to it.

And now, her brother stood before her as a stranger.

Kerothan said nothing. Even at a distance, she could see the harsh way he beheld her. He knew exactly who she was, and it was clearly a truth of which he wanted no part. Before anyone could respond to her utterance of his name, Kerothan turned and marched off in the direction he'd come. The third warrior—a massive hulk of a man—flashed a concerned look at the eldest before rushing after Kerothan. The remaining warrior gave one final glance to Xiekaro and Jalice before following his companions.

Jalice stared after them, even after the last had disappeared into the shadows. It had all happened so fast, and as the seconds ticked by, she wondered if she'd imagined it. Some hallucination conjured by her ailing mind and body.

Xiekaro realized Jalice either couldn't move or had no intention of doing so. He gently nudged her, bringing her out of her trance, and turned her again in the direction of her quarters. "Come, let's get you to that bed."

His voice broke the spell of her disbelief. "Was he truly there? Was that him?"

A beat of hesitation passed before Xiekaro replied. "Indeed, Kerothan has returned from the raid."

Jalice let out a shaky breath as she placed one foot in front of the other. Then her hand shot out, snatching Xiekaro with a sharp grip. "He was my interrogator. He pronounced my judgment. He…" She trailed off, swallowed, and whispered the rest. "He intends for me to die."

"Just keep walking," he said with an encouraging tone.

"Why would he do this?" she whispered, half-mindedly accepting Xiekaro's guidance down the hall. When he didn't answer, she grew quiet, letting her mind circle endlessly around the mystery of Kerothan's harsh exchange with her during what had been their reunion.

A horrible, sickening theory formed during the slow procession back to her room. Maybe Kerothan knew everything. Maybe he already knew the full extent of her betrayal—not only of the tribes, but of him personally.

Jalice fought against the nausea that washed through her at the thought. She grew faint, and in her quarters, she collapsed onto the cot before Xiekaro could ease her into it. A ragged sob shook her, and she twisted her head to face the opposing wall. She didn't want him to witness her tears. The drowning fear and shame over Kerothan's reaction doused whatever soothing words Xiekaro was offering. She ignored him, succumbing to the horrid possibility that her brother already knew what she'd done.

That she'd taken his beloved Hydrim from him.

Voices circled in her head like vultures. Words spoken within the confines of a past she wished to forget.

"Jalice, listen to me. I beg you. Hydrim is wicked. The Delirium is a facade …"

Then Kerothan's childhood warning died, replaced by a different voice. She cringed as Annilasia's disembodied words clanged in her mind.

"Kerothan is dead. Why are you aligning yourself with Hydrim? He's trying to enslave our tribe!"

Jalice pressed her eyes shut and sobbed, willing the voices to go away. But they didn't, and in the next breath, the phantoms merged with visions. A barrage of flashbacks cornered her, eliciting an undesired regurgitation of the past. In too many of them, she stood by in complicity as her husband—the chief of the Unified Tribes, the Sachem, her childhood friend—committed horrendous acts that sickened her stomach. She hated thinking about Hydrim. Nothing about him brought her peace or comfort like he once had. But even that past comfort was false. None of that endearment had been real. It had been a mirage of her own making—and his artificial affection a weak justification for marriage.

The flashbacks reminded her in painful detail of every mistake she'd made in her selfish conquest of Hydrim.

Including the betrayal of her own brother.

CHAPTER 13

"It was a massacre."

Kerothan's words struck like a viper. Those present in the meditation chamber held their breaths, perhaps wondering if the venomous bite in his tone would be scolded or permitted. He glared at his audience. Clanheads and clannite warriors of higher status than him, yet he didn't care how they regarded him. They needed to hear this. This crowd was a far cry from that of the last gathering. Too many had lost their lives down in the caverns. Their numbers had dwindled down to just a handful of clans and far too many orphaned clannites.

"Those valiant souls who entered the caverns didn't have to perish," Kerothan stated, his voice a pinnacle of solemn judgement. "I warned my clanhead of a possible ambush. Yet I was ignored. Instead, our brethren were ripped apart—physically and astrally. We watched as their skin disintegrated in the acidic waters. Listened to their shrieks as the twisters mutilated their souls upon their arrival in the Apparition Realm. How the latter was even possible defies my knowledge. The device we found must surely be some abominable technology to be able to accomplish such a horror. But it should not have happened at all."

The hush in the room persisted. Kerothan's eyes whipped to Cephus. The older man's face, still hard to read, creased with wrinkles of shame and irritation. But it was Orithmor, standing beside Cephus in the line of clanheads, who addressed Kerothan.

"There was every possibility that the cavern did not house an ambush, young Kerothan. Alerting your clanhead followed our customs, but if we acted on every concern brought to our ears, we'd tear ourselves apart going in diverging directions. Cephus may have erred, but to lay blame entirely on him is unwise."

Kerothan bristled. "Will no one be held accountable for the deaths of our kin?"

"Those responsible for their deaths will be held accountable," Orithmor affirmed. "The twisters who ensnared our brethren will be brought before Sahruum for justice."

"That isn't enough," Kerothan retorted, then quickly lowered his voice upon hearing his unchecked frustration. "If I can't trust my leaders to heed a warning of danger, to hear and respect me, then we will continue to have tragedies such as this. If Cephus had taken my words to heart, this gathering wouldn't be as empty and hollow as it is. I know that each of us can feel the absence of our kin who would otherwise be standing with us right now."

"That is impossible to know," Cephus stated. "The ambush may very well have already ensnared us by the time you voiced your suspicions. Do not patronize me with the supposition that your warning alone would have saved us."

Kerothan, unyielding, held Cephus's gaze. Souls were now lost because Cephus had dismissed him. Not for the first time, Kerothan wondered if the blunder could be traced to some form of jealousy plaguing the man. Perhaps under that stoic, cold facade, Cephus held some vendetta against Kerothan for desiring Ophim. But that was something Kerothan would not dare utter in mixed company.

"What disturbs me is the fact that our presence preceded us," said Tesritt. "How did the twisters know we were coming?"

Murmurs arose from the warriors gathered. "A spy amongst us," someone shouted from the crowd, and was answered with a chorus of shouts.

Tesritt held up her hands to silence them. "We've taken a prisoner, have we not?"

Cephus turned to her and nodded. "There were only three twisters at the machine's location. Two were slain, and we claimed the other. He was taken to the dungeons upon our return."

"Another injustice," Kerothan interjected. He ignored the harsh glares of the clanheads. "You speak of meting out judgement on those who are to blame for the massacre. Yet you've spared the life of one. Sahruum's justice must be brought upon him; he deserves the same fate he imposed upon our brethren."

"Justice will prevail, and judgement pronounced," Orithmor said with unmasked irritation. "But this twister can provide vital information on how they learned of our plans. Not only that, but we must glean the purpose of that machine."

"Templites have already been sent to investigate it with a small troop of our warriors," Tesritt announced.

"It isn't safe," Kerothan balked. "No one should be going back there."

"We have to know what the twisters are scheming," Tesritt shot back. "Would you have us keep blindly swinging our swords at every shadow in the land without knowing if our blades strike true? We were ambushed because the twisters are ten steps ahead of us; we can't afford to give them that advantage. Soon, we won't be gathering here in this chamber. We'll be underfoot as the twisters swarm over our dead bodies and overtake the free tribes."

"That will only happen faster if you keep one of them alive under our roof," Kerothan yelled.

"Enough!"

A tense hush fell over the crowd at Cephus's outburst. The clanhead glowered at Kerothan, whose face flushed with heat. Rarely did Cephus raise his voice to such an extent, and Kerothan knew he'd overstepped.

"What's done is done," Cephus stated. "We will grieve for our fallen, but we cannot afford to fight amongst ourselves. We have a prisoner, and we will use him for all he's worth."

"You aren't suggesting torture?" Orithmor asked with a hint of warning to his fellow clanhead.

"Of course not," Cephus agreed.

Kerothan bit his tongue, but it only worked for a mere second. "Why not?" he demanded.

The clanheads gaped at him in astonishment. "Because we are not them, clannite," Orithmor answered. "Torture is a twisted act of war that our enemies enact in their depravity. Sahruum would not have us tear apart what has been made in celestial glory."

"There's nothing glorious about a befallen twister," Kerothan countered. "They've lost the right to celestial birth status. Their auras are tainted, and they taint the auras of others. It is best to cut off such poisonous weeds before they infect those we care about."

Before the argument could continue, the doors to the chamber burst open. All eyes turned to the intrusive newcomer. Xiekaro stood inside the doorframe, eyes wide and swollen with panic. He surveyed the room, clearly flustered and unsure who to address. Upon seeing Kerothan, he wet his lips. "You must come quick," he urged. "Something's happened to her."

Kerothan frowned and grabbed for the hilt of his sword. "Has she escaped?"

Xiekaro waved his hands apologetically. "No, no such thing as that. She started speaking to someone who wasn't there, then a fit of spasms overtook her. She fell into an abrupt sleep—so fast I thought she might have died—and when I tried to wake her . . ." He trailed off, face crestfallen and solemn.

"It is the Endless Sleep!" someone shouted. "It's come for us all!"

Irritation boiled inside Kerothan. He moved through the circle of warriors to present himself fully to Xiekaro. "Is this true? Is it the Endless Sleep, or is the prisoner tricking you?"

Xiekaro gave an unsure shrug of the shoulders. "She's still in her quarters. I told the guards not to enter or let anyone else inside. Perhaps someone else should repeat my attempts to wake her. If it provides further proof, she *has* started whispering like the others."

Kerothan looked over his shoulder at Cephus, a new frustration burning inside him. "We should have never let her stay here. She should have been taken—"

"Be silent!" Cephus barked. "We've had this discussion already. Her wounds would not have permitted us to move her beyond here." He addressed Xiekaro next. "Summon Rejiett. She knows what to do. But have her wait until I've arrived. I'll be there shortly."

Xiekaro nodded but hesitated.

"There's something else," Kerothan stated, reading the restrained panic in the man's face.

Xiekaro swallowed and took a slow breath in and out. "I saw ..." He cocked his head, as if the words refused to leave his lips. "I saw ... something wicked in Jalice's quarters." He blinked as revulsion wrinkled his face. "It stood over her, like some terrible harbinger of death. Long fingers, with nails so sharp and long they seemed knives, touched Jalice's face." Tears filled Xiekaro's eyes, and his voice quivered. "Then the monster ... shushed me."

Kerothan's heart jolted. "I thought you said Jalice was alone. You're saying there was someone else in the room with her? Was it a twister?"

"No. It was a dokojin."

Alarmed murmurs filled the chamber but were silenced with Cephus's next words.

"That is quite the claim, healer," Cephus stated. "This Temple is cleansed daily by the templites. It is one of the purest sites across the lands. No dokojin should have the ability to tread in the Apparition Realm intersecting this place. Are you sure of what you saw?"

Xiekaro nodded, and despite the fear so obvious in his movements, a firm confidence exuded from him. "It stood over Jalice, looked at me, and brought one of its spindly fingers to its lips to—" A shiver ran over him as he failed to finish the statement. "Then it vanished."

"There can't be a dokojin here," said Kerothan. "There isn't a way for dokojin to enter the Terrestrial Realm with the Realms separated as they are. You must be mistaken. Perhaps Jalice is a twister and has conjured hallucinations to outsmart you."

Xiekaro shifted his gaze to Kerothan. "It is a strange thing to see a phantom, clannite. Once it is seen, it does not leave the mind. But it doesn't stay either. It skulks about in the mind like a rumor or a whisper. It teases and taunts—makes one wonder if they ever truly saw it to begin with. I saw enough to know I saw *something*. Beyond that? Anything is possible."

The room fell silent. The warriors turned from Xiekaro to the clanheads as they waited for a response to this fantastical account. Orithmor lifted his chin and brought his hands together in front of his chest. "We don't have time to argue the details of a phantom. We must attend to the Tecalica. If she is indeed in the Endless Sleep, we will move her to the Whisper Chamber."

Kerothan was already racing towards Xiekaro ahead of the crowd's dispersal. He gripped the templite firmly by the arm and dragged him towards the doors. "Come with me. I promise that she's tricking you. She's a master at it."

***

Jalice did not wake.

No amount of shaking or harsh words broke the sleep that had befallen her nor the string of whispers lifting from her lips. By the time Rejiett arrived at the Tecalica's quarters, Kerothan had given up trying to end his sister's trickery. The priestess found him sitting rigid and tense in the lone chair of the room. Xiekaro was kneeling at the bedside with a somber expression.

"So, the precious Tecalica has succumbed to the Endless Sleep," Rejiett mused as she went to join Xiekaro at the edge of the cot.

"Don't you fall for it too," Kerothan muttered. "This is all a scheme to escape justice. She'll wake when she thinks we've lowered our guards."

Rejiett cocked an amused eyebrow at the warrior. "She's whispering—a sure sign of this ailment. If I translate, and her aura is missing, then we'll know this to be more than a ruse."

Kerothan glimpsed the priestess's face under the drawn hood, and their gazes met for a brief moment. The dim grey eyes that stared back at him did little to detract from the youthful beauty etched in her chiseled face. A sharp jawline brought with it facets of power and control that augmented her demeanor and precise movements. Her skin was pristine, a far colder shade of white than even her cloak, and her head, shaved save for a small bit of ponytail unsealed by the hood, pulled all attention towards those dull yet intrusive eyes.

The priestess unnerved him. He wasn't sure if it was the fact that she'd mastered the same skills so flagrantly practiced by the twisters, or if it was something about her personality. He knew he wasn't the only one among the clans to feel this way. A strange dynamic eddied between the priestess and the clanheads.

The templites had pleaded with the clans of Heidretka to come to their aid at the border, and the clans had answered the call. But for all the urgency in that summoning, the clans had been met with unexpected resistance from the Temple's priestess. She insisted that no violence occur on Temple grounds, and had pressed the clannites to distance all skirmishes in service of this request. This proved difficult, and had resulted in many twisters breaching their defenses to disappear into the eastern lands.

Now, as Rejiett put a jeweled hand on Jalice's forehead, Kerothan couldn't help but wonder if she and his sister were colluding in some nefarious plot to infiltrate the Temple. His eyes caught on the gems set in her rings as they twinkled in the torchlight. A pang of jealousy and resentment passed over him. He envied how the priestess could boast such terrestrial gems and still translate without so much as a flinch of pain. It shouldn't surprise him though. A few rings on the fingers wouldn't cause much pain for someone who translated as infrequently as the templites did. Twisters had more to fear of such things because they interacted with the aether Realms on a daily basis.

As for him and the other clannites, natural translation wasn't an option. They'd ensured as much by piercing their bodies with numerous rings and metal jewelry. Part of him had embraced this—he wanted nothing to do with aetherwielding after what he'd seen twisters do—but there were times he wished he could study the skill so he might fight the twisters with their own weaponry. Not that the templites did that either. Using aether for violence was exactly what made that energy decay into aetherwaste. So, the templites used their skills only as a counteractive measure, such as for spying and healing. They never engaged in skirmishes.

Kerothan heard a buzzing in his ears, and his skin tingled. He watched as Rejiett stood over Jalice with eyes closed, unmoving as translation took her into the Apparition Realm. The vibrations stirring the room ceased. It wouldn't take her much time, but he grew impatient, shifting in the chair.

Xiekaro fidgeted his fingers. His eyes would at times flicker to Jalice's restless lips, and Kerothan wondered why the healer seemed to want her whispering to cease as much as he did. Minutes later, the room took on the subtle vibrational shift again, ending when Rejiett's eyes snapped open.

"Her aura is hidden," the priestess announced. "She isn't in the Apparition Realm, which means she is in whatever place the Endless Sleep takes its victims."

Kerothan sprang out of his chair in a surge of anger. It rocked against the wall behind him, but he didn't care. He fixed his glare on Rejiett. "This is a trick," he growled. "She's asleep. Just because she doesn't show up in the Apparition doesn't mean she ails with the Endless Sleep. Sleeping auras rarely show up there." His nostrils flared, and he cocked his head at her in a show of arrogance. "Bet you didn't think I knew so much about translation."

Rejiett regarded him with an unfazed expression. "I assure you, clannite, the Endless Sleep has taken her. I am skilled enough at interpreting an individual's vibrations to know whether they're merely asleep or if their aura has translated." She paused, eyeing him up and down, then a glimmer of excitement brightened those dull grey eyes. "You're the brother."

Kerothan said nothing but couldn't stop the heat warming his face under the priestess's scrutiny. Xiekaro looked between the two and cleared his throat before saying, "She should be taken to the Whispering Room."

Rejiett didn't break her gaze with Kerothan. The slightest curl at the edges of her lips implied a smile, the kind that made Kerothan squirm. "You could cause a lot of trouble," she said.

Kerothan's brow furrowed. He wasn't sure what to make of that statement, and out of the corner of his eyes, he saw a similar look of confusion come over Xiekaro. The healer cleared his throat once more, trying to catch the priestess's attention.

"Yes, yes, Xiekaro," said Rejiett. "She should be transferred by cot to the chamber with the other unfortunate sleepers. Go find someone to help this warrior complete the task."

Xiekaro shuffled towards the door, looking grateful to be leaving the tense room. Kerothan waited for the priestess to exit as well and grew anxious when she made no move to do so. Rejiett turned towards Jalice. A slender object slid out from her sleeve. Kerothan tensed, unable to hold back the faintest hiss of a gasp as he beheld the glass wand. The sound brought the priestess's attention back to him.

"Come now, clannite," Rejiett smirked. "Surely you are not so scandalized by the sight of a glass wand?"

Kerothan licked his lips as he glowered at her. "I usually expect them to be pointed at me."

"Don't play daft," she said in a mocking tone. "You know full well that the mirajin have blessed us templites to use these. We can't help that many of our own have stooped to aethertwisting and tarnished our name."

"That doesn't make me any less nervous around them," he said. "I've seen what they can do."

She looked between Kerothan and the wand, noticing something. "You're curious, aren't you? Just as much as you are unnerved by them, you wish you knew how it all worked."

Kerothan pursed his lips and said nothing. He couldn't deny it, but he wouldn't give her the benefit of that admission. Rejiett let out an amused chuckle as she held up the wand to glisten in the candlelight. Inside the glass, tendrils of light swam and danced in an endless stream of motion.

"They are curious tools, aren't they?" she commented. "We collect aether into them, and then we use the wand to release it. Aetherwielding is a matter of will. Emotion and purpose are often conflated, but it is purpose that manipulates aether. Emotion is simply the fuel."

Kerothan frowned, irritated with himself, but unable to resist the bait. He wanted to know more, and unprompted, he would have never actually asked a templite of their secrets. This was his chance to learn more. "If it comes down to a matter of will, why do you need the wands at all?" he asked. "Sounds like you could focus the energy with your mind alone."

Rejiett nodded. "A fair deduction, and not entirely erroneous. A strong enough will could manipulate aether without a wand. But a human with that kind of resolve and practice is beyond rare. I've known only a few, and they're long dead—inhabitants of the early Residuum era. The ability to bend existence, with one's own mind and resolve alone, is a hard skill to master."

"Don't the mirajin and dokojin do such things?" he pointed out. "If they can, why can't we?"

Rejiett's smirk grew as she eyed him with a look of surprised acknowledgment. "Another smart question. One that every templite apprentice asks. Mirajin and dokojin can indeed mold and twist aether to their wills as easily as we can swing our arms in the air. But that's because they're made entirely of aether in one form or another. They interact with that energy as casually as we drink, piss, and play in water. Not only that, but they evolved in it, just as we evolved out of water. They come into existence within the aether Realms, while we come into existence in the physical world."

Kerothan pondered this for a moment, too embarrassed to admit she'd lost him. He shifted his weight nervously between his legs. "All seems rather complicated," he muttered. He was prepared to let the conversation die, but his curiosity pushed more questions through his lips before he could stop himself. "I still don't see how the wands help."

"They act as conduits," Rejiett explained. "We trap aether inside them while we're translated in the Apparition Realm. It's easier to convince ourselves that this transparent, empty-looking material can be filled with something, even if that something is as intangible and abstract as aether."

"But aether is real."

"Yes, but our minds can better grapple with the glass since it exists here in a physical sense. We can see and touch and interact with it. Understand this: our minds struggle with intangible, invisible concepts. If we can't see or interact with something—like aether—then we engage with imagination in order to understand it. The problem is that, as we get older and exist longer and longer in the Terrestrial, the more our minds adopt a sense of truth that the physical is more real than the aether Realms. Convincing our minds otherwise becomes harder with each passing day. A templite's training is to unlearn this—to convince the mind that the physical is actually submissive to the will, a concept that is in turn applied to invisible aether."

"It seems like a dangerous thing," said Kerothan as he eyed the wand in her hand. "Convincing your mind of such ideas. Isn't it borderline delusional to believe the physical is not a base reality? Sure, the aether Realms exist, but this is where our bodies reside. This is what is real until we die."

Rejiett raised her eyebrows at him. "It *is* dangerous, at least given the state of things. With the Realms separated, it's harder now more than ever to impress the mind with a sense of duality. It's certainly not something to be apathetic towards. The mind can break if it's pressed too hard to believe something it doesn't see as true."

"No wonder the twisters have gone mad."

Rejiett flourished the wand at him in an accusatory manner. "Careful. Dangerous doesn't equate to wicked. Fire is dangerous, but we use it anyway. The mind is resilient, and if trained properly, just about anyone can learn to aetherwield."

"Dangerous can imply unwise," Kerothan countered. "But I suppose if the mirajin gave their blessing, then they must have expected some form of aetherwielding." He paused as he continued to study the simple outline of the wand. "But how do the glass wands even exist in both Realms?" he asked. "My understanding is that things in one Realm often don't translate to another. Or if they do, their nature changes entirely."

Rejiett gave an affirmative nod. "Your understanding is accurate. The mystery of the glass wands is one I don't have an answer to. The mirajin are tight-lipped about the origins and creation of the wands. Even the highest templites are not privy to those answers. Perhaps someday we will be. But there are countless secrets to unravel regarding the wands. What happens when a wand is left in the Apparition Realm intentionally? Does it vanish here in the Terrestrial Realm? Can the link that ties the wand across the Realms be broken? And why is it that aether is invisible in this Realm except when it's bound in these glass wands?" She shrugged, relenting to her lack of knowledge.

Kerothan remained quiet. He stared at the glass wand, marveling at the power—and chaos—such a simple object could contain and unleash. Soon,

Jalice's whispers overtook the ensuing silence. Kerothan tensed when Rejiett raised her wand over the woman.

"What do you intend to do?" he asked, his tone straddling respect and wariness.

Rejiett didn't turn, remaining hidden behind the veil of her hood. "Do you think me a twister?"

Kerothan licked his lips, unsure how to pry a straight answer from her. "You checked her aura. Wasn't that enough? What else do you need to do?"

Before Rejiett could answer, the door leapt open. Cephus and Ophim stepped in, and the two took in the strange tension of the scene. When Kerothan glanced back towards Rejiett, he found she'd hidden the wand again.

"Have you already checked on the Tecalica?" Cephus asked the priestess. "You were supposed to wait until I arrived."

Rejiett nodded slowly, ignoring his irritated tone. "It seems Jalice has been taken by the Endless Sleep. She should be moved to be with the others." The priestess swept towards the door, not breaking stride. The two men parted ways to permit her to pass, and she disappeared out of the room.

"Cephus and I can take care of moving her," Ophim offered as he looked to Kerothan. "You don't have to be a part of this."

Kerothan approached the cot and peered down at his sister. "No. As much as I want nothing to do with her, I will follow this through until she's tried for her crimes. I will bear the weight and inconvenience of her presence. At least she's trapped now. Her body will soon forsake her."

No reply came from his fellow clannites. Neither wanted to fight him on that callous statement. He heard shuffling behind him, followed by Cephus and Ophim approaching the bed with a mobile cot. Without another word, Jalice was transferred onto it.

The stifling journey to the Whisper Chamber left Kerothan's skin burning; not even the chill seeping into the Temple could stop his sweating. They passed through forsaken halls full of smudged windows covered in cobwebs and did not come across another soul until they came within sight of their destination. Outside the massive doors stood a cluster of white robed templites. At the head of this group was Xiekaro.

"She'll be taken care of," he said as the templites at his back moved to open the massive wooden doors to the chamber.

As if to counter Xiekaro's claim, a nauseating wave of sweat and body waste bled out from the chamber. The cloying sweetness of perfumes and incense—a meager attempt to overpower the horrible smell—drifted out with the odor. Kerothan flexed his nostrils as he resisted the urge to retch. He kept his focus on his footing as he and Ophim resumed their march carrying the cot, this time into the chamber.

If not for the stench or the makeshift beds lining both sides of the room, the chamber might have been inviting. Light bathed the space via windows fixed on the upper left wall, lending a serene quality to the space. It may once have seemed a peaceful place to convalesce. But the beds weren't claimed by people cursed with a sickness that would soon heal.

The beds were filled with the living dead. These souls would never wake.

As soon as Kerothan and Ophim lowered Jalice's cot to the ground beside the only empty bed in the chamber, Ophim fled the room with urgent steps that betrayed his unease. Kerothan lingered to stare down at his sister. A confliction of emotions warred within him. She deserved this fate—a fitting spell for someone who cared so little about those around her. She'd never wake. She'd be dismissed from the compassion of others. Though a burden still to the poor healers tasked with the impossible duty of keeping her alive for as long as possible, she at least couldn't wreak havoc on the Terrestrial world any longer.

Yet as his gaze rose to observe the others in the room, his stomach churned. Motionless bodies, riddled with sores and thick veins, occupied the beds. His fellow clannites. Those whom he'd traveled and conversed with since his adoption into the Heidretka tribe. Their bones pressed like sharp sticks against thin skin. The only movement among any of them came from their lips as the undying whispers croaked from their dry throats. No one knew what they whispered; only one word had cropped up amid the incoherent strings of mutterings. One single word that each had uttered at some point.

Spiracy.

THE SPAWN OF SPIRACY

A tug at his arm startled Kerothan out of his trance. He turned, surprised to see Ophim had returned and was now looking at Kerothan worriedly. The other man fixed him with a gaze that avoided the withering bodies on the beds. Kerothan nodded. They needed to leave. The healers would take charge of Jalice's care now. They would ensure she stayed alive.

Alive. That seemed too generous a word for those who'd been sleeping for months without end, whispering away, force-fed and cleaned by hands they couldn't acknowledge.

He followed Ophim out, unable to bring himself to take a final glance. He swallowed down the inkling of pity surfacing for Jalice. It quickly drowned beneath a wave of anger over her convenient escape from a more proper judgement.

Even in custody, she'd found a way to run from her sins.

CHAPTER 14

Awareness brought panic.

Darkness reigned in this indeterminate place, yet a faint, unsourced permeation of light allowed Jalice's eyes to adjust slowly. As they did, strange lines and shapes fleshed out. Lesser shadows slunk against the backdrop of utter void, and her mind pieced together the various shapes until, all at once, she realized she wasn't alone.

The murky outlines and details of a face mere inches from her own made her heart stop.

She screamed. But the jolt that should have sent her scurrying backwards did nothing. Her back met resistance. She threw force into her arms, attempting to lash out at her stalker. More panic rushed through her when she found that her arms and legs were restrained. All she could do was cower against the slab to which she was bound. She twisted her neck so that her cheek pressed against the smooth metal beneath her, wanting to close her eyes against the horror staring down at her but unable to.

If she closed her eyes, then it'd be able to see her while she couldn't see it.

Instead, she absorbed the details of the abomination. Fleshy membrane coagulated in a horrifying mockery of a face. A web of veins stretched beneath the grungy layers of translucent flesh, crisscrossing in an organic labyrinth of grey lines. Hovering within it were two lidless eyes of sheer oblivion. It was completely devoid of a mouth.

Ragged breaths punched through Jalice's chest, and she dry heaved as she pulled in the creature's putrid stench of rotten fish. Still, this didn't keep the shriek from building inside her and exploding. Another noise joined hers, and she fell silent.

A crude string of sounds gurgled out of the creature. It tried again, and she heard an unsettling familiarity in them. The sounds pitched in an eerie, panicked desperation. Much like hers. Jalice inhaled, swallowed the resulting nausea, and froze, eyes growing wide as she beheld the creature. Though it had no mouth, its perimeter expanded and then contacted as though taking a deep breath.

It was mimicking her.

She thrashed against her restraints and threw her head back against the metal slab. "Get me out of here!" she shrieked. "Get me out!"

The words echoed in the wake of their utterance, repeated by the creature. They were unarticulated, as if the creature wasn't sure how to say the words and could only manage the pitch of her vocals. It leaned in closer, its eyes inches from her lips. Jalice quivered and let out another scream, which the creature matched with near perfect pitch. Her lungs burned, and she went to inhale, but the air caught in her chest as she froze.

A crease in the facial flesh had parted, and the creature was copying her words again, this time with clearer, ungarbled vocalization.

A mouth. It had grown a mouth to better mimic her.

Jalice bucked wildly and shut her eyes. She couldn't take it anymore. She didn't want to see it.

A smooth, feminine chuckle from somewhere silenced the creature's eager screeches, and when Jalice snapped her eyes open to observe this new arrival, she found the monstrosity had vanished. In its place was darkness, out of which a new silhouette appeared, manifesting from the shadows. It stopped before Jalice could make out anything beyond the curves of a luminescent cloak.

"You'll need to provide more than primitive cries for my pet if it's going to learn anything."

"Please let me go," Jalice whimpered, her voice shuddering.

The chuckle came again—a lustrous yet deep sound that teased comfort but warned of death. "That's better. More words, Skinflake."

Garbled noises sounded from somewhere in the void of the space around them. Still wrong and uneven. But Jalice recognized her words, repeated back with excruciating deliberation.

"Leese leh ee goooo."

"Why does it keep doing that?" Jalice demanded. "What in the deep abyss is that thing?"

"Slower, Skinflake," the feminine voice said over the mess of noises the creature was making in response. "It can't keep up."

"Please make it stop," Jalice pleaded. "Let me go. I don't belong here. I don't know how—"

The voice shushed her, cutting Jalice off. More warped sounds followed, but Jalice didn't register them this time. She saw movement as her captor glided forward from the shadows. A grace imbued its movements, promising no misstep or clumsiness. It took a moment before Jalice realized that it hovered above the ground. Black pits served as its eyes, and the disturbing perfection that dictated every breath, every movement, every inch of its skin, told Jalice what she beheld.

The dokojin from her dream.

"You do belong here," the dokojin whispered, smiling at Jalice's discomfort as it grew closer. "Do you want to know my name? It might be best, since you'll be seeing quite a bit more of me during the transmutation."

Jalice opened her mouth but had no chance to protest.

"Spiracy. My name is Spiracy."

A chorus of hoots and clicks burst forth from above Jalice. She curled inward and searched the darkness from which the noises had erupted. Whatever it was numbered in the hundreds. Maybe thousands.

"My pets get excited at the utterance of my name. They know it is a herald of a liberation soon to come." Porcelain hands with razor sharp nails lifted to cup Jalice's face. "Would you like to meet them?"

Jalice tried to shake her head, but Spiracy's hands kept her head restrained. An orb of white light bloomed from behind Spiracy and soared upward through a thick fog that permeated the room. Jalice's eyes followed its illumination as it revealed just how massive the space around her was. The ceiling had to be a mile high.

But it was what hung from it that dropped Jalice's mouth open.

Far above her, crowding the upper regions of the chamber, hung large cocoon-like objects. Most appeared sealed and dormant, but those that weren't hinted at what they all held. The limbs dangling free and the oval-shaped heads peeking out were too far away to see clearly. But a shiver ran down Jalice's spine as some intuition told her what she was witnessing. These innumerable creatures were of the same breed as the one she'd already met. More embryonic monstrosities.

Jalice snapped her eyes shut once more. This nightmare had to end. She had to get out.

Sahruum, take me from this place. Show mercy on me.

"Now, now, none of that," Spiracy crooned.

Jalice's eyes pried open against her will, and she yelped at the pinch of pain. "How are you doing that?" she asked. "Stop controlling me."

Spiracy threw back her head and laughed. It was a confident and twisted sound. "One of my favorite moments. When my little Skinflake realizes we aren't in your nightmare." A cruel, slender grin crept across the dokojin's face. "We're in mine."

A roar of defiance surged through Jalice. The desperate desire to be free of this horror unhinged something within her. She *didn't* belong here.

And she was leaving.

The fog of the room imploded in a rush of wind that swallowed it up in an eyeblink. Spiracy watched it evaporate, eyes pinned to the motion with a look of wary concern. Out of the darkness that reigned, shrubbery burst from the ground at an exaggerated growth rate, and within a few breaths, the chamber was flush with flora and trees.

Jalice stared in awe, realizing that it was the first color she'd seen since arriving. With this color came an improbable light that washed across the forest scenery, warring against the shadows that persisted. Playful, innocent laughter skirted the air. She watched in stunned silence as a group of children entered her line of vision, skipping around the trees and brush. They passed by Spiracy, who watched them with seething disdain.

"What trickery is this?" asked Spiracy. "Why aren't they scared?"

The children ignored her, seemingly unaware of the nightmare surrounding their natural haven. They darted around, giggling and talking with a blissful disregard of the dokojin or the horde of creatures above.

Jalice knew who these children were.

Two boys. Hydrim, with his tan skin, on the cusp of manhood. Kerothan, who eyed the other boy with a shy admiration.

Three girls. Delilee, who wore an innocent grin but said very little. A deep sadness filled Jalice as she beheld her cousin, whose death at the hands of the Sachem months ago still pained her. Near Delilee, a young Annilasia bore a stern, confident look that rivaled the leadership exuded by Hydrim. She twirled a twig between her fingers to impress the boys, who attempted the same trick with less inspiring results.

Lastly, Jalice recognized herself amidst the group. Heat flushed her cheeks as she witnessed just how insecure and unsure her younger self seemed beside the other children. Just as she was about to look away in shame, her childhood reflection looked over and gave a knowing wave.

She heard Spiracy screech as the world shimmered.

"Get back here, you wench!"

The colors swirled, a wave of vibrations prickled her skin, and the sounds of the chamber—including Spiracy's words—dimmed to nothingness.

***

Reality claimed Jalice without mercy, punching a scream from her lungs. The action brought with it a sharp pain in her abdomen that had her doubling over. She panted as she waited for the pain to subside, letting her eyes wander.

A new darkness suffocated her, but she instantly recognized its difference. This wasn't the same void that had hosted Spiracy and her host of mimics; the smell of rotten fish no longer clogged her nostrils. A new stench assaulted her, one of waste and decay. She curled her fingers around the blankets beneath her. Giant windows spread out around her, but the world beyond them lay shrouded in night's shadow, giving her poor lighting. Her eyes fought to acclimate, desperate to search these new surroundings for threats.

Whispers tickled her ear—a cacophony of voices speaking over each other in hushed tones. The noise continued, rustling the air like a wind brushing withered leaves. She focused on the outline of a bed, pressed against the wall a few feet away and facing the windows. A still figure lay atop the bedsheets, and when she held her breath to listen, she realized some of the room's restless whispers were coming from the motionless stranger.

Jalice swung her legs over the side of her bed and slowly stood up so as to avoid making a sound. The pain in her stomach returned, and she inhaled sharply as she put a hand to the line of bandages underneath her tunic. With careful, delicate steps, she tiptoed the few feet separating the stranger's bed and her own.

No matter her focus, she couldn't make out the words fluttering in the air like bats. Even as she leaned her head in closer, trying to understand the stranger, their words whistled and scraped out at her, urgent but incoherent.

Muffling the whispers, her heart pounded in her ears as her adjusted eyesight took in more details about the stranger. Bones jutted from beneath a thin layer of skin, arms and legs no more than twigs ready to snap off at the faintest brush of a wind. If it weren't for the whispers, she'd have deemed it a corpse that she beheld. For a moment, she wondered if it truly was, thinking the eerie noises slipping out from it might be pockets of leftover air seeping free. But then she saw the movement at the mouth. Flat, cracked lips parted and closed in feverish succession.

Out of the nonsense uttered, she at last managed to make out a single word.

"... Spiracy ..."

Jalice tumbled backwards and crashed into the side of her bed. A sunburst of pain surged from her stomach, but she hardly acknowledged it. A newfound terror was overriding the pain. Now tuned to the hushed babbling that charged the room, all she could hear among the chaos was that word, that name. She gazed about, noticing the other beds containing other motionless forms.

All whispering that name.

Spiracy.

Jalice's eyes latched onto a tall sliver of light opposite her bed. She dashed towards the set of doors through which the light seeped, and shoved into them. Her shoulder took the brunt of the force, and she went reeling back, but the doors didn't so much as budge. She ran at them again, beating her hands against the wood as she shrieked.

"Let me out! Someone let me out of here!"

No one answered. No one was coming.

Time cracked under the strain of her panic. She wasn't sure how long she beat on the doors—long enough to bruise her hands though. Long enough that her cheeks burned with heat and tear stains by the time the doors finally groaned open.

She careened forward, unprepared to finally be liberated, and fell to the ground in the welcome light of torches. She stayed there for a moment, fighting to steady her labored breaths. A small gathering stood around her. She looked up at their shocked, silent faces, and recognized one to be her brother.

"Where am I?" she croaked, voice hoarse from shouting. "Where is Xiekaro?"

"We'll take her back to her quarters," Kerothan grunted. "We need to question her." His eyes flashed past her to the open doors. "Seal the chamber."

Two templites darted past her to heed Kerothan's command. Jalice stared up at him, fighting back a fresh wave of tears from the confusion and terror still swimming inside her. The pain that her panic had masked moments before surfaced back to the forefront of her senses. She moaned and put a hand to her stomach. A moist wetness caused her to draw her hand back and peer at it. Blood covered her palm and fingers, glistening in the torchlight. "What happened to me?" she asked. "How did I end up in that place?"

"We moved you here when you didn't wake," Kerothan answered curtly.

"What was that other Realm? It was too vivid for a dream." When his eyes narrowed, she realized he didn't understand. "The cave with the dokojin."

Kerothan stiffened and his hand instinctively flashed to his sword. "What in dying stars are you talking about, Jalice?"

She gawked at him. "It was the same dokojin that all those sleeping people are whispering about. Surely you know something. Why are they all in there? Why do they whisper its name?"

"Be silent," he snapped. "You babble about nightmares, nothing more." He motioned to the other warriors to collect her.

But this had not been a nightmare. And now, she wondered whether the dream she first had in her quarters had been a dream at all. She had seen this dokojin—a dokojin that had never before haunted her—and the cave in which she'd been trapped had not been the stuff of dreams or even nightmares.

It had been a vicious reality.

And so had the dokojin within it.

"You have to listen to me," she pleaded as firm hands gripped her arms and heaved her up. "It told me its name. It's here somewhere. We have to get out before it finds us."

Kerothan stood silent for a moment. "What name did it give?"

She opened her mouth, then hesitated. Just thinking the name soured her tongue, and her gums raged with a pain akin to blisters as she choked it out.

"Spiracy. It called itself Spiracy."

CHAPTER 15

Jalice just wanted to sleep. Her thoughts trudged through her mind like slugs, and her muscles caved as soon as she sank into the cot nestled in the corner of her quarters. But the audience cluttering the tiny space had demanded she stay awake and focused. She absentmindedly played with her hair, threading it into a familiar hair weave known to her tribe.

"It was a dream," Kerothan proclaimed, not for the first time.

He stood off to the side, arms crossed as he glared at her. She kept her gaze off him, wishing to escape the anger emanating from that part of the room. Instead, she looked to the other two men crowding the room. She'd seen them before, back when Kerothan had first spotted her with Xiekaro in the empty corridor.

Kerothan didn't seem to like the older man. He'd introduced himself as Cephus, and from what she'd intuited, Kerothan answered to him in some warrior hierarchy.

In between Kerothan and Cephus, and striking a balanced age between them, stood the bulkier fellow with tan skin. She'd heard Cephus call him by Ophim, and she wished it were this fellow taking charge of questioning her instead of Cephus and Kerothan. Despite his thick muscles and build, she found his face much kinder than the expressions worn by his companions.

"It wasn't a dream," Jalice murmured. She didn't have enough energy left for some forceful argument, and she didn't care if her voice didn't carry enough for them to hear.

"Tell us what happened before you woke," Cephus asked. "Do you remember anything?"

Jalice swallowed and let her gaze drift across the room to avoid eye contact. She cringed as she recalled the whispering corpses on the beds. The name on their lips flickered into her mind, but she swiftly buried it. She didn't want to dwell on that name. "The last thing I remember is Xiekaro putting me to bed after he took me to see the mirajin in their trance."

"Can you describe the dream you had?" asked Cephus.

"Why does it matter? You don't believe me." She hadn't bothered to tell them that this had not been the first time she'd met with the wraith-like dokojin. They didn't believe she could awake from the sleep that had apparently gripped her while in the cave. They wouldn't believe that something similar had happened before.

"We don't believe you because you're a liar, Jalice," said Kerothan. He ignored the reproachful look Ophim shot him.

"We're curious about what transpired," said Cephus. "We want to make sure you're not in danger here."

Jalice could hear the ulterior motive floating in that statement, but she closed her eyes and sighed. "I don't remember how I got there. I woke up in some sort of cavern, and I was trapped. Tied to a table. I think. I'm not entirely sure. The details are fading fast."

"Concentrate while they're still fresh," Ophim encouraged. "Did you see anyone there?"

Jalice stiffened. "Yes, but I'd rather not speak of that."

"You have to," Kerothan demanded.

Jalice hesitated. If they were right, and it had been a dream, then the more she spoke it aloud, the more power she gave it. She didn't want that. But she knew her brother would persist, and so relented. "It was a dokojin, as I said before." She opened her eyes, curious how the other men would react. Cephus's brow was furrowed, while Ophim looked alarmed. Kerothan simply glowered at her, as he had when she first exited the chamber. She continued on, watching their expressions. "I know they don't have genders like we think of them. They're astral. But this one . . . it was like it wanted to look human. Feminine. And beautiful. Only it wasn't. Its beauty was just . . . wrong."

"Wrong?" Cephus inquired.

Jalice shook her head in frustration. "I'm not sure how else to describe it."

"What did this dokojin do while you were in the cave?"

Jalice tightened her arms around her knees. "Please. I don't want to remember this. We need to leave here. If it comes back . . ." She trailed off, horrified at the prospect of that possibility.

The three men exchanged quick glances. Cephus cleared his throat and said, "Perhaps the trauma of your imprisonment here has had ill effects on your mind. Your wound has led to fevers, no doubt, and fevers can play awful tricks on the mind."

"I didn't imagine it," Jalice stated firmly.

Kerothan was fuming now. "No one else has ever woken from the Endless Sleep. Yet you arrive here and manage to do what our own templites can't do for the others. Doesn't add up." He drove his glare off her and over to his companions. "I told you it's a ruse. She's been sent here to infiltrate us, and this is some ploy."

"I don't understand," said Jalice. "What is this sleep you refer to?"

"She needs to know more," Ophim stated, looking to the other two men for permission.

Kerothan opened his mouth to protest, but Cephus threw his hand up to cut the man off.

"It might help her summon more details from her time in the Whisper Chamber," Cephus explained. He paused and looked at her for a moment, as if hesitating over what to reveal. "Some time ago, some of our members failed to wake from a deep slumber. In this sleep, they whispered words none of us could understand, and nothing would rouse them. In the nights that followed, it snared more victims—enough that we designated a chamber where we could sequester them and where the templite healers could attend to them until we could determine how to remedy the situation. That was the chamber you awoke in."

"How many are in there?" Jalice asked.

"Dozens. Too many to care for efficiently. Many have died already. Their bodies wear thin quickly. The healers have managed to keep some of the poor souls alive while in their comatose states, but it's only a matter of time before the lack of activity and the laws of nature finish off the sleeping victims."

Jalice considered this. "So, no one has ever woken from it? What does that indicate about me? To have dreamed of the dokojin twice?"

"Twice?" Kerothan seemed beyond outraged now.

"When I first awoke in the chambers with Xiekaro," Jalice explained. "I remember seeing it. But I—" It wouldn't be wise for her to mention the Black House or Dardajah. Not when Kerothan already hated her and was using that hate as reason not to trust her words. "I awoke to Xiekaro's calls."

"Another mystery indeed," Cephus rushed out before Kerothan could say another word about her treachery. "Perhaps now you can understand our curiosity—and caution—with your tale. Yesterday, you were placed in the Whisper Chamber because you entered a sleep that Xiekaro could not wake you from and you whispered like the others. But tonight, you awoke. We're hoping you can shed some light on how you managed a feat that no other victim has."

Jalice shook her head slowly, and her shoulders slumped under this new set of expectations. "I don't think I have an answer for you. Already, much of the dream has faded." She looked at Cephus, unable to meet her brother's harsh gaze. "You don't know what's causing it?"

Cephus shook his head and let out a heavy sigh. "It seems to strike at random."

"There is something far more wicked afoot than this Endless Sleep," Ophim said in a low voice. "What Jalice experienced? Seeing a dokojin? It sounds like the work of twisters."

Jalice wished she could give the large man a hug. *Someone* believed her. "You're having problems with twisters?" she asked.

"It's why we're here," said Kerothan with a resentful tone. He refused to look at her now, perhaps in denial of Ophim's belief in her story. Instead, he fixated on some point on the ground, arms crossed while he slumped against the wall. "Damn filthy things keep crossing the border. Can't seem to muster the decency of sticking to the land they've already infected."

In typical fashion, his words pulled the atmosphere taut again. Cephus cleared his throat, shifting on his legs and sharing the same uncomfortable expression as Ophim.

Jalice swallowed and let her eyes close again. The tension seeped into her bones. Her chest seized up as she struggled to breathe. A part of her joined in on the onslaught of blame and guilt that her brother's accusatory words had inflicted. She knew he was right to blame her for everything. If only she hadn't condoned her husband's violence. If only she hadn't married the Sachem and turned a blind eye to his reign of terror.

If only she hadn't made a deal with a dokojin as a child in a fit of jealousy.

"Jalice, are you alright?"

She kept her eyes closed. Sweat dripped down from her forehead. Her voice came out shaky.

"I just... I need some... where is Xiekaro? He has that pipe... He can help."

"What's happening?"

She shook her head and tried to stop from panting. "Sometimes when I get upset, it triggers these visions..." Her hands trembled, and she clutched at the blankets beneath her to try to ward off the anxiety. "Where is Xiekaro?"

Ophim sprang forward and knelt down so that he was at her eye level. "Listen to my voice. Stay here. Nothing can hurt you right now. Listen to my voice, and breathe." He sucked in a dramatic lungful of air and then exhaled long and slow. He repeated this, gesturing with his hand for her to join him.

Jalice tried to focus on Ophim. But by now, her throat was clenched tight, and she was fighting to get any air. Sobs threatened to send her into a fit that would strip her of the final sliver of control she maintained. Ophim inhaled and held his breath for a moment as she struggled to do the same. They exhaled together, hers a whistle of compressed airflow. He nodded at her in support, and the tension passed. Jalice let her head collapse into her folded arms in exhaustion. She heard Ophim stand, then felt the cot compress beside her where he sat down.

"Where is Xiekaro?" she asked in a tired, broken voice. "His pipe can help me. If it happens again—"

"If it happens again, just focus your breathing like we did," Ophim said with soft reassurance.

"I want Xiekaro," Jalice said more firmly. She lifted her head to look about the room and noticed the grim expressions on Cephus and Kerothan. She turned to Ophim. "What is it? What aren't you telling me?"

"When you woke up, we thought it prudent to fetch Xiekaro," Ophim explained. "He had mentioned seeing something when you first fell asleep, and we wanted to know if it aligned with what you saw. But when the clannite we sent came back, we were informed that Xiekaro could not be woken."

Jalice jerked her gaze between the three men in dismay. "What are you saying?" But she knew it before Kerothan answered.

"He entered the Endless Sleep."

Jalice sat forward. "We can't leave him there. That thing will torment him like it did me. It'll tear him apart."

"You don't listen," Kerothan snapped, gesturing curtly with his hands. "No one wakes up from that. Except you, by some cruel, messed up joke of Dardajah."

Cephus stiffened and barked, "Kerothan, that is enough. You are dismissed."

Kerothan froze, eyes wide with rage. He squared his shoulders, turned without making eye contact with any of them, and pushed past Cephus to exit, closing the door hard behind him. The tension in the room slowly dissipated some, much to Jalice's relief.

"I think this has been difficult for all of us," Cephus murmured. "If you wish for Ophim to remain nearby in Xiekaro's stead, I'm sure he'd be willing."

"I'll keep guard outside your door through tonight," Ophim confirmed. He turned from Cephus to look at Jalice. "I know it's not much comfort, but perhaps it will help you sleep."

Jalice nodded. He was right—it wasn't much of a comfort. But at least someone cared about her. "What if I go back?" she asked in a quiet voice. "What if that awful dokojin comes for me again?"

Cephus and Ophim said nothing. She could hear their unspoken uncertainty.

"If you escaped once, I think you could do it again," Ophim said. He stood up and went to join Cephus, who opened the door to step out.

The older man moved out of the way to let Ophim exit, then hesitated in the doorframe to regard Jalice. "Get some rest, as best you can. There will be more questions in the morning. You'll need your energy for it." With that, he stepped out and closed the door.

Jalice fell asleep seconds later, even with a head full of nightmarish imagery and phantom voices shouting blame at her.

CHAPTER 16

Annilasia stood perfectly still. A mere flinch would see her dead.

She couldn't see the dozens of spikes surrounding her, but that didn't stop her from envisioning them. Frozen pinnacles intent on nicking her just so she'd explode into a thousand tiny pieces. This close to them, her body prickled with needleskin.

The coven dungeons were a dark, unlit place, as they saw very little foot traffic. No need for torches when those condemned to the mountain's pit weren't intended to be visited. It wouldn't have been much of a view anyways—just slick walls, stalagmites, and pools of collected water.

As it was, she couldn't see the surrounding dungeon at all. Not locked in the twister's coffin, as the mentors called it. Constructed of iron, the coffin was lined with a sea of spikes, even the inside of the door that opened and closed to allow access into the hollowed insides. An itch crawled across her neck, the sensation quickly escalating to a feverish burn that demanded to be appeased. She growled in her throat, willing the pesky ailment to dissipate. Even if not for the wall of spikes, her bestowed cage would not have permitted movement enough for her to scratch away the irritation. The coffin held only enough room for her to stand upright, arms at her sides.

Dying stars, I will end that man for shoving me in here.

The anger came and went as it always did. She wasn't sure how long she'd been stuck in this forsaken cavern, but it had been long enough for her rage at Iveer to peak several times. Eventually the emotions would pass, replaced either by her intense focus on not moving or by a physical irritation like an oncoming sneeze. She could count on the hateful ruminations to return at some point though. Several times she'd even pictured how it would look when she shoved Iveer's blood-colored wand through the roof of his mouth and watched actual blood run over the glass.

Annilasia shivered as this imagery resurfaced. She didn't like how quickly her mind had turned so violent. She didn't think like this. Imagining how a man's skin would break as the tip of the wand drove into his skull and released a waterfall of glorious, beautiful blood. How he'd scream, or at least try to, amidst the fluid gushing down his throat and filling his lungs to slowly drown him.

"Stop that," she said aloud to herself. "This isn't you. You don't think like that. Twisters think like that."

But are you not a twister?

The question curled in her mind like a hooked talon.

"I'm not a twister," she whispered to herself.

"Yes, you are, Bloodspill."

Annilasia held her breath. She refused to admit that a voice had entered her head. That she'd heard anything at all but her own voice. She was alone. No one was down here.

"But you're never alone, Bloodspill. You have me."

She recognized the voice. It was all too familiar, marked by a tortured agony that sprang into glee at the mention of violence. It clawed at the insides of her head, and if it weren't for the danger of her cage, she would have struck her palms against her temples to banish this voice with a bruise's pain. Her lips quivered as she exhaled. "This isn't real," she said calmly, despite the edge of panic squirming around her chest. "It isn't here. It left you."

Her tone sounded far from convincing, and the fear undergirding it was validated when the sadistic response came.

"I never leave my shells, Bloodspill. I keep close when they promise blood and havoc. Your bones will splinter like dry-rotted bark, and your mind will shatter like ice blasted by fire when I strip you of control."

Inzerious had returned.

Annilasia's whole body trembled as the fear of brushing her skin against the spikes was joined by the terror of what spoke inside her head. She recalled Feliss—the fellow pupil's limbs flailing and knocking against the stone before severing into detached limbs and pools of blood.

The dokojin chuckled before tutting at her with a fabricated tone of reassurance and comfort. "Don't be like that. As much as I like to see you breaking, I can't have you flinging yourself to your death and taking from me what is rightfully mine. I need your bag of bones ready for my chaos when the times comes."

"I'll do it," she said. "I'll throw myself against these walls."

"No, you won't. You're too afraid. Perhaps not of the pain, but certainly of what would happen to your aura when it enters the Apparition Realm where I wait. I'd be so angry, Bloodspill. And a dokojin's anger can be quite the torment on an unfortunate aura."

Something far worse than an itch dragged across her shoulder. She let out a shrill cry as it seared with a fiery burn.

"You've made me oh so angry, Bloodspill. Keeping me muzzled like I'm some Ikaul canine to be controlled. I was so close to breaking you, and you had to go and do that."

A wet trail ran down her back. The dokojin had broken skin. "Stop," she pleaded. "I'll do whatever you want. Just don't maim me. Don't break me."

"That's more like it. Groveling will get you very far with me," Inzerious sneered. "But I needed to smell the blood. Feel it trickle down your scarred back. If I could only taste it!"

Its feverish tone invaded Annilasia, burdening her with a ravenous hunger for flesh. For murder. For death. Anything that would make a person scream and thrash like a trapped insect boiling under the sun.

"If you break me here, I'll die," she spoke quickly while fending off the inhumane cravings. She pictured Feliss bouncing on the rocks, bones cracking. "Your hijack would send me into a seizure that would only end with us both losing what we need."

Inzerious's teeth gnashed in her ears. "So clever. How do you propose we get you out of this silly containment before I melt what's inside your squishy little head?"

"Can you break me out?" she asked. "If I tapped into your aether, would it be enough to do the trick?"

"I suppose so," Inzerious grumbled. "After, we play, Bloodspill."

Annilasia suppressed the terror at that possibility, forcing her agreement through clenched teeth. "Deal."

She didn't waste time. Any moment, Inzerious's encroachment on her mind would send her into insanity. The cracks were already growing. She tasted blood in her mouth. Maybe it was her own from biting on her tongue or grinding her teeth too hard, or maybe it was Inzerious's cravings spawning phantom tastes. A horrible wail kept growing and then softening in her ears. It reminded her of her mother.

Those horrible sounds her mother had made during the Purge. When the aether had torn the woman to pieces.

Annilasia focused and tried drawing upon whatever aether might surround her. But, after years of twister presence, too much violence soiled this area of the Apparition Realm, which meant all she managed to do was tap into Inzerious's reservoir. Dread washed over her at the first, barest contact with the dokojin's aether, and she rushed to be rid of it before it in turn finished her off. She funneled the energy with force towards the sealed door. Under the amount of aether she unleashed, the iron creaked and bent like paper. The cold, hard surface of the cave floor met her as she tumbled out of the coffin. A race against the inevitable began, and she sprinted across slick rock with no light to guide her.

Already Inzerious was digging its claws into her. She screamed and fought off its assault.

"Time to give me what is mine, Bloodspill," the dokojin hissed.

Her mind buckled, but she pushed onward. She only had to find Iveer. He'd see her state and do what had to be done. She barely registered the light or the wind whipping around her as she surfaced from the cave and broke out into the leafless forest. Her movements were bizarre and uncoordinated. Foreign impulses rushed through her limbs at odd intervals, causing her arms to swing wildly and her feet to trip.

It was close. Inzerious would take her body any moment now.

Annilasia spotted a figure down a diverging path that led around the mountainside and away from the dungeon cave. She opened her mouth to cry out. Only a dry croaking noise broke from her throat. She limped after them, trying to summon a shout, a word, a whimper—any noise that might catch the attention of the retreating figure.

Turn around, you daft imbecile. Turn the blazing fuck around.

She would not remember every moment between when she first saw the figure and when she finally stopped running. As she trekked through the frigid terrain, all focus remained on resisting Inzerious, at mentally kicking and thrashing against its attempts to throw her into some void of a pit within herself.

A looming cave broke this intense focus. Annilasia plunged into the cavern's darkness, swallowed up like a pebble cast into the fathomless depths of the sea. Shadows engulfed her as she scrambled over slick rock and down a descending staircase carved into the stone. Torches lined the wall, their orbs blurry in her unstable vision.

She didn't at first notice the vibrations. Only when Inzerious's assault weakened from a frenzied onslaught to occasional viper strikes did she realize the change. The vibrations intensified, and she took the much-needed lull in the dokojin's assault to sprint farther down the staircase, where the vibrations continued to peak. A sharp hum crackled inside her ears before leveling out.

The vibrations had stopped. Inzerious had stopped its attack. She still sensed it lurking in the corner of her mind, its jaw gnashing and spewing muffled obscenities, but something about this place was keeping it back.

Annilasia came to the last step, where a crescent opening appeared. When she peeked around the edge of this opening, she froze. Beyond it was a vast, egg-shaped chamber with a high ceiling that rose into the darkness where the low torchlight could not reach. Unlike most of the journey, which had been riddled with stalagmites, this room had been cleared of natural formations to make way for the array of thin tubes that snaked across the walls and floor.

The display drove a spike of fear in Annilasia. The web of cords tickled her mind with an eerie familiarity, but she couldn't quite place where she'd seen it. All the cords converged at the very center of the room, where a gathering of cloaked individuals stood in a circle around an oddly shaped obelisk with a large cylindrical base. An emerald glow bled from this odd structure, bathing those gathered. The vast space acted like an echo chamber that carried their whispers to Annilasia, and she recognized them as the seven mentors of the coven.

". . . Evlicka is almost spent," one of them urged. "We need another conduit."

"We should have used one of the students who didn't return from the hunt. Waste not the talent."

"That would never have worked," said another. "We would have had to retrieve them from the Apparition Realm first to place them in a sleep rather than a cosmic meditation, and that might have taken much longer than Evlicka's expiration."

"Regardless, someone will need to be chosen, and their absence explained to the others."

Annilasia recognized the next to speak as Iveer, who said, "We can't keep Spiracy in the dream Realm forever."

At the mention of Spiracy, Annilasia's heart skipped a beat, and her chest grew heavy.

"The time is coming soon to birth her," another agreed. "Evlicka can be the last conduit; she will last long enough for the ignition of the Decayer device."

There was a pause in the conversation, and based on the next words uttered, Annilasia took it for stunned silence.

"What news do you know?" Iveer asked.

"The Sachem is hiding in Vekuuv," someone answered.

Annilasia held her breath, willing her ears to absorb every word uttered.

"My sources say he was sighted at the border after his disappearance from the Fortress months ago. Based off reports, the Sachem is ill. Or rather, the dokojin in him has nearly cracked his mind and body. Additionally, rumors abound from the Ikaul Fortress. They say he took their Elation Stone with him."

"Then the Decayer will indeed be turned on," another mentor voiced in awe. "Spiracy will be freed."

"She isn't powerful enough yet," Iveer stated. "If the Decayer device were to be utilized at this very moment, she'd be devoured by older, primordial dokojin like Dardajah. We have to accelerate her growth."

"Giving her more dreamers would be reckless and rash," someone protested.

"Speaking of dreamers," Iveer began, irritated, "why was her Realm projected here during the wand trials? One of our pupils got tangled in her nest."

"There was an incident at Editshi Temple that necessitated the switch. We had to transfer Spiracy's dream Realm here until they resolved the problem."

"Why wasn't I consulted about this?" Iveer demanded, looking around at what must not have been surprised faces. "Did you all know of this?"

"You were busy with that loner pupil. We didn't want to interrupt your time with her."

Annilasia caught the condescension in those words, and the irritation in Iveer's voice escalated.

"She's the very one who got caught in Spiracy's Realm during the trial," said Iveer. "A very dangerous situation not only for her, but for everyone else here at the coven."

"Annilasia is a dud," one of the others snapped. "She isn't worth our concern. You've already told us that she's got a parasite latched onto her. Now Feliss? She was a true loss. So much potential there."

"What was the incident that necessitated switching the dream's location?" Iveer asked with a heated tone.

"The warriors protecting that Temple located one of our Fence Posts."

"Did they learn anything more of our schemes?" asked Iveer. "Are we compromised?"

"Rejiett caused enough casualties during that raid. The warriors have had little time to study the Fence Post they found."

"Then it sounds like she's got things under control," said Iveer. "I assume we've switched Spiracy back over to the Temple?"

"Yes, but there is another oddity," one of the other mentors interjected. "Rejiett informed us that someone at Editshi Temple managed to escape Spiracy's dream lair. The dreamer entered Spiracy's Realm and brought with them elements of their own dream—something that hasn't ever happened. This same dreamer has managed to do this twice now."

There was a long pause. Annilasia grew anxious, wondering if they'd simply stopped talking or if they might be treading towards her.

"We are running out of time," said Iveer, his tone now more exhausted than frustrated. "If we wait too long, then Dardajah *will* conquer this Realm, and all of us will be doomed to a life of caged existence. Dardajah will free and birth other dokojin, and make no mistake, twisters will not be spared incarceration. Spiracy must be ready to face Dardajah, and from the sound of it, she's got blind spots. Who is this person who has evaded and confounded her?"

"The Tecalica."

Annilasia's mouth dropped open. As the seconds passed and the mentors continued to speak, she wondered if she'd misheard. It couldn't be Jalice they were speaking of. The Tecalica that Annilasia knew didn't have the kind of power needed to confound a twister scheme like this. Or the brains. It simply couldn't be her. She focused again on the echoing voices and found them arguing again.

"Iveer, what you're proposing could end Spiracy," said one of the mentors. "If we send that dreamer back in, Spiracy might not be able to cope with the dreams the Tecalica carries with her."

"If Spiracy can't adapt to a new challenge, then she won't be able to take on Dardajah," said Iveer. "If we expect Spiracy to defeat Dardajah, who pulled two entire tribes under its tyrannical rulership, then we need our child to be that much stronger. One single dreamer shouldn't be this much of a problem for her. Spiracy has to find a way to overpower her, whatever unique skills she might utilize."

"Piss of the abyss, you are insane, Iveer. If this is how you choose to proceed, then so be it. But if this fails, and I fully expect it to, then I'll be sure to throw you to the first dokojin that comes crawling to our doorstep, and I will enjoy watching them ravage you."

"I hate to interrupt," a softer voice said, one far more timid than the others. "But should we be concerned with the horde of pets our child herself has birthed? When Spiracy is freed, those creatures will be too. They practice an unnerving ability to mimic us . . ."

"Her spawn are weak," Iveer stated dismissively. "Simply byproducts of her dream Realm. The other dokojin will squash them like insects."

Annilasia waited for more, but no response came. Instead, a low hum broke from the obelisk at the center of the room, followed by what sounded like a moan. Her blood ran cold as the sound escalated to a high, crackly screech. An octave below it, a voice spoke in a confident, bold tone, but due to the hum and the disturbing howl, Annilasia couldn't make out the words. The scene died into silence when the speaker grew quiet, then the galling screech came again, immediately followed by the hum.

She was standing there, trying to make sense of everything she'd heard, when she realized the meeting was over. The cloaked figures had turned and were walking towards the entryway behind which she was hidden. She thought about retreating up the stairs so they wouldn't discover her presence but remembered what had brought her down here to begin with. Inzerious had nearly taken control above the surface. Only the vibrations of this chamber had ruffled the dokojin enough to force its retreat. She couldn't risk going back up only to have it pounce on her again. She straightened, walked through the open entryway, and stumbled towards the emerald light of the obelisk.

The mentors spotted her clumsy figure and halted.

"What in shite's breath is she doing down here?" one of them exclaimed.

Iveer stepped forward with a look of disapproval. "Who let you out of the coffin?"

She ran her tongue over her dry lips and cleared her throat. Her voice came out weak, but she managed to croak out the only words she knew to say.

"Inzerious is back."

CHAPTER 17

Annilasia detested the look on Iveer's face. She knew how pathetic she must look, a broken and trembling thing like on the day she'd first met him. "If Inzerious has returned, how is it that it hasn't overtaken you?" Iveer asked warily.

"I've kept it at bay," she said, "and this chamber has held it back for some reason." He nodded with realization. "It hasn't acclimated to the vibrations of the dream device. That won't last forever."

"I need you to cage it. Again." She waited for him to nod and close his eyes. Waited for the sweet relief that would come when he translated and caged once more the dreadful parasite attached to her. She waited, but Iveer did nothing but regard her with a stoic look. "What are you waiting for?"

"You can't leave here knowing what you do," said one of the mentors, an old, withered woman with fading yellow hair. "You know too much."

"Iveer already told me of Spiracy," Annilasia responded boldly. "What I heard down here is nothing more consequential than that. Keep me under lock and key, I don't care." This she directed at Iveer, fighting back the churning in her stomach at having to grovel. "Please, I just need to you do this."

"I'm afraid your doom is sealed and upon you, Annilasia," proclaimed Iveer. "Did you not hear? The Decayer is to be turned on at any moment now. When it is, Inzerious will take on a physical, flesh existence. Think about what that means for you."

She forced her mind, weary and broken as it was, down the path forged by Iveer's words. "If it's inside me . . . and we share my body . . ." She trailed off, unable to finish the dire thought.

"It will kill you. Shred you to pieces as it manifests in its Terrestrial form."

Annilasia fought against the fear unspooling within her. A guttural noise strained in her ear. Inzerious was moving again, skittering on the edges of her mind. "Just cage it, Iveer," she snapped. "Buy me some time. I can remove Inzerious before the Decayer is turned on."

Iveer shook his head slowly. "I'm not wasting any more aether on you, Annilasia. You are a lost cause. Accept your fate and be done with it."

Her fear entwined with rage. Inzerious cackled, and one of the scars on her shoulder cracked open to let blood soak into her tunic. "Cage it," she shouted.

Iveer raised his wand, and she knew already it wasn't to do her any favors. Her rage expanded, choking out the fear. Annilasia's heart slammed against her chest. This was it. Her end come early. Part of her wanted this end. Exhaustion riddled her body and mind. Too long keeping a dokojin's madness locked up. Too long studying poison and cruelty at this coven.

But another part of her, one that Inzerious clutched at, lashed out with the need to survive.

Invisible claws dug into the insides of her mouth and forced it open. A word, or a sound, or a forbidden vibration with origins in some unspeakable Realm, left her lungs and broke the air. Power rushed forward—a combination of her own emotions mixed with a dreadful energy of primordial genesis. An invisible slice of aether, like a wave rushing from the ocean to meet land, raced towards the mentors.

They had no time to react. Specks of blood spat out from red lines slit across their necks. For a mere breath, nothing happened. Annilasia stared at the handful of teachers, who stared back in motionless terror. Then, like weeds being torn from the earth by some invisible hand, their heads lifted up and detached from their necks. Blood rained down in thick globs onto the decapitated bodies, which, after a beat, collapsed onto the ground.

The heads went up, up, up. Annilasia's gaze trailed their ascent towards the shadowy ceiling. A voice that made her want to scream broke her nightmarish trance.

"Quite the exit, wouldn't you say?"

Annilasia shuddered. Inzerious's presence swarmed through her like tentacles. Its clawed hands raced across her back, sending pain searing through her whenever they collided with her open wounds.

"You've missed me, Bloodspill. You've been busy during my leave. Learning so many new tricks, strengthening our knowledge of aethertwisting. We couldn't have ended an entire group of mentors six months ago. I'm very pleased."

Annilasia watched the blood still dripping onto the heap of bodies. Her gaze latched onto a thin reed sticking out from Iveer's corpse.

His wand.

An idea flashed in her mind, and any hesitation lasted but a second. Annilasia settled her thoughts, breathed in, released the air, and translated. The world shimmered as she dove towards Iveer's bloodied corpse. Her hand clutched the mentor's glove, and she used it as a buffer to grasp his wand as the Apparition Realm manifested around her.

Vibrations rippled the world, traveled across her skin, and shifted her insides like slithering worms—it didn't matter how many times she translated, the journey never treated her well. She hated the sensation of her aura yanking out of her conscious perception and shifting to the aether-infested Realm.

Inzerious hadn't expected this bold action. It obsessed only over her cowardice, and although panic and anxiety gripped her, a confidence surged at what she knew to be her last chance at escaping a dreadful fate. The vibrations from translating quelled. The dokojin loomed a few strides away, but she didn't dare waste time glancing in its direction. She had seconds to perform the ward. Her arm shot out to point the wand towards her adversary, and she focused all of her intent on the aether swimming inside the glass. Fear overwhelmed her, slipping into her concentration as she fueled the aether's release.

As the plasmic energy sprang from the glass and soared towards the dokojin, she glimpsed the familiarly harsh details of Inzerious's form. Bulging, lidless eyes. A gaping maw of razor teeth. Bones slathered in obsidian liquid.

The dokojin's arms lurched forward to swing at her, but it was too late. The aether collided into it, and Annilasia heard the loud crack of bones striking one another under the impact. The ward's effects overtook the dokojin, and the cage surged over every disgusting inch of its form. She shuddered. In the span of an eyeblink, Inzerious had gone from a threat nearly upon her to a suspended wraith silently hovering inches from her face.

She didn't move. She had to be sure the ward had worked.

Iveer had taught her how to determine the ward's quality by observing just how murky the dokojin's details appeared underneath it. If done properly, the cage would render the dokojin as little more than an ill-distinguished form beneath a spectral sheet. The fewer details that could be made out, the stronger the ward. As time went on, the sheet would slowly disintegrate into a veiny lattice through which the dokojin's details would be clear.

Relief settled into her muscles as she noticed the cage's tendrils twirling through the air. The ward was holding. But as she looked up, relief dissolved into alarm.

Inzerious's form remained too vivid, too distinct. She could make out every bone, could see the pinnacles of gooey ichor frozen in place. Her gaze happened across its face, and when she found its sunken eyes, a spike of terror shot through her.

She held her breath. Hatred wormed out of the dokojin's eyes and sank into her aura like a sickness. Any moment now, and the eyes would blink or flinch—would show some sort of indication that her flimsy attempt at Iveer's ward had done nothing but slow the dokojin's descent upon her.

Annilasia wasn't sure how long she waited, but the dokojin's eyes never moved. Its jaw remained frozen too, suspended in an open yawn that would have driven teeth into her had she not caged it. Despite this, she knew her ward was weak. Only a film of spectral dust coated Inzerious's features. Thin and sinking, the substance was nothing like Iveer's mastery. This cage would collapse much quicker than those prior to it, and she estimated a handful of days before the dokojin escaped.

She scooted back from beneath the dokojin's looming form and scrambled to her feet. Turning away from the encapsulated horror, she took a moment to study her surroundings. The bleakness of the Apparition Realm rivaled the Terrestrial Realm tenfold, at least in spots sullied by a history of violence and debauchery, such as the coven grounds. A karst terrain surrounded her, barren except for the occasional leafless husk of a giant tree that had yet to collapse. Lakes of filthy water interrupted the valleys between the rocky shelves, and the sky held a dull grey, cloudless and leached of natural beauty. Bottled-up emotions lifted away from her and drifted like eels. She'd learned that trick fairly quickly. Aether Realms had an irritating effect of awakening emotions that normally lay dormant and compartmentalized while in the physical Realm. Here, they fought for attention and electrified the celestial stars in her aura to the point of eruption. Before her mastery over them, these emotional sieges resulted in bleak atmospheres and disturbing imagery of her own making. She'd learned some control though, particularly on how to disengage from them until it was safe to summon them back in slowly and one at a time. She didn't have to feel the bulk of any one emotion—just traces of them.

This wasn't always her strategy. Sometimes she needed the fuel of a particular emotion and would swallow it in overpowering measures to complete tasks. For now, she let them tangle in translucent threads around her aura.

She gazed down at the silvery chain wrapped around her right ankle. Irritation pinched her as memories flashed in her mind. She'd tried so many ways to sever the branching links that slinked off the root chain. Her vision traveled down the chain, following the branch until her eyes skittered across the ghostly figure it led to. She quickly averted her gaze from Inzerious.

Annilasia flicked her wrist and looked down at the glass wand grasped in her hand.

Iveer's wand.

Like the wand he'd given to her on the summit for the trial, this one sparkled with a crimson complexion, though a much dimmer one than before she'd used its reservoir of aether on Inzerious. She let the glass slide from the curl of her fingers into the dark silhouette of her palm, and back again. Unwanted flashes of the atrocity she'd committed in the cave surfaced in her mind. She recalled the frozen look of terror on Iveer's face as his head detached from his body in a blast of red fluid. But she also remembered what he'd said to her. What he'd intended to do if she hadn't stopped him.

Stupid, filthy twister. He deserved it. She clasped her fingers around the wand. *And this is my wand now. I've earned it.*

Her gaze landed on the illuminated sticks that littered the area around her—the other mentors' glass wands. They jutted up from the black sand, glowing with a kaleidoscope of rainbow colors. An idea sprang to mind, and she looked between the glass wands and the lifechain offshoot that ran towards the wraith at her back.

Iveer had hinted that aether might break a lifechain.

Annilasia focused her mind on identifying any particles and clusters of aether gathered around her. It quickly became apparent that the only aether around her was what little was gathered in the other wands. The Apparition Realm itself held none of the energy it had once hosted. Aether had been drained here, leaving only waste. Nevertheless, what the other glass wands held might be enough to test her wild theory.

She lifted the wand in her hand and willed the aether to sweep into the glass. Like the reedy bill of a dehydrated swamp herring, the crimson glass drank up the energy. The other discarded wands dimmed until they held none of their previous displays of light. The amassed aether inside Annilasia's wand sparkled with invigorated energy.

Annilasia permitted threads of hope to imbue her aura. Eagerness blossomed inside her, creating a high that left her trembling. Turning on her heels, she lifted the wand high in the air. The sharp tip angled downward, and she unleashed the aether onto the lifechain at her feet—specifically at the offshoot that linked her to Inzerious.

Sparks of every color erupted. Vertical waves sprayed forth, bouncing off the link.

The hope that had charged the eruption swiftly died. A twinge of despair and fury at the failing attempt entered her. She reeled in this thread of emotional fury, letting it overtake her previous elation. A shriek broke from her, full of a tyrannical demand for the lifechain to succumb to the force of the aether. The sparks increased in quantity, and their spray grew to the height of a mountain.

This had to work. Aether could break anything. Aether *would break* her chain.

There was a sputter. The funnel of aether energy flickered before cutting off entirely. The sparks subsided, and Annilasia stared in shock. The link remained unaltered. No dents or scars. It hadn't even moved under the pressure.

Annilasia stiffened as a faint, maniacal cackle crept into her ears. It died off, and in its absence, she wondered if she'd imagined it. She glowered at the chain, trying to accept her failure, before lifting her head to the ghostly figure at its end. Inzerious hovered above the ground draped in its pallid veil. She studied the eyes and waited to hear its cackle once more. It had seen her fail. Even now, its malice wafted off it like the stench of death.

Annilasia held her stare with it, locked in some unspoken duel of wills as the world around her shimmered. It was time to return to the physical world. Just before the Apparition Realm faded, she thought she saw a change in the dokojin's facial structure—the faintest grin bleeding out from beneath the murky cage.

Vibrations numbed her. The scenery changed. She found herself collapsed atop Iveer's corpse, his wand still clenched in her hand.

She waited, wondering if Inzerious's cruel words would scrape through her mind.

Nothing. Silence. The cage was holding, if only for now.

Wet fluid struck her back, and she turned over to find blood spilling onto her from high above. She crawled away from the bodies that littered the ground around her, and looked up in search of the decapitated heads. Too much darkness shrouded the ceiling from where the blood was descending.

Time slipped by as she stared at the macabre scene she'd created. The blood that soaked her clothes and lathered her face slowly dried. Her thoughts were a war between disgust at herself and sporadic spouts of glee over the carnage. As she beheld the corpses, a rush of euphoria drove through her.

It was art. The way the limbs of each corpse intertwined and layered with one another. The symbolism in the blood that splattered like a waterfall from the floating heads down onto the pitiful mound of headless bodies. Her eyes soaked in the beauty of it all, and her tongue darted out to lick up the crust of blood that had dried on her face. She tasted the terror of the mentors.

It occurred to her that Iveer had been right to deem her dangerous. Or rather, deem the parasite attached to her dangerous.

Eventually, the blood stopped dripping from above. Silence ensued, except for dull vibrations that filled the air with static. She pulled on Iveer's gloves and tucked his wand into the undergarments she wore—the damn bastard had stripped her of all outerwear before putting her in the spiked coffin. She stood up, looked at the obelisk at the center of the room where all the tubes on the ground met, and made her way towards the center. The same eerie familiarity from before rushed over her.

With the mentors dead, their final schemes were now her secrets, and she would see to it that whatever they had planned never came to fruition.

Starting with the obelisk.

CHAPTER 18

The obelisk turned out to be not some stone idol, but rather a machine. As she drew close to it, a hissing, emitted in long, drawn out intervals, filled her ears. A low clank preceded this sound each time, and it struck her as both organic and unnatural at the same time.

The machine was like some oblong, lifeless tree. Made entirely of metal, its base was not quite cylindrical as she'd first thought, but shaped more like a coffin. From it, a backboard rose up several feet into the air. Lights that had blended together at a distance lit up like firebugs across its surface, creating the green glow that bathed the cavern.

Annilasia looped around the object, stopping when she came to the opposite side of the backboard, which was mostly flat if somewhat curved around the coffin base. The round fixtures embedded in this side of the backboard connected to the wires that webbed across the ground. She resumed her trek around it, stepping over the tangle of tubes where they converged.

When she came around the other side of the backboard from which she'd started, her gaze latched onto the face of an old, malnourished person lying within the coffin. She froze, startled at this discovery.

This had been easy to miss upon first approach. The only part of this person's body that was exposed was the upper half of their face. The unsuspecting stranger had their eyes closed as if in a deep sleep, and their nose and mouth were sealed with a rubbery mask. A tube sprouted from this mouthpiece and snaked up into the part of the backboard that faced the coffin. The rest of this person's body remained encased in a rubbery black cocoon akin to a cretaceon's exoskeleton. Cylindrical pumps populated the curve where the coffin met with the backboard. These pumps moved up and down in rhythm with the hissing noise.

Disgust rolled through her and knotted in her stomach. Something was being pumped into the sleeping stranger.

She recoiled, taking a clumsy step back only to teeter on the wires that ran under her feet. As she regained her balance, she took in the machine as a whole, unable to shake how it reminded her of some parasitic beast coiled around its prey. She expected the stranger to wake from her presence, something she hoped wouldn't happen. Yet as the seconds passed, and nothing but the rhythmic compression of air through the machine followed, her pounding heart slowed. Curiosity replaced her anxiety, and she closed the little bit of distance earned by her retreat.

She peered down directly into the stranger's face. Their sickly, weathered condition made it impossible to guess anything about their age or gender. The skin was deathly pale, revealing more than a few red veins beneath the surface. The slightest movement behind the eyelids suggested sleep. Annilasia wondered how they had come to be connected to this device.

Whatever this is, it's not good. Some disgusting invention of the mentors. I've got to get this person out of here.

She prodded at the exposed skin of their face, trying to swallow down the revulsion that came when the skin dipped inward like a mushy crater and didn't spring back. No reaction from the sleeper though. Their eyes remained sealed, showing no sign that they sensed Annilasia's touch.

"Can you hear me?" Annilasia whispered. "Wake up. I'm here to free you."

Still no response. Annilasia balked at the machine, its wires and tubes. For all she knew, the ludicrous contraption could be keeping this person alive. Removing them from the mechanisms might do more damage than good. She looked back down upon the person's face and watched the eyelids twitch. Whatever sleep held them, Annilasia hoped it was more peaceful in nature than this cocoon appeared. Perhaps it was better to let them die in their sleep, on some undetermined day, undisturbed and unattended.

All alone. A victim of the twisters.

That last thought was enough to drive her into action. She sprang around to the side of the coffin and looked for any seam that might indicate a way to open the cocoon. Her hands happened upon what felt like latches, and she flipped these up. A gust of air broke from the coffin, giving her a sense of victory over the machine. The cocoon split where the latches were undone, and she heaved up the lid to reveal the full body of the sleeping stranger.

Annilasia straightened up, only to jolt still with horror.

What she noticed first were the dark red tubes—she'd counted six—lining the inner side of the lid and snaking down into the sleeper's arms and legs. Next, she saw the state of the sleeper. The same features that distorted the face—thin, weathered skin riddled with bulging veins—dominated the rest of the body.

Annilasia wondered if she'd made a mistake. This person couldn't be alive. This was a corpse on its way to becoming a skeleton. The bones were held in place by skin so frail and thin that it would tear if she attempted to move the person. She cursed the handiwork of the mentors, her nostrils flaring.

No. They don't get to have the final word with this poor victim.

She thrust her hand out and gripped the nearest tube, which was embedded in the sleeper's calf. She gently pulled, meeting resistance. The tube refused to give with every attempt, and finally she yanked back hard. It broke off from the calf, spewing blood from its open end. Annilasia held the tube away from her, letting the red fluid spill across the coffin's base and onto the floor.

As the spew slowed to a drip, she watched the machine for any indication that her action might have brought more harm. It continued its rhythmic hisses and clicks. Its victim continued to sleep. She didn't hesitate again.

More blood spilled across the floor as she worked on disconnecting the rest of the tubes. When only a few remained, the machinery finally reacted to the changes. It whistled in shrill protest, but she didn't stop for this, counting it instead as a sign of near victory. Only two tubes remained, each sinking into the stranger's shoulders. Annilasia reached for them.

The victim's back arched as violent spasms took hold of them.

Panic shot through Annilasia. Unsure of what this meant, she maneuvered against the thrashing to yank the final tubes free. Blood gushed forth, spraying in all directions as the victim continued to jerk about. At one point, their arms caught on the mouthpiece and ripped it free from their wrinkled face. Despite their erratic movements, they had yet to open their eyes. Something was keeping the sleeping stranger linked to this diabolical contraption.

Annilasia spotted a thick wire extending from the back of the victim's head. She dove for it, tugging on it as she had the tubes. It didn't give so easily. She dropped down to her knees, positioned herself at an angle to the head, and heaved with a defiant cry.

A loud click accompanied the wire's detachment. Annilasia shot onto her back. Above her in the coffin, the thrashing ceased. The air fell silent, no longer burdened with the machine's hisses or the thumps of the victim's spastic limbs striking the coffin.

At the same time, the static charge in the air dissipated. A shiver ran through Annilasia. She'd forgotten about the vibrations. She must have acclimated to them during her time down here, because now that they were gone, the space around her felt empty and dead.

A final, delayed compression of air exhaled from the machine before all grew quiet. She craned her neck up to find the stranger motionless. She stood to her feet and crept closer. The stranger's eyelids no longer twitched.

A dreadful thought set in. Perhaps Annilasia's efforts had killed the stranger. Her hands trembled as she realized it would be yet another death by her hands. The presence of the mentors' bodies at her back swelled in her mind. She clenched her hands into fists, rebelling against the shame trying to overtake her. Whatever the outcome, she'd live with it. She'd tried to save this victim of the twisters. If they died, it wasn't for Annilasia's lack of care.

She startled when a loud gasp erupted from the victim. The stranger arched their back, their shoulder blades meeting, before slamming back down into the coffin. They continued to twist and squirm while gasping. Annilasia sprang forward to grip their shoulders.

"Stop panicking. Just breathe." Annilasia inhaled deeply through her nostrils and exhaled in demonstration. "Breathe in with me." She repeated the technique under the rapt attention of the stranger, who stared up at her with wide, panicked eyes. Frail hands clawed at a reedy throat, but the stranger tried to follow along with Annilasia. A few more repetitions came and went before both were breathing in a calm, synchronized rhythm. The stranger closed their eyes, breathing in the air with sweet relief as they relaxed back into a reclined position in the coffin. For a brief moment, Annilasia worried they'd fallen back into a deep sleep.

"Do you know where you are?" she asked. "Do you have a name?"

The stranger's eyes slipped open with an exhausting effort that made Annilasia cringe. Their lips parted, but only a raspy croak emitted. Annilasia realized her mistake in assuming that speech would come easily for them, and quickly shushed them. "Never mind that. I need to go get you help."

It finally struck her that she hadn't thought this through. She had no herbs or healer necessities, not even a glass of water to offer the stranger's parched throat. As she backed away, anxiety gripped her. She had no way of knowing if the liberated victim would survive long enough for Annilasia to race to the coven grounds to get help.

If the stranger resented her retreat, they didn't have the strength to show it or protest. Annilasia took advantage of this and turned to run towards the exit. She passed by the decapitated mentors without so much as a glance.

A brisk, frigid wind greeted her outside the cave. Her feet pounded on the ground, her muscles and lungs burning as she sprinted as fast as her limp would allow down the path towards the coven. The face of the coffin victim remained fixed in her mind, spurring her on.

The twisters couldn't have another victim, at least not one capable of being saved.

She wasn't going to let this stranger die if she could help it.

CHAPTER 19

Annilasia bounded up the spiral staircase that wrapped around one of the pineoak trunks on the coven grounds. She bypassed the first hut platform and stopped on the second level of the three-tiered structure.

Bursting through the door, she entered a hut furnished with a number of shelves lined with various plant stems, weeds, and leaves. A small desk sat against the opposite wall to the door, behind which sat a young man. Drifter—the apothecary's steward when Mentor VeteVici was absent—lifted his gaze from an open book just in time to glimpse Annilasia's frantic entrance and cocked an eyebrow at her breathless state. His eyes traced the streaks of blood lining her face, but she'd taken the time to dress herself upon arriving at the coven, so he couldn't see that the lather of dried blood covered most of her body.

"I need you to come with me," she blurted.

Drifter scowled, lifting his head more to squint at her. The candlelight bounced off his black leather coat and reflected in his face, his brown skin golden in the dim lighting. Youthfulness gleamed in his earth-tone eyes, fed by a curiosity he'd been engaged in before her interruption. Out of all the pupils at the coven, he was the only one that Annilasia deemed worthy of asking for help. He'd at least spoken a handful of words to her during her stay. That was more than she could say about the others.

"What's the matter with you?" he asked, running a hand over his bristly hair, which refused to part under the push of his fingers. "You've got blood all over your face. And it's rude to barge in like this making demands."

"I don't have time for banter," she snapped. "There's someone who needs our help."

That caught his attention. "A fellow pupil? Or a mentor?"

"Not quite," she admitted. "Or maybe. I'm not sure what category they fit in. It was hard to hold a conversation given that they likely haven't spoken for some time, what with a mask and tube shoved across their mouth."

"Quite cryptic, Annilasia." He sighed. "Don't tell me you've found someone down in the dungeons. Whoever the mentors put down there, they're meant to rot. We don't nurse our prisoners back to health. Leave them be."

Annilasia leapt forward to slam her gloved palms onto the desk. She leaned into Drifter's space.

"Listen carefully because I'm not going to repeat myself. This person is malnourished. Very frail, very decrepit. They've likely been machine-fed only the bare minimum to keep them alive. I don't think they can walk, not without their skin tearing. So, gather whatever in the deep abyss you need to help with all of that, put some earnestness in your step, and come with me, Drifter."

He eyed her for a moment, and she could see him digesting the odd list of symptoms she'd thrown at him.

"If this is a prisoner of the mentors . . ."

"Don't worry about the mentors," she said. "Just get your shite, and let's go."

Drifter growled in annoyance but stood from his chair, darted around to retrieve various items from around the hut, and followed her out with a full satchel slung over his shoulder.

Twilight blanketed the forest. As they walked, their shadows grew in length, and the light that was muddled behind the curtain of grey clouds slowly seeped away. By the time they reached the cave, very little light remained. Drifter had thus far been willing to go at Annilasia's pace, which was slow due to her limp, but he stopped now outside the entrance.

"What's down there?" he asked warily.

Annilasia waved for him to keep following. "Don't worry, there's torches around the corner there."

"Is this some game or trick?" he asked. "The others have said you're dangerous. If this is some way to trap me . . ."

"Grow a pair and get down here. If I wanted to do something to you, I wouldn't have given a damn about you bringing leaves and cremes."

She turned and scrambled down a few steps, glancing back only to make sure he was following. The journey down took longer than she remembered, but she recalled that her initial descent had been under duress. Too much of that time had been nothing but intense terror and desperation to escape Inzerious.

When she came to the end of the staircase and breached the entryway that led into the chamber, she halted. Drifter's boots scraped on the stone floor as he scurried down to her. Her heart shot up into her throat as she stared at the pile of corpses. A curse tumbled from her mouth. This wasn't like her to forget something so intense.

And intense it was. The sight of pooled blood and headless bodies elicited a surge of adrenaline in her. What a glorious sight. So many blood bags piled on top of each other. Arm over leg, leg over chest, chest without a head—

"What is it?" Drifter asked as he came up behind her.

She swiveled around to face him and tried to block his view into the chamber. A shiver ran over her as the flash of euphoria she'd experienced morphed back into disgust at herself. "I need you to listen to me," she said, swallowing despite her dry mouth. "You're going to see something that is quite disturbing. I need you to understand that I didn't do it. I found this place, and when I came down here, this mess was already here."

Drifter scowled at her. "What mess?"

"Just promise me, whatever your conclusions, remember why I brought you down here. Somebody needs your help." With that, she turned and ran towards the obelisk. She didn't wait to see his reaction, but she heard him gasp upon seeing the dead mentors.

"What in bleak stars happened? Stop running and explain yourself!"

She reached the coffin and found the withered stranger lying on their back inside. Annilasia's heart pounded with a renewed urgency. "Get your ass over here, Drifter," she yelled over his panicked words. She heard him trotting across the web of wires to join her. His accusations and demand for answers ceased when he sighted the still form inside the coffin.

"Who are they?" he asked, shoving her aside to lift a finger to the stranger's nose.

"I don't know."

"Multiple puncture wounds," said Drifter, his tone taking a shift from his previous wariness to the analytical. "Looks like a lot of blood was lost." He glanced over at Annilasia with wide eyes. "Did you do this? Why were they bleeding out? Who put holes in their skin?"

Annilasia shot her hand out to grip one of the tubes and shook it. "They had these damn things lodged in those holes. The blood came from there. I guess maybe it was feeding into this contraption, but I don't know. I found this person wrapped in this cocoon or coffin—whatever in blazes you'd call this thing—and all I did was take off the lid and yank out the tubes."

Drifter groaned under his breath as he continued to test the stranger's organic reactions to his prodding. He lifted one of the eyelids to peer at the eyes.

"You're going to wake them doing that," Annilasia warned.

"They're in some sort of comatose state," Drifter countered. "No doubt the body is in shock." He turned away from the coffin to fumble through his satchel.

"Can you help? Are they going to survive?"

"Survive is a generous hope," he murmured as he swiveled back to the coffin with a large jar in hand. "There's so many ailments to treat, I don't even know where to start." He unscrewed the lid to the jar and overturned its contents into his hands.

"What is that?" Annilasia's stomach knotted at the sight of a bulbous, pulsating tumor twice the size of Drifter's hands. She watched in stunned horror as he lifted it over the stranger and squeezed his hands together. The tumor squelched, and a thick fluid poured out of it. Drifter repeated this several times until globs of black ichor covered nearly every inch of the stranger. Depleted and flattened, the tumor wailed sickeningly as Drifter flung it away into some shadowy portion of the chamber. He ran his hands through the muck to spread it into an even film over the wrinkled body.

"That was a gyrac spore," he explained "I thought to bring it when you mentioned malnourishment. Its sac holds fluid that's full of nutrients. When the fluid is spread across an organic surface, it osmoses via the pores. The lucky organism—in this case, our malnourished patient—absorbs the nutrients."

She glanced towards the corner where he'd flung the spore. "Why did it sound like it was in pain? Is it . . ."

"Sentient? Yes. Is that an issue for you?" he asked, though his tone clearly indicated that he didn't care either way.

"Do you treat all your tools in the apothecary with such mercy?" she murmured.

"If you think that was cruel, you would have hated mentoring under VeteVici. His apothecary was not known for its gentle approach." Drifter froze and grew quiet, and his eyes flickered to Annilasia just as she looked to him. They both spent a moment locked together to avoid looking over at the pile of bodies several yards away. Then Drifter set to the task of searching in his satchel again.

"Do you smell that?" she asked. She sniffed, inhaling a sweet scent that reminded her of lummie flowers.

Drifter shot her a revolted look before facing the coffin again. "Of course I smell it. I almost fainted walking in here. Between the drainage from our patient here, which I assume leaked into the bottom of this coffin, and the stench of the bodies, I'm surprised we haven't both keeled over."

Annilasia gaped at him, then blinked and shut her mouth. He didn't smell anything pleasant. Just as her eyesight had lapped up a violent artistry from the corpses, her nostrils interpreted whatever foul odors tainted the air as perfume. She couldn't trust her senses.

"So, you found this place?" Drifter asked, failing to hide his skepticism. "Any idea what did that to the mentors?"

"A dokojin. I'd recognize the handiwork anywhere."

Drifter retrieved a bottle of water from the satchel and poured some of its contents past the stranger's lips. "Sounds plausible. But these are the mentors we're talking about. They wouldn't mess with something that powerful. They aren't—weren't—stupid."

"I'm not saying I understand what happened," she stated, trying not to let her irritation slip into her words. She wished he'd drop it, but she couldn't suggest that. "I'm just saying, dokojin like violence. I'd say what happened to the mentors meets that criterion."

Drifter's eyes twitched some at that, though he continued to keep his eyes off her in order to monitor and prod his patient. "Where are their heads, I wonder."

The memory, fresh and gory, surfaced in her head—the heads of each mentor rising into the air, the blood draining onto their decapitated bodies. "Couldn't find them, though I didn't exactly go on a hunt either. I saw this machine, found this person inside, and went to get you."

"You don't seem entirely distressed by the coven's loss."

"Neither do you," she countered. She fixed him with a stern look, and this time he broke his concentration to look back at her.

"The mentors were cruel," he admitted. "VeteVici was a skilled, wise, demented excuse for a man." Annilasia waited for more, but Drifter turned back to the sleeping stranger in the coffin. "You know the others won't believe you," he said.

"About the mentors?"

He nodded. "The sister clique will raise hell for the death of Mentor Yulon. Turesque and Uvi aren't exactly the most sensible either. They'll kill you first and ask questions later."

"Then I guess it's a stroke of luck that I went to you and not them, and that you're the apothecary pupil."

"Your claim to luck will run out as soon as they find out about this place and about the decapitated bodies over there. My suggestion is that you lie when we go back. We'll tell them the mentors are away for meditation. It's a lie that won't hold for long, but long enough for us to think of our next move."

Annilasia regarded him, unsure whether to be comforted or wary of his blind willingness to help her beyond bringing healer supplies to the chamber. "Why are you willing to cover for me?"

"I'm not," he said. "I'm covering for me. If I leave here and arrive back at the coven at your side, then it implicates me in whatever horrid thing happened here with the mentors. The others won't buy my truth that you tricked me into coming here with no knowledge of the mentors' fate. The lie is as much for me as it is for you."

"I'm not staying," Annilasia stated. "The mentors are dead. There's no one else left to teach us. My time at the coven is over. I've got other problems to deal with."

Drifter turned, his eyebrow quirked again. "You think I'm going to take the brunt of this? You scamper off while I take care of this person you've flung at me, and while the rest of the pupils work to uncover the mess you left behind? I'll rat you out faster than one could bite."

"Then why help at all?" she asked. "If you care so little, why not let this stranger die?"

"I don't care if they live for the sake of their survival. I want to know what they know." He looked up and gazed at the backboard of the machine. "Maybe they can tell me what happened to the mentors. And I'd very much like to know the purpose of this contraption."

Annilasia looked down at the motionless figure in the coffin. The black film from the spore fluid masked some of the frailty and sickly complexion. Despite the plan she'd proposed to Drifter, she didn't want to leave just yet. There were too many secrets that taunted her, and all answers remained at the coven.

The secret of the mentors' schemes.

The secrets buried in the mind of this skeletal victim.

But most importantly, the secret to ridding herself of Inzerious.

CHAPTER 20

The plan was to keep the machine and the coffin's victim a secret, but they couldn't keep the patient inside the cave—not with the rotting corpses stinking up the confined space. Drifter decided it best that he stay behind in case the patient were to wake or show signs of distress, while Annilasia was to return to the coven for a portable cot.

When she emerged from the cavern, she found a layer of snow covering the ground and flurries sinking from the night sky. She swore under her breath and set to trudging through the altered terrain. It'd be a pain having to carry the cot back through it, and even more so while transporting the patient.

The coven grounds were quiet when she arrived. Annilasia paused before ducking behind a nearby tree out of instinct. She knew something wasn't right. It was too quiet. Night rarely meant sleep for every member of the coven. At any given time, someone was awake, studying rituals that could only be performed under the starry sky or using the time to delve deeper into the books of the twister library. But there were no candles lit in the hut windows—no movement, no footprints in the snow, no signs that anyone was even on the coven grounds.

The darkness blended it with the environment, but when she saw the mound lying at the bottom of one of the spiral staircases, it struck her as out of place. She didn't move towards it directly though. Whatever was at hand, she knew it unwise to move into the open area of the coven grounds. Instead, she left her post and crept around the tree line that surrounded the area until she found another trunk to hide behind with a better vantage point.

Still nothing. She waited, listening to the wind as it moaned through the trees and twirled the snowflakes in their descent. A visceral sense of vulnerability squirmed under her skin. If anyone was out here, hidden in the trees, she'd be an easy target now. But she still couldn't puzzle out the mound in front of the staircase, and with no sign of a threat, she decided to brave the eerie setting to find out more.

Hunched over, she darted into the cleared area of the grounds, stopping when she was nearly upon the mound. This close, it looked too much like a body on its side. Without a light source, she couldn't be sure unless she crouched and examined it. After a few anxious glances towards the tree line, she did so and leaned in.

The wind died for a moment, and the faintest hint of a sweet fragrance graced her nostrils. For a moment, she wondered if it wasn't a body at all. Corpses didn't smell like that. Then she remembered her skewed senses, and dread rolled through her stomach. She reached an arm out and pulled on the body's shoulder to lay it on its back. The stomach was blown out. Even in the dark, she could make out the hollow in its belly and the guts strewn in the snow. She bristled at the inner glee the scene brought her, and quickly directed her attention elsewhere in a swift attempt to disengage with that reaction.

No footprints tamped the area beside the victim. And the snow wasn't covering the body or its viscera. Perhaps that meant a long-distance weapon had been utilized. Or it meant the attacker was skilled.

Like an elusive shadow.

Her sense of vulnerability intensified. She scrambled into a hunched stance and glanced around.

An untrained eye would have missed the bulk of darkness ill-matched to the outline of the trees, assuming it an odd overlap of shadow or a rogue bush. Not her. Annilasia knew what to look for. Her life had once depended on becoming one with the shadows.

Aware they'd been spotted, the tillishu slipped behind a nearby tree, but not before unleashing an arrow at her. Annilasia was already ducking. The arrow soared overhead and landed with a whisper in the snow behind her.

Her heart pounded. She flattened herself in the snow and scanned for the tillishu warrior. Even with the snow, it was too dark. Not the moon nor the stars lit the night sky. The tillishu could have sprinted to the opposite side of the coven by now or climbed a tree for a better aim. The idea of lying flat for protection suddenly struck her as foolish. She sprang up and jumped over the corpse onto the spiral staircase. Her boots thumped on the wooden boards as she ascended.

There were other thuds. Arrows striking the stairs. She darted into the first hut and slammed the door shut as it vibrated with another thud.

The same soiled fragrance she'd smelled from the body below clogged the hut. She covered her nose with her arm and tried to ignore the splash of gore spread across the tiny space. The husk of a pupil littered the bed where they'd obviously been sleeping before meeting their grisly end. Like the other corpse, their insides were spewed all over—the outcome when a twister interacted too closely with terrestrial elements.

Everyone was dead. Every other pupil had been slaughtered.

Dying stars, they're here for me. Why else would they still be here?

Annilasia slipped the wand that was in her sleeve out into her gloved palm. It lacked any glimmer of aether. She cursed under her breath, knowing there would be very little, if any, natural aether to gather from the Apparition Realm here at the coven. It'd all be aetherwaste, especially after tonight's events.

The hairs on her skin stood on end at a new presence in the room. The pieces fell into place seconds before the attack. The hut had a window.

Her dormant instincts, cultivated by her own tillishu past, saved her from yet another fatal strike. She spun as the tillishu's arm shot out. The unseen blade in their grip sang as it swung through empty air. Annilasia's foot rose and struck the tillishu in the chest, sending them careening into the front corner of the hut.

She had seconds. The tillishu would recover more quickly than a typical warrior. Her muscles and mind moved as one. The need to survive pushed her onto a dangerous precipice. There was no external aether to fuel the wand. But there was her own aether—the natural source from within her aura. It would, however, come with a cost.

She didn't even use the wand. The tool was pointless under the strain that this amount of aether would bring. The need to survive and her rage at the tillishu's persistence fueled the aether gathering at her fingertips, and she forced the onslaught onto her attacker.

The walls and ceiling of the hut exploded in a sea of shrapnel as they broke off from the platform into a vortex of snowy air. The tillishu was propelled away from Annilasia. She watched their form become engulfed in the night's shadows, then heard a loud crack when they struck one of the trees.

The tornadic debris crashed to the ground. Annilasia blinked as flurries brushed across her face. The wind stirred her hair, whipping it furiously. Dread crawled beneath her skin and depleted her of the strength to stand. She dropped to her knees, choking back a wail. The aftertaste of the tainted aether soured her thoughts. Death beckoned to her, and she thought about crawling to the edge of the platform and casting herself to the ground.

She'd made a mistake summoning that aether. Iveer's warning surfaced, echoing and burning in her ears. He'd warned her that using her own aether meant tapping into Inzerious's too, but never before had it sickened her like this. Perhaps it was because the cage she'd created was so weak. Too much of the dokojin's aether had slipped in with her own.

Fear bled into her mind when she realized she had crawled to the edge of the hut's platform. The ground pulled at her from below. She didn't want to jump. She wasn't going to.

Her muscles moved without her permission, and she rose to her feet. Her toes inched over the edge.

A cackle of malice and mockery reverberated in the confines of her head. She squeezed her eyes shut and let out a groan.

No. Inzerious doesn't control me. This is a trick—a side effect of using tainted aether. Step the fuck away from the edge.

Annilasia staked her dread with this truth and scrambled backwards towards the center of the hut, where she panted from exhaustion. Lying on her back, she watched the snowflakes appear from the void above and twirl downward. She knew she needed to get up and locate the tillishu. A collision with a tree was no guarantee the assassin was dead. But whenever she mustered up the will to move, her muscles refused to cooperate. A heavy weight pressed into her chest. By the time the depression lifted, tiny icicles weighed her eyelashes and her face quivered from the cold.

Checking her footing with every step, she descended where she thought the tillishu had plunged. and trod through the snow in search of a body. It took time in the dark, and it was only by stumbling across a tree slick with goo that she found her attacker. Her gaze followed the trail of blood up the tree until she spotted the motionless body skewered on a high branch.

It was a small mercy that the tillishu was alone. If there'd been others, Annilasia would have known by now. She thought about finding a way to get the body down in case she might be able to glean the motivation behind their attack on the coven. But she dismissed this idea. She knew how tillishu operated. There'd be nothing so compromising anywhere on the body—no parchment, no sigil. Tillishu were shadows—knives in the dark with no purpose but to kill.

If she had to guess, though, the tillishu had come for her. After all, Annilasia was still wanted for her crime of kidnapping the Tecalica and taking her from the Sachem's Fortress nearly half a year ago. It was a miracle the Sachem's assassins had taken them this long to find her at the coven. Now that one had, more would come.

Annilasia abandoned the corpse and trudged back to the monastery to retrieve the cot she'd been sent to find. She found small comfort in the fact that the massacre here was not by her own hands. The pupils had been killed by an assassin—not like the mentors, who'd met their end because a weakling puppet couldn't control the parasite trying to hijack her body.

**

Drifter's eyes widened when she arrived with the cot. "Why do you look like a horse kicked you in the stomach? Surely the cot wasn't that heavy."

Annilasia dropped the cot to the ground at the foot of the coffin. "The other pupils are dead."

Drifter's mouth dropped open. He took a step away from her, hand yanking down sharply so that his wand dropped out of his sleeve into his bandage-wrapped hand. "What in Dardajah's shite did you do?"

"I didn't do anything," she countered. "I got to the coven, and there were no signs of life except a tillishu, who tried to kill me."

Drifter eyed her with obvious distrust. "I don't suppose you have proof?"

"There's an assassin's body in a tree. That should be proof enough for you."

Drifter turned away to look down into the coffin, but she could hear his mind churning. She followed his gaze and studied the elderly sleeper for any signs of change.

"Did they wake at all?"

Drifter blinked and shook himself out of his thoughts. "No. I don't expect them to for a while. They're too weak to stay lucid. My guess is that it'll be some time before we can communicate. We'll take them back on the cot, settle them in near the apothecary so it's easy for me to transport my tools, and then we wait as I nurse them back to health." He paused and glanced at her. A flicker of dismay crossed his face. "I suppose you'll be leaving now that the others are dead."

Annilasia considered this. He was right. Nothing held her here anymore. But she'd heard Inzerious cackle in the moments after the attack in the hut. The cage was thinning fast.

"No. I have to stay. There's a problem that only the mentors could have fixed, and with them dead, I have to scour this place for a solution of my own." She squinted at him. "Why do you care if I go anymore? With the pupils dead, it doesn't matter what happened down here. There's no one to accuse you of anything."

Embarrassment swam across Drifter's features before he could control them. "Call me weak, but I don't want to be abandoned at a coven where everyone is dead and a tillishu came to call. At least until I can nurse this stranger back to the waking world, I'd prefer to know there's someone else here."

Annilasia huffed. What comfort could her presence possibly provide him? She was a dud. She was the coven pariah. The one everyone had wished would fail. "You're a damn twister. Don't act like you can't take care of yourself. Now help me lift the sleeper onto the cot. It's cold in here, and I'd like to get back before my blood freezes solid."

As Drifter moved to the opposite side of the coffin, Annilasia stared down at the sleeping stranger. Much of the black film from Drifter's spore creature had absorbed into the skin, leaving it tinted a subtle purple. No longer confined to the exoskeletal cocoon, they looked rather peaceful in their slumber.

Yet secrets waited beyond those closed eyes and within that resting mind, and Annilasia wondered if the stranger truly was a victim. Perhaps when they woke, they'd admit to playing a willing part in the mentors' schemes.

CHAPTER 21

Mygo scrubbed at the blood that slathered his ebony skin. The trickle of water falling from overhead wouldn't last forever, and he didn't have the patience to go fetch more. It was a trek to the nearest lake with clean water, so it was best to make efficient use of what little was left at the bunker. He'd been generous enough to let Vowt wash before him, which had left him with remnants.

The chilled water sent a shiver across his skin. He watched it splash onto the floor, taking with it the blood. He heard a groan behind the walls and looked up at the hole overhead.

No more bathing water. He swore under his breath and shook his arms to unleash a spray of droplets. Beneath his feet, a drain in the floor gurgled as it drank up the red-stained liquid until only a moist film layered the ground. The sound made him shudder as he recalled what the drain had already choked down.

It hadn't just been blood covering Mygo when he'd first stumbled down into the underground chamber. Loose innards, slimy and pale like worms, had tumbled off him when the water struck, only to become lodged in the drain. As the pile of chunky gore started to grow around his feet, he'd forced his toes to scrape and crush the guts until they were small enough to disappear through the grates.

Mygo reached for his towel and patted at his arms and chest, dismayed when he drew it back and saw bright red splotches staining the white linen. But there was nothing for it. By the time he finished drying, several crimson streaks covered the towel. Mygo threw it towards the corner of the windowless room. The cloth landed on the growing pile of laundry, emitting a slap that made him cringe. He needed to gather up the laundry soon and set to washing. Otherwise, he and Vowt would have to share the last clean towel next wash.

As he was tying his loincloth fast around his waist and stepping into his pants, a low rumble caught his ears. He froze. The walls muffled the sound but couldn't fully buffer the screeching on the other side. Mygo shook himself out of his uneasy trance and finished dressing. The screeches continued, refusing to cease. His only escape came when he barreled up the stairs to the upper level of the bunker. He couldn't hear the flayers with that level of separation.

The iron door at the top of the staircase groaned against his push. Beyond it, candles illuminated a circular room cluttered with cabinets, desks, and a plethora of personal items such as books and jars. Mygo stepped inside and shut the door behind him, sealing off the last, distant screeches seeping through the walls. He approached one of the desks, behind which sat his companion. Vowt spoke up before Mygo could.

"I—I hear the flayer s-screeching."

Mygo put a comforting hand on the stout man's shoulder. "You've got better ears than me. Can't hear the poor thing all the way up here."

Vowt looked up from his work and peered at Mygo from behind a set of spectacles that amplified the size of his eyes. Mygo smirked, always amused by the comical look the glasses created on the chymist's face.

"Don't—don't laugh."

Mygo put up his hands in playful defense. "Not laughing. Carry on."

He stepped back, but Vowt didn't return to whatever had held his attention on the desk. The other man leaned forward in his chair to fix thinned eyes on Mygo. An expression of dismay troubled his face, which was half obscured behind long strands of dark blond hair. He looked small then, and it wasn't because he was half the height of Mygo. Defeat had morphed the wrinkles on his pale face and had hunched his shoulders. Despite his youth, being a bare few years past the period of growth spurts and voice changes, Vowt's time in the bunker with Mygo had worn him in a very visible sense.

"We failed again," said Vowt.

Mygo sank into one of the lone chairs in the room and let out a heavy sigh. His muscles relaxed some, though there was a permanent stiffness that riddled his shoulders and back. Perhaps it could be attributed to age. But it was more likely his line of work. Catching and dissecting deformed beasts no doubt took a toll on his body in ways he'd never be able to undo. Age probably just made it worse. Unlike Vowt, he was well into the seasoned period of his life and couldn't attribute all of his wrinkles to stress.

"We'll try again," he replied.

"We're almost out of—of—of the fluid again."

The words took longer to leave Vowt's lips than was typical in conversation, but Mygo had long ago learned to be patient with the chymist's way of speaking. Sometimes words tripped Vowt up, and he'd stutter or repeat a word until he found a way to keep the sentence going. Other times the words came out in bursts of phrases with long pauses in between.

"As long as we've got flayers to dissect, then we've got more of that damn green goo to work with," said Mygo.

Vowt nodded, but it was obvious the chymist didn't share Mygo's optimism. "I didn't like seeing it d-d-die."

Mygo cringed and shifted in his seat. "I wish you didn't have to see any of that. If I could do this alone, I'd spare you that trauma."

Vowt scowled at him. "I'm brave like you. Don't p-p-patronize me."

Mygo pursed his lips and averted his gaze. "I didn't mean it like that. I wish neither of us had to go through this. Some days I wish we'd never agreed to help that mirajin."

Vowt shook his head. "It's good to help. And if we can s—if we can save just one flayer . . ."

"It will have been worth it," Mygo finished in a tired sigh. "Don't you worry though? About if they'll ever come back?" It'd been months since the mirajin and the Tecalica had departed for the Heidretka border. A place miles away, with uncountable dangers between here and there. For all he knew, Elothel and Jalice might have made it no more than a mile before an Ikaul warrior struck them down. Just one potential fate out of a thousand that could have befallen them.

"We're doing all this work, taking all these risks, for someone who might never return. We might even be able to save more flayers if we didn't have to extract the serum during the procedures. And even if we do succeed, it might end up being a waste of time."

Vowt shrugged. "Not if we s-s-save a flayer."

Mygo didn't respond. It wouldn't have mattered too much, except for the stubborn fact that he actually cared. Somehow, that damn woman's plight had plucked at heartstrings he hadn't even known still existed in him. He hated to admit it, but he wanted Jalice to find peace. If part of that peace required somehow restoring her husband—the star dying Sachem himself—to some resemblance of sanity, then Mygo was going to make that a reality.

Sahruum's infinite ass, I've got too much altruism in me. Gotta carve that out before it gets me killed.

So, here he and Vowt were, stuck in the damn forest only a few days' travel from the Ikaul Fortress, trying to create an impossible antidote to the Sachem's madness. As Mygo understood—which was a stretch of the word considering how convoluted the whole thing sounded—the Sachem's madness could be boiled down to three issues.

A disease, a curse, and a possession.

The disease came from some type of poisonous serum that Jalice had given the Sachem long ago. It had altered his mind and given him an unhealthy fixation on Jalice. A strange obsession that couldn't be broken without an elixir.

The curse originated from the binding aether agreement between Jalice and the dokojin, to whom she'd promised the Sachem. There were a number of prerequisites to break it, and Elothel had not spoken to Mygo much about what it all required.

Finally, the possession was the dokojin's actual inhabitance inside the Sachem. The curse may have given Dardajah claim over the man, but the possession was the actual hijacking of the body. Once again, the mirajin had explained little of what could be done about this.

It was all enough to make Mygo's head swim, and on most days, he tried hard not to puzzle through it all. He'd leave that up to the Elothel and Jalice. All he'd been tasked with was the disease portion, and even that held far too many mysteries for his own liking.

He and Vowt had started off with a single vial full of green fluid. Elothel had claimed fae'd retrieved it from the Black House, and had explained that it held the same serum that had bent the Sachem's mind towards obsession over Jalice. Vowt had tried to use the green fluid to concoct a cure, but enough failures had eventually dried up this source.

But along the way, by happenstance, they'd discovered something curious. When they dissected a flayer, the same green goo was secreted within the creature's skull around the brain matter. Vowt, through his odd and peculiar chymist ways, had confirmed it to be the very same fluid that had been in the mirajin's vial—the same green goo. A promising find that meant they had more substance to work with.

And, as it happened, more substance to fail with.

It was a morbid consolation that with every failure at saving the flayers, Vowt at least still had their fluid to work with.

It, of course, required that Mygo track down and capture flayers. That wasn't exactly a pleasure. But Vowt wouldn't let him give up, and Mygo couldn't, not even if he wanted to. He couldn't live knowing that he could have saved the Sachem and, in turn, Jalice. If she could confront her own sins and seek out her brother miles away just to redeem herself, then Mygo could do this from the comfort of his home.

Even if it meant wearing blood and guts.

"Are you l-l-listening to me?"

Mygo blinked and grunted. Vowt was frowning at him.

"What were you saying?"

Vowt threw up his hands. "I need to concentrate, and I can't—can't—can't think with you stinking it up in here. D-d-did you even shower?"

Mygo growled and got to his feet. "Fine. I'll go on another hunt. Might help clear my head of the awfulness we just witnessed."

"When you get b-b-back, we try with the other flayer."

"Are you sure you're up for it?" Mygo asked. "We've never done the procedure twice in one day."

Vowt gave a confident nod. "We try again. Just g-give me time to think first."

Mygo headed for the door, grabbing his thick fur coat along the way.

"We can do this, Mygo," said Vowt.

He glanced over his shoulder and gave his companion a forced nod. "If anyone can find a cure, it's you, Vowt." With that, he opened the door to the bunker and stepped out into the frigid cold of Wither Season.

CHAPTER 22

D ecay surrounded Mygo.

It infested the forest like termites, poisoning the air. In the very way the mud languished beneath his boots and the morning light got lost in the trees, his bones curdled in the decay that wormed its way under his skin. It sank its teeth deep, gutting his mind.

These days, thinking was difficult. The last several months had ushered in a change in the land, a deeper misery than even before. Mygo blamed the Sachem. According to his sources at the Flock of Tents, no one had seen the tyrant in some time, and if Mygo were to guess, the Sachem had taken the tribe's Stone of Elation with him to wherever he'd run off to. Not many knew the true purpose of such Stones, but Mygo knew enough to attribute the invisible decay to the absence of such an artifact.

The change had affected the way he viewed the forest, and the way the forest viewed him. The trees were watchers now, waiting for him to misstep so they could curl their devouring roots around him and feast. Very few critters remained in these parts, either exterminated by their new predatory neighbors or driven to abandon this land for their usual migratory patterns. It made hunting game difficult, and often meant he had to look to other markets for provisions. What little wildlife remained never showed itself to him, as if they waited for him to succumb to an ill fate that would allow them to again show themselves and nibble away at his corpse.

The change had even altered his relationship with Vowt. His companion's quirks and fidgets had gotten worse, provoking quicker tempers and harsher tongues. For the most part, they navigated through it and remained close companions. But the decay had made this challenging.

Mygo crouched low and studied a trail of imprints in the muddied earth. To an untrained eye, or even a well-versed tracker, the subtle impressions and ridges in the mud might easily have been dismissed as the natural work of rain. Nothing about it suggested the trample of paws or hooves. But he knew better. A long decade of work in these forests lent him a certain expertise in such markings.

Flayers had crossed this way.

That deduced, he hesitated. Tracking flayers was no science. The creatures were unique from each other—one might be a chimera of a bird-like nature, while another might be bipedal and mammalian. It made it difficult to determine whether the tracks belonged to one single creature or a pack of them.

Based on what little he could gather, two had passed this way. One particular cut in the mud betrayed a different kind of track, one that didn't seem to match the others. The dominant trend appeared canine—long strides and paws, shifting at times from all fours to a bipedal lunge—but this lone incision, different from those canine tracks, seemed a reptilian feature.

Mygo let the deduction rest in his head. It was entirely possible the collection of marks was from the same creature. Perhaps it had slid here in the wet dirt before carrying on. Perhaps the creature he tracked was just that—a single creature with a triadic nature. A chimera within a chimera.

He looked up from the earth and surveyed the trees. A small meadow lay beyond, surrounded by an endless, barren forest and a light fog. Nothing moved, and as unnerving as that was, he'd grown accustomed to it.

A howl broke the silence.

He stiffened. Usually, sound out here meant only one thing: the hunter had made a mistake and become the hunted. Mygo's hand shot to the axe at his side and then froze when the noise repeated. He calculated the distance. It was a mile off and didn't seem to have come any closer since the first cry. He dared to wonder at the strangeness in its tone. It sounded surprised. Hurt.

Hesitation gripped him. This scenario usually ended with him retreating back to the bunker. He only took on a flayer if he had the element of surprise, which was a rare advantage. But something about those howls struck him as odd. Not the agony—the poor creatures always sounded like a dog kicked one too many times or a grimalkin burned alive.

No, the surprise in the howl was different. Something had startled it. Flayers weren't ever known to be caught off guard.

When a third howl broke through the trees, followed by loud hoots and snarls, he set off towards the source. He made sure to trot slowly and deliberately. As much as he wanted to catch the creature before it could vanish, he wasn't going to announce his presence with noise.

A few more grunts bled through the leafless trees. Every instinct in him told him to turn around and go back. He suppressed this and pushed on until he spotted movement, then slowed and hunched over behind a tree.

Three warriors, clad in armor he didn't recognize as Ikaul, stood in a circle with their backs to each other. The blades of their weapons pointed out towards the treetops as if they expected an attack from above. Something large lay at the center of their circle, a splatter of dark fluid glistening across its surface. Mygo came out from behind the tree and trotted towards the troop. When they noticed him, their blades swept through the air to point in his direction. He slowed and raised his hands.

"No need to startle," he stated. "Where's the beast?"

Their eyes darted from him to the treetops. One shook like a leaf in the wind, and Mygo thought the young man might faint right there on the spot. The other two, a seasoned male and a middle-aged female, clenched their weapons with white knuckles, but Mygo could see the slight tremble even in their grips.

"Where is it?" Mygo asked with a stern tone.

"It came out of nowhere," the lone female spoke. "Sliced our comrade's arm clean off and then bit off his head."

Mygo gazed down at the body behind her. Blood soaked the armor and clothes where the arm had been torn off, and a pool of the red fluid flowed from the decapitation wound. Mygo turned on his heels to eye the treetops.

"You keep looking up," he pointed out. "I assume it can fly?"

"No, I don't think so," the elder of the group stated. "But it can damn well jump."

A shadow was all Mygo saw. It swept out from behind a tree like a sheet of void and dove atop the young warrior who had yet to speak. There wasn't time for him to scream. Blood spurted across the others in unison with the rip of torn muscles and crunch of crushed bones.

A stench like rotten meat assaulted Mygo. He had time enough to glimpse vague details of the flayer in the aftermath of its attack. The meager sunlight reflected off a brown exoskeleton barbed with tiny thorns. The flayer stood on two legs like a human, but a giant spiked tail, made up of bulbous metasoma segments like that of a scorpion, curled from its hindquarters. A sharp stinger at the end of this tail protruded through the back of the impaled warrior. Blood and innards slid off its tip to plop onto the ground.

Most notable, yet most expected given his foreknowledge of the creature, was the tattered cloak that hung across its back and shoulders. He doubted the other warriors had identified the material in the mere seconds that passed, but he already knew its origin.

The cloak was not a part of the flayer's natural hide.

It was human skin.

Some poor traveler had crossed the creature's path in days past, and the encounter had ended with them being stripped down to the muscle. The flayers wore these skin coats like prizes, though Mygo doubted that it was pride that motivated this abominable behavior. There was something more complicated, more tragic, that fueled the need to wear the skin of their victims.

The female warrior cried out and swung her blade. The flayer moved much quicker. Its tail retracted, searing more flesh from the young man as it tore free. The creature emitted a series of clicks and hums as it sprang again. Unlike her dead companion, the warrioress had time to scream. The sound ceased with a sharp gurgle when the flayer's jaw ensnared her entire head. Rows of teeth clenched together above her shoulders. More blood stained the forest floor as her body sank to the ground without a head.

Mygo somersaulted away before the flayer could decide he was next. He dropped his axe, and his hands fumbled at his belt as he turned on his knees to face the creature. His fingers found the pipe tucked between his belt and his tunic, and he brought it to his lips.

The last surviving warrior let out a high-pitched shriek. The flayer dove at the elderly man and pinned him to the ground.

Mygo blew air into the hollowed pipe. A dart flew out from the opposite end. *Guide the need, Sahruum.* It was a quick prayer. He hoped it would make a difference.

The flayer arched its tail. The stinger twitched in the moment when it would have descended through the warrior's head like a blade through melon. Mygo stood, prepared to run. If the dart hadn't broken skin, the flayer would hunt him down next.

The tail fell, limp and deflated, as the flayer swayed with an anguished moan. The dart's paralyzing effect took hold, and the creature collapsed sideways onto the ground. The liberated warrior scrambled up and ran towards Mygo to hide behind the wilderman. The two watched as the flayer thrashed until it grew still.

Mygo traveled a few feet to retrieve his axe, all the while watching the creature. Its presence defied even the paltry warmth of the sunlight overlaying the forest. Even in the midst of the decay, it struck him as wrong to see it in the daylight. These were the things of nightmares, belonging to the shadows and the darkness of night. Seeing its deformity midday only added to the dread these things conjured in him. Perhaps it was the frigid cold that was to blame for the flayer's diurnal presence. With its reptilian and insectoid features, it likely didn't fare well in low temperatures.

"What did you do to it?" the surviving warrior asked. "Is it dead?"

"No," Mygo answered. "It succumbed to a extract from the cythamprow flower. Learned a while back that it's the safest way to take one of these down. Carved myself a nifty blowpipe and coated the darts in the flower's extract." Satisfied that the flayer would not stir or fight off the paralysis, he turned to regard the sole survivor of the warrior troop. He frowned.

The man's skin was pasty, stealing away any lingering qualities of youthfulness that might have been present despite his older age. A rash circled his eyes, and a restlessness swam in the warrior's gaze. Mygo had previously interpreted this as fear of the flayer, but though the threat was gone, the agitation still remained. The sickly features put Mygo on edge, and he took a reflexive step backward to put a bit more distance between him and the warrior.

"Never heard of that kind of plant," the man said. He craned his neck as a shiver twitched his spine. "Is it sanctioned by the Sachem?"

Mygo chose his words carefully. "The Sachem doesn't care what happens out in these parts. Flayers make it hard for me to follow civilian sanctions."

The warrior returned his cautious stare. "Are you Ikaul then?"

Mygo sighed. "I grow tired of games quickly. I'm no Ikaul, and I'm no friend of the Sachem. If you're here on his behalf, let's get this tussle over with."

A new voice crept out from within the forest.

"You may have taken down the creature, but you can't take on a whole troop."

Mygo twisted around to see a number of warriors, clad in the same armor as the sole survivor of the flayer encounter, emerging from the trees. His shoulders sank. He wouldn't escape this crowd even if he could take down a few. They far outnumbered him.

One of the warriors stepped forward, a clear indication this individual held some sort of leadership status. The same light breeze that carried the stench of the dead bodies tousled the man's wavy brown hair. Black skin ink peeled out from beneath his tunic to crawl across his face. The pattern curled around his eyes, which held a sternness within their muddied depths.

Most unsettling was that same restless movement in his gaze, which drifted away from Mygo at times in a lazy, chaotic rhythm. Despite his darker complexion compared to the survivor, his brown skin still betrayed the same red rash around his eyes.

These people are sick. Or soaring higher than a kite during a storm. "So, you are Ikaul," Mygo grumbled aloud. "Enough ink to claim a new skin color." *Skipped the feather greeting though,* he noted to himself. *That's odd for an Ikaul.*

The man scowled at him. "If I were Ikaul, that comment would have ended with your head severed from your neck. It's not wise to loosen the tongue these days, old man."

"And that comment is enough to earn you the title of shithead in my book."

A snarl twitched on the leader's lips. "Who are you? What are you doing out here?"

"Well, for one, I just saved your daft kin over there, who thought it wise to take on a flayer."

"Looks to me like you let three of my warriors die," the man retorted.

"You can't hold me accountable for the lives of your warriors. I'm not their clanhead nor their leader. Just be grateful one of them lived to tell the tale. Now, if you're not Ikaul, then what stupidity drives you to wander flayer territory?"

"You've got a sour tone, old man, and it'll earn you nothing but trouble. I'm Yetu, second elder of the Vekaul tribe. This forest belongs to the free people of the Fractured Tribes. The Sachem and his abominations don't have claim over what they never had."

The Vekaul. Mygo had heard of them—a ragtag tribe of rebels in opposition to the Sachem. Made up of Ikaul defectors and escaped Vekuuv slaves, they lived like nomads in a secret place not far from the Sachem's Fortress. For the longest time, Mygo had believed the tribe to be nothing more than a rumor. When he'd go to trade for supplies at the Flock of Tents, some would mutter of troublesome warriors hiding in the forest. He had yet to personally encounter a Vekaul until now, and his first impressions left a bitter aftertaste.

He spat on the ground. "Well, Yetu, you're in for a rude awakening when you press on and find your numbers dwindling to shite as the flayers lay waste to you."

"You mean this pathetic beast?" Yetu moved past Mygo and closer to the flayer. "Is it still alive?"

"He used some sort of paralyzing agent on it," the surviving warrior stated. "I think he's a twister. Look at the rings on his fingers."

Yetu turned to more closely observe Mygo. "Is that true, old man? Are you a part of the twister revolt? Raise up your jeweled hand."

Mygo did nothing. If they wanted to see his rings, they could cut them off his fingers. "Some shiny rocks on my hand doesn't make me a twister."

"Don't play us for fools," Yetu barked. "Those rings are only worn by priests, and all the priests defected."

"It seems likely that whatever my answer, you're not going to accept it," said Mygo. "Let's give it a shot though. Name's Mygo. I've lived out here longer than you have, and thus have got more wits about me when it comes to flayers. Here's a free piece of advice: run when you can, hide when you can't."

"Is that why three of my kin are dead, yet the creature remains alive with you standing guard beside it?" Yetu challenged. "Seems more like you ran to the aid of the creature."

Mygo shook his head and grunted. "Like I said, you don't want my answers. You want your fake truth, whatever in Dardajah's spit that might be."

"Then you won't have a problem with us killing the creature." Yetu signaled to the surviving warrior, who raised his spear.

Mygo stiffened, unable to keep the protest from leaving his lips.

"Stop!"

The warrior froze with the spear raised over his head. Rage entered Yetu's glare. His hand went to the sword at his belt, and he unsheathed it to reveal a grand weapon that took Mygo by surprise. The pristine white blade radiated with an impressive halo of shimmering shadow. It was an aether weapon known only to the hirishu who guarded the Ikaul Temple.

"So, you are a filth of the Sachem," Yetu grunted, aiming the tip of his blade at Mygo.

"Quite a sword you've got there," said Mygo. "I've only known Ikaul to wield those."

"It's a trophy," Yetu snarled. "We stripped it from the filthy shite who wielded it before casting his screaming body into a fire of judgement. It serves a more righteous purpose in my hands. But, of course, it makes sense that you recognize a hirishu blade. Only an Ikaul would be so familiar with it."

"Believe whatever you want of me," said Mygo. He pointed to the flayer. "But we need that creature alive. It holds the secret to undoing the wickedness that infects this land. It can restore the Sachem to sanity."

"Only an ally of the Sachem would care for a fate other than the tyrant's death." Yetu raised his hand in a strange salute and then drove it down. The signal meant something to the survivor, who thrust his spear into the flayer's neck. Blood spurted from the wound.

Mygo returned Yetu's glare. "You just murdered a tormented human."

Yetu's anger morphed into an incredulous expression. "It's a killing monstrosity. These things have slaughtered hundreds of innocent people during their infestation of the forest. We can't let these things continue to destroy the wildlife here. We can't let it shatter the sense of safety for those trying to leave Ikaul."

"I'm all for making these parts safe," said Mygo. "But you're dealing with something of which you have no understanding. You killed a tortured soul out of pure animosity for it, and that only creates the very aetherwaste you so oppose. This is an intricate matter."

"Maybe you're not a twister. Are you some sort of crazed Tamer?" Yetu asked. "These aren't the critters your kind were tasked with befriending. These things are the work of the Sachem, and are as forsaken as dokojin."

Mygo shook his head. "So many things wrong with everything you just said. First off, I'm not a Tamer. Second, they're nothing like the dokojin. Third, there is, in fact, a part of this creature that is indeed native to this land. The only thing you said that came anywhere close to the truth is that the flayer's deformity is the Sachem's doing."

"Enough," Yetu shouted. "The Vekaul will not tolerate anyone deemed loyal to that man. You are now a prisoner for acts of treason."

"You're making a mistake," Mygo growled.

Yetu strode up to him and leaned in to whisper into Mygo's ear. "We execute twisters, old man. We execute the traitorous Ikaul. And we execute those too friendly to either. You should have killed the flayer. Your fate is sealed."

CHAPTER 23

The rash-eyed bastards thought a blindfold would disorient Mygo.

He found it laughable, but went along with the charade. He pretended to be disoriented even as he kept up with every twist and turn they took. He almost snorted when the blindfold came off and he found himself at the entrance of a grand grouping of tents nestled in the forest. The daft warriors hadn't even tried to make circuitous their route to disguise the location of their camp. He knew exactly how far his bunker was from here, and precisely which direction to run to get to it. These people were going to get themselves slaughtered by the Ikaul if they acted like this with their prisoners. Mygo kept his mouth shut though. He'd learned already that Yetu wasn't one to take sound advice, so it wasn't worth trying to bestow any upon him.

Yetu and a few of the warriors from the troop led him through the main pathway created by the lines of tents. Nothing of fixed permanence stood out. From the tents to the furnishings, everything was minimalistic and designed for swift deconstruction.

"Very nomadic," Mygo muttered to himself. His sarcasm vanished when he noticed the pikes jutting from the ground along the edges of the path. Dark stains lined the wood, and at the top of each sat a severed head fixed with a frozen expression of horror and pain. Many of the faces were marked with skin ink.

"What in Sahruum's good voyage is the meaning of this?" he blurted. The warriors at his back prodded him on without so much as a glance to the morbid display.

Yetu, on the other hand, smirked at the spiked heads. "Our people have a healthy thirst for justice, and Geshar and I do our best to appease it. With the Sachem gone, the Ikaul are weak. Soon this land will belong to us instead of their defiled tribe. Many have already fallen into our hands, whether by fate or by force. We hold trials for these treasonous filth, and Abisholo bathes in their blood."

"Who in damnation is Abisholo?" Mygo spat on the ground, hoping it would liberate him of the sour taste in his mouth. "This has to stop."

Yetu barked a mirthless laugh. "Scared you'll meet the same fate? You probably will, old man. Tremble, and fear the judgement of Abisholo."

Mygo's arrival was marked with curious stares and distrustful scowls from the citizens of the camp. He returned these with his own glares. He wondered how these folks could mill about, completing chores and labor in the midst of the impaled heads mere yards away. He noticed how most of the Vekaul's attention went to the beast dragged by the warriors. Murmurs and gasps erupted as the flayer made its rounds throughout the camp until the procession arrived at a giant four-peg tent into which the creature's corpse was dragged.

"We'll dissect it like the abomination deserves," Yetu stated with a sneer. "Maybe you'll get a similar sentence, Sachem lover."

Mygo refused to rise to the taunt, remaining silent as Yetu led him to the only hut in the camp. Smoke with a flesh-pink hue poured from several openings in its ceiling. Two warriors stood stationed at the door, which they opened at the instruction of Yetu, allowing more smoke to escape. Yetu grabbed Mygo and dragged him inside.

The odor that swelled in his nostrils was sweet at first. But with each inhalation, a tangy after-smell lingered, and could only be quelled by more inhalation of the smoke. Mygo squinted and tried to blink away the burn in his eyes that was summoning a stream of tears. This wasn't hopper's weed. "Dardajah's bleak ass, what is this stuff?" he grumbled.

"Don't worry, you'll adjust," Yetu murmured. "Just in time to die."

"Is that you, Yetu?" a feminine voice asked from somewhere in the fog. "You've returned early from your scout."

Mygo stumbled forward at a push on his back. He pressed into the smoke until he saw the thin silhouette of someone sitting cross-legged on the ground. Yetu prodded him until they stood a few feet away from the stranger.

Her details were hard to make out, but he observed blurred scars across golden skin, similar to the one that marred his own face. The dark skin ink on her forearm indicated her Vekuuv slave status and was the only other marking. Dehydrated blonde hair framed her head, adding a sense of detachment that was mirrored in her restless gaze. Like every other Vekaul that Mygo had seen thus far, red circles were forged around her eyes.

"Who is this fine fellow?" she asked with a hungry grin. "Looks about as rough at the edges as we do. The forest isn't kind to those of us who try to live in it."

Yetu gripped Mygo by the wrist and jerked his arm up to display the finger jewels. "He's a damn twister. Don't coddle him, Geshar."

Her smile slipped some. "Did you consider that maybe he chopped off a twister's hand and stole those shiny rocks? Think beyond a lake's surface, Yetu. You carry a hirishu blade. Doesn't make you an Ikaul warrior."

Mygo could feel the frustration wafting off Yetu as he replied. "He came to the rescue of one of the forest beasts. A flayer, he called it. The encounter cost the lives of three of our warriors, and the one who survived explained that this man showed up under the guise of aid, only to put the flayer into some sort of sleep. If it hadn't been for us arriving, he'd have probably released the damn thing back into the forest."

"He put it to sleep?" she asked, and her twitchy eyes fell upon Mygo. "So, you are a twister."

"If I may speak for myself without repercussion," said Mygo, "I could correct your companion's false conclusion."

Geshar's smirk returned in full. "Speak at your own risk. I have no more control over the second elder than he does over me. But I'll hear you out, for what it's worth."

"I did indeed place the flayer in a paralysis, but not by means of twisting. I used extract from a flower I've found growing in these parts."

"The plants of this forest drink the aetherwaste," said Geshar. "You're a fool to think extracting them doesn't come at the expense of purity."

Mygo gave a clipped nod. "Perhaps. But it's effective against the flayers, and not many things can boast that. Those creatures are durable, and they aren't easily neutralized."

"Then you'll have to give us the recipe for it," Geshar said. "If it stops the beasts, then it's worth the hypocrisy in its creation. But it doesn't explain why you left it alive. You've a soft spot for these abominations?"

"They're not quite the abominations you think they are," he said, uncertain how to navigate this part of the conversation. "My companion and I have studied the flayers for quite some time now. You'll be surprised to learn the truth behind their origins."

Geshar cocked an eyebrow. "Enlighten us, then, wilderman."

Mygo swallowed, but kept a confident, stern expression. This might not go over well. "The flayers are chimera—a nefarious experiment that blended man and beast. It's why each carries unique physical traits. None of them look the same because they aren't of the same blood. They're not a species."

Geshar and Yetu scowled at him. "Are you saying that these things were once human?" Geshar asked, a clear unspoken warning in her tone that told him she wouldn't like his answer.

Mygo shook his head. "They *are* human. And creature, also. The flayers are the Sachem's attempt at creating an army of his own through aethertwisting. No natural threat can properly challenge them. They have incredible strength and endurance, and have little need to feed like they once did in their natural forms."

Geshar's hand flashed to quiet him. "Stop this nonsense. You have no proof."

Mygo regarded her with pity. "You're upset because it means you've slaughtered what you thought were antagonists, when really they were victims. They are your fellow kin."

"Suppose what you say is true," said Yetu. "That doesn't extinguish the damage and terror these flayers have unleashed over the years. They've taken far more lives than the two souls the Sachem fused into one. They can't go unpunished."

"You say the Sachem intended to form an army with these beasts," Geshar said. "Yet they roam the forest unattended, and the Ikaul have not claimed them as their own. Nothing points to them as weapons for the Sachem's reign."

"This whole tale you've spun doesn't make sense," Yetu added. "It sounds like a convenient lie."

Mygo sighed in frustration. "I didn't say the Sachem's attempt was successful. He abandoned the poor things out here. Perhaps he couldn't control them as he'd hoped. I'm not the Sachem, so I don't know."

Yetu released an angry growl. "This is lunacy, Geshar. He's spinning a tale so absurd that it doesn't even hold together. Sentence this man, and let Abisholo's judgement erase his lies."

Mygo suppressed the urge to squirm as Geshar appraised him. The rash around her eyes created a sunken look that he worried he might fall into. Something in the smoke had slowly numbed his legs and arms. The ground beneath him no longer registered under his feet, and every few seconds, the sensation of flight washed through him. The smoke veiled the perception of depth—the walls of the hut had vanished—and Mygo wondered if they now occupied a space of infinite proportions. If he ran, would his flight simply take him into the unknown regions of a smoky nightmare?

He thought he glimpsed something beyond Geshar—the faintest lines of a figure lurking at the edges of his vision.

"Abisholo is indeed hungry for another sacrifice," Geshar said.

"Who is this Abisholo person you mention?" Mygo asked.

Geshar chuckled. "Not a person. A mirajin."

Mygo stiffened. That didn't sound right. Mirajin didn't ask for or enjoy sacrifices.

The figure hiding in the smoke crept closer. A shiver ran down Mygo's spine, and he lifted upwards in flight. The sensation came and went so swiftly it made his stomach roil. "Is there someone else in here with us?" he asked. An urgency bled into his voice, but he didn't care. Panic surged as movement continued behind Geshar. It looked like a figure on all fours, crawling like an insect. "There's something behind you."

Geshar squinted at him curiously, then looked over her shoulder. She let out a surprised cry, but it wasn't in fear. "Abisholo has graced us!" she exclaimed as she prostrated herself.

Yetu did the same, falling to the ground to kneel and lower his head in reverence. Mygo wasn't sure how to move at this point. He couldn't feel his legs, his arms, his chest—anything. He simply existed in the smoke—a voice with no body, a mind of disjointed emotions. Unable to control the panic, he let out a distressed whimper.

"What in dying stars is that thing?" he asked in a shrill cry.

It wasn't a person. Only red muscle fiber without skin, collected into mush that defied the laws of motion. Two sunken pits absent of eyes hovered above an open gap where a mouth should have resided. Connective tissue stretched in strands across the opening, the pockets between them permitting sound to escape. The entity came up to Geshar and let out a wail. The Vekaul elders trembled at the sound and wailed back.

"Hail Abisholo!" they shouted in unison and repeated their praise several more times.

"*That's* a dokojin." Disbelief masked the fear in Mygo's words. "Have you fools lost all sanity?"

The entity lifted its head to regard him. Mygo wanted to flee in that moment. Yet the lure of death drove through his instinct to survive. Death meant escape. Escape from the dokojin's stare.

"Abisholo wants to feed," Yetu said as he looked up at Mygo. "You will be honored as faer meal. Fae will cleanse you of your lies and your sins. Justice will prevail over you."

Mygo shook his head in protest. "No. I can prove what I've said. I'm not your enemy. I can prove the flayers are human." He was tempted to look back at the danger in the room. The dokojin's presence demanded his focus, if only to make sure it hadn't moved closer to him. But fear kept him from looking back—if it had moved, he didn't want to see it close up.

Geshar's voice addressed him, but he refused to look at her either. She was too close to it. "Abisholo wants your aura, wilderman. We won't refuse it."

Mygo turned and ran. Or floated. Or took flight. He wasn't sure if he even inhabited a body anymore, he just moved away. The smoke could go on forever, and he wouldn't care. He would not go to his demise willingly.

A defiant cry scratched from his lungs as he sprinted towards the hut's exit, or at least towards where it should have been.

Daylight blinded him when he broke free of the smoke's embrace. He shrieked as he grasped the dull knowledge that he'd broken his retreat to collapse in some way. He writhed under the blinding light and thrashed when hands fell upon him. Their presence returned to him an overwhelming sense of touch and depth.

Slowly, the light separated into distinct colors. The blue sky bloomed above him, as did the shadowy shapes of faces. He wasn't sure if it was Geshar and Yetu, so he pretended for the sake of his own sanity that he'd escaped them.

"I can prove it," he said. He twitched with violent spasms as the numbness left his body, replaced now by the sensation of needles across his skin. "Don't give me to that—that thing. I can prove what I said about the flayers."

Geshar's voice spoke, but he still couldn't make out details in the shadows over him. "We are generous, wilderman. If you can prove your claims, we will spare you. Abisholo only devours those who deserve it—the treasonous, the liars, the hypocrites. Are you any of these?"

Mygo shook his head, and the rest of him shook too.

"Good. When the detruid subsides, you will take us to your companion, and you will prove yourself."

Tears flowed from his eyes, and his eyes burned again. Or perhaps they had burned all along and only now could he feel them again. His mouth was dry, and he wondered if he'd been crying inside the tent the entire time too. He inhaled a shaky breath at Geshar's next words.

"I hope for your sake that you are truthful, wilderman. But if you are not, Abisholo will cleanse your aura."

CHAPTER 24

Yetu waited with Mygo inside a small vacant tent as the effects of the smoke wore off. The Vekaul elder glowered down at him as Mygo shivered with feverish chills. "There's far more to your tale than you're letting on," said Yetu.

"Everyone's got more to their story than they tell strangers," Mygo mumbled in between his teeth chattering. His arms were wrapped around his chest in an effort to conserve heat, and he rocked back and forth on the cot. "What was in that smoke?"

"You inhaled burnt detruid seeds. It's what enlightened us to Abisholo and faer justice."

"You keep using that term—*faer*—as if that monstrosity is a mirajin. I hate to be the one to tell you, but that's a damn dokojin. You need to stop smoking that shite and communicating with that monstrosity."

Yetu snorted with an amused, mocking smile. "The mirajin is pure of intention, demanding justice for the atrocities wrought by the Ikaul."

"I promise you, whatever it's selling you, that thing doesn't want justice. It wants blood, and you're freely giving it."

Before Yetu could protest more, an anguished cry stole their attention. The flaps to the tent parted as three figures charged inside. The commotion made it difficult for Mygo to make sense of the newcomers. Two women gripped another by the arms and were dragging her towards the only other cot in the tent. The captive tried and failed to escape with a dash towards the tent flaps that proved too slow. Her captors shoved her onto the cot and pinned her down by the wrists and ankles.

"What is the meaning of this?" Yetu exclaimed.

"We found her wandering around the camp," said one of the women. "Look at her red hair. It's the Tecalica. We've found her, and now she can face judgement for her crimes."

Yetu leapt over and pushed the two women off the other. They looked disgruntled at his interjection and glared at him. He retrieved a black feather with a red stripe and held it up for display.

"You are sworn to secrecy," he hissed. "Take this, and do what you wish with it. But speak nothing of this woman to anyone."

The two women exchanged glances before one snapped the feather from Yetu's hand. They disappeared as quickly as they'd appeared. Mygo's attention latched onto his neighboring bedmate, fighting off the temptation to believe their outlandish statement.

It couldn't be the Tecalica. Jalice was leagues away from here. They'd made a mistake.

He stiffened as he observed the woman. Her skin curled and caved into pockets of craters across her exposed body. An ill-fitting dress did little to hide the fact that these scars left no portion of her untouched. Her eyes were closed, and an expression of pain contorted her face further.

"What happened to her?" Mygo demanded. "Answer me!"

"A terrible accident," Yetu answered in a low, grim voice. "She's been under our care for some time now."

"Did you do this to her?" Mygo asked. He saw disdain enter Yetu's face but didn't care. If these people were responsible for this, he needed to know.

"Of course we didn't," Yetu spat. "How dare you accuse us of such a thing?

"Then how did it happen?"

"She was one of our spies in the Fortress. The Sachem discovered her, and she paid the price for treason."

Mygo's eyes narrowed. "The fate for treason is death. How did she escape such a sentence?"

"We found her before she could succumb to her wounds. But the pain and scars have taken their toll, and she experiences a constant agony beyond what any of us could imagine." He sighed down at her. "On top of that, she's lost her mind."

"How do you know?"

"She can't retain memories. Whatever life she led before is now lost to her."

The woman's lips gaped wide in a silent moan or perhaps a shriek frozen somewhere in her chest. Orphan strands of red hair trailed from a few patches on her otherwise bald scalp. Mygo paused on these, recalling Jalice, and pointed at them.

"That color is rare. Surely you've identified her clan?"

Something swept through Yetu's eyes, and the wrinkles besetting his face tightened ever so slightly. He gave a solemn shake of his head. "Rare indeed. So rare we have no one in our tribe who bears such colorful threads."

"Those who dragged her in here claimed she was the Tecalica."

Yetu blinked. "You shouldn't trust everything that's uttered."

Mygo cocked an eyebrow. "Have you at least considered she could be related?"

Yetu turned away from Mygo to gaze down at the woman. "Possible, but not probable. Besides, what good would it do her? The Tecalica has vanished, and her whereabouts won't heal this fragile skeleton of a woman. It's best that we keep our focus on tending to her."

Mygo straightened, not taking his eyes off the woman. "What do you call her then, if she has no tribe and no kin?"

"Delilee."

The name sparked an elusive familiarity in Mygo. It came and went so fast that he wasn't able to summon it back. "Her wounds look dire," he said. "Perhaps there's something my companion can concoct to help ease her pain. He's well-versed in remedies and alchemy."

"Should he find the time in between producing his miracle to save your lives from judgement, then I'm sure she'd be grateful in her silent way," said Yetu. "But if you can't prove your claims about the flayers, this stranger's fate will be the least of your worries."

"You forced those other women into secrecy," said Mygo. "Why?"

"Because there are many in the camp who would make the same mistake of misidentifying Delilee as the Tecalica. They'd call for her head, not knowing that this poor, broken thing is not the treasonous wench they want."

Mygo didn't respond. He couldn't look away from Delilee's scarred features or the patches of red hair. He kept seeing Jalice's face in his mind.

An unnerving thought refused to leave him.

What if this *was* Jalice?

As outlandish as that seemed, he couldn't shake his worry that somehow Jalice and Elothel had failed, and that the Tecalica had found herself back here after some unfortunate accident. Yetu had a story conjured to explain the woman's wounds, but Mygo trusted almost nothing the Vekaul elder said. This woman could be anyone.

Even Jalice.

His mind spun. If this was Jalice, it could mean that the task set to him and Vowt was now void. She was the only one who truly wanted the Sachem redeemed—the only reason Mygo cared about his redemption. If it so happened that this was indeed Jalice lying opposite Mygo, and she couldn't even remember her own past, her own husband, her own name . . .

"I ask again, is something the matter?"

Mygo startled at Yetu's voice. He fixed the other man with a scowl. "If I learn that she came to this fate by your hands, I swear on every mirajin's shiny asshole that you'll pay the commensurate price for her suffering."

Yetu glowered down at him. "I don't take threats lightly, wilderman."

"That's wise," Mygo grumbled. His muscles spasmed with the last shivers of the smoke's waning effects. He peered up at the Vekaul elder. "'Cause I make good on my threats."

***

A troop of three Vekaul warriors accompanied Yetu and Mygo on the trek to the bunker. The group set out from the camp while the afternoon sun still reigned, and it wouldn't be until dusk that they'd arrive. Mygo spent most of the trek in silence, obsessing over how events might unfold once they reached the bunker.

In his desperation to escape a fate decided by the Vekaul's insidious communion with Abisholo, he'd made a promise that might be far too difficult to follow through with. In order to prove his claim to the Vekaul—that the flayers were a melding of human and animal—he and Vowt would have to perform the very ritual they'd continued to fail at. A ritual to separate the two—to unmake the flayer.

Thus far, that'd proven fatal to the beasts. Perhaps if he and Vowt had been less interested in saving the flayers, this wouldn't have been an issue—they didn't need the separate entities alive to prove their point to Yetu. And, for that matter, they didn't need the flayers alive to extract the fluid for the elixir.

But Vowt had a tender heart, and Mygo wasn't a merciless man either. Seizing the fluid from the flayers without trying to save them in the process struck him as violent and heartless. As he saw it, the flayers deserved every chance at survival through the ritual.

Only now, much more was at stake. If they couldn't successfully separate a flayer, then they might not get another chance at their elixir. Despite his flagging faith in such things, Mygo offered up a few urgent prayers to Sahruum in hope that a miracle might happen this time.

The journey passed rather quickly due to his preoccupied mindset, but on several occasions they had to stop so that Yetu and his kin could inhale detruid through their makeshift pipes. The Vekaul elder offered him some with a smirk, but Mygo declined with an unamused scowl. During one of these breaks, Mygo took the opportunity to relieve himself. Yetu sent one of the warriors with him, and the pair strode off a few feet away from the others. While he was letting nature run its course, Mygo spotted a peculiar marking on a nearby tree. He tucked in his shirt once finished and went over to investigate. If it was what he presumed, then it could spell trouble.

"Don't think about running," the warrior barked at his back.

Mygo gave the man an irritated wave before he crouched down at eye level with the scratch marks in the tree. He heard rustling and craned his neck to find Yetu and the others approaching.

"Heard someone shout," said Yetu. "You giving my warrior trouble?"

Mygo ignored the baseless accusation and gestured to the tree trunk. "Take a look."

Yetu joined him and peered down, unimpressed by the scratched bark. "Looks like a bearolf took a liking to it and sharpened its claws on the tree."

Mygo shook his head. "Follow the marks. They're quite intentional." He ran his fingers along the seemingly random scratches, showing how it formed a crude symbol.

Yetu frowned. "You're seeing patterns where there aren't any."

"Your eyes aren't trained to see such symbols," Mygo countered. "These beasts are intelligent, and the language of their previous lives seeps out, like what you see here on the tree. The symbols don't necessarily communicate anything yet. Not enough time has passed for them to have developed a language so sophisticated as our own. But it's the beginnings of one."

"You're trying to ascribe intelligence to a beast that flays its victims and wears their skins like coats."

"And that doesn't seem intelligent to you?" Mygo asked.

Yetu shrugged. "Critters and beasts do odd, intricate things. It doesn't make them any more human."

"Indeed. But frame it like this: if the flayers did have some human in them, wouldn't it be a small leap to say that perhaps they wear our skin in a crude attempt at feeling human once again? That perhaps the skin coat is the closest they can get in their broken state to their old lives? It might not even be a purposeful action. It might be an instinctive grasp at the old life they lost."

"And you're grasping at stars," said Yetu. "I find it appalling that you defend these creatures when they slaughter anyone they meet. They deserve death for such atrocities."

"Yet these creatures are subject to greater torture than you or I can see."

"And that makes them innocent? Absolves them of every murder?"

Mygo pursed his lips and considered this. "Not necessarily. But we must take into account the state of existence they are in. They aren't of sound mind, and it was by someone else's hand that they came to be this way."

Yetu's eyes left Mygo to study the forest around them. "I very much doubt that. Regardless, we should get a move on. If you're right to attribute those markings to a flayer, then we may very well be in danger."

Mygo straightened and surveyed the forest. "The claw marks look old. The flayer that left them is long gone. Doesn't mean there aren't others lurking about though. I agree. We need to get to the bunker."

CHAPTER 25

The day's shadows congregated as a giant cloak of darkness. The last etchings of light streaked the horizon and webbed through the decaying foliage. When they arrived at his homestead, his shoulders slackened in a release of tension. As confident as he was in his knowledge of the flayers, it didn't make him fear them any less.

Taking down a flayer in daylight was one thing. It was nearly a death sentence to encounter one at night.

Upon seeing the bunker, Yetu halted his troop. "This feels like a trap, wilderman. Only the Ikaul work from structures such as these. Your claims seem less and less truthful with each revelation about your life."

"Take your pick," Mygo growled. "Stay out here with the flayers or come in at the risk of an ambush. I, for one, am going inside." He strode towards the door despite the tension wafting from the Vekaul, but paused at the iron door. Vowt had no idea of the trouble Mygo brought with him, nor of the expectations these strangers carried. Mygo gripped the door handle and squeezed it until his knuckles burned, struggling to bring himself to intrude on the oblivious peace Vowt currently enjoyed.

"Make haste, wilderman," Yetu hissed as he and the other warriors came up behind him. "It isn't safe to linger out here."

Mygo sighed and, with a great heave, pushed the door open. Light struck them, and he blinked as he stumbled inside.

Vowt didn't turn away from his equipment. Flexible bellows pumped furiously while pressurized air charged through tubes and vials. A high-pitched whistle pierced the air as steam erupted from the peculiar contraption connecting the segments of the experiment. Slowly, the whistle died off and the pump came to a stop. Only then did the short man turn and startle at the guests.

"Who—who—who are they? Why are they here?" Vowt's spectacles amplified his eyes as he regarded the Vekaul. He pulled off his rubber gloves and wrung out his fingers.

"They mean us no harm," Mygo assured him, hiding his own uncertainty for the sake of his companion. He tried to force a hint of optimism into his voice to keep Vowt calm. "They've come to see our progress."

Vowt's hands continued to writhe in a restless ball of nerves. "P-p-progress on what?"

"They want to see the flayer," Mygo said. "They want us to save it."

Vowt's eyes widened. "Save it?"

Mygo licked his lips. *Please don't make a scene.* "They want us to separate the flayer back into human and critter."

"We haven't d-done that yet," Vowt said with a frown, not catching Mygo's frantic expression of warning.

"What's he mean by that?" Yetu asked, stepping forward and crossing his arms.

Mygo rushed to explain. "It's not something we've succeeded at yet, but we've gotten close." He turned back to Vowt, hoping his companion would catch his drift. He didn't want Vowt spewing their true intentions—that they'd been tasked by a mirajin with finding a cure for the Sachem's mind. That would make things messy.

"Isn't that right, Vowt?" he added. "This time it'll work." Vowt stared back at him with obvious confusion, but the short man slowly nodded. Mygo continued. "I've told these people that the flayers can be saved. If we can show them, they might be able to help us capture more so that we can heal those too."

Vowt's head tilted. His fingers twisted around one another like snakes. "It's d-d-dangerous."

Mygo nodded. "I know."

"How so?" Yetu asked.

Mygo turned to the Vekaul elder. "The flayers were created in a disjointed sequence. There's two aspects to their existence. One is their chimera meld—an action accomplished with aether. But their minds are also skewed. The Sachem poisoned them against external influence. Made them loyal to him."

"These things still answer to him?" Yetu exclaimed.

Mygo nodded. "Witnessed the results of that myself. One day they were afraid of fire, as all living things naturally are. Then they changed overnight. Fire no longer fazed them. They overrode their own instincts and allowed their very flesh to burn despite the pain."

Yetu didn't look convinced. "That doesn't sound like something you can attribute to any loyalty to the Sachem. Sounds like the flayers simply adapted."

"Not that fast," Mygo insisted, but he said nothing more on it. Like with every other claim about the flayers, he didn't need Yetu's agreement to be convinced himself. He'd connected the pieces, and they fit all too well. When Mygo had joined Jalice and her companions at the Black House, the Sachem had somehow been present there too. On that same day, within that same hour, the flayers had shown an odd reaction to Mygo's fire tactics—tactics that had always worked before. It couldn't have been a coincidence. The Sachem had worked his aethertwisting on them—had made them unafraid of fire—and they'd bent to his will.

"So, what does that all mean?" Yetu asked. "Can you address both problems?"

"I m-m-made an elixir," Vowt interjected. "It's intended to—to—to alleviate the flayer of its duty to the S-Sachem." He shook his head with an uncertain look. "The disunion of human and critter though—"

Mygo jumped in before Vowt could cast more doubt on their work. "The chimera issue is harder, but I'm certain we can succeed this time. We know what mistakes to avoid." He gave Vowt a quick glance, hoping it communicated his request for silence.

Yetu didn't respond, his eyes fixed on something across the room. "Are those schematics hanging there on the wall?"

Mygo caught himself before he could release a verbal obscenity. He clenched his teeth and forced the irritation off his face. *Damn nosy shitehead needs to keep his curiosity in check.*

He, of course, wasn't going to explain what the schematics entailed nor share that the mirajin, Elothel, had been the one to create the massive canvas of instructions.

THE SPAWN OF SPIRACY

They detailed how to build a duality chamber—a space where the Realms could meld together via vibrations. It'd taken him months to build. Mygo had been able to follow the schematics enough to construct the chamber, but the science behind it all went far beyond his comprehension. It was an old, archaic construction—something that would have existed during pre-Residuum times.

What he *did* know was this: the Apparition Realm and the Terrestrial Realm met within the confines of this chamber and interacted temporarily. In the overlap of these Realms, it was possible for Mygo to attempt separating the flayer.

But Yetu didn't need to know any of this. In fact, Mygo bet that the Vekaul elder would once again accuse him of being an aethertwister if he found out how the chamber functioned. Instead, he said, "I think we should concentrate on our task at hand."

Yetu cocked his head to consider this, then nodded. "I'm assuming you have one of the beasts here?"

Mygo gestured with his chin towards one of the iron doors that lined the circular wall of the room. "Beyond there."

"And you've kept it alive?" Yetu asked, still not convinced of Mygo's claims. "I want to examine it before we initiate this strange ritual."

"The s-s-sedation has worn off," Vowt stated. "It won't be s-s-safe to—to—to get close."

"Agreed. We can't sedate it again if you intend for us to perform our ritual. Such medicines interfere with the mechanics we must put in play."

A clanging noise bled through the walls, muffled but shrill.

"It's fighting the restraints," Mygo stated. "We need to go down there before it does damage to the clasps or to itself." He squared himself in front of Yetu. "Listen to me closely. What you see down there is going to frighten you. It's one thing to see a flayer dead or lying immobile on the ground. It's another to see it alive and up close. It's going to make a lot of noise, and it's going to act out. It doesn't like being locked up any more than you or I would."

A growing look of unease swept the Vekaul warriors. Their hands flexed on the hilts of their swords. Yetu stared back at Mygo, unable to hide the briefest twitch of hesitation on his face.

"Don't interrupt us," Mygo added. "You won't understand everything you see. We can answer your questions afterwards. What we don't need is our focus broken and everyone getting their arms ripped off."

That got their attention. All four Vekaul stiffened.

Pounding erupted. The faintest pitch of a howl leaked through the bunker walls.

Mygo turned and followed Vowt towards the door. He pushed back the giant lever, which clanked as it unsealed the lock. The door cracked open, the noises amplifying even before Mygo heaved the door wide to let everyone pass. The Vekaul startled at the onslaught of shrieks scrambling up from the depths of the chamber.

Mygo didn't hesitate, sweeping down the flight of metal-reinforced stairs. As much as he hated what he was about to encounter, he couldn't let the others see his hands shaking.

CHAPTER 26

At the bottom of the stairs, Mygo picked up a lone candlestick and lit the wick with a match. The sizzle brought with it a cowardly light that hesitated to breach the engulfing darkness. Only the few steps preceding him were illuminated.

A tense silence followed. The others froze on the stairs, unable to bring themselves to set foot into the chamber itself. The animalistic sounds bellowed moments earlier had ceased at the sound of the struck match.

Mygo took one step forward.

A shriek drove him back and jolted the others. The sound teetered between guttural and pitchy, a strange mixture of growl and wail. Like the noise, the emotional drive behind it couldn't settle on agony or rage.

"Where is it?" Yetu hissed behind him. "You swear it's restrained?"

"Yes," Mygo murmured just before another, less resounding shriek bled from the back right corner of the room. He reclaimed his lost step and moved farther. His boots thudded dully on the stone blocks. The candlelight slid over a weathered cabinet braced against the side wall, which hosted Vowt's supplies and equipment.

Mygo prepared himself for the only other furnishing in the room. A few more steps revealed a metal-framed table and the faint outline of something massive stretched out across it. The flayer saw him long before he could make out its details. He flinched when the flayer's head snapped towards him, unhinging its maw. Its shriek echoed in the chamber and rang in his ears after the creature grew silent. He pushed forward, even when violent bangs erupted as the flayer struggled against its restraints. The table, bolted into the ground, didn't move with the protests, but Mygo wondered, as he always did, if it would hold. One of these days, a flayer would surely prove strong enough—enraged enough—to break the table's anchors.

The outline solidified as he inched closer. A giant emerged, its limbs and back thrashing against the ten-foot slab. Its eyes glowed in the darkness—two orbs of greenish blue that crystalized with a pointed intensity. The candlelight flickered on its face, revealing a greasy mane of velvet black. The dark fur plunged into sheer obsidian where it ran down the rest of its body, thickening at the limbs and receding some across the chest. Perhaps from a distance, it might have looked like a man cursed with too much body hair. But truly beholding it bent the mind towards comparisons of wolves or grimalkin. The shape of its face and snout emphasized such attributes; paradoxically, its heels jutted harshly into elongated feet that helped it run like a human.

Mygo had already incinerated the wretched skin coat that had belonged to this particular flayer. Gazing down at the flayer now, he couldn't help but find it off-putting not to see the creature donning it. He shivered at that thought. Had he grown so accustomed to these monstrosities that he could even excuse their macabre choice of clothing?

The flayer's mouth curled upward in a snarl; it bared its teeth, its two massive canines seeming to stretch forever. Phlegm dove from its mouth as it shrieked again. Its ragged breath brushed across Mygo, the rush of heat urging him to turn and sprint across the stone floor, back up the stairs, and past the door. Flecks of spittle struck his face. Not for the first time, he was grateful that this flayer didn't possess acidic properties in its saliva like some of its kin.

The noises swelled to frantic grunts and desperate howls as the frenzy of its struggle escalated. Mygo risked a quick glance back at Vowt, reminding himself that the flayer couldn't touch him. Still, he didn't like taking his eyes off of it, even if he hated to behold it.

Vowt stood over at the cabinet, where he gripped a lever hidden behind it. Over at the staircase, the Vekaul had managed to broach the chamber's space, but hadn't dared distance themselves more than a few feet from the false safety of the stairwell.

The shrieks at Mygo's back begged for his focus, but he kept his eyes on Vowt. Not many things frightened Mygo. But he wasn't so arrogant that he hid his doubts and nerves from his companion when down here. This chamber, thus far, knew only death and pain. It bred terror. It held secrets of death. Even when no flayers tainted its space, he swore he heard howls and growls from within it, like phantoms of long-dead creatures come back to haunt him.

Vowt nodded, and Mygo marveled at the younger man's resolve even as the chamber echoed with the flayer's horrible sounds. Mygo gave a clipped nod back. Vowt leaned into the lever. Had the space been quieter, the sound of clicking and grating would have followed the motion. But the flayer howled on.

He noticed then the alarmed behavior of the Vekaul. From their position farther away from the commotion, they would have heard the iron door sealing at the top of the stairs. The meager light from the common room above vanished, handing the responsibility of illumination over to the lone candle. Given room to shine, the candle's light offered more depth, and the flayer's form sharpened.

Yetu waved his hands at him, but Mygo ignored the gesture. He and Vowt had come down for a task. Now wasn't the time for Mygo to give his suppressed fear any leeway by retreating towards the cowering Vekaul.

A buzzing sound was growing in Mygo's ears. The lever had done more than just seal the room. It had awakened the chamber's purpose. The hairs on his skin stood on end as the vibrations amplified around them. Numbness took his body, starting with his fingers and toes until eventually it swam over his head. He resisted the urge to hurl, knowing that he'd adjust soon enough.

The flayer's thrashing lessened with this new shift in the room. It arched its neck, casting about in an attempt to identify the source of this change. The vibrations peaked, and the buzzing petered off as the room acclimated. An invisible tug ran from Mygo to the flayer, a pull the creature sensed keenly. It snapped its jaws and snarled before running a long, hungry tongue in his direction. He cringed as it wagged at him in a desperate attempt to have a taste.

He did his best to ignore the fear coiling out of him—to ignore how the flayer lapped at it with a feverish hunger. This, as it always did during the semi-translation, proved difficult. Like trying to ignore a knife being shoved into his back.

He watched Vowt experience the same phenomenon. His stubby hands punched the air between him and the flayer as his face wrinkled. Mygo stepped forward and placed a gentle hand on his companion's shoulder. The touch did the trick, shaking Vowt out of the uncomfortable exchange enough that he looked up to Mygo and remembered their task. Vowt twisted to the cabinet and grabbed a few items from the mess of objects, including a short stool.

The two turned and together approached the table. Vowt wrapped around to the head of it while Mygo came to its side. He kept his focus on Vowt as the short man climbed atop the stool to loom over the flayer's face. One misstep, one finger brought too close to the gnashing jaws of the flayer, and his friend would end in a fountain of blood. Still, he made no move to stop Vowt.

The chymist had to do his part.

Vowt stretched his arms out over the flayer's face, a vial in his hands. The creature arched its neck and growled as it tried to touch Vowt with the tip of its nose. Its snout trembled with the effort, but a manic purpose drove it to try. If it got close enough, all it would take would be one quick lunge, and Vowt's hand would snap off.

If Vowt was unsettled by the creature's intent to bite him, he didn't show it. With steady hands, he tipped the vial upside down and let its contents pour out. Green liquid splashed across the flayer's teeth and dripped down its throat while the creature's tongue flicked in a hopeless effort to negate the sour taste.

Mygo squeezed the candle. The whole thing wobbled in his quivering hands, and the flame swayed from the motion. He focused until his trembling stopped. If Vowt could brave the danger with steady hands, then so could he. Unsure how long he could keep up the facade of bravery, he pushed the candle towards the flayer.

This was the moment of truth. If Vowt's elixir had worked, the creature would fear the fire as it should. All living things feared fire, unless a crazed madman like the Sachem twisted their natural instincts.

The elixir will work. Vowt was so close before. He's got it this time.

The flame grew closer to the flayer's fur. Mygo slowed the candle's approach. His heart pounded. With every inch lost between the flame and the flayer, doubt grew inside him. Every flayer that had laid on this table had abided the flame's heat. Mygo never let the fire touch them though. He had no intention of torturing the creatures. But pushing the fire as close as possible was the only way he knew to test Vowt's elixir.

The flayer grew quiet. The flame was nearly upon it. The tremble returned to Mygo's fingers, and the flame tipped close enough to singe the fur.

The flayer jerked back.

Mygo backpedaled away from the table. A heavy sigh left him. He heard Yetu shouting at him, demanding to know what had just occurred, but Mygo ignored the man's pestering.

The elixir worked. The flayer feared fire again.

Vowt was clapping his hands but stopped when the loud noises agitated the flayer back into its thrashing and screeching. The chymist retreated to where Mygo stood a few paces from the table.

"Now it's your turn," Vowt said, his words barely audible over the flayer's shrieks.

Mygo said nothing. He knew he had to approach the table again. But this part was worse. Worse than the fire test. Worse than anything he'd ever done in his life.

He swallowed down his fear and strode towards the edge of the table. A brief flex of his muscles commanded his trembles not to return. He inhaled deeply. With a slow exhale, he rallied against the chaotic energy writhing before him. Despite this best effort, his eyes darted to the flayer's face. Their eyes locked, and it fueled the creature's rage. As it sank its back into the slab over and over, the metal cuffs around its wrists buckled. Its howls swarmed Mygo's ears. It was all he heard.

With calculated movements, he lifted his hands together in front of his chest. He hoped the Vekaul were still at a distance. He knew full well they wouldn't be happy with what they'd see next. The fingers of his right hand crept into the sleeve of the opposite and pried out a glass wand.

That morning, well before his run-in with the Vekaul, he'd performed a blessing to fill the wand with purified aether. The ritual had taken hours of uninterrupted solitude. The only reason he even knew such a skill was because of a priestly apprenticeship that he'd abandoned years ago. Rarely did he utilize the knowledge of aether and translation he'd learned during his time as a templite, but this task with the flayers demanded it.

The wand glimmered in his hands. Unlike twisters, who spent too much time in the aether Realms and made themselves vulnerable to physical elements, he could handle the glass without fear of death. He resisted feeling dismayed at how little aether swirled within the wand's confines. Aetherwaste tainted too much of the forest, too much of this room. His blessings had done little to combat it. It also didn't help that he and Vowt had exhausted some of the wand's aether during their first attempt earlier in the day. He hoped what remained would be enough.

Mygo held the glass wand over the creature's lower torso and initiated a string of scripture quotes. His whispers weren't audible over the flayer's unending howls, and the only proof of their utterance were the warm breaths that left his lips. That, and the reaction the aether had to them. The wand's contents spiraled towards its tip. Colors leapt out from it and washed over the flayer like mist. With their appearance, Mygo inched the wand upward in a slow ascension as he continued the ritual. The area of the flayer's torso directly under the wand rose in sync with it, as if tied to it by string.

Focus was vital. One misspoken word or the slightest flinch of his wrist would undo the entire ordeal. But in the back of his mind, where dark curiosity and horrified awe refused to be stifled, he noticed the effect that the ritual had on the flayer. As the creature curled its back to follow the wand in a forced ascension, its mass grew.

This defied logic. An object could not create more of itself. Yet the flayer's chest expanded in depth and substance to meet the demands of the wand.

The absurdity in this fought hard to break Mygo. On previous attempts, it had won out, and his loss of focus had proven fatal to the flayer. He pushed away the desire to watch as the hide flexed, tore like threads, reassembled, tore again. The higher his hand moved, the faster this restructuring occurred.

The flayer's shrieks devolved into coughs and gurgles. Bile and blood spewed from its mouth as a spasm of seizures gripped it. Skin sliced apart.

From these open pockets, muscle and bones jutted forth. Blood spilled across the flayer's fur and onto the table. Bones were forced to choose between staying in the original mass of the flayer or joining the ascending portion obsessed with the wand. They burst out of the ascending clump of muscle, skin, and blood like an urchin expanding.

Trembles returned again to Mygo's hands. He quickened his words, but his arm now hovered as far as it could stretch. For a moment, even as he continued to whisper, he observed Vowt's figure out of the corner of his eye. Vowt stood with a vial at the head of the table, hands outstretched beneath the flayer and covered in a thick layer of blood. Mygo thought he saw a flash of green fall down towards the vial.

He snapped his focus back to the ritual and closed his eyes to avoid further distraction. Shut off from the repugnant sights, his ears homed in on the gurgling and the cracking of bones. He didn't have to witness it. He knew already the flayer had split. Two forms now existed—one on the table, covered in a waterfall of blood and visceral fluid descending from the form floating above it. Muscle and skin still dangled and stretched between the two in a last effort to resist Mygo's work. A low groan broke from the table while a synchronized, higher pitched wail screeched from higher in the air.

Nearly there. Mygo's lips pressed out the words as he came to the end of the scriptures. Victory washed over him. This time, it had worked. He and Vowt had done the impossible.

His wrist flinched as his trembles matured to a spasm. He felt the flow of the aether surge, and energy slammed out of the wand. Too much, too quick. His eyes snapped open to witness the horrid outcome.

The contrasting sounds—the wail and the screech—spat out a last protest as the suspended body crashed down. The agonizing symphony ceased as innards and bones collided. Blood gushed out across Mygo's and Vowt's faces. A dreadful quiet settled over the chamber, interrupted only by the trickle of fluid falling from the table onto the floor.

Mygo stared at what he'd created. Nothing familiar remained of the flayer. Twisted and curled shapes were spread across the metal slab. He couldn't make sense of them. He knew blood, he knew bone, and he knew innards. But the carnage before him defied his senses. It caved in his mind, and all he saw was the most horrible death to befall a living, breathing thing.

He turned away from it, doubled over, and unleashed a single obscenity in an anguished, enraged scream.

He had failed.

CHAPTER 27

Days of endless questioning had left Jalice more exhausted than when she'd first awoken from Spiracy's lair.

The clanheads had been persistent. She'd relayed her experience to the entire assembly of them at one point, only for each to later grace her chambers individually to ask a slew of questions they'd left unspoken during the gathering. Many of these private conversations repeated each other, and she voiced her opinion that it'd be more efficient to address them all in a second gathering. This suggestion went unheard. They simply continued to barge into her quarters at sporadic hours.

Although all of these encounters had left her spent and strained from the stress, one in particular stood out from the rest. In the dead of night, a woman veiled in a white cloak and hood slipped into her quarters without so much as a breath. Jalice had startled out of sleep to find the stranger standing over her in the dark. Before she could scream, the woman had struck a match, lit a candle, and introduced herself as Rejiett, a templite priestess.

Rejiett's questions were unlike those of the clanheads. They were pointed, specific, and laced with a knowledge like secrecy, as if the priestess knew more about Jalice's confounding escape from Spiracy than even Jalice herself. The encounter ended as eerily as it had begun. The priestess blew out the candle and vanished with the same stealth as her entrance.

Aside from Rejiett, only Cephus left as deep an impression, and for less unnerving reasons. He was usually joined by Ophim, and sometimes even Kerothan, though not nearly as often. During these interactions, she engaged more and tuned into the nonverbal language exchanged between the three. From what she could gather, Ophim and Cephus were married—or joined by some equivalency to marriage. She heard the term *lebond* dropped once or twice, which seemed to denote their union but was an unfamiliar term to her. The Heidretka observed different customs than Ikaul and Vekuuv, many of which Jalice didn't know or remember from childhood lessons.

Another intriguing observation was that Kerothan appeared to be enthralled by Ophim. At first, she thought it to be some shared comradery since they were of the same clan. But during interactions when all three were present, she grew wise to this rash deduction. Anytime Ophim spoke, which was rare compared to Cephus, Kerothan's eyes would dart over to the other man and soften. Other times, she'd catch him inhaling deeply, chest puffed out, as he admired Ophim from his corner of the room.

Whenever Cephus spoke, however, Kerothan did nothing but scowl at the ground with his arms crossed.

What she couldn't quite tell was how Cephus or Ophim felt in return. Ophim showed no signs of awkwardness around Kerothan, and she found it hard to believe that he didn't notice Kerothan's lingering stares. It was odd that neither he nor Cephus discouraged Kerothan from this behavior. Not that Kerothan was necessarily doing anything unethical or wrong. It all just seemed like a game they were playing at—Kerothan pretending to mask his admiration of Ophim, Ophim's casual restraint with Kerothan, Cephus's bland reaction to the two men's subtle flirting.

All of this she'd gleaned from their initial meetings, but as the days had passed, Kerothan's visits became less frequent. This had prompted her to ask Cephus for a private audience with her brother, but she'd known better than to let her hopes rise.

"I'm sorry, but Kerothan has refused your request," Cephus was relaying to her now.

Jalice nodded her head in quiet acceptance. She would have asked again, but she wanted more energy for her encounter with him anyway. Today, she felt like a leaf trampled under the hooves of too many horses.

Cephus cleared his throat. "It is indeed miraculous what you've managed. Our warriors and clannites remain trapped in the lair you've described, yet you managed to escape with your life." He paused, hesitating. "Your fate is to be decided at the Teftiki Valley, where every tribe will be represented. Make no mistake: you are a prisoner here. But there also lies an opportunity now. If you cooperate with us, there is a slight chance that some sort of mercy might be extended your way. I ask that you please consider it. If your victory over this dokojin can somehow lead to the liberation of the other victims... well, may Sahruum show you mercy in the next Realms, and you may find some in this one as well."

Jalice didn't speak at first. After the initial shock dissipated, she sifted through his words again. He wasn't promising her freedom. He simply wanted to use her to help his kin, and it didn't mean anything would bode better for her by extending him this aid. Her thoughts drifted to Xiekaro, and she shivered. She couldn't leave him there in that horrible Realm. He'd cared for her, talked with her, listened to her—and he'd been repaid with a death sentence he didn't deserve.

By Sahruum's grace, I will not let more people die because of me.

"I'll do whatever you ask," she said softly. "But I'm not sure I will be of much help."

"Wherever this lair exists, I doubt it's here in the Terrestrial," Cephus stated. "More than likely, it's in the Apparition Realm. Would you be willing to translate there and see if you can find it?"

Jalice stiffened. "I wasn't expecting you to ask something so dangerous of me."

"We've run out of options. My kin are trapped, and you're the only one familiar with where they are and what it might look like from the outside. Rest assured, we'll be translating with you. You won't be alone."

Jalice tried to calm herself. She didn't want him to realize how terrified the concept of translating made her. It wasn't just the lurking dokojin in that place that frightened her. She herself was a danger. Her memories posed too much of a threat. Translating would surely provoke a flashback of some sort. The Apparition Realm thrived on emotional baggage, and she wasn't arrogant enough to deny she carried enough with her to cause unintentional trouble. As such, she'd given up translating. She didn't even know how to do it, which had made this an easy solution.

These strangers already judged her for the crimes they attributed to her. If they glimpsed one of her Black House memories, that judgement would surely be amplified.

"You've gone quiet. Is this a sign of your refusal to help?"

Jalice swallowed. For so long, she'd escaped responsibility of any kind. Thousands of people had died because of the ignorance she'd embraced. This was a chance to do what she couldn't do before—to potentially save others from a fate of doom.

"I'll do it," she said, relieved that her voice held a resolved tone. "I can't promise anything will come of it, but I'd be remiss not to try."

Cephus gave a nod and stood. "Then follow me. May Sahruum's eyes guide us to our kidnapped brethren."

***

The room was much like the one Elothel and the other mirajin occupied—square tiers leading down to a level platform. Nothing special, and actually rather ominous without the glorious glow from the mirajin lighting up its space. Wooden boards covered a portion of the upper wall, but Jalice wasn't sure if they were covering a window or something else.

Upon her entrance, Kerothan ignored her, pretending to be engrossed in an important conversation with Ophim. Both he and his fellow clannite were bare-chested and wore only lengthy loincloths, leaving exposed muscular physiques fashioned by the grueling life of a tribal warrior. Something else was different, and it wasn't until she spotted the piles of discarded metal near the two men that she realized they'd stripped themselves of most of their jewelry. In addition, their glass swords were placed atop these piles.

She was surprised that Kerothan would be translating with her. If a memory surfaced during translation, and he saw it . . .

But the less she thought about such an outcome, the less likely it would be to occur. She refused to let a memory be conjured just because she'd fixated on negative thoughts.

Her muscles tensed as she beheld Rejiett, disengaged and separated from the warriors, standing in one corner of the lowest tier. The priestess craned her head ever so slightly, a lone, grey eye peering from beneath her hood. Whereas Kerothan refused to even glance at Jalice, Rejiett followed her every move down the tiered steps. Jalice waited for the priestess to address her, but Rejiett said nothing.

Cephus joined Kerothan and Ophim on one side of the lower platform and gestured for Jalice to do the same across from them. Jalice moved to do so, ignoring the tension between her and the hooded priestess she now stood beside. A plinth at the center of the room hosted a glass sculpture that resembled a large flower, its curled petals outstretched in full bloom.

"We're grateful for your willingness to help, Jalice," said Cephus with a formal tone. "I'm not sure if you've been introduced to the Temple's priestess—"

"We've met," Rejiett cut in, her unblinking eyes still latched onto Jalice. "The Tecalica's tale of a dokojin ruling some secret lair here on our Temple grounds has certainly captured my attention."

Cephus cleared his throat, no doubt startled by Rejiett's abrupt and terse interjection. "Rejiett is here to guide you into the Apparition Realm. Myself and my clannites here must use a more intrusive route of translation that you will be spared."

As he spoke, Kerothan and Ophim sank to the ground to sit with their legs crossed. The clanhead stripped down in similar fashion to his clannites before joining them on the ground. Jalice looked to Rejiett for guidance but received nothing more than the same blank stare. She turned in time for Cephus to glance up and notice her confusion.

"Apologies, I forget our customs and rituals are foreign to you. No need to disrobe. You're not burdened like us, and can use a different means of translation. But do join us in sitting. I'm not sure how long we'll be translated, and no doubt your body will thank you for a more comfortable position."

Jalice lowered herself to the ground, then noticed the identical set of bowls in front of each of the men. Nothing of the sort was present near her. To fill the awkward silence, she asked, "Why must you remove the jewelry?"

"The more natural metals on the body, the harder it is to stay translated," answered Cephus. "But as you notice, we've kept on pieces of greater significance, which can't be freely removed. Our tribe frowns upon untrained translation that could be interpreted as allegiance with the twisters. Only templites should translate, as they've been trained to do so properly through meditation. Those of us untrained in such skills infuse our bodies with metal to signify our bond to the Terrestrial."

"I don't recall Heidretka requiring that sort of practice before the Sachem's reign," Jalice noted.

"That's not quite true," Ophim responded. "Our tribe has always valued body art. But the twisters have forced us to morph what was once art into necessity during these troubling times."

Jalice didn't respond. As was the case anytime negative connotations were attributed to the Sachem, shame washed through her. She knew these men blamed her just as much as they blamed her husband for the twisters and every other atrocity of the last few decades.

"Since you have no such burden, you won't be needing what's in these bowls," said Cephus.

"And what do they hold?" she asked.

"Kykaleeches, though they're more mollusk."

A shiver ran down Jalice's spine as she recalled her encounter with the parasitic worms when Annilasia had snuck one onto her. She hated leeches.

"This particular mutation comes from Ikaul," Cephus said. We conduct underground trade with some Tamers and Gardeners over there. These nasty critters facilitate translation for those of us with metal in our bodies."

"I don't understand," she said, eyeing the bowls warily.

"The Apparition Realm, at least while separated as it is, doesn't take kindly to natural elements. That's why twisters, and sometimes templites, are so sensitive to metals." Cephus gestured with one hand to the line of rings piercing his opposite arm. "When we translate, it must be short. Eventually, the pain of our bodies becomes too much, and our auras are inevitably drawn back them. When we return, our bodies have been in a state of pain for so long in our absence that seizures and unconsciousness sometimes beset us."

"Then why are we doing this?" asked Jalice. "If it's going to hurt you . . ."

Cephus pointed to the bowl. "That's why we have the kykaleeches. They'll numb our bodies. Whatever pain the metal induces won't be felt while they're attached."

"Won't they drain your blood?" she asked.

Cephus nodded. "Indeed, it comes with a price. We'll be weak due to blood loss, and we can't stay connected with the leeches forever. But they will allow us a longer time in the Apparition Realm."

"Enough talk," Kerothan snapped, breaking his silence. "She doesn't need this explanation of our ways. She isn't even using a leech to translate. Let's get this over with."

Kerothan lifted the lid to his bowl. No sooner had it separated from the base than a furious splashing erupted from within. Speckles of water soared as writhing tentacles lashed out from the confines of the bowl. Kerothan showed no concern over the leech's agitation. He retrieved a set of tongs that were clanging about inside and used them to extract the leech. The creature squirmed, a spasm of appendages that flopped wildly as Kerothan lifted it into the air. The rapid succession of wet slaps sickened Jalice's stomach.

Cephus and Ophim followed suit. They lifted the lids to the bowls, extracting leeches just as violent as the one Kerothan held, and lifted them up. Ophim turned his back to Kerothan, who extended his suspended leech towards the other man's exposed back. The leech reached out hungrily, tentacles feeling out the smooth skin once within reach. Barbs flexed out, boring into Ophim's flesh and eliciting a wince from the large man. His face quivered like the serrated feelers of the leech. Using its barbed hold, the leech yanked free of the tongs, closing the final inches between it and Ophim and nestling into his skin with pleased suckling noises. Blubbering oozes escaped from it as it burrowed.

Jalice could see the repressed pain clawing across Ophim's face, but without any further sign of discomfort, he swiveled around towards Kerothan, who in turn exposed his back to Ophim. The other leech extended towards Jalice's brother with eager and erratic thrashing.

"Rejiett will assist in your translation," Cephus said. "Follow her instructions, and we will meet again shortly." He turned and handed his tongs to Ophim, then swiveled so that his back was to his clannite. Ophim extended the last free leech towards the clanhead's exposed skin.

Jalice averted her eyes this time and flinched when she heard the leech latch onto Cephus with a chorus of squelches. When she glanced back, she found all three men facing forward again in a rigid posture with hands placed on their knees.

"You may initiate the hypnosis, Rejiett," said Cephus.

Without a word, the priestess glided up the tiered steps towards the wall where Jalice had noticed the wooden boards. Rejiett grasped a thin piece of rope hanging from the upper boards and yanked. Light poured into the room through a now unblocked window and struck the glass atop the plinth. Colors erupted across every surface, painting the room with rejuvenated energy. Jalice gasped in awe.

Rejiett descended the steps and approached the plinth. "Stare into the glass and focus only on the colors and light. Free your mind of worry and thought. If you do so, your aura will liberate from your body and translate to the Apparition Realm."

The priestess reached for the glass flower, gripped one of its pristine petals, and gave it a forceful push. The sculpture whirled in place, sending the rays of colorful light spinning in a euphoric dance. Jalice found it dizzying until she concentrated only on the spinning flower rather than the beautiful chaos around her. She suppressed her thoughts until nothing remained in her mind, and a deep relaxation settled into her muscles.

The glass continued to spin. Colors leapt all around her.

The room shimmered.

And vibrations raced across her skin.

CHAPTER 28

Greenery spread out before Jalice in lush extravagance. A garden of immaculate proportions stretched all around her, interrupted only by a humble cobblestone path that curved and forked in diverging directions. A rainbow of flowers sprouted from vines and trees, coloring the otherwise endless green.

Above her, the sky swam with nebulous clouds. Celestial bodies fluctuated in size when her gaze fell upon them, coming into focus as if she had telescopic vision. Unlike in the physical Realm, the backdrop of the galaxy wasn't an endless void. Too many nebulas and stars congregated to leave even an inch of it a bleak darkness.

The scene took her breath away, and she didn't hear Cephus's voice at first. When she managed to hear him, she turned towards him only to peer again at the garden in further admiration. She saw the Editshi Temple far beyond, glistening in augmented glory under the light of the stars.

"How do you feel?" he asked.

She finally focused on Cephus, noticing his altered form. Against the backdrop of vivid colors, he stood out in stark contrast with a constitution like the night sky, an endless and vast shadowless darkness. Within this void, a sea of colored orbs and flashing sparks floated and spiraled. It was as if the man had absorbed the expanse of the universe and formed his body from it. The sclerae of his eyes were white, but within them, the iris reflected the dominating color of the orbs that swarmed within him—a healthy yellow that flared like the sun. At his side, his glass sword hung by an invisible belt.

Beyond him were two other forms boasting similar glass swords and starry expanses, though the colors of their orbs varied. Ophim, recognizable by his familiar bulk, contained playful orbs of light blue. The other figure, Kerothan, displayed something more restless—brilliant red orbs that pulsated and flashed about like shooting stars set ablaze.

"It's been so long since I've been here," she answered Cephus, looking down at her own starry form and at her lifestone and lifechain. "At least, on a lucid level. The last time I translated, I wasn't quite aware of everything. I was . . . lost. Trapped in some sort of nightmare." She paused as she continued to absorb her surroundings. "Something like this shouldn't exist during Wither Season. I suppose the Apparition Realm isn't subject to the laws of the Terrestrial, but even so . . ."

"You're standing on holy ground," he explained. "The grounds of a Temple are some of the most sacred, purified places in the world. Templites spend their waking hours performing rites and meditations that rejuvenate and restore the aether here. In the days of our parents, the Terrestrial reflected the same grandeur you see now. But these days, it is difficult to mirror the aether Realms in the physical world. We're fortunate that the results of our templites' dedication thrives here in the Apparition."

Jalice stood speechless. That such a wonder could exist in a place of desertion and desolation left her in awe. Her focus inevitably drifted back towards the magnificence of the sky. "It's been months since I've surveyed the night skies. I used to dedicate most of my time to searching it for messages."

Cephus followed her gaze. "That doesn't surprise me. I recall that the Vekuuv were fond of divining what mysteries the Celestial Drift contains."

"I'm not too proud to admit that my obsession with the Star Alignment in recent years was an escape. If I spent all my time looking up, I could ignore the sins taking place around me." Jalice paused. "I think I'm learning that my time would be better spent addressing the problems I've caused. Maybe one day I can care again about the Alignment."

There was a brief moment of quiet before Cephus spoke again. "Come. We don't have much time—at least, not as long you might."

"How do you expect me to find the lair?" she asked, tearing herself from the reverie that the stars had drawn her into. "I never journeyed in or out of it. I have no directional basis."

"I assumed as much. But unlike in the Terrestrial Realm, where we're bound by the limitations of distance and time, here we can subvert those.

The lair that we seek isn't a physical destination. It's more like a memory or an emotion. It's fear manifested. What you need to do is search inside yourself for what that place made you feel—how it seeded you with anxiety and terror. If you access those, then it's possible you can be led back there while in this Realm."

The heavy weight of expectation crushed Jalice as he spoke. "What if I can't find it?"

"Don't think like that. Maintain a sense of determination. Doubt will only keep it locked to us."

Jalice grew quiet, unsure how to banish the sense of imminent failure. She focused her mind on what foggy recollections she still had of Spiracy's lair. She conjured the gloom, the dank air of the cave, the suffocating darkness, the awful sense that death lurked just out of sight in the shadows.

She shook her head. "It's not working. This place is too . . ." She paused, searching for the right word. "It's too pure. Nothing like the lair could exist here."

Cephus considered this. "Let's try something else." He turned towards Ophim, but quickly his demeanor changed. Cephus's orbs, previously an inviting yellow, shifted to a sickly green, some dripping like mucus while others fizzled with an erratic charge.

Ophim and Kerothan stood together, facing each other. The flares of their silhouettes radiated a calm carmine. The dancing orbs within them burned the same red, many with searing white centers. Most notable, however, were the bands wrapped around their necks and the giant key each man held in his hand. The mysterious objects glowed a brilliant white, untainted by any other color or speck of darkness.

"What's happening?" asked Jalice. "What are those keys meant for?"

Cephus didn't answer and instead addressed his husband with a firm tone. Jalice noted the odd mix of hierarchical command and personal irritation in his voice. There was another element though. Sadness, maybe. Or perhaps jealousy.

"We need your skills, Ophim. Join us."

Both Ophim and Kerothan turned their heads to regard their clanhead. The neck bands, along with the keys the men held, vanished. Kerothan's orbs shifted to a furious crimson, a static charge propelling the orbs into fervent trajectories. Some collided in exaggerated fashion, blooming into bright flashes that frustrated Jalice. At the same time, Ophim's form returned to a serene blue, turning Jalice forlorn and embarrassed. Only then did she faintly recall that emotions could be shared, even unintentionally, in this Realm.

"How can I assist?" asked Ophim as he strode towards her and Cephus. Kerothan remained behind and regarded the group with obvious disdain.

"An aerial view may help Jalice perceive the lair's location," said Cephus.

"Understood." Ophim extended his hand towards Jalice, palm up.

She hesitated. "What's going to happen?"

"Ophim's meditative disposition within this Realm has lent him the ability to defy the concept of gravity," said Cephus.

Jalice eyed the large man with awe, tentatively taking his hand. "You can fly?"

Ophim smirked. "It's a skill many of the templites of the past possessed. But nowadays, it seems something only a few can master. Rejiett claims it's something to do with my aura. Says my natural disposition to be patient and compassionate is intertwined with the ability." The blue orbs in his form gushed a brief orange, and Jalice realized he was embarrassed by the unintentional compliment he'd paid himself.

"So, you're just going to lift me up?" she asked, not caring so much for the reasons why Ophim could do it. She didn't want him to drop her, and the idea of soaring to an unmitigated height set her on edge.

"Just hold my hand. As long as you've got a hold of me, you won't notice much of a difference."

Jalice inhaled sharply when Ophim slowly rose up, his feet slanting to point at the ground. She watched him ascend, and when it came time for her to follow, she squeezed his hand. She waited for a shift, some sort of resistance in her body to the pull of gravity. But when she noticed the trees passing by her, she looked down to find the ground several yards below and realized no change had occurred. The transition had been seamless.

Cephus and Kerothan shrank in size, and the garden's vastness expanded. Jalice stared silently at the brilliant landscape, a wild beauty allowed to thrive without threat. Colors splashed and mixed, a prism unrivaled in the Terrestrial Realm. In every direction, as far as she could see, a lush array of life sprouted from the ground.

"Quite a sight, isn't it?" Ophim murmured. "It doesn't go on forever. The twisters have tainted the garden's outer edges. We don't go into those parts now. Too much risk of encountering dokojin. Some of the templites are permitted to scout out there, but they're specifically chosen by Rejiett."

Jalice opened her mouth, but words escaped her. Fragments of her childhood sprang to mind. Back then, the forests had mirrored this brilliance. She hadn't seen anything like it since. Guilt trickled into her at that thought. Hydrim's reign had crippled this beauty. The forests had lost their radiance during his reign.

Ophim's voice broke her from the trance. "Do you see or feel anything beyond the garden? Try accessing the emotions and vibrations you experienced in the lair. If you're able to, you might perceive its whereabouts."

Jalice stared out over the garden as she conjured her fading memories of Spiracy and the cave. Revulsion at the dokojin's pet and the way it'd mimicked Jalice, the sense of disorientation within the cave, the inability to recall how she'd arrived—all these sensations crept over her. She closed her eyes, wondering if perhaps the distraction of the scene's beauty might be diluting the horror of her memories. After a long moment spent forcing herself to replay the lair's scene again, she let out a beleaguered sigh. She opened her eyes, and her gaze latched onto the Temple.

Filth and blood. Screams of the innocent heard only by the wicked. A string of vile deeds desecrating all that touched it.

"What is it, Jalice?"

She blinked and tried to speak. Dread flooded her. "The Temple . . ." she managed to whisper.

Ophim twisted his head to view the grand structure. "What of it? Should I take you over there?"

The idea of getting closer sent a spike of panic through her. She almost let go of his hand in an attempt to move farther away from the Temple, even though there was plenty of distance between them and the structure already. "We shouldn't go there," she murmured.

It made no sense. The Temple appeared to be the center and source of the lushness around them. Whatever repulsion she had surely couldn't be attributed to the very place that the templites prayed from and cleansed.

"Let's join the others and see what they have to say about your discovery," said Ophim. He guided them back to the ground in a slow descent. The trees of the garden swallowed them up until their feet smoothly touched down on the cobble path.

"Anything?" Cephus asked.

"She experienced something regarding the Temple," said Ophim. "I think we should investigate."

Confusion and doubt radiated from both Cephus and Kerothan. But Cephus said, "If that's our only lead, then we take it."

Jalice followed the warriors reluctantly. The dread never left. With each step towards the structure, she wanted to turn and run. The more they walked, the more the garden around her struck her as fake, as a facade. The luster she'd experienced upon arriving shriveled up under her mounting anxiety. This beauty wasn't real. The ground beneath her churned with a vile poison. She envisioned the roots of the plants, sharp and barbed like knives and oozing with blood.

Soon, the Temple towered above her. She forced herself to look up at it as they entered. If the ground contained the poison, perhaps the sky might offer solace and calm. But the view only intensified the sense that the Temple would come crashing down. Its cornerstones were fragile, placed only to flaunt a false strength.

It, like the garden, was a fraud.

The group wandered the empty corridors. Despite the clean floors and the ceilings free of cobwebs, the pristine elegance didn't impress her. Light poured in through the windows and glistened on the tile floor, offering a warmth that seemed suspiciously inviting. She searched for shadows, and upon finding them absent, she became convinced they had fled. Shadows were too natural to be contained in a place of such elevated forgery.

"Do you still feel something here?" Ophim asked her.

Jalice stopped to reflect. The Temple here certainly made her uneasy—something she hadn't experienced in the physical Realm. Its halls and decor were the same, albeit shinier, but she couldn't shake how foreign it seemed.

"This place feels like a mirage," she said. She pursed her lips, knowing that wouldn't suffice for the men. They needed more from her. "I can't explain it. It's a lovely palace, just as it is in the Terrestrial. But at the same time, it puts me on edge. I feel like we're treading into a trap, one that lies beneath the Temple itself."

The men exchanged glances, clearly unimpressed. Cephus opened his mouth to speak, but a question sprang to her lips. "Is Elothel here?" she blurted. "Aren't the mirajin translated?"

Cephus shook his head. "I'm afraid you'll find nothing if you look for the mirajin here. When they translated here, they vanished into the sky and joined the stars above."

"They abandoned us?" she asked, unable to accept that possibility. "Elothel wouldn't do that."

"They are likely to return," Cephus assured her. "The mirajin hosted inside the Temple are bound to their physical shells. They can't soar the aether Realms undeterred like their brethren. They can only visit."

"Then where have they gone to?" she asked. "Why did they leave at all?"

"The ways of the mirajin are beyond us," said Ophim. "Best to just trust their judgement."

Jalice wasn't sure how to respond to that, and said nothing. She trusted Elothel. But her time with the Sachem had soured her opinion of the mirajin because of their subjugation of humanity. These others who had taken Elothel away from her might not be trustworthy.

"If she's got nothing more than a bad feeling, then this has been a waste of time," Kerothan blurted. "I told you it was a nightmare she had. Nothing more."

Jalice cringed at the spite in his voice. "I told Cephus that I wasn't confident this could help."

"Just admit it," Kerothan snapped. "You've come to infiltrate us in the name of your husband. This has all been a ruse to distract us."

Jalice faced him, bristling at the sparks and static that crackled within his aura. "I am telling you the truth," she urged. "I came for you, Kerothan. I came because guilt pressed me to find you."

"You liar!" he shouted. "Everything you say is a lie. That's how it's always been."

Shame flooded through her, and from the glow emanating from her starry orbs, she became vaguely aware of her own aura shifting in color. "I'm not lying."

"Then why me?" he demanded. "You've hurt so many more. Have you sought out the families of every Vekuuv sentenced to death by the Sachem? Have you pleaded with your kin for mercy?"

"You are my kin," she whispered, and shrank back when he yelled in response.

"No, I am not! I disowned you, just as you disowned me all those years ago. I have no sister!" He rushed forward, pressing his face towards hers even as she turned away in fear. "Tell us why you came. Admit your purpose!"

His aggressive posture broke her resolve. She couldn't withstand the assault of words and accusations. A surge of emotions, tied to memories that she'd worked hard to rebury, clamored up within her.

"I came to save Hydrim!" she shouted.

As the shrill words left her lips, portions of the corridor abruptly morphed. Steel framework appeared, jutting out of the stone at odd angles. The light pouring through the glass windows dimmed as if veiled by clouds.

Before Jalice could understand what had occurred, Ophim pointed and yelled, "What in dying stars is that?" All eyes turned to a massive cylinder of glass upheld on a metal stand. Inside it, feverish, bloodshot eyes peered back at them from behind curled, leather wings.

Jalice stumbled back, a scream catching in her throat as she tripped and fell to the ground. Swords unsheathed, and the men shouted as they brandished their glass blades. Yet their words didn't register. Jalice's attention tunneled towards the creature inside the cylinder.

Dardajah.

Before anyone else could understand what they were seeing, a figure flashed into existence directly in front of the cylinder. The men's shouts broke off into stunned silence.

A young girl stood before the cylindrical encasement. She didn't acknowledge Jalice or the men or the crude, disjointed landscape of metal rods splintering the tiled corridor of the Temple. Unlike those around her, the girl was fully fleshed, her features as they'd appear in the physical Realm.

A deep, guttural voice clawed out from within the glass.

"Bring the boy here."

"What will you do to him?" the girl asked. "Will any of this hurt him?"

"Pain is an illusion," the creature responded. "It evolved alongside everything else, and it serves a purpose. But it is no more real than the dreams your sleep bestows upon you."

Jalice instinctively sprang back to her feet. "No! Stop!"

She wasn't sure if her command was directed towards the girl, the creature, or the very scene itself. This was exactly what she'd feared—a memory conjured into existence, on display for everyone here. She willed it to be gone, but it persisted. This couldn't be happening. Not here, not now. Not with Kerothan present.

She risked a quick glance to her brother. Even given his translated state, she could read the recognition in his face. He knew as well as she that the girl before them was a younger Jalice. His years spent separated from her had not erased his past, and this was evident by the way he observed the mirage of his sister. He looked between the two—the younger, oblivious Jalice and the all-too-lucid adult beside him—with wide eyes of disbelief.

Jalice turned back to the glass cage and gasped, nearly choking. In the time she'd taken to glance at her brother, her youthful self had vanished. Now a youthful Hydrim stood beside the cylinder. It was strange and startling to see the Sachem there, especially in a form younger than when she'd last seen him.

A man she'd tricked. A man who'd married a lie.

Hydrim looked at her as if he could see her, which was impossible. The Hydrim before her was a fragment of a memory—a phantom projected from inside her. He wasn't actually there. And yet, wearing a concerned expression, he addressed her.

"Why didn't you tell us about this?" asked Hydrim.

Jalice jerked her head back to Kerothan to catch his reaction. Her brother quivered, the orbs inside him sputtering and exploding in slow bursts. She jerked her head back to Hydrim, who was looking back at her expectantly.

Behind him, the glass cage shattered. The leather-winged creature leapt out and tackled Hydrim. Jalice screamed, but the creature ignored her. It reared its head and plunged its jaws into the boy's neck.

Cephus shouted and rushed at the creature, sword poised behind his head and ready to strike.

The creature lifted its head towards Jalice, blood gushing from its mouth. *"Dardajah is free."*

Jalice screamed again. Violent vibrations besieged her. The world around her shimmered, and she sank away from the scene into oblivion.

CHAPTER 29

Swimming arrays of color snapped into Jalice's vision. She scrambled across a cold stone floor, jerking her head about frantically. She was back in the meditation chamber. Rejiett, who stood over Ophim with an odd scowl, sprang back when the man jolted awake in a fit of labored breaths.

Jalice met Ophim's gaze before turning and sprinting out of the room. She had no idea where she was going. All she wanted was to get away. She didn't want to be there when Kerothan returned to his body.

Her feet slowed when she came alongside a set of giant glass windows overlooking the Temple landscape. Tears swelled in her eyes, and she let them fall. Beyond the windows stretched that mockingly barren wasteland. She saw nothing of the lush growth she'd glimpsed in the Apparition Realm. Thick grey clouds shut out the sun, further shadowing the desolate terrain of black rock.

She stood there, fixed in place as the tears swept down her cheeks. Pounding footsteps echoed behind her, but they slowed when the person spotted her. She didn't turn, knowing these were her last moments before facing this reality.

"Are you alright?"

When it was Ophim who spoke, her shoulders sank in a release of tension. At least it was him and not Kerothan. Still, his question conjured a new storm of tears, and she brought her hands up to cover her face.

"I—have to—get out of here," she gasped in between sobs. But before she could act on this, other footfalls reverberated in the corridor. She lifted her face to find Kerothan and Cephus barreling forward, both still bare-chested like Ophim but wearing trousers now. Her heart thudded against her ribs and in her ears. The expression on Kerothan's face told her all she needed to know. A history of pent-up resentment tugged at the wrinkles and muscles of his face. His chest flexed with the same seething hatred that was curling his lips into a snarl.

Jalice could no longer hide from this confrontation. He knew her secret. This was it. And knowing this, she battled every instinct still telling her to run.

"So many secrets," her brother spat, halting a few feet from her and Ophim. "And they spilled out for everyone to see. You wanted to speak to me. Well, now you've got my attention, Jalice. Better make this worth it because I'm never going to engage with you after this."

Jalice choked down the sob clawing up her throat. She inhaled, squared her shoulders. "I don't know where to start."

"Start with explaining what just happened. You saw what we saw, but you know more. It looked like a memory. Don't take me for a fool. I recognized that girl to be you. Same with . . ." Kerothan pursed his lips, unable to utter Hydrim's name.

Jalice gave a clipped nod. "Memories, yes, if somewhat disjointed and incomplete. I've suffered flashbacks for months, and at times they hijack my mind. I find myself lost in them, both when awake and during sleep. The mirajin lent me faer aid, but the relief never lasted. The ailment still plagues me. I think the memory you saw was provoked by your accusations. The onset can be unpredictable."

"A dangerous ailment to have, and much more so when translated," Cephus said. He no longer maintained the stoic warmth he'd afforded her until now. Instead, he beheld her with a sternness that offered no comfort. "So, what was that in that cage?"

"A dokojin," she said quietly. She swallowed, summoning the courage to confess. "I made a bargain with it many years ago. I asked for . . ." She stared back at Kerothan as tears blurred her vision. "It told me it would give me Hydrim's affection. In exchange, it wanted a host that it could exist within. It chose Hydrim."

Shock washed away Kerothan's anger. "Dying stars, you did what?"

"I didn't know what it was," she explained. "I was young. I just wanted Hydrim to love me back."

"So, that's how the Sachem became possessed," Cephus murmured. "And he rose to power with the aid of a dokojin."

"Surely you must have realized your mistake," Ophim stated, eyeing her warily. "The malice of the dokojin couldn't have escaped you for long."

"That would be disheartening," Kerothan added with dark sarcasm. "Because that would mean she knowingly condoned and permitted every atrocity that the Sachem committed."

Jalice shook her head. "Hydrim did something to me shortly after. Or rather, Dardajah did. It planted one of its kind inside me—a dokojin that somehow skewed my perceptions. I wasn't truly aware of all the chaos and death happening around me. I lost access to my memories too."

Kerothan closed his eyes, and his voice shook as he shouted at her. "Enough! I'm sick of your excuses."

"But can't you see?" she pleaded. "Hydrim isn't to blame for any of it. It was Dardajah. It overtook him. Hydrim would never hurt anyone."

"Only, he has," Kerothan stated firmly. "How convenient—a couple of dokojin to blame for your mistakes and Hydrim's crimes. I suppose every Terrestrial misdeed can be chalked up to astral entities lurking over our shoulders."

"That's not what I'm saying," Jalice insisted. "I made a mistake, and it led to further sins. Shame has followed me every step of the way to your doorstep, Kerothan, but I confess these things." She paused, taking a deep breath before continuing. "What I am saying is that there is yet hope. I'm free of the dokojin that muddled my wisdom and hid away my memories. And Hydrim can be saved as well."

Kerothan shook his head, a smirk of disbelief twisting his lips. "You truly are a naive little—"

"Elothel can attest to it," Jalice said firmly.

Kerothan threw up his hands. "The mirajin who accompanied you here is indisposed. We can't seek an audience with faem."

"Then we wait," she said, unwilling to relent to his cynicism. "I didn't come here only for my brother's forgiveness. I came here to petition for your help. Hydrim is under the control of a dokojin, and we can save him. If you won't do it for me, then do it for Hydrim." She hesitated, then added: "And for what he once meant to you."

Kerothan's expression faltered, and a pained tenderness surfaced above his anger. He clenched his jaw but said nothing. She understood this to be her one and only chance to truly apologize.

"I'm sorry."

Her chin quivered as the words caressed the air and traveled through the tension to Kerothan. She studied his face for any reaction—anger, empathy, curiosity. She saw no change, though, and found herself filling the silence. "I rehearsed this conversation in my head every day for the last six months. I played it over in my head, envisioning how you'd react. This wasn't how I wanted it to happen." She sighed, her breath shaky. "Nothing seems adequate now except I'm sorry."

"I've never wanted this conversation," he said, simmering with rage. "I never wanted to reunite with the sister who betrayed me—who betrayed my family. I fled, and I never thought of going back."

"It doesn't have to stay this way," said Jalice. "I know I wronged you. Wronged so many others. I can't undo what's sealed in the past, but I've seen the error of my ways. I've come to atone for my sins and to seek . . ." She trailed off, unable to say it. She could see the answer in his eyes. He hated her—hated every word that passed her lips, hated the very space she used up.

"What is it you seek?" he asked, a painful, dreadful knowing lacing his words.

Jalice forced the admission from her mouth. "I seek your forgiveness, brother."

A sneer curled his lips. "If you truly knew the extent of your damage, if you truly understood what your decisions cost me . . ." He shook his head, judgement pouring from his eyes. "You wouldn't dare be asking for such an impossible thing. I barely escaped the Purge that took our parents, though some days I wish that had been my fate. Then I wouldn't have had to endure the cruel knowledge that came later—that the Purge was nothing more than a ruse. The Delirium too. All part of some wicked scheme by your power-hungry husband."

Jalice fought off the tears drifting in her eyes. She wasn't going to keep crying. She'd expected this malice from him. "You have every right to be angry with me," she said. "But I need you to forgive me."

"I don't have to forgive you," he spat, nostrils flaring. "There's no cosmic law that compels me to do so. Perhaps I should, as far as Sahruum's mercy goes. But as one human to another, I don't owe you anything. Especially after everything you've done."

Jalice could hardly keep the tears at bay. They flooded her vision, but she wouldn't let them fall. Her voice broke as she spoke. "You don't understand. It's not for my sake."

Kerothan huffed. "It's always been about you, Jalice. That's the trick. Or more accurately, the trap."

"What if it's the only thing that could save him?" she asked.

Kerothan's eyes narrowed. "Surely you did not just say what I think you did."

"He can be saved, Kerothan," she stated more firmly. "The mirajin told me as much. A disease, a curse, a possession—those are what keep Hydrim shackled to Dardajah." She paused, waiting for her brother to respond. He simply stared at her, his face blank save for a few twitches. He looked to be in shock. Unsure if this was progress or not, she pressed on. "An antidote to the disease is already underway. I found a wilderman and chymist who are working on that right now. And the mirajin will take care of the possession. We just need you to break the curse."

Kerothan's brow furrowed. "A curse?"

She nodded. "When I made the deal with the dokojin, it sealed a bargain—a curse. It gave Dardajah claim to Hydrim. Even if we cured Hydrim's disease of obsession towards me and even if the mirajin exorcised him, the dokojin would still own Hydrim. Hydrim wouldn't truly be free."

"What does that have to do with me?" Kerothan asked, his voice low and gruff.

"Curses are complicated," she admitted. "They're bound with aether, and Elothel isn't sure fae knows the truest conditions to break this one. But it's likely tied to you . . . and to me. To both of us." She swallowed, forcing the words out. "It would require reconciliation between us, and for you and him to reunite. Forgiveness and redeemed love would break his curse."

Out of the corner of her vision, she saw Ophim and Cephus shift their focus from her to Kerothan. She held her brother's gaze, determined that he would see and accept the urgency of all this. He had to save Hydrim. He just had to.

Cephus stepped forward to angle himself between her and Kerothan. "You've given us much to consider, Jalice. We need time to deliberate over these revelations. Given the uncertainty of your ailment, we'll no longer require that you journey to the Apparition Realm."

"I'm sorry to have failed you," Jalice said solemnly. "I wanted to help."

Cephus didn't acknowledge her apology, turning instead to address Ophim. "Are you well enough to escort her to her quarters? I know none of us is accustomed to such a swift detachment from the leeches."

Ophim nodded. "I'm a bit lightheaded but am steady on my feet. I can escort her."

Jalice stared past Cephus at her brother, who'd averted his gaze. She yearned to hear words of affirmation, words that would validate her quest. She waited even as Ophim nudged her to follow him towards the opposite end of the corridor. Her feet dragged as he turned her around. She craned to look over her shoulder one last time.

Kerothan never looked back in her direction. He and Cephus departed through the doors at the corridor's opposite end. He looked worn out. Tired. Defeated.

As Ophim guided her down winding hallways and past windows overlooking the glum scenery outside, the conversation with her brother played out again in her head. None of it had gone like she'd hoped.

But if she was being honest, it had gone exactly as she'd expected.

CHAPTER 30

"**S**he has to be lying."

Kerothan winced at the fiery pain in his shoulder as a damp cloth pressed against an open wound. The numbing effect of the kykaleech had worn off considerably, and the leech's barbed touch had left punctures across his shoulder blades and lower back. As was customary after enduring the leech's detachment, he and Cephus had journeyed to the Temple bathing pool to clean and sterilize the wounds.

Boasting the same elegance as the rest of the Temple, the bath chamber cultivated a calm and tranquil environment that fought hard to unknot the years of stress now tightened inside Kerothan. Steam rose from the water, warmed by some feat of the templites, who were tight-lipped on how they accomplished such a luxury. Marble tiles, divided by thin lines of mortar, lined the ground, and a high glass ceiling, rounded to form an upturned canoe shape, permitted soothing light to enter.

The space was quiet. Kerothan imagined that in the days before the Sachem, this was a popular place to retire after a grueling day of study or labor. During his time here, his presence had only once or twice overlapped with other clannites wishing to soothe their bodies in the inviting water, though this was in part due to Kerothan's care in choosing less popular hours to frequent it. At the moment, it was just him and Cephus, who was at his back as Kerothan dangled his legs in the pool.

"What if she isn't lying?" Cephus asked. He squeezed the warm water out of the cloth to wash away the trickles of blood running down Kerothan's skin. The residue soaked into a towel he'd laid beneath himself. "What if the Sachem is redeemable?"

Kerothan flinched as the water seeped into his open gashes. "I don't think that word could ever describe the Sachem. No amount of remorse nor tragic story could cleanse that man of the sins that grease his soul."

"But he's possessed," Cephus reminded him. "Can actions truly be attributed to a man when it's a dokojin pulling the strings?"

Kerothan groaned. "Spare me the philosophy."

"You like philosophy," Cephus chided.

"This is serious. I'd appreciate it if you could acknowledge the gravity of my sister's claims."

"Your sister admitted her sins," said Cephus. "She came for your forgiveness, and she wants to undo her mistake. I think it's you who isn't feeling the gravity of that heavily enough. You'd rather cling to the pain she's caused you so that you can brand her as malicious and abandon her. But is your sister as irredeemable as the Sachem? Will you not at the very least consider her sincerity? What I saw earlier was a woman who wanted to atone, not initiate a sinister plot against you."

The warm cloth left his back. Kerothan gripped the side of the pool in anticipation of the searing pain to follow. When the vinegar-soaked sponge touched the first wound, he tensed and hissed through his teeth.

"So, the Sachem meant something to you?" asked Cephus.

Heat flooded Kerothan's body, and he briefly forgot about the pain inflicted by the vinegar. He didn't want this conversation, especially with his clanhead. Out of all the nonsense Jalice had spewed, he wished she could have left out that bit about Hydrim. Ophim and Cephus weren't daft; he knew they'd pick up on what she'd meant, which was now made more obvious by Kerothan's reaction.

"My sister misspoke," he muttered.

"I don't think that's true."

Kerothan fought off the urge to slink away from the clanhead's touch. A sense of vulnerability dismantled his previous indifference to being unclothed. He was suddenly very aware of his nakedness—aware of how his wounds weakened him and of how Cephus knew something about his past that he would have never admitted on his own.

As if sensing this, Cephus shifted behind him and came to sit beside Kerothan. The older man sank his legs into the water. Before further exchange could commence, Kerothan shuffled backward and positioned himself behind Cephus to treat his back. Now he didn't need to worry about his clanhead watching him like a hawk, waiting for his eyes to pour out some weak emotion or, stars forbid it, tears. As much as Kerothan didn't want to acknowledge it, the topic of Hydrim made him sensitive. He hadn't actually heard the name in years. Everyone referred to that man as the Sachem. Hydrim was a name lost in the years of chaos, a boy stuck in a past that Kerothan rarely thought about.

Silence reigned between the two men as Kerothan focused on treating his clanhead's back. He was no stranger to Cephus's features, but seeing the splotches of blue marking his skin always made him queasy. The patches looked like massive bruises and covered sporadic areas of the older man's body. According to Cephus, the odd skin discoloration wasn't painful nor the result of any injury. Kerothan wasn't sure if that was true or not, but he knew better than to comment on them. Cephus couldn't help the splotches—they were simply a part of him and had no bearing on his ability to lead a clan.

Just when Kerothan thought he'd escaped the conversation, Cephus spoke up again.

"You've carried this anger with you for so long," said the clanhead. "Your sister is giving you the chance to let it go, and you have the opportunity to save someone you cared for. I ask that you not throw all that away simply because the past hurts."

Kerothan's hand paused. His fingers clenched the cloth in a tight, forceful grip. A gush of water ran across Cephus's back, and he watched it fall onto the towel on which his clanhead sat, taking blood with it. New red stains blossomed over the white towel. He couldn't get Hydrim out of his mind, nor the image of the dokojin as it pounced on his childhood friend. Its guttural voice swam in his head, dragging its claws as it repeated one phrase over and over again.

Dardajah is free.

"You have no idea what this feels like," he said in a low, hushed voice.

"You're right," Cephus admitted. "I don't. But I hope you take my words to heart. As a member of my clan, you have my care. I wouldn't push you towards this if I thought it would break you. In fact, I think it will help you heal. And Kerothan—you deserve to heal."

Kerothan flung the cloth into the water bowl and retrieved the sponge. He pressed it into Cephus's open gashes, somewhat vindicated when the older man arched his back and let out a sharp sound like a muffled gasp.

"Dokojins' claws, take it easy," Cephus growled.

Kerothan didn't respond. Maybe that would put a stop to this absurd exchange. He finished sterilizing the other wounds, enjoying each hiss and groan from his clanhead, before placing the sponge back in its bowl. He moved to stand, hoping to make a quick retreat from the bathing chamber.

"Come, sit." Cephus patted the ground beside him.

Kerothan stifled a groan and moved back to the ledge, dipping his legs back into the water.

"I witnessed the aura bond between you and Ophim."

Kerothan stiffened. The steam's heat swarmed into his face. He could see Cephus staring at him from the corner of his vision, and Kerothan in turn kept his own gaze on the water. "That wasn't an aura bond," he blurted. "The Apparition Realm is complex. There's no way to know what happened there between us."

"Don't play me the fool, Kerothan. It doesn't take a templite to know what that was. You clearly carry some level of affection for my lebond, and it slipped free while translated."

Kerothan dissected the man's tone. Cephus sounded level and calm, but there existed some degree of accusation in his words. Kerothan held his tongue, hoping the clanhead would betray his motivations in broaching the subject.

"Your fondness for Ophim isn't news to me," Cephus continued. "Despite what you may think, he shares quite a bit with me, including the interactions you two have had in the past. You desire a particular arrangement, but Ophim has relayed to you what such an arrangement would require." He paused, letting the implications sink in. "Ophim is linked to me."

"I am clear on Ophim's status," said Kerothan. "You won't have a problem from me."

A short pause lingered before Cephus spoke back up. "I humbly ask that you convey to me your grievances with our stipulation. What is it about me that you refuse to engage with?"

Kerothan remained quiet as his mind raced. He wasn't prepared for this conversation any more than he'd been prepared for the one with Jalice. He'd never spoken with Cephus about such intimate matters, though it appeared Ophim clearly had. Kerothan chewed on the memories that surfaced—those of when he'd told Ophim his reservations about entering any sort of intimate relation with his clanhead.

He turned and faced Cephus, braving the man's intrusive gaze. "You don't respect me."

Cephus's brow furrowed. "I beg to differ. But please enlighten me, clannite."

"You don't respect anything I say or feel. As recent as the cavern expedition. I expressed to you the dangers I suspected, and you did nothing. Then, when I thought it best to leave no survivors among the twisters we found, you dragged that imbecile back to our Temple."

Cephus opened his mouth, then shut it, frowning. Kerothan watched as the other man mulled this over.

"I believe there's truth to your statement," Cephus said, choosing his words with care. "But I think your unwillingness to enter relations with me extends much deeper than that. You have an aversion to me—whether it is my age or my demeanor. I sense a great deal of animosity towards me, but I can't imagine what it is I've done to deserve that." He drew in a long breath, his chest expanding fully before he exhaled heavily. "Whatever it is, I humbly ask your forgiveness. But in the spirit of raw honesty, be aware that your aversion to me delivers its own pain. To have someone extend affection towards my lebond but so venomously reject me in turn is . . . difficult to reconcile."

Kerothan stared back, unsure of what to say. Shame washed over him, but so did confliction. He didn't like Cephus; he found the clanhead too stoic and controlling. And regardless of what Cephus claimed, respect indeed meant a lot to Kerothan. It would be ludicrous to enter any sort of bond with a man who clearly didn't care for Kerothan's opinion on matters. Despite this, a flicker of temptation danced in front of Kerothan. Cephus wouldn't be saying these things unless a willingness existed to attempt relations. That meant Kerothan could finally get a chance to be with Ophim.

"What is it that you're trying to convey, clanhead?" he asked cautiously.

Cephus swallowed, clearly nervous—a rare sight, and one that puzzled Kerothan. The clanhead lowered his head, unable to meet Kerothan's gaze. "You want to be with Ophim, and my lebond desires you as well." He hesitated. A war waged across his face and threatened to seal his lips. He opened his mouth, but it took a second more for the words to come. "I mean to say I'm blessing that desire, both as clanhead and as one who is linked to Ophim." Knowing the vulnerability that came with such a confession, he rushed on as he jerked his head up to Kerothan.

"But this comes with the same condition as it always has, Kerothan. If you enter relations with Ophim, so also do you enter relations with me. I'm not asking you to summon the same affection for me that you have for him. But I do ask that you abolish your disdain of me and express a willingness to share yourself with both of us."

Kerothan's jaw dropped, but he quickly gathered himself. "Is this something we have to consult the others of our clan about? Those back home? Custom dictates that new links be acknowledged by every member of that clan."

"In due time," said Cephus. "The others are far away though. It wouldn't be fair to offer you this gift but force you to wait. As clanhead, I'll allow this exception to tradition."

Hope and excitement surged inside Kerothan. His heart raced as he lifted his chin with solemn determination. "I can't promise I'll ever think of you as I do Ophim. But with the stars of my birth as my witness, I will try—"

He didn't get the chance to finish. A thunderous boom rocked the room, splashing water over the pool's edges and onto the marble floor. Cephus scrambled to his feet, slipping on the slick tiles as he headed over to their pile of clothes. Kerothan leapt to follow but found the ground just as difficult to maneuver. When stable enough on his feet, he darted towards Cephus and began dressing. His clothes clung stubbornly to his wet skin as he tugged them on.

"Are we under attack?" he asked.

Cephus shook his head, but Kerothan could see no certainty in the answer. "Go check on Ophim and Jalice. Make sure they're safe." With that, the clanhead darted out of the room.

Careful not to slip and crack his skull on the film of water under his boots, Kerothan clipped on his belt, stumbled out of the bath chamber, and headed towards Jalice's quarters.

CHAPTER 31

Kerothan found nothing but an empty chamber. Jalice and Ophim were nowhere to be found, and the corridors were more vacant than usual. He came across no guards, no other clannites. This wing of the Temple was deserted.

With no hints as to their whereabouts, he decided to head towards the source of the quakes. Soon after, his ears perked at the sound of panicked cries and the clash of blades. He followed the noise, his path taking him towards the Grand Hall, which connected most of the main passages of the Temple.

As the passage approached its intersection with the Grand Hall, he came to a halt. The walls were plastered with blood here, and several bodies littered the ground. He took the last strides of the corridor slowly, eyeing the scene in shock. A warrior lay prostrate, a sword still in hand, head missing. Opposite him, the robe of a templite was stained a dark crimson where their stomach had imploded and burst as they'd fallen to the ground.

He came into view of the Grand Hall and stopped again. He couldn't process the carnage at first. All he heard were screams and the frantic movements of desperate warriors. Slowly, the scene came together. Limbs flew about as they were ripped free from motionless bodies. Innards splattered pillars and walls in unnatural patterns. Mounds of indiscernible flesh and bone vomited dark fluid.

He wasn't sure how long he stood there watching the chaos unfold. Warriors swung their weapons at figures that moved with impossible grace despite the scene around them. It took him a moment to realize those evasive foes were templites.

Templites. The very ones Kerothan had spent months conversing with and working alongside. Many of them had healed his wounds after skirmishes with the twisters. He'd witnessed them pray, awed by their dedication as they diligently strived to cleanse the Apparition Realm of waste around the Temple grounds.

Now, the white robed bastards were brandishing their wands and slicing his comrades into tiny pieces.

It dawned on him then. These weren't templites anymore. These were twisters. Aether erupted sporadically, the room a constant shimmer. Pockets of the invisible energy surged into existence at the behest of the templites, who hurled it towards the warriors. Howls of fear or pain were cut short when the aether obliterated their bodies. Throats gurgled as they snapped. Stomachs opened up to spill their contents across the floor.

Not all was lost for the warriors though. The blades of their weapons, forged from the same glass as the wands of the templites, absorbed the onslaught of aether when possible. Every blade shimmered with the energy, though none among the warriors knew how to discharge it back at the templites. Which meant none of them had much time before their swords could hold no more.

A number of warriors had formed clusters throughout the Hall, banding together in meager thresholds of strength. The outer line of the formation comprised the sword-bearers, while a few archers stood in the center and targeted the twisters that swarmed the room. Their glass-tipped arrows shot through the air, periodically repaying a twister with a horrific end of combusted flesh.

Urgency stirred in Kerothan. A deep rage at the loss of his brethren ignited. His cry ripped free as he unsheathed his sword and entered the fray, knowing death surely awaited him in some grisly fashion.

Kerothan's blade absorbed flashes of aether that dove through the air. He fully expected at any moment for the energy to crash into him and sever his body into a million pieces like so many of his fallen kin. His sword swung wildly at the nimble templites, but many glided off the ground and into the air with the aid of carefully utilized aether. He earned a few lucky strikes, basking in the spray of blood that erupted when his sword touched flesh.

The fight didn't last long. A few final explosions contributed more casualties to the body count that overflowed the room, and then an eerie quiet fell. Kerothan stood poised with his sword, chest heaving. Blood coated his face, the red fluid dripping off the metal rings embedded in his skin.

He picked up on the lingering noises of the banished chaos. A few moans, the gurgle of air bubbling in blood, the thumps of failed attempts to move. A horrible dread crept up from the depths and choked him. Possibilities, slippery with uncertainty, dove into his mind.

He'd never find Ophim.

Desperation overrode his rooting despair, and he searched the faces of the fallen. Many were mangled or contorted, no longer bearing any semblance to the warriors Kerothan knew. These were especially difficult to observe, but he couldn't stop. He would stare at every imploded face, every shred of skin pasted to the floors and walls. He wouldn't rest until he knew without a doubt that Ophim wasn't among the sea of bodies littering the Grand Hall.

Though he hardly acknowledged them, the other surviving warriors huddled in various corners and intersecting halls. Puddles of bile surrounded some, while others held their faces in their hands to hide the sobs shaking their bodies. Kerothan spotted empty expressions of disbelief and shock on some, who stared in any direction but the morbid scene. One warrior, trembling and sputtering out choked sobs, stood locked in an embrace with another. When the crying warrior bent his head lower, Kerothan saw the man who was trying to comfort him: Cephus. Kerothan dashed over to them.

Torn between respecting his fellow warrior's distress and learning the fate of Ophim and Jalice, Kerothan leaned close and whispered to his clanhead. "I can't find them."

Cephus peered over the shoulder of the warrior, worry filling his eyes. "They weren't in the prison quarters?"

Kerothan shook his head. "We need to scout the Temple. How many can we task with this? There's too much space to cover myself."

Cephus face fell. "Look around you. These are our only survivors."

Kerothan blanched, twisting around to glimpse the dozen or so warriors in the Grand Hall's vicinity. "This can't be all that's left," he said, turning back to Cephus.

A sadness weighted the clanhead's face. "Are we certain they aren't among the fallen?"

Kerothan stiffened. "No. They can't be. Ophim wouldn't have left Jalice, and he wouldn't have led her into danger. They have to be in the Temple somewhere."

"They aren't," a shallow voice croaked.

Cephus and Kerothan craned their necks towards a man sitting against the nearby wall. Tear stains and splotches of blood marked his face. He didn't meet their gazes, instead choosing to stare absently at the ground.

"You saw them?" Kerothan asked.

The warrior nodded slowly, as if the motion required too much energy. "They went with the traitor."

Kerothan and Cephus exchanged a confused, somber look.

"Are you accusing one of our own of betrayal?" Cephus asked. "Be careful with such accusations, clannite. This is no time to spread rumors."

"I saw Rejiett's wand rip apart my clanhead," the warrior replied. "She strode across the Hall with those two in tow—the Tecalica and . . . and your lebond, Ophim. Their faces looked terrified, but they went willingly from what I saw."

Kerothan looked to Cephus with alarm. "Has the priestess been accounted for? Can anyone corroborate this?"

Cephus slowly leaned the bereaved warrior off of him and onto the wall, whispering hollow condolences and comforts before straightening again. "This is beyond troubling, but it goes in hand with what happened here. The templites turned on us. Rejiett no doubt led the charge. But why take captives? Were Jalice and Ophim intentional?"

"We need a plan," said Kerothan. "We need to search the Temple for them."

"If Rejiett took them, they're no longer here," said Cephus. He turned to look at the warrior who'd previously addressed them. "Has the prisoner been accounted for? The twister we took captive during the raid near the northern caverns. Did Rejiett free him?"

"I'll find out, clanhead," the man stated. He rose and departed the corridor with a teetering gait that betrayed the lingering effects of post-battle shock.

"Why do we care if the prisoner is alive?" Kerothan asked.

"Because that may be why this happened," said Cephus. "Perhaps Rejiett intended to free the twister. Considering the templites turned on us, I now consider them all twisters. Perhaps they attacked to rescue their comrade."

Kerothan considered this, but it didn't strike him as a viable theory. It didn't explain why the priestess had taken Jalice and Ophim rather than killing them. As he pondered the meaning behind the attack, an idea wormed its way between his thoughts.

"If the prisoner is still here, then we can use him."

Cephus frowned at him. "How . . ." His eyes widened. "Sahruum's stars, you don't mean to . . ."

A dark, pensive look came over Kerothan. "Spare me your judgement."

"We don't do that," said Cephus. "*They* do that. We don't defile ourselves through—"

Kerothan's irritated groan cut him off. "We don't have time to debate morality. Look around us. Tell me we can still keep the twisters at bay. They're here, Cephus. Our efforts to bar them passage into the Eastern tribes has failed. We need to get ahead of this before any more of us are slaughtered. Ophim included."

Cephus shook his head, his mind already decided. "No. It's a sin before Sahruum. We don't torture our enemies."

"This is war," Kerothan countered. "We no longer have the luxury of abstaining from the sins our enemy freely commits. If we can't stain our hands with their blood, then we'll continue to pay with our own."

"Would you propose this if it were anyone else that she'd taken?" Cephus asked.

Kerothan leaned forward, invading the other man's space. "I won't let them have Ophim. If Sahruum expels me to the void for what must be done, so be it."

Cephus glared down at him in disgust. "Your violence will stain the Apparition Realm. You'd so flagrantly desecrate the gardens the mirajin and priests have maintained, for the soul of one?"

"Don't act like you aren't thinking of doing the same," Kerothan said in a low, harsh whisper. "If I'm willing to damn myself, how much more would you bend to get him back? Or are you prepared to see him die? To see him be killed? Torn apart, sliver by sliver, until he begs for the dokojin to consume him? Because I guarantee that's the kind of fate that awaits him in the hands of twisters."

Kerothan watched the vivid imagery of that description burrow into Cephus's mind—watched the subtle twitch that flexed the older man's facial muscles.

"I refuse to let you justify this," said Cephus. "Torture is torture, and it will produce the same aetherwaste that this carnage did."

"You refuse it, even if it would save Ophim?"

"Ophim would never condone such violence for his sake," Cephus retorted. "If you knew him as well as I do, you'd understand that."

Kerothan clenched his open hand into a fist. "I'll let him tell me that after I've saved him. Abstain from this unpleasantry if you must." He moved to stride away, but Cephus gripped him by the arm to stop him.

"I'm going to be there," said Cephus. He closed his eyes and let out a long sigh. "If this sin is to be committed for Ophim, then I take on this burden with you."

Kerothan gave a clipped nod. Part of him had hoped the clanhead would refuse further, which would leave Kerothan unsupervised and unhindered in his efforts. But he also admired the pious man's dedication to Ophim. When it counted most, the clanhead was willing to bend his moral compass for the sake of his lebond.

"May Sahruum forgive us for these necessary means," Cephus murmured.

Kerothan turned, knowing Cephus would follow. As he did, he quoted a scripture that hadn't graced his mind in years but now seemed fitting.

"*Sahruum courts the night of the wicked with a siege of judgement.*"

CHAPTER 32

An unhinged cackle sprang at them when they opened the door to the prisoner's quarters.

Kerothan entered the room with hesitant steps, unsure if a trap like that in the Grand Hall awaited inside. He flexed his hands open, then closed, wishing he still wielded his sword. Cephus had advised against it. The room was vacant of aether, but walking in with charged swords would be exactly what the twister needed to slaughter them and make an escape.

The dungeon cell was far too generous a space for the likes of a twister. It had been a space for solitude once—a retreat where the senses could be deprived of light and spared the bustle of the Temple. Now it hosted someone bent on desecrating all the Temple stood for. At least it was windowless. The filth it caged didn't deserve to partake of the daylight.

The clanheads had expressed concern at keeping a twister locked up within the Temple. It was difficult to envision what would keep the prisoner from simply translating into the Apparition Realm to sow chaos or to simply extract aether to wield.

But Rejiett had convinced them that the twister couldn't translate. The Temple grounds, blessed by the dedicated prayers of her fellow templites, were too concentrated in pure aether. For a degenerate such as the prisoner, translating into an aether Realm here would be like a thirsty cricket hopping into scalding water. Further, while one might still see it as a minefield from which to extract aether, the twister had no wand. It would take a master in aethertwisting to pull that sort of aether into the physical Realm and utilize it without a conduit.

Kerothan pondered this as he slinked farther into the darkness of the room. Rejiett had said many things, but she'd also betrayed them. How many of her claims could he trust? Maybe the prisoner would unleash a torrent of energy that would splash his guts across the walls like his kin in the Grand Hall.

Ahead, in the center of the room, a figure sat limp in a chair.

Kerothan heard the strike of a match behind him, and candlelight illuminated the room. The figure's details became clearer. The prisoner was middle-aged with a closely shaven head, much like Ophim's, and the faintest outline of facial hair framing the sharp edges of his face. Tiny pockets crossed from one eyebrow down into his cheek, absent of any rings but more than hinting that he'd once proudly hailed from Heidretka. The twister lifted his eyes but kept his head bent forward. A nefarious smile already twitched at his lips. Sweat dripped off his forehead, and his drabby looking cloak appeared drenched under the arms.

Kerothan approached slowly. He heard Cephus close the door behind him. The clanhead did not move to follow Kerothan in farther but instead lingered in one of the front corners with the candle in hand.

"I haven't had many visitors since you flung me in here," the twister croaked, coughing out a chuckle. "Haven't even translated since then. Rejiett, she told me, she said, 'Aruzz, you won't be free like you were out there. The aether here is too damn blessed to translate into without going mad for someone like you.'"

Kerothan held his tongue and glanced back at Cephus to see if his clanhead thought it wise to respond. The older man beheld the twister with a dark look but made no move to intercede or offer guidance, so Kerothan turned back to address Aruzz.

"It's too bad she didn't let you out during her little retreat out of the Temple. I'm sure you felt the quakes. Did she at least stop by and commend you for your sacrifice?"

The twister's head twirled on the axis of his neck like a blade of grass bent by the wind. He let out a snort. "I heard the chaos upstairs. Managed to make out a few of your people's screams. How many of your clannites died? I imagine it's hard to count when they're shredded beyond recognition."

Kerothan's nostrils flared. He brought himself in front of Aruzz and loomed over him. His hand dipped into his pocket, sliding out to show off a thin golden needle. Aruzz's eyes caught on it, and though his smug grin remained, anxiety flashed across his face before his mask of arrogance returned. He flickered his eyes between it and Kerothan, chuckling.

"You think a tiny little piece of metal is going to scare me?" he crooned, rocking back and forth in the chair. "Or perhaps you mean to teach me to sew!"

Kerothan wasted no more time. He ripped the twister's cloak back to expose the skin on his shoulder and extended the needle before Aruzz could retreat. Frantic, primal screams erupted from the prisoner as the tip hovered inches above his shoulder.

Kerothan's cheeks quivered from how hard he was clenching his teeth together. Aruzz's skin rose like a flower to the sun, papery as it stretched from the muscle and bone beneath it in some unnatural desire to grip the needle. Where the needle traced too close, though, the skin buckled instead, curling and caving. It was as if the tiny object was some magic paintbrush, etching impossible canyons and mountains into a leathery canvas without ever making contact.

Kerothan heard Cephus bark his name, and he withdrew the needle. He tore his eyes from his handiwork. Shame and revulsion caused him to step back. He'd wanted this. He'd wanted to make this imbecile pay for all the horrid sins he'd committed. Pain was a just sentence for a twister. But the sounds scratching from the man's throat and the way his legs thrashed and pummeled the ground out of sheer muscular reaction to an overwhelming pain sickened Kerothan. He closed his eyes and breathed out. The prisoner couldn't be permitted to see his resolve crumble. It would steal away his authority, regardless of what the needle in his fingers could unleash.

Aruzz panted, his entire body trembling. His eyes pressed shut so tight that deep creases formed at the corners.

"Where are the twisters?" Kerothan asked. "Did the templites intend to join them? Is that where Rejiett has gone?"

Aruzz's eyes shot open, wide and brazen. Kerothan flinched, unnerved by the sight.

The grin, wilder than before, crested the twister's lips again. "Do you miss them already? You must enjoy the sounds of your comrades' screams.

I'm sure my brethren will return to finish off what's left of you." A chuckle thudded from the man's throat, but it ceased when Kerothan jerked his hand up to display the needle prominently.

"Despite what you might think, I don't want to watch your skin writhe beneath this needle," said Kerothan. "So, let's be civil. You talk. I listen."

Aruzz's grin cracked open into a smile as his eyes rolled off the needle to land on Cephus. "What's your name, gramps?"

"Whatever foul scheme was at play is now over," the clanhead announced to Aruzz. "We know the twisters had a plan. We found your device, and most of the templites at your disposal were slain earlier today. We'll find our friends and we'll stop you, just as we always have. The twisters will not breach this defense."

"All in vain," the man wheezed, grinning maniacally up at Cephus. "Have you seen her lurking? Lingering in the backdrop of empty corridors that once festered with life? She watches you and takes your precious kin into deep, deep sleep." He let out a gleeful cry, gnashing his teeth. "She's powerful enough to project from her cocoon now. I know you've seen her!"

"What do you know of the Endless Sleep?" asked Kerothan.

The wild eyes flashed to Kerothan, and he winced beneath their heaviness. "Who have you lost to it?" Aruzz asked. "A brother? A mother?" He paused. "Maybe a lover?"

"Why do they sleep?" Kerothan demanded. "If you tell us what you know—about the Sleep, about where Rejiett has taken the captives—then we'll stop hurting you."

The prisoner sneered, craning his neck as if trying to pop his head loose. "You think pain is a threat? Give it to me! All of it," he cackled. "Let's make aetherwaste together. Spiracy will be so pleased."

Cephus gave Kerothan an alarmed look at the mention of the dokojin that Jalice had claimed to have witnessed in her nightmare.

"Spiracy," repeated Kerothan, turning back to Aruzz. "Is it a dokojin?"

The man's eyes lit up. "So, you *have* seen her. Many of us have not yet beheld the glory of our laborious sacrifices. But we've heard blessed things.

Of a terrible beauty that lures the weak into a lullaby sleep." His awe twisted back into an expression of mockery. "But you haven't seen her. No, if you'd witnessed her, you wouldn't be here right now. You'd be in her lair, strapped to a table, begging to go back to your precious waterbag of a body."

Kerothan raised the needle towards Aruzz's face; the twister grew rigid, pressing against the chair yet still maintaining his grin even as he eyed the sharp object.

"No more riddles, Aruzz," said Kerothan. "I'm not afraid to end you, and you won't get the luxury of sinking into the void in the next Realm. We'll have mirajin waiting there to collect your aether. They'll take your stain and polish it for eternity until your aura is cleansed."

A snarl licked at Aruzz's lips, and Kerothan wondered if the twister could see through his bluff. The mirajin were indisposed. Such a fate for Aruzz after death seemed doubtful. More likely, he'd just evolve into aetherwaste in the next Realm after his physical demise, tainted as he was.

"I can't wait to see one of those nasty pets of Spiracy try and mimic your arrogance before it eats you up like a tasty platter." Aruzz licked his lips and cackled.

Kerothan leapt forward, yanked more of the cloak off of Aruzz, and hovered the needle over the man's skin again. He closed his eyes as Aruzz's screeches broke out once more. It seemed they'd never stop, and when they did, Kerothan opened his eyes to find the man's upper chest swollen with boils. The skin had tunneled in at some places, drying and withering to form craters. Kerothan turned away, muscles shaking as he concentrated on not hurling. He couldn't keep doing this. No wonder Cephus wanted nothing to do with this sort of practice.

"You want aetherlick."

Kerothan looked up at Cephus and regarded him with a puzzled expression. But the clanhead wasn't talking to him.

"I recognize the twitching, the sweats," said Cephus. "It isn't just the needle that's wreaking havoc on you. Your body is trying to purge itself of its addiction. It was doing so even before we set foot in here."

Aruzz only stared back, an animal cornered.

"We can give it to you," said Kerothan, eyes flashing to Cephus. The other man gave an affirming nod, and Kerothan looked back at the prisoner. "Tell us what we need to know, and I'll deliver the stick to you myself."

Aruzz's fingers twitched feverishly. "I'm no traitor," he wheezed. His tongue shot out to scrape at the edges of his mouth. "But I suppose it won't do much harm to tell you what you're going to discover on your own anyway. Your end is nigh, and this knowledge will sink into your grave with you."

Kerothan said nothing. To do so might risk interrupting the man's eroding defenses.

"I know nothing of who was taken," Aruzz continued, "but my brethren do not take prisoners. This exception means they've got plans for your friends." The grin returned, and he moved his jaw as if crunching on something delicious. "And plans like that happen at a very specific spot. At a Fence Post."

"Fence Post," the clanhead repeated back. "That's how your kin referred to the device—the one we found in the cavern. Rejiett was supposed to decrypt its purpose . . ." The clanhead trailed off, eyes narrowing in deep thought.

Aruzz gritted his teeth. "I was promised aetherlick. Where's my treat?"

"Not until we get all our answers," Cephus stated firmly. "Tell us about the device we found. This thing you call a Fence Post."

"You haven't figured that out yet?" Aruzz threw back his head and hollered, kicking his legs like a child. "No wonder we've got a blanket pulled over your eyes. Not very well-versed in pre-Residuum mysteries, huh?"

Kerothan caught Cephus's attention and shot him an incredulous look. They were there to find Ophim, not to inquire about some pointless machinery. If Ophim was at the Fence Post, they needed to get to the caverns now.

"Respect your elders, child," Aruzz mocked as he witnessed their silent exchange. "He's much wiser than your tiny mind can comprehend, and he's onto something." He winked at Cephus.

"What do you mean by that?" Kerothan asked.

Aruzz leaned forward as if to tell a secret. Rivulets of blood gurgled from his boils and flayed skin as he moved, but the twister seemed immune to the pain, or at least ignorant of it. "Because as I said—your friends are being taken there. To a Fence Post."

Cephus and Kerothan stared at him, dumbfounded.

"But we already found it," Cephus said slowly, unwillingly to walk into a word game that would result in him looking foolish. "The twisters wouldn't be taking them to a location we've secured."

An impish, knowing look wrinkled Aruzz's face. "You're missing my point."

"There are more of them," Kerothan uttered quietly, piecing together Aruzz's elusive hints. "They're being taken to a second device."

"So, you're not a full imbecile." Aruzz laughed. "Though, being that you didn't know the Temple's secret, you have asked the wrong questions."

Kerothan glanced at Cephus and saw his own alarm mirrored in the clanhead's expression. "The Temple's secret?" Kerothan asked. "You mean the twisters are somewhere in the Temple?" He didn't want to believe that Jalice's little show during translation was the truth.

"Deeper than the Temple," Aruzz corrected. "Deeper and older places exist on these grounds. You'll never find them. The metal tunnels below are a labyrinth too confounding to navigate in one lifetime. It would take years for you to find the Fence Post down there, and your friends would be long since sacrificed in the name of our glorious Spiracy." He cackled again before his glee vanished into a dark glare. "Now, where's my aetherlick? If you've lied about it, then you might as well pop me like a mud bubble with that needle you've got. I'm done answering questions."

"Not until you tell us exactly where this other device is," Cephus growled.

Aruzz's grin returned. "That'll cost you extra."

"We'll get you the aetherlick," Kerothan assured him.

Aruzz shook his head, still smiling cruelly. "This secret requires a different gift. I want to see the massacre."

Cephus and Kerothan stared, at first unsure what he was asking. Dread washed over Kerothan when he realized what was being requested. "You horrible monster," he whispered.

Aruzz sneered up at him. "Blood and gore, or you can kill me right here, 'cause that's my price. In exchange, you get a grand tour led by me, your fearless guide."

Still confused, Cephus looked to Kerothan. "What's he talking about?"

"He wants to see the Grand Hall," Kerothan stated.

Cephus's face fell for a moment before it contorted into rage. "You sick bastard!"

Kerothan stepped in front of Cephus to stop the man from charging at Aruzz. "Just let him see it. We need to find Ophim. Clear the Grand Hall of any wands so he can't bring the Temple down on us."

Nostrils flaring, Cephus snapped himself out of Kerothan's grip and marched back towards the door without another word.

Kerothan looked to Aruzz one last time, growing tense under the man's gaze.

"I'd like my treats now," Aruzz sneered. "Then into the labyrinth we go."

CHAPTER 33

The chaos of the Grand Hall eradicated Jalice's hope that someone would save her. She willed the warriors to recognize her state of distress. She had no way to cry out, no way to dart into the fray and force someone to whisk her to safety. An aether ward of some sort prevented her mouth from opening. Anytime she tried, a fiery pain pierced her lips. Another ward incapacitated Jalice's ability to move her muscles freely and forced her to follow Rejiett without resistance.

The priestess had ambushed Ophim and Jalice on their way to Jalice's quarters. Ophim, stripped down with no armor and protected only by the glass sword he carried, hadn't stood much of a chance against Rejiett's surprise attack. She'd quickly disarmed him. Jalice had tried to flee, but it'd been too late. A pair of passing warriors had witnessed this, only to end as limp corpses on the floor after a horrific demise full of shrieks and writhing, courtesy of Rejiett's aethertwisting. Then Rejiett had pointed her wand—glowing brighter with what Jalice could only assume was energy from the now dead warriors—at her and Ophim, rendering them unable to move at will. Unable to speak or flee.

Now, the pair were trapped in the clutches of aether that obeyed Rejiett, and the priestess was showing no signs of losing her hold on them. They could only follow her away from the Grand Hall and down the empty corridors as she dragged them to a hidden passage. They disappeared through a secret door that opened onto a thin corridor nestled behind the Temple's walls.

Jalice's resolve broke further. No one would find them here. This secret corridor was obviously rarely used. The passage was dingy and layered in cobwebs. Torches lit the way, but they were few and far between, leaving most of the length veiled in darkness. The farther they traversed it, the rarer torches became. At one point, Rejiett retrieved one from the wall at the top of a descending staircase.

Down they went. Eventually, the walls shifted from the stone layers of the Temple into the natural formation of a cave. Stalagmites and stalactites spiked from the ground and ceiling of the steep pathway down which they continued. Pools of collected water sat in corners, some an unnaturally bright pink.

Her feet ached by the time the ground leveled off. The large flat area, though still cluttered with natural cave formations, had a maneuverable path leading to the edge of a drop-off. Jalice's heart quickened at the sight. The torch Rejiett carried did very little to reveal what lay beyond the drop-off, but she could imagine the gaping shaft with no ground in sight.

Perhaps Rejiett intended to push her and Ophim off it. No one would ever find their bodies. With each forced step towards the edge, her mind screamed at her to turn and run. If only she could.

The faint outlines of new figures gathered a few yards off; behind them, a strange contraption was suspended in the air over the cavernous shaft. A few more steps, and the torchlight revealed better details. The figures were clearly in league with Rejiett. They donned black attire rather than the pristine white robes of the templites, but after what Jalice had witnessed in the Grand Hall, that meant nothing. They held glass wands; that was enough to determine who they served.

Perhaps the templites here were all twisters. It had all been a ruse.

Beside these figures was a capstan, coiled with a rope that, at its end, spanned the vast canyon. Running alongside the outstretched end of the rope was a wooden bridge that led to a square platform, above which the rope that sprouted from the capstan was fed through thick boards.

A mechanism that would lower them down into the dark abyss.

Jalice wasn't sure if she should feel relieved at the discovery. It hinted that Rejiett didn't intend to cast them off to their deaths. But it meant descending farther into the cave, and further from salvation.

The priestess exchanged no words with the hooded figures, but one of them extended an arm out to bestow her with strange looking gifts. Rejiett took these and resumed her march onto the wooden bridge. Jalice and

Ophim followed with no other choice. Once they were all on the platform, Rejiett grew still and waited alongside her captives. Jalice couldn't watch from the vantage point where Rejiett's aether had placed her and Ophim, but she heard the grinding of mechanisms that snaked the rope over their heads through the boards that hosted it. The platform jolted. Rejiett stood poised and unfazed. If not for the aether keeping them frozen in place, Jalice imagined she and Ophim would not have remained as steady.

The descent began. Slowly the platform edged down into the darkness, with Rejiett's torch offering meager insight into the passage below. A brief vibration swept over Jalice, and her muscles atrophied. Now released from Rejiett's aether cage, she collapsed onto the boards. An anguished groan broke from her lips, and she heard Ophim unleashing his own series of pained noises beside her. Boots thudded on the wood nearby, and Jalice startled to find the priestess looming over her. Rejiett crouched down, wrestling against Jalice's subsequent struggles.

"Hold still," the priestess snapped. She forced a rubbery mask across Jalice's mouth before wrapping a strap around the back of her head. When it snapped into place, Rejiett stood and backed away.

Jalice clawed at the constraining mask as she struggled to breath. Air filtered into her lungs through the mouthpiece, and her exhales pressed out of it with a low, garbled sound. Her hands trembled as she ran them along the strange item that muzzled her.

"It's a ventilator," Rejiett said as she watched Jalice panic. "You need it for where we're going. Without it, you die. Stop fighting it, and relax."

The priestess turned and approached Ophim. He tried to maneuver away, but the immense pain from his unattended kykaleech wounds, along with the muscle cramping from Rejiett's merciless aether ward, had him clumsy and uncoordinated. Rejiett forced the mask piece over his mouth with the same ease as she had with Jalice. The clannite flailed weak arms and tried to rip the piece off, which quickly ended with him collapsed on his back and breathing heavily.

Jalice stared at Ophim, catching his gaze when he rolled his head over to reveal a set of wide eyes swimming with panic. His whole body shook in the frigid chill permeating the cave. She gifted him her best expression of calm to try to ease his nerves, and she saw what might have been a nod of gratitude in return.

The sole torch Rejiett had brought revealed very little of the chasm that swallowed them as they plunged further down. Sharp mysterious pipes and rods jutted from the walls like rigid snakes.

"This place is old," Ophim murmured with suppressed awe, his words coming out clipped due to the chill. A layer of crackles masked his voice, something Jalice figured to be an effect of the mouthpiece.

"Old is an understatement," said Rejiett, her voice crackling. Jalice glanced at the priestess to find she, too, wore a mask over her mouth. "This stretches back to the age before the Residuum. The templites who built the Temple with the mirajin must have thought it wise to maintain a way to access the forbidden artifacts in the ground. This shaft is a crude entryway. It cuts through much of the ceiling of the ancient structure we're soon to enter. I'm not sure why those ancestral templites decided to do it. Surely the mirajin would not have condoned any sort of possible connection to the forbidden tech from before the Last Great War. Regardless of those ancient intentions, the twisters have found it beyond useful."

As she spoke, the walls squeezing the platform suddenly broke away. A vast space overtook them. Positioned far too close to the edge for her liking, Jalice scrambled to a safer location towards the center of the platform.

"We've now entered the forsaken chasm of our ancestors," Rejiett announced.

"What exactly is it?" Ophim asked.

The priestess smirked. "The archives we've studied claim it was a factory—a place where machines were manufactured by machines."

"Machines?" Ophim inquired.

Rejiett's smile broadened. "A place where the miracles of the Mechanical Age were born. Our ancestors, those whom the tribes have shunned and redacted from the histories, created alternative lifeforms here made of tubes and metal chips—some no larger than the size of your pupil—that governed thought and perception."

"No one should be down here," Ophim said, eyeing the darkness around them as if expecting to glimpse some ghost of an era long deceased.

Rejiett wore an expression of admiration and triumph. "The twisters have reclaimed this place as their own. The secrets of our ancestors will be revealed in places such as this. We've unearthed some already. The age of regression is over."

"You're playing with fire," Ophim warned.

Rejiett let out an amused cry and regarded Ophim like a parent does a naive child. "As we always have, clannite. Templites are innovators, trained as we are with the gifts and skills of the aether Realms. But I don't expect someone like you to understand. Like so many of our contemporaries, you hold archaic beliefs force-fed to you by the mirajin."

"Do you mean to awaken every dokojin still in existence?" Ophim asked incredulously. "That's what our ancestors managed. Through their arrogance, they permitted the dokojin a means to infiltrate the Terrestrial Realm. It brought about the Last Great War. You'll obliterate human life if you persist in this ignorant reasoning."

Rejiett cocked an unconvinced eyebrow. "We have the wisdom of history on our side. We won't make the same mistakes our ancestors did."

"Every naive generation thinks that," Ophim stated. "*History outside of memory has a tendency to repeat.*"

"You spout regurgitations," Rejiett said with a tone of mockery. "The mirajin tainted our age with misdirects and lies. The history you think you know isn't accurate. Myself and the other templites refuse to live in subjugation to those corrupted accounts any longer."

Ophim said nothing more. He curled his body in to try to stop the shivers assaulting him and stared at Rejiett darkly for the remainder of the descent. Eventually the lift came to a stop, and the platform struck the ground with a thunderous boom. The torchlight refused to give light beyond a few yards in any one direction, but Jalice managed to glimpse smudged pieces of shattered glass and valueless rubbish littering the ground. A layer of dust stretched across everything in sight.

"You're about to observe relics of a glorious age now gone," Rejiett announced. "A museum of untapped potential for our generation."

Jalice and Ophim followed her reluctantly into the darkness. They lingered a few feet away from her to exchange hushed words before Rejiett could notice.

"Should we run?" Jalice asked.

Ophim gave a quick shake of his head. His teeth chattered as he spoke. "We have no light without her damn torch. We're leagues away from the surface, and I have no idea how to work the lift for that platform. We'd end up lost down here, and I don't think that's something we want."

"Then we're trapped."

"Until we know more about where we are or until we can obtain some sort of light source, we're at the mercy of the priestess."

In agreement over their predicament, the two fell into file with Rejiett, all the while glancing about at the occasional mysteries the torchlight revealed. For the first hundred or so yards, the darkness conceded very little. It wasn't until a giant wall appeared that their surroundings took on more distinction. Rejiett led them into a hall that cut through the wall, and here the forbidden elements of a bygone age began to crop up.

As they passed by the massive glass windows of various rooms, Jalice gaped at what each space hosted. Giant tubes descended from ceilings. Flat, box-shaped objects with sheeny black surfaces lined the walls, sometimes accompanied by other unusual pipes and vats of thick liquid.

"The materials they used have long since expired," Rejiett explained, pointing to her mouthpiece. "Thus, we wear these for protection. The air isn't breathable otherwise."

"Aren't you worried you'll come across something here more dangerous than bad air?" Jalice asked, finally braving a conversation for which she felt she had no pertinent knowledge.

"You mean materials that prove explosive or fatal?" Rejiett clarified. "We've already lost our share to this place's unpredictable elements. But without loss, there would be no gain. Innovation and the mastery of nature come at a price."

"Have you awakened anything else?" Ophim challenged. "Any foes of old that you couldn't restrain?"

"You'd like to think us befuddled buffoons, but we have a lot more knowledge of the ancient mechanisms than you might think. Archival materials are easy to digest once a foundation of understanding is established."

Jalice glanced through a window into yet another room. Her muscles froze. The odd mouthpiece compressed her scream. She shot against the wall at her back and pointed towards the room. Ophim, who had been a few steps behind her, bounded forward to get a glimpse and froze as though caught in an archer's line of fire.

Rejiett came up beside them and chuckled. "Take a gander at that. What glorious creations our ancestors devised."

Behind the glass was a room similar to those they'd already passed. Vats and jars of spoiled fluid occupied one side of the room, while the other hosted an array of black glass-like surfaces in thin bezels. A thick metal pipe ran down from the ceiling.

It was what the metal pipe connected to that terrified Jalice.

A bulbous skull of massive proportions hung suspended from the pipe. Jalice figured it had to be at least as tall as herself, giving it mind-boggling dimensions that didn't match any living humanoid she had ever seen. Its jaw gaped open as if emitting an endless cackle of malicious origin. Empty eye sockets stared at the black screens it faced.

Jalice's heart raced in her chest. She feared that at any moment the skull would jerk its enormous head to direct its silent cackle at her.

"It's not organic," Rejiett said in a tone far too casual given the horrific sight. "Some of the material you see is certainly organic in composition, but this marvelous creation was not birthed by natural means. A machine built it, and as such, it is a machine itself. Notice the transparent portions along the cranium? Those are synthetic—that is, they're not natural."

"I don't understand," Jalice whimpered. "Why a skull if it isn't organic? Where is its body?"

"Those questions have answers that will only add to your confusion. I can already tell that what I've explained makes no sense in your limited minds. You can't comprehend the intentions behind this creation."

"This is what the dokojin hijacked," Ophim said, his voice shaking. "Our ancestors built these abominations, and then the dokojin possessed them. They gave these dead machines life with their auras."

Rejiett raised her hands and gave a slow, mocking round of claps. "Bravo, clannite. You're much smarter than I give you credit for. No need to fret though. We aren't foolish enough to keep building such machines as this. We don't want the dokojin unleashed any more than you do. But there is knowledge and machinery down here that is still worth utilizing."

Jalice rose up off the wall and brushed past Rejiett to escape the sight of the room. She stopped a few feet beyond it and shuddered. "Let's get on with this. I don't want to look anymore."

Rejiett glided past her to take the lead again. "Fine, then. Not a surprise that you have no appreciation for what this museum conserves."

"This isn't a museum," Ophim muttered. "It's a mausoleum of horrible decisions."

Eager to put some distance between her and the giant skull, Jalice followed Rejiett with rapid strides. Ophim swore under his breath as they walked past other discoveries, but Jalice kept her eyes glued on the ground in front of her.

The monsters of the past could remain buried down here. She didn't need to know their purpose.

She just needed to find a way to escape them.

CHAPTER 34

Aside from the scuffle of their boots, silence suffocated the abandoned chambers and corridors. Jalice couldn't shake the desolation that every dust particle emanated, from the unnatural tubes and vats to every forsaken corridor. She found it surreal at times. A place such as this existed in her mind only as a long-forgotten legend that she'd always believed a fiction. The Elders' oral histories recounted an era that could have hosted a factory that manufactured abominable things, but those retellings had always struck her as saturated with time's inevitable exaggerations.

Yet here she was, treading down hallways built over a millennium ago.

After miles of journeying, the trio came to a passage that glowed a sickly yellow. Jalice peered over Rejiett's shoulder as they walked, glimpsing the open chamber from which the light spilled forth. Rejiett stepped inside and out of the way, but Jalice and Ophim paused where the corridor ended, not yet willing to breach the entryway. Dozens of twisters stared back at them, robed in either the black cloaks associated with twisters or the white robes of templites. All of them wore the muzzle-like mouthpieces. Jalice, desperate to escape their haunting glares, studied the chamber's peculiar centerpiece.

The giant machine looked like a planet frozen in a timeless explosion. A shiver ran down her spine. Its materials looked far too similar in composition to the Black House. Sheets of black metal reflected the room's light, and a center core hung suspended in the air, supported by some of the long cylindrical pieces sprouting from it. Its size intimidated her, its pinnacle stretching several yards above her. Under any other circumstances, she might have regarded it as art and nothing more. But Ophim's reaction told her to be nervous.

"That's the same thing we found during the raid," he whispered.

Rejiett picked up on his hushed words and chuckled. "I suppose it's not much to tell you now, given your encroaching fate. It serves as a sort of perimeter for Spiracy's lair. We needed a way to translate a sufficient field of victims to Spiracy's dream Realm. So, we built a perimeter of sorts around the Temple. It's invisible to the naked eye, but it's marked by what we refer to as Fence Posts." She gestured to the machine before them. "These serve as anchor points, but they also vibrate at a very specific frequency—the same frequency at which Spiracy's dream exists. These Fence Posts create a sort of bubble by connecting with one another, and anyone within their perimeter is susceptible to entering Spiracy's Realm. Think of it like a trap, and of the Fence Posts as the outer edges of it."

"So, they create the dream?" Jalice asked. Her head hurt. This was too much to take in. "They're the reason I entered that nightmare with those dokojin?"

"Not quite." She pointed towards the center of the chamber. Easy to overlook even in front of the star-explosion piece, the smaller machine she indicated was still at least twelve feet tall. Emitting from it was a sound like heavy, labored breathing. The base looked like an oblong coffin made of a thick rubbery material, and from it, metal sheeting peeled upward. Yellow lights flickered and glowed across this metallic surface, and hundreds of thin tubes sprouted off of it to snake out in various directions across the room.

Yet Rejiett was likely indicating for them to look inside this structure. Because within it, a pale, veiny scalp peeked out from the rubber base, nearly lost in the mask wrapped tightly around the lower half of the face. The material encasing the individual was connected via tubes to a set of cylinders that pumped in rhythm with the aggressive gusts of air.

"Courageous, valiant Torrou has served us for many weeks now," Rejiett said, her tone mocking.

Ophim's face paled and his fragile facade of bravery slipped into horrified disgust.

"He dreams for us now," Rejiett said with a satisfied grin. "A dream that hosts Spiracy."

"That isn't Torrou," Ophim said, face quivering. He shook his head. "He went missing months ago. This can't be how . . ."

Jalice turned back to the husk of flesh strapped to the machinery, trying to picture someone other than the nearly dead man in front of her. "What did you do to him?" she asked quietly as she absorbed the nightmarish setup.

"It takes quite a toll on the body, sustaining an entire Realm for such a long period of time," Rejiett answered cryptically as she, too, looked down at the man trapped within the coffin. "Who better to brave the task than the most talented clannite amongst the warriors? Someone who'd shown untapped potential in the Apparition Realm? He was much like you, Ophim. His aura is unique and efficiently structured, and it permitted him abilities that few possess. Naturally, the perfect kind of aether for us to harness to fuel Spiracy's lair."

"What is it doing to him?" Ophim shouted, voice cracking as he glared at Rejiett with wide eyes. "Get it off him! Get him out!" He rushed at Rejiett only to be roughly stopped by a pair of twisters.

"Oh, we plan to," Rejiett stated with a hollow comfort in her voice. She looked at Ophim with pity. "But if we do, someone else has to take his place." She grinned darkly.

A heavy dread dropped in Jalice's stomach as she picked up on the implication. Ophim had gleaned Rejiett's meaning too; he bucked against the hands that restrained him, but this didn't stop the twisters from dragging him off into an adjacent room. Jalice yelled in protest and moved to follow, but another twister stepped into her path, and she abandoned her attempt. Ophim disappeared out of sight, his defiant shouts echoing until distantly closing doors muffled the sounds.

Jalice turned back to Rejiett. "This is why you took us? To feed us to this abomination?"

"We needed a replacement, yes," Rejiett answered. She cocked her head, eyes traveling up and down Jalice as if sizing her up. The others in the room bore the same bizarre fascination, and Jalice wished she could shrink away.

"What is it you're doing to Ophim? At least give me the mercy of knowing what fate awaits me."

Rejiett shook her head slowly. "No, you misunderstand. Ophim's fate is not the same as yours. We have other plans for you." As she spoke, an elderly man draped in dark robes came up beside her. Jalice noted that Rejiett's posture shifted some at his arrival, as if allocating some respect for the newcomer.

"The man you brought is wounded," the old man grumbled disapprovingly to Rejiett. "He's got punctures all across his back."

"He'll do just fine," Rejiett responded. "They're only kykaleech wounds. Besides, he's about to have a hole drilled into his head and tubes shoved into his skin. Those leech wounds are nothing of consequence."

"And what of Aruzz? I notice he does not accompany you."

Rejiett clenched her jaw, obviously irritated by the older man's tone. "There wasn't time to extract him. It was either him or the Tecalica, and our plans with Spiracy are far more important than Aruzz's comfort."

The old man pursed his lips but said nothing more on the topic. He turned his attention to Jalice, an eerie curiosity dripping in his words. "So, this is the troublemaker?"

Rejiett nodded. "The Tecalica of the Unified Tribes, no less."

"I have no quarrel with you," Jalice blurted, a glimmer of hope sparked by them knowing who she was. "Whatever this is, I'll stay out of your way. Just release me and Ophim."

"Ah, but you've already caused your share of trouble," the man stated. "We wouldn't have gone through all the inconveniences of extracting you from the Temple otherwise."

"I don't know what you're talking about," Jalice said, desperate to make them understand. "If this is about the pair of twisters whom I traveled with over the border, I had nothing to do with—"

Rejiett clicked her tongue. "Stop talking." She turned to her companion. "Papallas, what does the Orphan Coven advise?"

"I have not received further instruction from that coven since our last conversation. Iveer advised us to put the troublemaker back in with Spiracy to challenge our child. He believes Spiracy must overcome this obstacle if she is to become cunning enough to overthrow Dardajah."

Jalice bristled at the names thrown about. Spiracy. Dardajah. The elderly man spoke them with such casual indifference, yet she knew better. Those names represented power. Horror. Death. Her eyes darted wildly between Rejiett and the decrepit old man.

"How do we put her back in?" the priestess asked.

"I'll send someone into the lair to tell Spiracy our plan," said Papallas. "She'll come for the Tecalica like she did last time. Our child is getting stronger. She can project herself to ensnare new victims."

"Wait," Jalice interjected. "You speak of the dokojin that tormented me. This Spiracy. I want nothing to do with that. I won't go back there."

"You nearly undid our laborious months of planning," Papallas said with a frown. "Care to explain the power you wielded while visiting our precious child?"

Jalice shook her head. "I don't even remember most of it. It's like a nightmare that has faded into the void. But whatever you think I did, you're mistaken. I possess no special power or skill. I barely escaped from that place—from that thing."

The two twisters stared at her, unconvinced. "We'll uncover your secrets soon enough," Papallas murmured darkly. "Spiracy will find a way around your tricks in time for her birth into our world. She and her spawn will usher in a new era for those of us who wield aether."

The cryptic threats, filled with nonsensical accusations and declarations, pressed in around Jalice. "I won't go back."

A thin, demeaning smile creased the man's lips. "I'm afraid you have no say in the matter, Tecalica."

Commotion from another part of the room stole their attention. Ophim stumbled in, his head hanging limp and his muscled arms swinging loosely with his awkward movements. The same pair of twisters that had dragged him off now assisted him as if he were a drunkard unable to support himself. As they led him towards the strange coffin-like contraption, Jalice saw Ophim's back.

In addition to the kykaleech wounds, a trail of blood now stained his neck. It had streaked from a large hole drilled into the back of his head. A socket of metal plugged this new aperture, sealing off any further blood from leaking out, but the damage done was obvious.

"What did you do to him?" Jalice asked, but she received no answer.

One of the twisters bent down and retrieved a loose wire near where Torrou's head lay. The wire was brought to the socket in Ophim's skull, and it clicked into place. Ophim went rigid, then fell entirely limp into the embrace of the other twister.

Jalice shrieked. "What have you done?"

Still no one answered her. She thought of running up to Ophim but knew that nothing would come of it. She couldn't stop an entire coven.

A few of the twisters near the machinery began fiddling with knobs and levers. The pristine metal hissed in compliance, and the rubber encasement that cocooned Torrou released with a sucking sound like a squid's tentacle unbinding from an object. The shell's lid hinged open, revealing the rest of Torrou's body.

Jalice inhaled, lifting a trembling hand to her face as she fought back tears at the sight. What little skin the man retained now clutched to bone with greedy desperation. Veins pressed up like mountains, and sickly splotches dotted the body. It reminded her of the bodies in the Whispering Room, but severely progressed.

After ripping long, red tubes free of the man's body with sickening pops, the twisters lifted the corpse out. Jalice resisted the urge to hurl at the shriveled body they held, and instead watched as Ophim was placed inside the open coffin in a position identical to how Torrou had lain. They gripped the dangling red tubes and pressed them against various spots of his body, releasing them only after a clipped noise indicated their talons had sunk into his skin. The rubbery shell descended with a smooth groan, and once lowered, the twisters fitted it around Ophim's frame. A few other levers were pulled. Air hissed, and the rubber shrank up against Ophim in a tight embrace. The thrumming air compressors resumed their rhythmic pace.

"Transition of hosts complete," one of the attending twisters stated. "The expired host can now be detached."

Those holding the shriveled body of Torrou disconnected the wire still attached to the back of his skull. Unlike with Ophim, Jalice didn't see any change occur—the man appeared as dead now as he had before the wire's detachment.

In the coffin, Ophim's face appeared serene, showing no hint of pain. She tried to take solace in this. Maybe he was in blissful ignorance of the surgery the twisters had performed on him. Maybe he felt nothing and simply slept. She hoped these possibilities were true.

"He's the last to be so honored," Papallas said, looking down at Ophim with empty apathy. "Spiracy's time is nigh."

"Please let him go," Jalice said, voice hushed and trembling. She gaped in horror as the machine squeezed out air and held Ophim like a snake coiled around its prey. She opened her mouth to plead again, but this time failed to muster the resolve to speak.

Rejiett and Papallas turned to her, and she suddenly wished she hadn't commanded their attention.

"Now it is your turn to serve us, Tecalica," Papallas said. "And like your friend, it is time for you to sleep."

CHAPTER 35

The smell of burnt flesh traveled with the mountain wind.

Annilasia stood several yards away from the massive pile of corpses, but this did nothing to mitigate the overpowering aroma burrowing inside her nostrils—a smell she knew she should despise, but rather enjoyed. Still, she wanted to watch. She wasn't sure if this was a side effect of Inzerious's influence over her, or if she just truly hated the mentors that much. Probably a little of both. She couldn't place all the blame on Inzerious; the dokojin was caged. No, more than likely, this was a festering rage and resentment she'd brewed on her own.

Either way, she reveled in the way the blood sizzled in the flames, the way the innards and flesh bubbled from the heat. She wished she could watch their faces melting in the fire, but the heads of these corpses still floated inside that mysterious cave she'd discovered weeks ago.

The bonfire was rewarding enough though. That, and her pillaging of the bodies. It was a fair trade. She'd had to drag their old asses up those damn stairs and out of the cave, and with a limp. That had been no easy task. Drifter had offered to help, but she'd seen in his eyes that he wanted nothing to do with the bodies. Perhaps he still feared that any involvement in their deaths would come back to haunt him.

Fine by her. Made it easier to pocket her findings without him wanting in on the treasures. Most of the mentors had carried nothing of value. A few shiny rings that she could sell at some point. Vials of blood that likely belonged to unfortunate individuals indebted to the mentors in some fashion. A few odd trinkets that had purposes she couldn't guess.

Her greatest find, however, was the card in Iveer's cloak.

It was exactly like the one she'd found in Korcsha's book all those months ago. At the time, she'd not understood what kind of power such an item held, and had wasted it at Inzerious's prodding. She wouldn't make that mistake again.

For there were only a handful of such cards in existence.

Her time with Iveer had hinted at that—and at their worth. On top of his irritation that Korcsha's book had missing pages, he had raged over the missing card that should have been tucked within it. He'd interrogated her for days, sure that she knew exactly what had become of the precious item. By some miracle, she'd managed to sway him into believing that she truly knew nothing of the card or why the book had been tampered with.

Ever since, her curiosity had been piqued over the card's importance. Scouring the coven library revealed very little about it, and finding ways to broach the topic with Iveer proved futile. He either got enraged again over the misplaced card or grew quiet. Perhaps because he hadn't wanted her to know that he, in fact, was in possession of an identical card.

Annilasia retrieved it from her pocket now and studied it. No, it wasn't identical. Just similar. It had smudges, the corners were frayed or bent, and ink splotches dominated its surface. But the whispers—those were different. So were the shapes the ink formed as she stared at it.

She tore her gaze from the card and shoved it back into her cloak's pocket. The whispers faded. A sick feeling swam in her stomach. The last card she'd utilized had obliterated everything in its wake. She had no idea if this one would do the same—or something entirely different.

What she knew without a doubt was that the card was powerful, and if she stared at the moving ink too long, she might bend to the will of its insidious whispers. For now, she'd keep the card secret and safe. Someone else had to know of its purpose or origin, and she intended to find those answers.

Her stomach churned. The burnt flesh no longer pleased her.

Annilasia turned from the bonfire and tracked through the snow back towards the coven. It wasn't only dead bodies that she could plunder.

There was an entire coven to be raided.

***

As Drifter attended to their mysterious companion, who had managed only to croak out indiscernible utterings, Annilasia spent her days reading anything and everything pertaining to mirajin, dokojin, and lifechains. Despite Iveer's claims that the library sourced answers, her search for a solution to severing Inzerious had proven arduous. The twisters' collection was less concerned with mirajin, who were referred to in derogatory ways, and more invested in darker topics like dokojin, which were viewed alternately as pesky nuisances or revered entities worthy of praise.

Lifechains and lifestones in general didn't come up very often. The twister knowledge affirmed that lifechains could extend to include objects and entities that were bound to the aura through aether, which explained how Inzerious was tied to her. She'd inadvertently invited the parasite to share her body, a tie represented by the extra chain attached to her lifechain.

But there was nothing on altering a lifechain. Perhaps because there wasn't a way to break them.

When she came across works written during the peak of the Residuum era, she took greater time to review those. One particular passage caught her attention due to its reference of mirajin. It read as such:

The celestial mirajin sing in a foreign and befuddling tongue. When asked what music they were partaking in, they explained the Music came from a greater Realm, where humans only go once they've discarded their emotions in the Apparition. When pressed about this Realm, the mirajin eyed us with open suspicion and said nothing more of it.

Music. It tickled her memories until she summoned one of Elothel—that damn coward of a mirajin—mentioning how fae missed some star-blazing Music from the Ethereal Realm. With this new keyword at her disposal, she gathered a new pile of books that might possibly broach the topic. As she'd come to expect, all but one ended up useless.

But in that one book, she found an intriguing entry.

The Music of the Spheres
Not much is known of the mysterious music that mirajin claim hails from the Ethereal Realm. They mention it in passing, as if in casual acknowledgement of

some new color or sound that exists in a higher vibrational Realm. Yet when we inquire further, out of innocent curiosity, the mirajin's lips seal tight, and they cling to this aforementioned Music as a starving critter does to a feast. What little has been learned has been collected here, and constitutes so brief a section of this tome that it is as a drop of water in an ocean, easily overlooked and deemed unimportant in comparison to the better cultivated topics.

The Music is a constant in the Ethereal Realm. Whereas music in the Terrestrial Realm begins with rhythmic and recurring noises being melded into a coherent string of pleasant sounds, and then ends with the cessation of these produced noises, the Music of the Spheres accompanies the ongoing existence of those within the Ethereal. It never ends, and that is because of its attributed source.

Like some things that translate from one Realm to another—changing state but not quite losing their definition of existence—so too do the celestial bodies that drift through the void. Planets, star-streaks, moons—these things exist from one Realm to the next, in one form or another. Evidently, their presence, or rather their churn and spin in the Ethereal, produces this Music. It is the result of their movement against the aether energy within the Ethereal that is the passion of the mirajin.

Sadly, as mentioned, this is as little as we know. In summary, the celestial bodies exist in the other Realms, their movement through aether produces Music, and the mirajin hold it in such high esteem that they refuse to divulge its secrets further.

A few more days passed. She pondered the passage, all the while battling a mounting anxiety over Inzerious's impending escape from its cage. It was while entrenched in this quest, head bent over an open book and eyes absorbing more knowledge than would prove useful, that Drifter approached and startled her with his voice.

"You look horrible."

Annilasia glared up at him, but he only returned it with an incredulous expression.

"Don't pretend you're okay," he said. "Something obviously isn't right with you. You look almost as malnourished and pasty as our friend from the mystery machine."

"Why are you here?" she demanded.

"She can speak now."

Annilasia's eyes narrowed. "She?"

"Our patient. The sleeper you liberated. She wants to talk to you."

***

During the previous few days at the coven, Annilasia had not seen much of Drifter. Or rather, Drifter hadn't seen much of her. While she was locked away in the library, he'd spent his time attending to the aged individual they'd rescued from the mentor's machine. Aside from a few passing exchanges, the only time she'd taken care to observe his comings and goings was when he spent one evening gathering the bodies of the pupils to cremate them. She hadn't offered to assist. Her mind was bogged down by other troubles. But she'd watched him nonetheless in an absent-minded manner as he dragged the corpses away into the forest.

Even now, as he led her to his private quarters in one of the coven huts that occupied the pineoaks, her thoughts continued to return to her dilemma. Eager to give her mind a moment's rest from obsessing over Inzerious, she welcomed the distraction of Drifter's chatter.

"There's something you should know about our new companion," Drifter said over his shoulder as he led them up the stairs that spiraled up the tree. "When she first managed to convey words—albeit scratchy and rudimentary—she made it clear that she didn't find light comfortable."

"What exactly does that mean?"

"I guess light hurts her eyes."

"Wait. Is she blind?"

There was a pause before Drifter answered. They'd reached the door to his hut in the trees, and he turned to her. "I think it's best if you let her explain. She sees things, but . . . they're not what we see."

"That's beyond cryptic."

"Just ask her yourself. I'm not good at explaining it. Another thing: she's not exactly energetic or mirthful. She's understandably very tired. Her time hooked up to the device has not been kind to her. Keep that in mind." He opened the door and disappeared inside, where darkness reigned. The windows were covered with sheets that blocked all light from seeping in. A lone candle was lit and sitting on the dresser.

Annilasia entered with a wary gait, closing the door behind her without taking her eyes away from the figure huddled in the corner on Drifter's bed. A wrinkled face peeked out from a swaddle of blankets, then two spindly hands curled out from the cloth to pull the protective barrier tighter.

"Annilasia, this is Evlicka," said Drifter. "Evlicka, this is the person who found you down in the cave. She woke you up from your sleep."

A pair of milky eyes stared at Annilasia, and from their lack of movement, she deduced that her initial guess had been right. The old woman was blind. She cleared her throat to properly announce her presence. "Stars' blessing upon you," said Annilasia. "I hope my companion here has taken kind care of you."

Evlicka did not respond. She simply stared in Annilasia's direction.

"Maybe that's her way of saying you didn't," she muttered to Drifter.

"You did not come alone, Bloodspill."

Annilasia stiffened and sharpened her gaze on the woman. "What did you just call me?"

"That's its nickname for you, isn't it?" asked Evlicka. Her voice croaked, and phlegm garbled her words. "The parasite that's latched onto you."

Drifter turned to Annilasia, alarmed and confused. "What is she talking about?"

"No doubt she's still a bit delirious from her time in that horrid machine," Annilasia murmured. Her heart pounded in her chest as she dared to address the stranger again. "Just be grateful I woke you from such a slumber."

Evlicka huffed. A tired, disgruntled expression tugged at the meager amount of face exposed by the blankets. "Perhaps I am. Such a nightmare can do horrible things to the mind. Maybe the entity I see is lingering residue from my nightmare." She paused in consideration of this. "But I doubt that. I can hear the fear in your voice. You know to what I refer."

Drifter glanced between the two, still perplexed by the conversation. Annilasia turned to walk towards the door but halted when Evlicka spoke once more.

"Its cage is nearly gone. You have days. Not months, not weeks. Days."

Annilasia turned back around, eyes wide in disbelief at how this complete stranger knew her darkest secret.

"I can see it," Evlicka explained. "It haunts your presence. A horrifying knot of black ichor and bone. Its eyes never blink. It's seen terror, and it's caused terror. It consumes the fear it provokes out of unfortunate souls."

"Is she talking about a *dokojin*?" Drifter exclaimed. He backed away from Annilasia towards the opposite corner of the room. "Dying stars, you've got a *dokojin* attached to you?"

"I've got a plan for it," Annilasia hissed, unsure if she was trying to convince them or herself. "It won't be with me for much longer."

"You can't get rid of a dokojin," said Drifter. "Once they've latched on, they're there to stay."

"A mirajin can break the lifechain that connects me to it," said Annilasia. She looked between Drifter and Evlicka, wishing she sounded more confident, and somewhat hoping one of them would affirm her outlandish idea. "I know a mirajin would never aid a twister, so that's why I've got to trick one into helping me."

"You can't trick a mirajin," Evlicka croaked. "But you *can* trap one."

"That sounds just as impossible," said Drifter. "And where in the endless universe are you going to find one of those in time? Evlicka just said you have days left." His eyes narrowed as he realized he had no idea what the countdown even referred to. "Days until what exactly?"

"Days until it ends her," said Evlicka. Her milky eyes remained fixed on something just over Annilasia's shoulder. "You said you had a plan. But all I've heard is an idea."

Heat swarmed Annilasia's cheeks. "Sounds like all I need to do is trap a mirajin. I think I know what might entice one to me." She paused and summoned the courage to voice yet another flimsy idea. "They're attracted to the Music of the Spheres. I could utilize that to lure one."

Drifter scowled at her, clearly unconvinced. Evlicka offered a grin, meager and timid but full of appreciation for Annilasia's bold statement.

"How in blinding stars are you going to conjure *that*?" demanded Drifter.

"I just need more time to figure that part out," Annilasia stammered. "From what I gather, the Celestial Drift in the Ethereal Realm creates the Music."

"Yet another impossible element of your plan," Drifter sneered. "I don't see how you're going to reach the Ethereal Realm, much less find a mirajin to trap once there. That's not even taking into account that you'd be dragging your dokojin with you, and that alone will tip off any mirajin to your trap."

Annilasia balled her hands into fists and glared at him. "You got a better idea?"

"No, and that doesn't matter," said Drifter. "It's not my problem."

The words struck her harder than she'd thought possible. Her fists unclenched as a wave of despair pummeled her. She tried to summon anger, to feel even an ounce of irritation at his pessimism, but the sheer magnitude of her dilemma drowned out her rage.

He's right. It isn't their star-blazing problem. It's mine.

And it was a problem she still had very few ideas about how to solve. A problem that would end in blood for her if she couldn't figure it out.

"Maybe it's not your problem," Evlicka said to Drifter. "But I'm going to make it mine." She coughed into the sheets, phlegm splattering out, and cleared her throat before speaking again. "You saved me, after all. The very least I can do is try to save you in return. I've not got much to offer. My body is withered, and my mind has melted away during my time in captivity. But perhaps—"

"I didn't ask for your help," Annilasia interjected. She crossed her arms, trying to regain a composure of power. They—or at least Drifter—didn't need to see her as weak. "Besides, you heard him. It's a rather impossible quest."

Another coughing fit seized Evlicka. She smacked her lips in its aftermath. "You're feisty. I like that." She inhaled and then exhaled, which came out scratchy and sputtering. "Music of the Spheres, you say? I know a little of that. My mother was a priestess, and she passed on her knowledge to me and my siblings. From what I recall, the Music is indeed created by the Celestial Drift. As the planets, the stars, and the comets pass through aether, it creates a melodious sound. I don't think any human alive has heard it, but the mirajin are somewhat obsessed."

Annilasia sighed. "My understanding is that only the deceased who have spent ample time in the Apparition Realm can pass into the Ethereal."

Evlicka nodded, sheets rustling with the movement. "That is accurate."

Silence fell over them. Annilasia shifted her weight from one leg to the next, and as time slipped by, the hope that Evlicka had ignited faded.

"Couldn't you make a model of it?" asked Drifter. He shrugged under the scrutinizing gaze of Annilasia. "I don't know much about what you two have mentioned. I was a pupil learning medicinal alchemy after all. But I was just now reminded of a childhood memory. I made a small-scale model of our village from sticks and stones, then built a small moat in the dirt to mimic the water. I speared tiny bits of paper on twigs for trees, and when I blew on them, they really sounded like leaves rustling in the wind. Maybe you could do the same here. If the planets and stars moving in aether makes the sound, maybe we could recreate that sound with a model." He grew quiet, shrugging his shoulders. "Or maybe that's just nonsense. The connection there is fragile at best."

A brief moment of quiet followed, in which Annilasia frowned and struggled to take his idea seriously. "How absurd," she finally muttered.

"Brilliant," Evlicka countered in the same moment.

Annilasia snorted. "You think a mirajin is going to be fooled by a crude mimicry of their beloved Music?"

"It's better than nothing."

"I don't know enough about the heavens to make a model of them," said Annilasia.

Evlicka's expression brightened a little, though it still wasn't free of the heaviness that tugged on the wrinkles around her eyes. "No, but you're either forgetting something or you don't know it exists. There's a planetarium here. You could use it to create the model."

"What the hell are we going to use for material? The model has to translate to the Apparition Realm, where I'll go to lure the mirajin. The only thing I know of that translates from here to there is—"

"Glass," they all said together.

Annilasia shut her eyes and tried to absorb the new plan. It seemed absurd and outlandish, a fool's attempt at something beyond their comprehension. But she was on borrowed time. It was this, or head off to the Decayer device with the earnest and shallow hope that the Sachem did not turn it on before she could stop him.

The odds were not in her favor. Then again, she realized, they never were.

Annilasia let out a protracted sigh and opened her eyes. "So, where is this planetarium?"

"Mentor Drenciophous was secretive about it," Evlicka stated. "Only his pupils were permitted access. I suppose all the mentors were like that with their areas of expertise. It's a blessing of the stars I happened to be one of those pupils."

Drifter and Annilasia struggled to respond, both staring at Evlicka in confusion.

"You studied under Drenciophous?" Drifter asked, clearly skeptical over the claim. "But you must be twice his age, and he was an old croak."

Evlicka nodded slowly. The tiredness intensified in the small patch of face exposed to them, and she swallowed heavily. "I am far younger than I appear. My time in that exaggerated sleep was not kind to me."

The statement lurched Annilasia back to questioning the whole reason for the obelisk and its coffin. "We haven't even talked about any of that."

Evlicka lifted a thin, reedy hand from out of the blankets. "Another time. To be honest, I'm grateful for the distraction. About time someone else's nightmares became my focus. I've spent too much time in mine." She pulled the blankets around her and closed her eyes for a moment. "Forgive me, but my mind is not what it once was. This conversation has worn me down. I will tell you how to get to the planetarium, but I can't join you. It seems sleep and rest still demand my time."

Annilasia nodded. "I owe you a great debt for your aid."

Evlicka nodded slowly. "I think the debt is paid on both ends. You awoke me from a prison. I only hope I can somehow help you escape the fate that your dokojin intends for you."

CHAPTER 36

The planetarium, it turned out, was to be found in yet another cavernous chamber within the mountainside. Annilasia was convinced by this point that the mountain was hollow. With the number of caverns that the coven evidently utilized, she wondered why the mentors even bothered with the measly huts they'd constructed in the trees. Maybe it'd been in an effort to remain exposed to the sun—a weak theory considering the mountains rarely seemed to escape the clouds that clogged the sky. Perhaps, then, it was a ruse in case anyone ever discovered their whereabouts.

"How is it she could see the dokojin with me?" Annilasia asked Drifter as they trudged through the snow up the mountainside. "I can only see it when translated, and the only reason Iveer ever could when translated was because he learned how to vibrate at the specific frequency of my aura."

"I don't know much more than you. She was more talkative with you around. She must like you." Drifter looked at her over his shoulder. "Can't understand why that would be the case." He turned back and resumed marching up the incline towards their destination. "If I were to guess, I'd say her mind was subjected to vibrations at a more intense frequency than what exists here in the physical world. I don't know how long she was in there, but it must have been quite a while for her to have lost her eyesight. Now her senses are attuned to vibrations that are typically attributed to the aether Realms."

"Did she know anything about the machine? Why it's here? Why she was sleeping in it?"

Drifter shook his head. "If she does, she hasn't said anything. I imagine she'll explain in her own time."

The two came up on an area where the terrain flattened into a meadow-like area. Carved into the mountainside was the gaping cave entrance, just as

Evlicka had claimed. The mountain wind howled, lifting snow off the ground to batter them.

"Do you trust her?" asked Annilasia.

Drifter turned and shot her a confused look. "Why wouldn't I?"

"Well, twisters aren't typically known for their honesty or trustworthiness. She could be leading us into a trap."

"Do you distrust me then?" he asked.

Annilasia rolled her eyes. "Don't pretend. We both have a healthy wariness of the other. I think it should be extended towards Evlicka too. We know her less than we know each other, which isn't saying a lot, but still . . ."

Drifter was quiet, and she realized he was mulling over something. Before she could inquire, he raised his eyes to hers, his expression now solemn, and spoke.

"We're not all imbeciles, Annilasia. I'm not so hard-headed not to objectively realize that twisters are some of the most selfish, maniacal individuals that infest the tribes. But not all of us came to this life with sinister schemes." His eyes flickered away, and he stammered over his next words. "I—How do I—" He sighed, closed his eyes, then opened them and looked at her again. "I'll just say this. I trust you. I know that sounds insane, and maybe I am. But I got this feeling over time, as I watched you among our peers, that you weren't like the rest of them. Something troubled you. At the time, I didn't realize it was a star-blazing dokojin, but that revelation doesn't change what I saw. You'd been through far more shite than the rest of us, and trust me, I've been through a lifetime of trauma. I think it's made you distrustful of others, perhaps rightfully so. But if I may offer some advice: you can't go through life never trusting anyone. You'll die alone and lonely if you do."

Annilasia scowled at him. "Quite a speech from someone who knows nothing about me. Maybe we do have to trust each other right now. But don't act like we're in some sort of blood-bound pact of friendship. For all I know, you're a mass murderer with his own schemes to take over the tribes. For all you know of me, I'm planning the same. You won't survive much longer if you're as trusting as you are with someone like me. You shouldn't trust Evlicka either. She may look old and weak, but looks are deceiving."

Drifter clenched his jaw. "Say what you will, but you trust me, even if it's just a little. You wouldn't have come to me for help with Evlicka if you didn't. Maybe it's because, unlike anyone else here, I offered you help in tiny ways. When the others would leave you behind, mocking you for your limp, I'd remain behind. Sometimes I didn't even approach because I knew you'd snap my head off. I'd just linger, making sure you didn't come across trouble. I imagine you never noticed this. You were too wrapped up in your own issues—your dokojin dilemma, no doubt. That's fine. But deep down, some part of you recognized my presence over the months here at the coven. A part of you knew that I wasn't like the others either. I'm different. I'm not a twister because I want to hurt others. I'm a twister because I didn't have a choice. My best guess is that the same can be said of you."

Annilasia bit her tongue. This was immense vulnerability that Drifter was showing her, but she didn't have time for this. Regardless of what he spouted, they hardly knew each other. "What a load of shite. I'm not going to fetch you a friendship feather, if that's what you're hoping for. And stop comparing me to you. I'm not a twister. I'm here to learn aether, but not to abuse it like you would. I don't go around hurting people—" As soon as she said this, she thought of the decapitated mentors. Heat bloomed in her face, and she gritted her teeth before putting an end to this absurd conversation. "Enough. Just stay alert when we get in there. Evlicka strikes me as a conniving wench."

Drifter sighed heavily, an indication he would submit to Annilasia's aversion to any honest response to his confession. "If we die, we die."

"Easy for you to say," Annilasia muttered. "You don't have a dokojin waiting for you in the next Realm." She strode forward, bracing against her limp, to brave the darkness ahead, and Drifter followed without protest. The air was chilled inside, and the tunnel was vacant of flame or light aside from the torch that Drifter had brought, which he'd lit once they were out of the wind's domain.

Evlicka had relayed specific directions on how to reach the summit housing the cave, as well as the path to take within the cavern. To Annilasia's surprise, the instructions proved accurate. A part of her had suspected that the frail woman's weary disposition was a ruse so she could act on a smoldering grudge. Had it been herself awakening from that coffin, Annilasia would likely have been homicidal to find her eyesight altered and her body so cruelly aged.

The chamber they found was nowhere near as vast as the one in which Evlicka had woken in. By means of the meager torchlight, Annilasia could make out a smooth dome ceiling above them. She saw no drawings or tapestries that would indicate the chamber's purpose as a planetarium, but Evlicka had prepared them for its drab appearance.

Drifter placed the torch in a sconce fastened to the wall before making his way to the lone shelf carved into the cave wall. Along the shelf were various objects, many of them metallic cylinders. Evlicka had explained that they would need the cylinder on the far left—the first in a sequence. Drifter retrieved this, stumbling under its unexpected weight, and then strode over to a podium that stood on the outskirts of the chamber. He heaved the cylinder up, all the while muttering about its weight, and shoved it into the empty socket bored into the highest edge of the podium. The cylinder slid in, then a burst of bright rays erupted. Shrapnel of light sprayed across the chamber's empty space before settling into a precise arrangement of orbs and rings that initiated a slow orbit through the air.

Annilasia stared in awe at it. "It's the cosmos."

"All of it?" Drifter asked skeptically. "Forgive my ignorance, but there doesn't seem enough here to equate to the stars I see overhead each night."

"That was only the first cylinder in the sequence." Annilasia gestured towards the other cylinders lining the shelf. "Those others probably display other portions. She told us to run a palm across that piece there." She pointed to a hemisphere jutting up from the tabletop portion of the podium, right beneath where the cylinder's bottom stuck out from its socket in the top edge. Drifter dragged a hand across the piece, which moved beneath his touch like a ball slipping through water. As he did, the display of orbs and rings moved and reformed, shifting into new patterns and shapes.

"Where did they get this equipment?" Annilasia asked, marveling at the sea of information swimming in front of her, all being projected from one small cylinder. "This has to be pre-Residuum. Forbidden technology."

"*Ancient* technology," Drifter corrected her. "The mirajin called it forbidden. It's best not to repeat their manipulative labels." He took a step back to observe the podium's structure. "Seems unlikely it was just sitting here, ready for use. The mentors somehow restored the tech. Or rebuilt it. It's not impossible to reverse-build machinery."

"I wonder why they kept this place so secret. I've been here for months and knew nothing of its presence."

Drifter shrugged. "It's normal to hoard knowledge. Knowledge lends power, but the more it's lent out, the more diluted that power becomes."

They grew quiet as they beheld the rays of light. Annilasia's kin, the Vekuuv, had valued the stars. Supposedly, the Celestial Drift held secrets to the mysteries of life itself. But the need for survival had torn that academia away from them. There wasn't time to study the night sky when the day was full of cruelty and enslavement. Annilasia had been among those too busy trying to stay alive to bask in the glorious expanse that revealed itself at night. Maybe someday, when the world was pure and at peace again, she'd take up the pastime.

"I'm not sure how far the glass will spread," Annilasia said. She saw Drifter's confused look. "I stashed away the mentors' wands. That'll serve as a source for creating the solar model. But it's obviously not an infinite source. I have no idea how large the model needs to be to produce a sound that even remotely mimics true Music, nor do I know if the glass on hand will be enough to accomplish that." She let out a heavy, exasperated sigh. "But I'm out of options, and I'm out of time. I'll just take a guess and go from there."

"Molding glass is outside my skill set," Drifter stated. "But the good news is that there's a kiln on the coven grounds."

Annilasia was quiet for a moment, summoning enough humility to override her pride. "What would be your price for helping me?"

Drifter cocked an eyebrow. "A trade, eh? You know it's not going to come cheap; we're twisters after all. Such conniving bastards . . ."

Annilasia groaned. "Just get on with it. What's the price?"

"The card in your pocket."

Annilasia's heart skipped. She licked her lips, trying but failing to wipe away the shock that had sprung across her face. "What card?"

"Don't. You asked for a price. I'm giving it. I want the card."

She gritted her teeth, wracking her mind for a way to play the situation off. "What's a bent up, smudged piece of paper mean to you?"

Drifter didn't answer. He stared at her. Waiting.

A growl crawled from her lungs to burn in her throat. "Fine. You get the card."

He nodded in satisfaction. "I don't see a need for an aether binding. If you fail to deliver, I'll just sabotage your efforts."

"You'd loose a dokojin on me for not handing over a damn card?"

"We both know it's not just any card. And yes, I would. You'd expect nothing less of me evidently. Can't trust a twister, so I guess I'd better play the part."

She bared her teeth at him. "Then you're proving me right."

"Says the woman who's a twister herself."

Annilasia marched towards the exit to the chamber, ignoring the bait of another argument. "Time is slipping out of my favor. Let's get the glass and make the model. I'll be lucky if I make it to the end of the week."

She wasn't lying. Thoughts of mutilation—of carving up Drifter into tiny pieces until he was nothing but grub for the birds and critters to eat—had hounded her throughout their conversation. She despised Drifter's deal, but she didn't hate him enough to truly wish that end for him. At least not yet.

No. This was Inzerious, slithering into her thoughts and desires.

The dokojin was nearly free.

CHAPTER 37

Kerothan gripped his sword, positioning it behind the bulk of himself to hide the glow of the blade. Aether swarmed inside it, collected during the massacre in the Grand Hall. It would be easy to spot in the darkness of the cave. He looked over at the other side of the pathway that cut through the stalagmites, where Cephus stood with a knife to Aruzz's neck. The clanhead gave him an assured nod; they could initiate their attack.

Beyond them, the path ended at a clear area that preceded a sharp drop-off. Stretching over the abyss was a wooden bridge, with two hooded figures posted on either side of it. Kerothan had spotted them a few paces ago, spurning him and Cephus to seek cover while Aruzz giggled like a deranged child. Only when Cephus had promptly retrieved a knife and threatened Aruzz with it had the twister gone quiet. A pasty grin still wrinkled his face though.

Kerothan flexed his fingers around the hilt of his weapon. He pushed away the fear that kept trying to worm its way past his courage, trying not to dwell on the fact that his blade held more aether than he liked. It could absorb a bit more, but its brightness indicated that it would reach its capacity sooner rather than later. If the hooded figures turned out to be twisters as he suspected, he'd be vulnerable to their aether assaults.

Reaching a point of numbness over these worries, he took the opportunity and rushed out from behind the massive sheet of flowstone that had served as his hiding spot. He swallowed down the cry that wanted to break free in a release of anxiety and tension. Sometimes in battle it worked as a startle tactic. But for this attack, he needed the element of surprise.

The twisters were ready. Wands slipped out from their sleeves into gloved hands. Their arms curled in fluid movements. The wands swelled with light, and ripples of translucent energy raced from their glass tips. He pivoted as the aether drove at him, and used the momentum to lunge forward and swing his sword. The blade gained speed, and as he finished the twirl, it sliced clean through the first twister's neck. The head bubbled as it fell to the ground, where it splattered like a rotten melon. The decapitated body collapsed. Neck and shoulders melted away into pools of disintegrated fluid.

Bracing for more aether energy to charge at him, Kerothan turned toward the other twister. As expected, the hooded figure stood with arm raised and wand poised. There came a holler from behind Kerothan, and the twister's attention split. Their discharged aether buzzed by Kerothan, and the hairs on his arms raised as charged vibrations rose and fell. Rock exploded where the energy collided against the cavern's formations.

The momentary distraction was all he would get. Kerothan leapt over the collapsed body of the first twister and fell to one knee, bringing his sword up in a skyward ascent. He heard flesh separate as the intrusive glass plunged into the twister's stomach.

It took only seconds for the agitation from the glass to shred apart the twister. The cloak bulged out as the torso exploded. Chunks of flesh, soiled in blood, slapped onto the cave floor before the maimed corpse joined the other on the ground with a wet thud.

Kerothan stood, covered in blood and other unfavorable fluids, and turned away from the carnage his blade had wrought. Already a horrible stench wafted off him from the accumulated slime he'd earned from his victims in the Grand Hall, and now the odor intensified with his new adornments. Such was the prize of warring with an enemy that succumbed to explosive ends. It'd taken intense training to overcome the disgust that always followed.

Kerothan darted towards the corpses to retrieve the glass wands while Cephus marched into view with Aruzz. "Your kin didn't stand a chance," Kerothan grunted to Aruzz as he cast the wands down the shaft and into shadow. When he faced Aruzz, he found the twister's grin gone, replaced by a repulsed snarl after what he'd observed.

"Time to cross the bridge then?" Cephus asked.

Aruzz did not acknowledge the inquiry with a response, but he did stride through the pools of blood and onto the boarded walkway. "You'll want their masks," the twister called to them without turning. "Can't breathe down here without them."

"I don't see any masks," Cephus murmured.

Kerothan's stomach lurched. "The twisters were wearing them." He bent down to the decapitated head of the first twister and turned it upright. Sure enough, a rubbery mouthpiece wrapped around the lower portion of the head, which was now more like a shattered pumpkin oozing pulp. He swallowed bile as he pried the item off and shook it free of the blood. Behind him, Cephus swore violently as he did the same with the other mask. With these new items in hand, the two warriors strode down the length of the bridge to the wooden platform on which Aruzz stood. They came to a stop, and all three stood in a brief moment of silence.

"Now what?" Kerothan asked with irritation.

Aruzz cocked an unamused eyebrow. "The lift won't work unless two turn the capstan." He lifted an arm to point back in the direction from which they'd come.

Cephus cursed under his breath. "We obviously have no one here to turn it for us, and we can't separate. You knew this would be the case. You've stalled us."

Aruzz leered and threw back his head to chuckle. His throat gurgled with phlegm.

"One of us will have to go back and bring some extra hands," said Cephus. He looked to Kerothan with a question in his eyes.

"You should go," said Kerothan. "We already shouldn't be down here without the blessing of the other clanheads. Whoever you're going to rope into this will need to be convinced. They won't listen to me. But they'll listen to you."

Cephus frowned. "Can I trust you not to kill our guide?"

"As much as I want him dead, it wouldn't make sense to do that given our circumstances. Go. We'll be here when you return."

Cephus turned without another word and sprinted down the bridge and out of sight into the cavern's darkness. Kerothan faced his prisoner, keeping his sword unsheathed. In addition to it being their only source of light, he hoped it would keep Aruzz in check while they waited.

The twister sat down, hissing as he peeled his cloak away from where the needle had maimed him. Tumors and boils sprouted across inflamed skin, but no more blood seeped from the open cuts. "Don't suppose you've got any more of that aetherlick?" he finally asked.

"I don't use it, so no, I don't have any on me," Kerothan growled.

"You might be less cranky if you did," Aruzz sneered. "Helps make life a little less drab."

"Life's plenty exciting without screwing with my mind. Besides, you look rather glum coming down from it. Not sure the flight to the sky is worth the sharp drop."

"If you would give me some, I wouldn't be so glum. Our first meeting left me with some nasty wounds. Aetherlick would help alleviate the pain."

Kerothan sighed in frustration. "Just go back to being quiet."

"Or what? You'll cut me down? Your righteous clanhead wouldn't like that. Guess that means I can do just about anything."

"I dare you to make that mistake. Damn whatever commands I've received."

"What I can't wrap my head around is why you care so deeply for two kidnapped prisoners," said Aruzz, ignoring Kerothan's threat. "We sacrifice our own every day for our cause. We aren't bound by the hindrance of altruism. That type of thinking can wait until the world is molded into the most desirable format. No more mirajin manipulating and hoarding aether. No more devotion to a passive deity that forsook this world. Humans can finally reign free and explore our untapped potential. My death doesn't have to be some tragic loss. I played my part in the twisters' rise to power, and I don't fault my kin for leaving me behind. Struggle for existence demands such sacrifices. My death in the grand scheme of eras past and eras to come is insignificant—lost in a wave of grander events."

"That's a cruel perspective," Kerothan argued. "Every life has value. The clans would be nothing if not for the individuals who make them up. When one is lost, the clan suffers."

Aruzz squinted at him. "That's not why you're gallivanting off after these kidnapped prisoners. Your quest boils down to guilt. You can't live with the idea that someone died because you didn't try to save them."

"It's not a matter of guilt," Kerothan snapped. "I'm doing what's right."

"But you slaughtered two people back there. You don't know their names. Their families. Their pasts. You treat your enemies like they've no identity at all. Yet isn't that what you're accusing me and my kind of doing? Of being willing to sacrifice lives, our own and others, for the cause? Seems to me you're willing to sacrifice others too—just not those you know by name and virtue."

"Shut up!" Kerothan snarled, nostrils flaring. "You're defending those who abandoned you when they had a shining opportunity to rescue you. People who treat others so carelessly, especially their own kin, deserve whatever violent fate awaits them. Those two twisters who met my blade polluted the aether Realms with waste and took innocent lives as part of their selfish schemes. I don't feel guilt over those deaths. Those are the deaths that are insignificant in this grand timeline you've framed."

"You should be helping us, clannite. Our reign is inevitable, and you don't want to be on the wrong side of victory. Besides, we've got a solution to the Dardajah problem. What you're trying to stop right now is what will save us all from a fate of dokojin obliterating our world. We're going to overthrow the Sachem and end that pesky dokojin inside him."

Kerothan scoffed at him. "So, you twisters want to take down the Sachem, even though he's the reason you can twist away without consequence? You do realize that only a few decades ago, twisting was something of a sacred practice reserved for templites? Though back then, it wasn't twisting in the sense you know it. It was a pure practice, a symbiotic exchange between the Terrestrial Realm and the aether Realms."

"Do you take me for an unlearned idiot?" asked Aruzz. "Everybody knows that. You and I may only have faint, foggy memories of such times, if any at all, but it's not like the generations before us are all dead. They whisper, they talk. Maybe not openly—there's quite a few decrees that would get them souldrained in some nasty ways—but I've heard enough to piece together that it wasn't all it was cracked up to be. The purists—all of them damn Vekuuv, mind you—claim it was a golden age. They complain that the Sachem's decrees of unrestrained aetherwielding tainted an otherwise pure practice. But us twisters know the truth."

"If you're referring to the claim that the mirajin were overlords bent on keeping us in subtle enslavement, you're trying to convince the wrong person."

"Aether can do so much more than what they were teaching us," Aruzz insisted. "The mirajin were scared of our potential. Scared of what we could do with their precious substance. Well, now look at us. We ran those scum out of our lands, and we can twist as much as we want, until we're as powerful as they were."

"Then why rail against the Sachem? Sounds like his vision."

"Because he's in bed with a fucking dokojin. He embraced the opposite extreme, taking on a role with his companion in the same way that the priests allied themselves with mirajin. The entities of the aether Realms are too unpredictable—dokojin and mirajin alike—and we've become willing pawns in their schemes."

"But your kind created their own dokojin—this Spiracy," Kerothan pointed out. "That seems like a paradoxical step in your fight against dokojin rule."

"True," Aruzz conceded. "But unlike the primordial ones, our dokojin is a means to an end that we can control. She doesn't harbor some delusion of superiority to us."

"I think it's incredibly stupid to assume that," Kerothan stated. "You expect to reign over an entity meant to take down the Sachem? You mean to create something more powerful than Dardajah, yet expect that entity to remain subject to you?"

"Spiracy has been taught to serve us. This is different. The more powerful she becomes, the more powerful we become."

Kerothan shook his head and let out an incredulous laugh tainted with disgust. "I think your lunacy proves exactly why we needed mirajin to guide us in peace and unity. Evidently, when we don't have that guidance, we think we can reign over aether entities like they're nothing more than demoralized pets."

Aruzz pointed up at Kerothan. "You're an ignorant fool. You wanna believe the dokojin only bring chaos? Fine, no argument here. But the mirajin *were* overlords, not guardians. We weren't allowed to question them, and we weren't allowed to tap into our potential. They made sure we never stepped over the line that would have made us greater than them. If that's not tyranny, then I don't know what is. You aren't willing to acknowledge that what you call extreme—twisters enlisting dokojin—is no worse than you enlisting their counterparts. Mirajin and dokojin are two sides of the same feather."

Kerothan shook his head. "It doesn't matter if they're both corrupt. What I'm fighting for does not align with what you twisters condone and celebrate. You sacrifice lives, spill blood and don't care that you create aetherwaste while doing so. You thrive in chaos and violence. I don't stand for that. My clan will lay down their lives for each other. We're rescuing our own. Your kind can't say the same, and I don't want to live in a world where that kind of behavior is standard and expected."

Aruzz studied Kerothan until the clannite bristled. "You're a zealous soul," Aruzz finally said. "You hold to personal creeds just like the rest of us. But it is guilt channeling your rage and devotion. Perhaps you started off as someone devoted to an honest cause, but now some guilt teems inside you. That's what keeps you marching on—not some altruistic philosophy. You want to atone—and for more than your own deeds. Perhaps your penitence is over what others have done, as if you alone could have stopped them."

Kerothan squeezed his fingers around the hilt of his sword. He quivered as shaky breaths broke past his lips. "I'm the last person who should feel guilty about any of this."

Aruzz's grin widened, his eyebrows arcing into false sympathy. "No, certainly not. The world owes Kerothan, brother to the Tecalica! Everyone around him betrays him, but surely none of it is his fault." A chuckle croaked from his throat. "You play victim as well as I do."

Kerothan shot forward a few steps before stopping himself. His limbs trembled. He couldn't separate logic from instinct; though he wondered how the twister knew of his relation to Jalice, the question suffocated under his rage. His mind screamed at him to raise his sword and cut down the twister. Aruzz didn't flinch at the near attack. Nor did his grin falter. "Struck a nerve, have I?"

"My sister betrayed me. She turned Hydrim against me and got our family—our *tribe*—slaughtered or enslaved. There is nothing in that tale that demands guilt of me."

Aruzz leaned forward, his sunken eyes accusatory. "But you ran, clannite. You didn't stay behind. You didn't try to save your people or undo your sister's decisions. You didn't even try to save your lover. You *ran*."

Kerothan's sword swiped up.

Damn this twister to a fate worse than death.

"Kerothan!"

He jerked his head to see Cephus running across the bridge towards him, a torch in hand. Beyond him at the edge of the cave, two clannites were positioned at the capstan. Kerothan brought his arms down, letting out an uneasy breath as he shoved away from Aruzz. Cephus joined the pair on the platform and grew still.

Kerothan waited for his clanhead to scold him, but the rebuke never came. The platform jolted as the other clannites turned the capstan wheel. Once the trio on the platform were steady on their feet with the lift's motion, Cephus and Kerothan put on the masks. Kerothan grunted at the way the material pressed against a few of the metal rings that lined his cheeks, aware of the indentations already forming in his skin.

"We only have two masks," Kerothan grumbled, his voice distorting through the mask's filters.

"Guess it's time to test this altruism you boast." Aruzz leered at them. "Or will you let me die for my cause?"

Kerothan responded without giving Cephus a chance to decide. "Altruism doesn't extend to murderers and degenerates. You brought on your fate."

"Kerothan! We need him alive." Cephus weighed the impossible calculation. "How poisonous is the air down here? Would it permit us to take turns with the mask?"

Aruzz shrugged. "Poison is poison."

For once, Cephus's impassivity wavered some, but it returned in force. "My clan's safety comes first. We'll share the masks. But you'll take the greater risk—longer exposure to the air with no mask."

Aruzz sneered up at the clanhead. "So be it. I don't care if I die down here." His eyes flickered to Kerothan, a dark, knowing look entering them. "For my death ushers in the reign of the twisters. I've played my part."

Kerothan's blood boiled, but it seemed to neither intimidate nor please the twister. So, he funneled his rage instead into his resolve to find Ophim. They would find him alive and unharmed. If they didn't, it wouldn't matter that Aruzz had no mask. The same fate would befall him. Kerothan would ensure it himself. Already he was picturing the twister's boiled body exploding into a million pieces as Kerothan's blade ended him.

The beauty was that, even if they found Ophim alive, Kerothan's sword might still slip.

CHAPTER 38

Hours spent wandering empty corridors and vast chambers with no ceiling in sight was taking a toll on Kerothan. Every time he or Cephus inquired as to their distance from where Jalice and Ophim had been taken, Aruzz would assure them they were nearing their destination.

Then more time would pass. The cycle would repeat. They'd ask, Aruzz would answer, they'd proceed on.

With each step, a growing sense of claustrophobia set in. Kerothan found himself glancing over his shoulder more and more, trying to make sense of where they'd come from and to note any landmarks that could serve as beacons for the exit. Nothing stood out; everything was either bathed in utter darkness or vacant of details to commit to memory. The few sceneries that did make an impression repeated: giant vats of fluid and rooms swarming with wires and tubes.

His skin crawled. This place was from a forgotten time. A time of forbidden machinery and diabolical knowledge. He wanted to be done and out of here as soon as possible.

But not without Ophim.

Eventually, even stoic Cephus lost his patience. He stopped Aruzz, who was in the lead, to confront him. "We've been down here too long," the clanhead grunted. "I'm beginning to think you're not leading us anywhere."

"Rest assured, I'm—" Aruzz broke off into a fit of coughing. He'd developed a hacking cough not long after they touched down on the surface and departed the lift's platform. He wheezed, fighting for the air he needed to continue talking, but never gaining enough in his lungs even to breathe.

Kerothan interrupted the harsh noise. "No more lies. It's got to be the middle of the night by now, maybe even early morning. There's no way the twister base would be this far from where we entered. You're trying to get us lost in here."

Aruzz, hunched over and still trying to regain control of his breathing, lifted his bulging eyes to Kerothan. His facial muscles tightened from a lack of air as he spoke. "I . . . need . . . your mask again."

Cephus stepped between them. "No. I've had enough of your tricks. You don't get a mask anymore. Either you swear to get us to the base within the hour, or you die from suffocation. You get the mask only if we arrive in that timetable."

Aruzz's face contorted into rage, but his head snapped downward with more hacking.

"He's no use to us now," Kerothan muttered. "Unless we're close, I don't think he'll last as long as you've graciously given him."

"We've been walking for miles," said Cephus. "Maybe he needs rest."

"You'd risk the life of Ophim to abide this man's weakness? We need to find them."

"It doesn't matter how badly we want to do that. If he's led us away from the base, we'll never find it. We probably couldn't even find our way out of here now."

Kerothan didn't respond. Cephus was right, and though he'd never admit it, his own muscles demanded rest from the grueling trek. The little energy he'd retained after the skirmish in the Grand Hall was all but depleted.

Despite Kerothan's protests, Cephus took the dwindling torch and wandered away in search of more material to burn for it. With only the glow of his sword to light the area, Kerothan watched Aruzz curl up on the ground. In time, the twister's wheezes relaxed into more productive breaths, ragged though they were.

Cephus returned with nothing to show for his quest. "We've only got enough material to keep the torch lit another cycle," he informed him as he sank to the ground. "A few more hours, and we'll be at the mercy of the aether in our blades."

"At least we've got them," said Kerothan. He joined his clanhead on the ground, keeping close to share the meager warmth wafting from the flames of the torch. Silence took over for a few minutes as the two sat in their own thoughts.

"I suppose Aruzz would be missing a head had I shown up seconds later than I did, back on the bridge."

"I'm sorry, if that's any consolation," said Kerothan. "The stress of being down here . . . it got to me."

"Caverns can be claustrophobic," Cephus affirmed. "Perhaps it triggered you. But I think there were other stressors the twister found."

Kerothan shifted his weight. He wasn't going to admit that Aruzz's accusations—that Kerothan sustained a profound guilt coiled around his past—had indeed provoked him.

"I can hear your thoughts," Cephus said quietly. "We don't have to be translated for me to know what's worming through your mind. There's no need to feel ashamed, Kerothan." Cephus paused, hesitating over something.

Kerothan braced himself, unsure what would come next. Already this encounter had him on edge, regardless of Cephus's calm reaction to his near loss of control earlier. Embarrassment flooded him as he attempted to anticipate his clanhead's next words. A hand fell across his knee. Surprise evaporated his dread, but his body remained strict and rigid. He knew what Cephus meant by the touch—he'd heard the comfort and affirmation in the man's voice—but everything else told him that this vulnerability was dangerous.

Vulnerability meant weakness. Weakness brought pain.

A memory, frayed at the edges but quick as a knife striking in the dark, blazed in his vision.

Hydrim standing over him, Kerothan's blood dripping from fingers that Hydrim had clawed into his skin.

The memory came and went like a flash of lightning, though the rumble of its thunder echoed through Kerothan's mind. Cephus remained still during this, no doubt fighting for his own courage to broach the sensitive topic.

"I think we should talk," said Cephus. "About your sister, about Ophim, about you and me. Too much has happened in such a short amount of time. It's no wonder you've been straining to keep up without breaking."

"I'm not breaking," Kerothan whispered back tersely. The hand on his knee flexed as Cephus sought to ease away the tension coursing through those words.

"I didn't mean it like that," Cephus apologized. "I only meant . . . I want to help, clannite. Let me. Tell me what you're thinking. Tell me what troubles you."

As if they held some sort of power, the words loosened Kerothan's muscles. Part of him still remained tense and ready to flee at the slightest sign of danger, but Cephus's offer was too apropos to deny.

"I don't like it down here," Kerothan said, voice low to keep Aruzz from overhearing. "Everything down here is lethal—the air, the machinery, the shadows. And I can't help constantly reminding myself that Ophim is down here, alone. I keep imagining how frightened he must be. If I feel this anxious, with my own clanhead to keep me sane, then he must be terrified."

"He isn't alone though. Your sister is with him."

Kerothan groaned. "Her presence doesn't mean anything. He might as well be alone."

"Why are you still so ready to discount your sister like that? Have you thought nothing of what we spoke of before? Your sister wouldn't be a prisoner to the twisters if she were on their side."

"How do you know she *is* their prisoner?" Kerothan challenged. "The whole ambush might have been part of some scheme she orchestrated. She may very well have been the one who got Ophim kidnapped."

"I don't think that's true. And I think, deep down, you know that too. Whatever sins your sister committed in the past no longer seem to drive her actions in the present, at least not in a cruel way. If anything, they drive her towards a sense of atonement."

"It's so easy for you to say that and believe in it," said Kerothan. "She isn't your sister. She didn't betray you like she did me." He paused, failing to escape the newfound revelations bubbling to mind. "You saw the same thing I saw when translated. She deceived Hydrim, and it cost him . . . everything. His aura, his body, his freedom. And it cost the tribes everything too."

As soon as he spoke of the Sachem, he knew he was opening a door to a conversation he desperately wanted to avoid. He clenched his jaw, bracing for the words already slipping from Cephus's lips.

"Hydrim must have meant a lot to you. When he betrayed the tribes, it seems you took it personally. Or perhaps that larger betrayal hides within it a more intimate one against you."

Kerothan let the words sink in, absorbing them slowly. Cephus grew quiet, patiently waiting for him to respond. "I don't think it's a secret at this point that Hydrim indeed meant something to me." Kerothan inhaled deeply before adding, "Something beyond friendship."

"Is that why your sister thinks you can help?" Cephus asked.

It was a leading question, but Kerothan took the bait. "That's where my sister is truly wrong," he said without holding back the spite. "She thinks that bonds from ages ago still intertwine us—me, her, Hydrim. As if all the pain and deceit hasn't torn those ribbons of union to shreds."

"If those bonds were truly gone, do you think you'd have reacted the way you have since her arrival? Anger and rage are still powerful emotions, and they seem to have lived inside you all these years. I think you're bound to Jalice and the Sachem, even if it's through resentment."

Kerothan jerked his knee away. "Why does it matter? I want the Sachem dead. I want my sister gone. Whatever it is she thinks might bring me back, it isn't there. Why are you doing this? I didn't ask for you to pick apart my emotions and motivations."

In his clanhead's silence, Kerothan once again readied himself for a fight. He watched the wrinkles around Cephus's eyes tighten and the ever-so-slight dip of his eyebrows. This was it. He'd finally stopped his clanhead's interrogation.

"I think those things are true," said Cephus. "You want the Sachem dead. You want your sister to leave. But I think there are deeper truths beneath them. You want Hydrim back—the version of him you knew in your past, before his tyranny. And you want your sister to be right—for there to be a chance to save the Sachem and undo some of the destruction you've endured. I think that if you believed those truths more than those you've erected on top of them, you could forgive her."

Kerothan stared back, stunned. His mind came up blank, and instead a wave of emotions swept out of the depths of a vault he'd sealed over the years.

Tears welled in his eyes, and an inevitable sob rushed up from his chest into his throat. The mask across his mouth now seemed suffocating. His hands trembled as he scrambled to yank it off his face; deep breaths shuddered through his body when he managed to do so.

Seeing his distress, Cephus boldly moved them into a tight embrace. Kerothan buried his face in the man's chest, muffling his soft wails in a hopeless effort to conceal them from Aruzz. The onslaught gripped him for some time, and all the while Cephus rubbed his free hand across Kerothan's back. After instinct dwindled, rational thought returned. Kerothan grew quiet with fresh embarrassment. He raised himself out of Cephus's embrace and turned away to face the outstretched torch, sniffling while swiping at his eyes.

I'm a grown-ass man sobbing like a child in front of my clanhead. Dying fucking stars.

He heard movement beside him. A hand gently swept beneath his chin and nudged his gaze back to Cephus, who had removed his own mask. Kerothan, too emotionally weak to resist, let the man's touch linger. He expected an awkwardness in the clanhead but saw only a fiery passion.

"I think there is hope, Kerothan. Your sister's plea is genuine, and if there's a way to redeem a man chained in the throes of possession, then you—we—should pursue it."

Kerothan saw Cephus's gaze flicker down ever so slightly before it flashed back to Kerothan's eyes. It happened again, and a rush of adrenaline drove through Kerothan. His pulse quickened, and he swallowed the lump that had collected in his throat. Cephus leaned forward, bringing their faces a breath apart. Kerothan thought to protest. Uncertainty clouded him.

He kept quiet.

Their lips met, and Cephus took the lack of resistance as invitation, pressing deeper into the kiss. Kerothan, whether by shock or satisfaction, didn't draw back. He inhaled Cephus's passion as if a transference might occur between the two. The musky scent of sweat and its bitter taste intoxicated his senses as their lips grazed against facial hair dewy with perspiration. Warm breath brushed across Kerothan's face when Cephus exhaled through his nose, stirring in him an inexplicable excitement that burned down his chest and into his loins.

The want, the *need*, to reciprocate and join in the kiss rushed into Kerothan—just as Cephus ended it and leaned back. Kerothan blinked, flooded with conflicting emotions. He'd enjoyed it. Despite every moment when he had resented his clanhead—all of them now racing through his mind as if to remind him how irritating he found the man—Kerothan wanted those lips back on his.

He wanted Cephus to lean back in and kiss him again.

A smug grin brightened Cephus's face, though by the taut posture of his body language, something akin to embarrassment gripped him now. Absent his sturdy composure from moments earlier, he gave a clipped nod to Kerothan. Only then did he resume the normal, stoic demeanor of a clanhead.

"No doubt you're tired, clannite. We won't be resting for much longer."

"I'm fine," Kerothan said, clearing his throat to steady his voice. He brought the mask over his head and positioned it over his mouth again. "The twister appears to have regained control over his breathing. We need to push on and find Ophim."

A fresh wave of embarrassment and shame washed over him then. He wasn't sure why though. No one had crossed any boundaries, not after what he and Cephus had agreed to earlier. And he still wanted Ophim, more than anything or anyone. But the kiss with Cephus had stirred in him a similar passion, one a bit strange and unexpected. He let the heat of these thoughts drive him to his feet. His legs wobbled, and he shook them to bring back their blood flow. Cephus grunted as he followed suit while simultaneously replacing his mask.

Kerothan crossed over to Aruzz's still figure on the ground and nudged him with his boot. "Get up. Last chance to find your way, or we leave you down here to die."

CHAPTER 39

Jalice couldn't recall how she'd arrived in the cave. She wracked her mind, trying to retrace what steps and decisions had resulted in this setting. But nothing gave any hints beyond a few fuzzy images and muffled voices that she only faintly recognized.

"Welcome back, Skinflake."

That voice she remembered. It was cold. Insidious. A voice so sharp in concentration that it lacked a true infusion of emotion. It sounded human, but it wasn't. A mimicry that contorted and dismantled the very thing it attempted to copy.

Spiracy's form crystallized in the darkness, gliding towards Jalice in an ominous procession—a wraith of impossible beauty, so vivid and pristine that to see or touch such elegance would be to shatter oneself in the grip of inferiority. The dokojin's face rippled between pale and shadowy features as though it were a water-logged canvas brushed with weak paint. Wispy hair lifted with Spiracy's movements like seaweed swaying in the currents of the ocean, while long nails spiked from her fingertips in a vicious reminder that every kind of beauty came with a dangerous thorn. Radiant lips remained pursed, unwilling to part unless to bestow upon a listener a string of horrifying curses.

A wraith forged by ill intent, created to mock the beauties of human flesh. A mirror of humanity's frailty, ready to shred to pieces anyone foolish enough to behold it.

Jalice pressed back in an attempt to flee, only to find herself restrained across an angled metal frame.

This had happened before. But why couldn't she connect the pieces?

She knew Spiracy. She knew this place. But what had happened here?

Another presence lingered where light breached the darkness, following in Spiracy's wake. Jalice's vision fought to amalgamize the newcomer's conflicting features—patches of pasty pink skin like that of a newborn's splotched the vivid reds and purples of exposed muscle. In other areas, raw tissue peeked out from beneath a translucent shell, as if still in the process of some internal mitosis. A gooey liquid film coated the figure, and the indeterminate light source above it glistened off the sickening sludge.

When its face came into view, she screamed, craning her neck sideways and pushing back in an attempt to avoid it.

This isn't real. It's just a nightmare. Sahruum get me out of here!

It had been her own face looking back at her. Or rather, elements and patches of her face. She recognized her ocean blue eyes, but on this imposter, they were ringed with translucent goo. Despite its crude, makeshift skin, she recognized the unmistakable shape of her face. A few patches of red hair, though not nearly as elegant or lush as Jalice's own, sprouted from atop the head.

Color. It struck her then that this inclusion was new. What little impression she retained of her previous visit, she knew that color had been absent, a place painted only in shades of black and white. Now, somehow, it made an appearance.

Spiracy graced the nightmarish creature with a sinister smile. "A masterpiece in the making, is it not? Look at the details. I marvel at my own creation—that it's able to mimic its victim so well, and so quickly. One visit, and my pet mastered the bare bones of your form. And the color . . . a vivid gift from the new dreamer sustaining my Realm."

"What is this?" Jalice shrieked. "Get it away from me!" Noises erupted from the creature, strange hoots and moans eerily reminiscent of the words Jalice had just uttered. It was something out of a nightmare she once had. Or was it a memory?

Spiracy glided closer, craning down to leer in Jalice's face, and shushed her. "Stop that now. This way is better. You roam about in the Terrestrial Realm, flamboyant and naive as you waste your time and presence there. You don't deserve such privilege." She glanced at the creature, glee and admiration inflating her tone. "But my pets retain the honor of your making. Your looks and sounds. Humans won't be entirely forgotten. Your legacy, as pathetic and wasteful as it was, will live on in my spawn."

The creature tilted its face, studying Jalice with primal eyes. With *her* eyes. "Why does it look like me?" she whispered. She prayed that her voice didn't carry enough for the creature to hear her and try to mimic her words.

"It has to learn somehow," Spiracy explained. "My pets need subjects to mimic. Once they learn enough and can replicate their victims' forms, their potential unlocks. Soon, this one will be able to shift into any human it desires. But first, it must learn from you."

Jalice couldn't speak, petrified by the monstrosity looming in front of her. Only her mind screamed out, willing the creature to be gone or for its stolen similarities to somehow dissipate. This thing couldn't have her. Couldn't be her.

Wouldn't be her.

"Let me out!" she screamed, thrashing against her restraints and bent on repeating the plea until her voice gave out.

"Not this time, Skinflake," Spiracy said, her grin widening far too much in identical arcs up into marble cheeks. Eyes of black pools bore down on Jalice, poisoned by a craving for authenticity but burdened with an overwhelming cruelty. Too much dokojin, not enough human.

The words sank in, and Jalice abruptly stilled. *Not this time.* Recollection swirled, elusive but almost within grasp. She *had* been here before. How had she escaped this place? Something to do with a memory . . .

A pleasant memory. She'd summoned a pleasant memory.

Jalice concentrated, ignoring Spiracy's ensuing monologue and the creature's attempt to copy her breathing. She needed to think of a moment from her childhood—before the Sachem, before the Black House. Spiracy hissed, inevitably breaking Jalice's concentration.

"A nasty little trick," Spiracy seethed. "But it won't work this time."

Jalice turned, the shock of her freedom only briefly setting in. She wasn't restrained. The metal slab was gone; it had vanished like it had during the previous visit. She remembered that too. But this revelation dissipated when a giant structure sprouted in the center of the cavernous chamber—a looming pyramid of black metal.

The Black House.

A figure emerged from the structure's base, stumbling as it sprinted towards them. Her red hair bobbed side to side. Tears streaked the young girl's face as she sobbed violently and ran.

It was the moment Jalice had fled the scene of Hydrim's possession. The moment after her betrayal. Hoots stole her attention away from the girl. Like its master, the creature was fixated on the younger Jalice. Perhaps it didn't realize what was happening—Jalice herself wasn't quite sure—but it slowly took steps to follow the fleeing girl. When the younger Jalice passed by, it let out an excited chirp and galloped after her into the darkness. Spiracy shouted at it to cease its pursuit, but the creature ignored this command.

Jalice grew rigid when Spiracy's rage shifted onto her.

"A nasty, nasty trick," Spiracy spat, revealing rows of crystalline teeth sharpened to points. "But it's not enough to save you this time. This is my Realm. I control what happens here. Not you."

The Black House shattered with a thunderous boom. The fractured pieces rained down like star-rocks plunging towards the earth. Jalice braced for impact, her eyes darting between the giant debris bearing down on her and Spiracy. Yet nothing of the structure touched either of them. The boulders collided with the cavern floor and disintegrated into motes of dust. Thunder shook the ground and overwhelmed her ears. Seconds later, silence ensued.

A green glow bloomed where the House had stood, a faint pillar of color amidst the shadows. Jalice eyed it warily, certain this wasn't part of any memory of hers.

"Let's take a closer look at that," Spiracy said tersely. Her thin arm snapped out and gripped Jalice's wrist. In a flash, the two were transported from their edge of the chamber to a location near the light.

Jalice squinted against the green glow, blinded by the sudden change in lighting. Slowly, her vision adjusted to behold an odd machine, eerily reminiscent of an insect carapace, with a face peeking out from inside of it. Her mind stumbled in an attempt to place the familiarity she felt.

"Let me help that foggy mind of yours," Spiracy hissed. "I've learned his name is Ophim. I believe he's a companion of yours. A fellow victim of my lair. Only, he serves a far more direct purpose than you. He is the dreamer that keeps my Realm in existence."

The name jolted Jalice. Ophim. He'd been with her during the twister attack. He'd tried to protect her.

"You see, Skinflake, my reign is inevitable. All will fall to me. Warriors and queens and cowards alike."

Jalice heard a snap, and in an eyeblink, the scenery around her changed. Huddled figures pressed in around her. She screamed, flailing desperately and pedaling backwards on hands and feet until she smacked against the farthest wall from the others.

The new space had a low curved ceiling that forced those within it to either stand with a hunch or accept a place on the floor. A single wall wrapped in a circle around them, and there were no doors or windows aside from miniscule holes punched in the ceiling that admitted speckles of blue light.

One of the strangers from the group rose and sprang towards her. Jalice shrank back, jerking her hand in the air at the assailant as if that single command would stop it. Surprisingly, the figure took her discomfort to mind and slowed its approach. But the way it moved alarmed her; it swayed on its legs as if uncertain of its balance, and its arms loped from side to side.

Finally, her mind focused, and she recognized the face peering back at her. Xiekaro. The templite healer.

He examined her worriedly, looking her up and down for signs of injury while he knelt beside her. Dirt and open scratches smeared his face, the dark stains of blood webbing through the black soot, and a weary strain had smothered the light in his eyes.

His hand went towards her knee, and for a split second, her mind flooded with relieved anticipation of his touch and the comfort it would bring. This shattered when his skin met hers. She stiffened and looked down at his hand. Nothing struck her as abnormal, but her skin crawled in revulsion as if she should fear him. His voice stole her attention away, but the feeling of wrongness had overwhelmed her senses. She looked up into his face, failing to recall what he'd just said to her.

"Where are we?" she asked instead. "What is this place?" She studied the others, still huddled in the center of the room, unsure what to make of how their terrified faces scrutinized her with the same intense uncertainty. Most of them wore the bare minimum of clothing to shield their privates, leaving bony limbs and sagging skin exposed. Their faces were hollow, their beady eyes sunken into the folds of their wrinkles.

"Where have you been?" Xiekaro asked, dodging her questions. "I've been waiting to see you here with me ever since I arrived, but only now you show. Has she kept you away from us all this time?"

Jalice struggled to keep up with his questions. She shook her head. "I escaped here before. Then I came back . . ." She trailed off, unable to piece together the chain of events that had led her here once again. "I think I got kidnapped by the twisters. Then I woke up here." Her ears pricked at the sound of whispering. She looked back to the huddled crowd. Their agitation seemed to be growing.

"Who are these people?" she asked. "I don't like the way they're looking at us."

"They're paranoid," said Xiekaro. "Sometimes new faces mean . . ." He trailed off and grew quiet.

"How do we get out of here?" Jalice asked, her hand clutching his shirt to tug his attention back to her.

The weariness in his eyes deepened, and his face crumbled into wrinkles. "If I knew, I wouldn't still be here, Tecalica."

She refused to let his words prevail, tightening her hold on his sleeve. "I've left this place before. That means I can do it again. I just need to figure out how I managed it last time."

An admiring curiosity wiped away his defeated expression. "That's quite a claim. No one here knows of another who's managed to escape. You're the only one. Are you sure you escaped and that it wasn't some trick of the mind she's played on you?"

"I may not remember everything from before my return, but I know without a doubt that I've been here before and that I somehow got out." She paused. "It has something to do with my memories. The dokojin didn't like it when the

Black House appeared out of nowhere. It was like I had a flashback, triggered by fear or some other emotion, but this time, it didn't help. I didn't escape."

"Is there a difference between the memories?" Xiekaro asked. "Something that helped you escape the first time that this new moment lacked? Think hard on this."

"I don't know," she said with frustration. "At first I thought it had to be a happy memory, but I'm not even sure I chose it. I just need time to think."

"Time is not a luxury known to this place," said Xiekaro. "Spiracy's reign is imminent."

That didn't sound right—not in the sense of his voice or tone, but in the chosen words themselves. As if he aligned himself with the claim within them. It disturbed her how easily he uttered the dokojin's name, and in association with the other words in that sentence.

She heard a whimper from across the room. The huddled group had shuffled to the far wall, leaning into it just as she had into the slab that had restrained her in the presence of Spiracy. Something had changed; a renewed fear charged them with the goal of steering clear of a present danger, and the farthest they could get from it was the opposite wall. She stared a moment longer before realization crept over her.

They weren't staring at her in terror, and their whispers might not even have been about her.

They were staring at Xiekaro.

Out of the corner of her eye, she could make out the frame of his jawline, the edges of his face. The skin lacked its normal texture and was vacant of color. Instead, a translucent white exposed the dark muscles and veins beneath it. No hair. No bones. Just cartilage.

She couldn't look back at him. Maybe when she did, she'd see Xiekaro again. But she didn't want to look and see in full what her peripheral vision had revealed. All she knew was that this wasn't Xiekaro. It explained his strange words. It explained why his touch made her skin crawl.

She didn't think. She just reacted. Her arm shot out, striking the imposter square in the face. Her fist met with a gelatinous substance, and she recoiled at the sensation. Moving fast, she scrambled away towards another part of the room. She resisted the temptation to join the other frightened strangers—maybe they were imposters too.

The creature loped over, still boasting Xiekaro's clothes and body. But its face, mangled where she'd struck it, now only vaguely imitated the man. Where it didn't, blood spilled across veiny diaphanous skin to form the red outline of a cartilaginous skull. Gurgling noises bubbled from it, like a drowning rat trying to squeal in mud. Jalice screamed at it, hoping the shrill sound might keep it back. A whistle, short and haunting, brought the creature to a sharp halt a few feet away from her. It hung in place like a doll on strings, limp and ready to collapse at the slightest brush of Jalice's breath.

A disembodied voice echoed throughout the chamber.

"You're not so dumb after all, pretty bones," said Spiracy. "Though I suppose the obvious panic of your fellow captives was quite the hint. But is it not impressive? You thought it was your friend for a while there. A near perfect replicant of that prior specimen. This one though—this one obeys me. My spawn aren't vulnerable to such weak inklings as rebellion or liberation. They aren't hampered by human insecurities."

Jalice shut her eyes. If she could just summon a memory—of her childhood, of her friends, of anything other than this place. She concentrated, but the harsh imagery of Xiekaro's face, mangled and deformed to fit another creature's flesh, thwarted her efforts. Still, when she pried open her eyes, she hoped to be somewhere else. She dared to hope she might have escaped.

The face of Spiracy's minion swarmed her vision, now pressed in right against her face. It opened its mouth, the gaping chasm lined with elastic pillars of flesh. The pitch and tone of Xiekaro bled out but lacked coherent words. It sounded more like the anguished moans of the man she'd known.

The sound of Xiekaro frightened in his last moments of life.

Jalice sucked in a breath, her body readying an inevitable shriek. When it left her lungs, the cry joined in a jarring chorus with the mimic creature's awful lament and Spiracy's tinkling cackle.

Pleasant memories eluded her, and in turn, so did her escape.

CHAPTER 40

Annilasia could no longer see. A vivid red had seeped into her vision over the previous hours until the crimson hue had blurred all distinction of shape and color. Whispers scratched in her ears. She heard howling too, like from prisoners in a stuffed dungeon begging in screams and manic groans to be killed. These howls haunted her days and nights.

She wasn't sure how much time had passed since the onset of these symptoms. What she did remember was that she and Drifter had been close to finishing the glass orbs. Each moment that passed took her closer to a fate with Inzerious. It seemed the dokojin's influence had returned with a vengeance. Where her eyes couldn't see, her mind conjured horrible imagery instead.

Bodies flayed with such gruesome violence that she couldn't make out the identity of the victims. Rivers of blood swarming over villages and drowning all manner of residents and wildlife. Maggots frothing from the mouths of the dead, who decayed in such rapid timelapses that she witnessed every stage of the process.

She thought she felt a hand. Maybe. Touch had left her too. A distant luxury.

The red around her shimmered like a quake upsetting a glass of wine. Murky shapes tumbled about until greys and blacks broke through the veil of crimson. Trees formed around her. Light coalesced into a muddled sun veiled behind an endless sheet of clouds. The land, as if it wanted nothing to do with the sun's meager attempt to bless it with its presence, clung to a shadowy overlay that permeated every inch of the terrain. She existed in a night that happened to be day.

Canyons teemed with writhing motions. Giant lakes sloshed about as if some organism swimming within them had rebelled and desired to escape onto land. Logs and reeds tumbled about, breaking the surface with chaotic randomness.

The faintest pitch whistled in her ear. She willed her ears to pick up more. More shrill sounds. A chorus of them.

Some of the logs pushed down on others, while those on the borders of the lake struck the shores with a frantic vigor only to be pulled back into the churning waters. When she realized what it was she was seeing, she turned away to escape the scene.

Those weren't logs. Those weren't whistles.

She rolled over, finding the motion strange as she couldn't recall ever having lain down. A figure crouched over her, and she startled even as they shushed her and held up their hands in a sign of peace. It took her a moment to realize it was Drifter, for some reason in his translated state—a night expanse for a body filled with suspended orbs that swirled and sparked.

"We've translated," he said. "You weren't aware of the journey, I'm sure."

Another voice stole her attention—a low murmur slipping through the foggy darkness. She spotted a presence lurking behind a set of boulders a few yards off. Unblinking eyes, nestled at the top of black bones slathered in ichor, stared back at her. Her eyes traveled the length of the silvery cord that ran from the creature to the lifestone at her side.

"What's it saying?" she asked with urgency. "Can you hear it?"

"I can't even see it," said Drifter. "Only you can. Is it still in its cage?"

Annilasia studied Inzerious's form. She saw the faintest remnants of the spiderweb material etched over its bones and peeling skin. "It's nearly free," she murmured. "I'm out of time."

"You're only out of time when it's completely free," said Drifter. "Look here."

Annilasia tore her gaze from the dokojin, which felt like too much of a risk, to look over to Drifter, who pointed behind him as he moved out of the way. Beyond him lay a pile of translucent globes of various shapes and sizes.

"I used up the last of the glass we had. You lost touch with the Terrestrial Realm for a few hours—looked trapped in a trance, and your eyes were glazed over with blood. You muttered some, but I stopped listening when I realized what it was you were saying."

She looked up at him. "What did I say?"

Drifter's eyes, glimmering the same velvet that backdropped the stars swimming within him, peered down at her with what she guessed to be concern. "Nothing that should ever be repeated. Dark things, no doubt a result of your companion skirting toward freedom."

Annilasia glanced back at the distant lakes populating the terrain around them. "Who are all those people?" she asked in a haunted tone. "Why are they stuck?"

"I imagine that they are auras that the coven has tortured and enslaved over the years," said Drifter. "Those aren't normal lakes. They don't allow their victims to escape."

"Shouldn't we rescue them?"

Drifter's glowing eyes met hers. "Do you think we have time?"

She knew the question was rhetorical. There wasn't time. Not for her at least. "Can they even be saved?"

Drifter shrugged. "Maybe. But it wouldn't be a quick or easy task."

Suddenly another figure manifested a few feet away. Annilasia jolted, realizing in that moment that she held a glass wand in her hands. She pointed the weapon at the unexpected intruder but was relieved upon seeing a celestial form, which meant the newcomer was human. Unlike Drifter, this figure boasted fluid hair that twirled about as though free of gravity. In one hand, a glass wand stood out in stark contrast to the canvas of darkness that made up their form

"What a nasty little bastard," the newcomer said, their black eyes on Inzerious.

Annilasia recognized the voice even though it lacked the scratchy phlegm that she associated with it. "Evlicka? You look so . . . young. As far as looks go while translated, that is."

"You don't have much time," the other woman stated. "As much as I'd like to bask in your awe at my youthfulness, we have more pressing matters."

"Wait. You can see it?" The dokojin let out a low rumble as its eyes met hers.

"I'm in tune with the bastards now," said Evlicka. "Spent too much time with a whole disaster of them. Now, it seems, I'm cursed to always see them, no matter what frequency they vibrate at."

"Can you interact with it?" asked Annilasia as she got to her feet.

"That I don't know," Evlicka answered. "Guess we'll find out if it tries to interrupt us."

Annilasia followed the example of the other two and began setting the glass orbs in the predetermined sequence they'd mapped out prior to translation, and prior to Annilasia's unexpected comatose state.

"What are we going to do about aether?" asked Annilasia. "This whole place is rife with aetherwaste."

"You weren't the only one to hide away wands," said Drifter. "Plenty of the pupils gathered aether during the wand trials. I gathered that source up while you were busy plundering the bodies of our mentors." He stopped and held up his own glass wand, which shimmered with colorful tendrils of energy.

"Well, then let's get to it," Annilasia said.

The group completed their task of arranging the glass globes, and Annilasia looked over their handiwork once the last one was placed. Evlicka took it a step further by flicking her wand. Aether rushed into the display with eagerness, lifting the globes up at various heights and depths.

Estrelda. The Iron Shield. The Doomsday Clock. The Metal Warrior. Higher Tooth and Minor Tooth. The Dancing Feathers. Sahruum's Grace. The Lost Tears.

Together, they formed miniscule projections of their far more glorious counterparts that graced the skies at night. After a few tweaks—pressing certain globes closer together or inching others to a more proper placement— she told her companions to put them into motion with the collected aether in their wands. The model came to life, and she watched in awe as the globes raced through the air in their proper orbits.

She braced for the Music. They waited in tense silence.

No sound came.

"Why don't I hear anything?" Drifter asked, voicing the panic growing inside each of them.

"This is mimicking a sound of the Ethereal Realm," Evlicka reminded them. "I doubt it>s something we'd hear, even were it not at this miniscule level."

Annilasia's panic over the lack of Music compounded with another anxiety. The idea of trapping a mirajin suddenly frightened her. A mirajin. An entity of pure aether, wielding energy that could crush her with a mere thought.

And she intended to trap such an entity. As she stood there, watching the model of constellations twirl about, the goal struck her as ludicrous.

Before she could voice her apprehension, a blinding light erupted in their midst. Out of the halos that broke into existence, radiating in slow bands, Annilasia could make out the faintest outline of a figure. It hovered above the model like a wrathful ruler over its disappointing kingdom. She couldn't take her eyes off its brilliance. Without even moving, the mirajin emitted a fluid elegance that surpassed any found in nature. Where legs would have sprouted in a human, faer form flowed into a large tendril of energy, like a plume of smoke tricked into solidity. Colors swirled amidst white light, rays of rainbows frolicking.

Pure aether.

When fae spoke, Annilasia trembled. The tranquility contained within faer dual tone of masculine and feminine frequencies held a judgement that threatened to unlace the very essence of her aura.

"What mockery is this?" fae asked. "Whoever dared to taunt us with this blasphemous rendition of the Music will answer to Sahruum and face a fate of well-deserved doom." Faer gaze fell upon Annilasia. "Was it you who interrupted my quest? You shall return with me to the Editshi Temple. Elothel and Besholaut can decide what to do with you."

Annilasia hesitated. But it didn't matter if this mirajin knew Elothel. Fae wouldn't be able to tell faem what she was about to do here. This was her moment. The mirajin was distracted, lured successfully by her crude model. Blasphemous or not, the sound had beckoned faem from the depths of the universe. Still, all resolve to capture this mirajin withered as she beheld it. Mauling this entity would be beyond a travesty. She'd be laying waste in a way that far exceeded any violence or debauchery committed by the twisters. Maybe even by the Sachem.

A roar of defiance thrashed the air. Plumes of darkness disrupted the halos bathing the hovering globes. Out of the smoky veil, a monstrous form sprang out. Inzerious shrieked as it collided with the mirajin, and aether blasted through the air in every direction. Annilasia fell to the ground as the energy wave streaked over her and across the bleak terrain. When she managed to force her head up, she found a grand scene unfolding above.

Aether streamed out in flying rainbows from the mirajin as fae tried to force the dokojin away with beams of plasmic energy. The black ichor that covered every inch of the dokojin took on a life of its own, lashing out in lithesome tentacles that sucked up the mirajin's aether into tiny tunnels of darkness. Yet some of the mirajin's light was breaking through, evoking anguished howls as it struck Inzerious.

"Annilasia! Do it!"

Drifter, who lay on the ground several yards opposite her, waved his wand frantically at her, his eyes huge. Beyond him, Evlicka was rising up off the ground from where the initial blast between dokojin and mirajin had launched her.

"You have to be the one to get the mirajin!" Drifter yelled over the thunderous emissions of aether. "Only you can see your lifechain!"

His words settled quickly. Annilasia scrambled to her feet and squared herself with the mirajin and dokojin. She focused her will, her determination, her terror of Inzerious's impending liberation.

She willed the mirajin into her wand.

On the opposite side of the battle, Evlicka worked the aether from her own glass wand to send the entire collection of globes charging at Inzerious. The dokojin tumbled under the assault and crashed into a mountain of boulders, which spat dust that rose to conceal Inzerious. Annilasia fought off the streak of panic that came with this obscuration, hoping that Evlicka would keep the dokojin occupied whenever it appeared again.

The mirajin attempted to flee. Fae angled upwards and would have shot into the sky—had it not been for the intense pull of the wand holding faem in place. The war between the wand's pull and the mirajin's sputtering aether created a horrendous droning like a ball of fire fighting to stay aflame in a torrent of wind. The earsplitting bass was pierced through by the mirajin's frantic screech as fae stretched faer arms towards the murky clouds above in desperation. The wand dragged the mirajin back inch by inch, slowly closing the distance between faem and its tip. Faer terrified shrieks intensified. Annilasia held steadfast, even as the wand threatened to snap out of her hand under the sheer intensity of the energy at play.

The tail end of the mirajin slipped into the wand. With a rush of aether, fae stopped, shaking in the matched tension between faer energy and the wand's. Then fae tried to blast forward, but the motion only ended with faem falling farther into the wand. Half of faem disappeared into the glass. Faer arms pressed at the edges of its soon-to-be prison. For the briefest of seconds, fae glanced back at Annilasia, bestowing upon her an expression of terror.

A wave of revulsion swept through her. She was the source of that desperation. That fear.

But she could not dwell on that. Instead, she thought of her freedom from Inzerious. She envisioned the dokojin's rage when she finally cut the cord connecting it to her. So strong were these desires, these *needs*, that they became the needs of the glass.

The mirajin's final shriek cut off abruptly as it shot inside the wand. The incessant humming, the drag of the wand, the mirajin's resistant fountains of aether—all crashed into silence. Within the wand, aether swirled with an angry vigor.

Annilasia suppressed the guilt that threatened to swarm her focus, instead clinging to her surging triumph over the mirajin's capture. She looked up with a sense of reinvigorated purpose. That confidence vanished immediately.

The terrain had gone from an indistinct shadowy setting to a cankerous field of violet tumors that spurted thick ichor. Eerily organic, the mounds pulsated and quivered as they merged with each other to form massive ulcers.

A rush of wind pushed against Annilasia. She raised an arm to her face to block the slime in the gust. A few yards ahead, amidst the newborn chaos, she made out two humanoid figures.

Towering beyond them was Inzerious.

The dokojin had evolved into a massive terror. Its bones were the size of tree trunks, grinding like a landslide as it moved. Eyes the size of small moons leered down at Drifter and Evlicka as Inzerious hunched over to bring its giant head closer to the them. The dokojin grinned, baring teeth that could easily skewer the twisters clean through from head to toe. Evlicka and Drifter both unleashed a torrent of rainbow prisms at the dokojin, which did little aside from provoking their foe. A waterfall of black ichor poured from Inzerious's mouth, and the two sprinted in opposite directions to escape the onslaught.

Annilasia fought against the wind and charged towards the scene. The ground palpitated under her feet, and black ichor erupted from the nearby spores. She shielded her face as it splashed her. The glass wand slipped from her grip and bounced off a veiny polyp before striking what little was left of solid ground. It landed with a clink.

The sound caught Inzerious's attention. "Too little, too late, Bloodspill," it roared. Black slime splattered off its bones with its movement, joining the puddles already lathering the malignant terrain. "My cage is gone. My reign inside your body starts now."

The towering mass of rotting bones dove at her. Annilasia's mind played out the imminent doom. She wouldn't be able to retrieve the wand in time; it lay too far away.

A volley of colorful aether struck the dokojin in the side of its exposed jawbone. Inzerious drew up short and howled. Another streak of energy burrowed into its skull like a woodmite. Its thunderous screech reverberated as the dokojin turned to locate Evlicka and Drifter. The twisters continued their assault; Annilasia didn't waste the precious time this earned her. She scrambled towards her wand and her fingers wrapped around it. The glass gleamed with anticipation as Annilasia traced the length of her lifechain, searching.

The ground quaked. A writhing in the corner of her vision told her Inzerious approached. No amount of aether would hold it back now. A skeletal foot the size of a hut smashed into the ground a few yards off, spewing ichor in seismic eruptions. Annilasia gripped her wand tightly. She refused to lose it again.

She spotted the offshoot chain and unleashed a defiant scream as she tipped the wand to point at it. The will to be free of Inzerious drove the aether out of the glass. The mirajin's wails returned to split the air but were drowned out by the dokojin's roar and Annilasia's own shriek. The aether's power, so strong that she slid backwards through the slime, collided with the lifechain in a flurry of sparks. A crescent rainbow spray bloomed at the point of collision.

Inzerious howled, its foot stumbling away from the spray. Its toes sizzled where a few sparks had landed and eaten through skin and bone, much like an ember on a leaf.

"You will be nothing without me," the dokojin shouted over the crackle of the aether. "You will shrivel up and die. No more power, no more future. You will fail, Bloodspill! Only I can defeat Dardajah for you. Only I!"

The lifechain snapped. Though no sound confirmed this, and though she couldn't see the chain through the blinding aether spray, the release of negative energy was apparent. The disconnection broke her. All strength evaporated, and her hand dropped with the wand still clenched within it. The flow of aether ceased. The squishy ground met her, and ichor swelled over her aura.

Her head flopped to the side, and she saw the dokojin. Inzerious no longer towered tall, now shrunk down to a hunched skeletal frame. Rage bled across its face as it entered a vengeful sprint at her. Razor-tipped claws stretched toward her with violent intent.

She didn't move. Agony crippled her. A moan croaked from her lungs.

Appearing from some other direction, Drifter and Evlicka interrupted her view. They crouched down at her side, and with their presence came a shimmering that spread across every inch of her vision.

Emptiness and weakness clung to her during the translation. Inzerious's form bled away, disappearing with the rest of the sickly ulcer-infested land.

She waited for the whispers in her head. She braced for the claws that would carve her skin the moment she returned to the physical world.

But the whispers didn't follow. Nor did the claws catch.

***

Annilasia wailed upon sinking into her physical body.

The clouds overhead passed by, apathetic to her pain, but she wailed at them again anyways. She ran her hands over her clothes and ripped at their edges, desperate to remove them. The emptiness, the pit of despair yawning open, had to go. Fingernails met with skin, but she didn't feel pain. Only the slimy texture of blood. She plunged her nails in deeper.

Someone else's hands grasped at hers. She thrashed against them and resumed her digging only to meet the same resistance. Muffled voices spoke. She understood the words to be protests. She heard the desperate plea in her shouted name. She ignored them. More blood on her hands.

The despair burrowed deeper. She had to extract it. She'd yank it out, rip its barbed roots from her aura and crush it in her fist. More blood. Almost had it.

A sharp pain wormed through her focus. Foreign hands grasped her wrists and pinned them down. She screeched and bucked against the restraint as a heaviness descended upon her chest. Through the dark shroud of her resolve, Drifter's face came into focus.

"Get off of me!" she shouted. "I have to get it out."

"Stop moving," Drifter commanded. "Listen to me. You have to calm down."

Annilasia thrashed harder. Drifter, who sat across her chest, pressed his weight into her. This brought a searing pain to the forefront of her senses, and she grew rigid. Stars danced in her vision, and a numbness sank into her muscles.

"Don't faint on . . ."

Drifter's voice disappeared, and she succumbed to an empty darkness.

CHAPTER 41

Annilasia's eyes fluttered open. She squinted against the light, then closed her eyes again. The smooth touch of satin and wool pillowed around her. A moan rose from her chest as pain broke through the pleasant sensation of blankets.

"I swear, if you try to claw out your own guts again, I'm going to knock you out."

Annilasia tried prying her eyes open again, this time fighting to let them adjust. Drifter's face came into focus, framed in front of a window through which the sun shone. From the snow-covered branches outside, she knew she was back at the coven. A shudder passed over her and she forced herself to exhale through her nostrils. "What happened?"

"You did it," a creaky voice said from a different part of the room. "You broke the lifechain."

Annilasia swiveled her head, a motion she instantly regretted after the pain it brought, to find Evlicka propped up on a cushioned cot against the wall. It was odd seeing the wrinkled woman in daylight and not swaddled in sheets. Thin, frothy hair sprouted from her head, and a timid grin curved upward against her wrinkles in a paradoxical expression amplified by her milky eyes. To Annilasia, Evlicka looked impossibly frail and weak compared to her vibrant and nimble aura. It was difficult to regard her with that uncomfortable reminder.

Yet that reminder came with another: the image of aether eating away at the chain that had connected her to the dokojin.

Relief flooded her even as she waited to hear whispers full of malice, or a barrage of horrid imagery. Her back tensed as she waited for the dokojin's invisible claws to reopen the old wounds across her shoulder.

But only quiet answered her. A peaceful, solitary quiet.

"I did it," she breathed. A release came from self-induced tension unraveling inside her. Her throat swelled up as she choked back a reflexive sob, and she turned her face away from the others to hide the tears swelling in her eyes.

Endless months of torture, of madness, of terror. The dokojin had nearly broken her. She had scars to prove it. One unfortunate incident so many months ago had brought her a lifetime's worth of pain and misery. It'd stolen her away from her pursuits, had taken her into a den of twisters.

Now, she was free.

Embarrassment finally managed to overpower her other emotions. She wiped the back of her hand across her eyes before turning back to face the others. "I thought you didn't like light," she said to Evlicka.

"I'm adjusting," Evlicka murmured, voice scratchy and burdened with malaise. "My healer here says I need to get used to it if I'm to grace the world with my presence again."

Annilasia winced and brought a hand to her chest. "I don't remember getting hurt."

Drifter's look was strange and unreadable. "We journeyed you away from the Apparition Realm," he explained. "When we got back and you grew conscious again, you began clawing at your chest. I couldn't get you to stop, and you only did so after you fainted."

Annilasia frowned and pondered this. She couldn't even remember the incident. "Maybe it was a reaction to severing the connection. Dokojin are aether after all. It probably wasn't easy for my aura to be suddenly altered that way." She ran her hand across the bandage that covered her upper chest. "Is it bad?"

Drifter sighed. "Just scratches. Deep scratches, mind you, but nothing life threatening. Will sting for a while. I've got some ointments that will help with that. It could have been a lot worse."

"You both saved me back there," Annilasia murmured, glancing between the two twisters. "I owe you both a great deal."

"We're even." Drifter raised his hand to reveal a thin piece of paper pinched between his fingers.

"So, you took the liberty of taking your payment before I awoke," she noted with disapproval.

"I might have been a bit eager after battling the dokojin," he responded dryly. He eyed her up and down. "But I am glad you're free of that thing. No one deserves to be possessed by those parasites."

Annilasia gave a grateful nod. An awkward silence settled as she grappled with all that had occurred. She was free. Finally and truly free. Part of her felt the significance of this. A weight had lifted, and she no longer sensed an invisible presence lurking over her shoulder or in the recesses of her mind. But another part of her felt spent. Scarred. Marked in a way that made her wonder if she'd ever feel herself again. Maybe this was who she was now. Dokojin touched. A mind and body that had housed the darkest filth known to the Realms.

"I need to leave." She took in their confused looks. "No one is safe as long as the Decayer device stands. If it hadn't been for that damn dokojin inside me, I would have already been on my way to Vekuuv to stop the Sachem. He can't be allowed to turn on that device."

"If it's the Sachem you want dead, there's no need to rush off," said Evlicka. "The Decayer device will meld the Realms. Dokojin will manifest in the physical world."

"That's my point," said Annilasia, irritated by the unhelpful input. "I have to stop that from happening."

"But have you considered that the Sachem is about to kill himself?" Evlicka pressed. "He's about to face the same fate that you would have met. A dokojin lurks inside of him. When the Realms come together, the man you know as the Sachem will perish, and only the dokojin that possesses him will exist here."

Annilasia envisioned it: Hydrim blown into a hundred pieces from the inside out, reduced to mere slivers of flesh as Dardajah emerged and entered the Terrestrial Realm.

"I take it from the look on your face that you didn't think of that," Drifter commented.

"I only thought of myself when I realized that particular danger," she admitted.

"Does that at all change your drive to go?" asked Evlicka. "If it's the Sachem you want dead, the job's already done for you."

Annilasia took a moment to ponder this before shaking her head. "No. The dokojin must be stopped. The Decayer device cannot be turned on."

Evlicka frowned. "This sounds unwise."

"It's downright foolish," Drifter broke in. "Not to pat myself on the back, but you couldn't even take down your own dokojin without some help. Now you want to try it again alone?"

"It's different this time," Annilasia countered. "I have the advantage of stealth. Dardajah won't know I'm coming. The leftover mirajin aether in my wand should be enough to take it down."

"Will it?" Drifter asked. "It was enough to break a lifechain, but you don't know that it's enough to conquer a dokojin itself. What we did offers no proof of that. We didn't defeat Inzerious. We escaped it."

Annilasia didn't answer. Heat flushed her cheeks. He had a point. She refused to concede though. She couldn't let the world fall into chaos without trying to stop it from happening.

Dying stars, I didn't sever myself from Inzerious only to give up my quest. The Sachem will not turn on that device. Dokojin will not infest the tribes.

"We've all three seen firsthand what kind of chaos the dokojin bring," she stated. "And the twisters are no better. They trapped Evlicka in a machine, and they are birthing a dokojin of their own that will be unleashed when the Decayer turns on. If you think that what you saw in the Apparition Realm earlier is an abnormality, then you're star-touched. Dokojin will bleed this world of everything. There won't be anyone left after they're done."

Evlicka's face fell, a sudden departure from her timid warmth, and she let out a sob as she flung her face into her hands. A shocked Drifter rushed over to lay a hand on her shoulder as the withered woman shook.

"She's right," Evlicka wailed, voice croaking with strain. "It was horrible in there. Whatever nightmare the mentors put me in, I wouldn't wish it on anyone." Her hands trembled as she pried her face away, milky eyes staring off. "I don't want to remember anything more than I already do."

"Then you must understand why I need to do this," Annilasia insisted. "I don't care what the mentors thought. There isn't a way to control a dokojin. Their plan will fail. Someone has to stop the Sachem before he melds the Realms. Once the dokojin are here in the Terrestrial, it'll be too late. They'll reside in physical shells until someone slays them, and even then, with the Realms joined, they will persist. There's no telling what they'll be capable of. They will want to keep their physicality once they have it. They might even regrow shells, again and again, to continue their terror."

"You're wounded," Drifter said sharply. "And not to be ableist, but your limp hinders you. Do you really think you can take on the Sachem, who has a dokojin empowering him? How will you even find him?"

"He's gone to Vekuuv already," she said. "I may be too late already. But I have to try. I don't think anyone else is going to."

Drifter glared at her. "You can't do it alone."

Annilasia didn't miss a beat. "I don't have much of a choice."

Evlicka sniffled and wiped away the snot dripping from her nose. "Take Drifter with you."

Drifter shook his head. "No. I can't leave you here without aid. There isn't anyone else left at the coven to attend to you. I refuse to abandon any patient of mine."

"How noble for a twister." Annilasia immediately regretted her words as she remembered the aid he and Evlicka had graciously given to save her. She pursed her lips under Drifter's disapproving gaze.

"You better hope you're enough of a *twister* to take on another dokojin," said Drifter. "'Cause *this* twister won't be there to save your ass this time."

The words stung. She swallowed, held by his fixed glare until he turned away toward Evlicka. Annilasia watched him assist the aged woman in lying down on her back, after which Evlicka quickly descended into a fit of snores.

Drifter moved towards the door but paused at the foot of the bed that hosted Annilasia.

"We aren't all wicked," he said quietly. "Some of us fell into this practice.

Orphans with no parents, no food on the table to fill our stomachs. We wave these glass wands around to stay alive and nothing more."

"There are other ways to survive," she murmured.

"Perhaps. But then again, here you sit, as much a twister as those you malign. As much a twister as those you've slaughtered and those who battled your dokojin so you could break free. Twisters are like any other clan or tribe out there. Wicked is in the heart, not the label. Try to remember that the next time you come across another one of us." He strode to the door, opened it, then hesitated once more within the doorframe. "Do you plan to rescue him?"

Annilasia's brow furrowed in confusion. "Rescue who?"

"The Sachem. I only wonder because we now know the link can be severed. I think it's safe to assume that enough mirajin aether could liberate the man from the dokojin, just as it liberated you. I think there's more hope of that than the leftover aether slaying Dardajah outright."

Annilasia opened her mouth, then closed it, unsure what to say. She hadn't thought of that. The idea curdled her stomach, but it refused to leave.

When she took too long to respond, Drifter snorted. "Guess you've got some things to think over. Try to rest. It sounds like you'll need all the strength you can muster."

He shut the door and left her. Only Evlicka's snores disturbed the quiet. For a while, Annilasia mulled over Drifter's piercing observations. On the topic of her trajectory here, he was certainly right, as much as she hated to admit it. It was easy to blame Inzerious for the path that had led her to the coven. If not for the dokojin, she would have finished her quest to slay the Sachem. Instead, she convinced herself that only the twisters could banish the dokojin from her—a belief that ended up being only partially accurate. But beyond that, she'd convinced herself that twisting was the only way to conquer the Sachem. A dokojin would only respond to aether. And there weren't any templites in the land anymore. Only twisters.

So, she'd learned twisting to survive, and she'd learned it for the task ahead.

Her mind snagged on that thought. The task ahead—another subject Drifter had managed to muddle. For years, she'd held to the belief that the only way to save the tribes was to kill the Sachem. Then, she'd realized it was a dokojin that she'd need to contend with. Still, she'd reasoned that the Sachem needed to die anyways—that he'd meet the grisly end he deserved when she came for the dokojin within him.

Now, she wasn't so sure the two went hand in hand. A way to save that wretched man existed. The idea sickened her. She wanted nothing to do with it. But it simply wouldn't leave her be, and it haunted her into the sleep that exhaustion eventually brought upon her.

CHAPTER 42

Mygo fiddled with the thick knots in the string wrapped around his wrists. When his fingers fell upon something much smoother than the threads, he paused, letting his fingers rove across it; only then did he let his muscles slacken. There wasn't any point in struggling if they'd used wire along with string. He listened to the drums thumping outside the dimly lit tent and the hoots and hollers that accompanied the beat.

They'd been held captive like this since the debacle at the bunker days ago. Marched back to the Vekaul camp promptly by Yetu, they were slated for trial by the two elders. Now the day for that trial had arrived, and already other prisoners—Ikaul from the looks of them—had been dragged out of nearby tents while screaming their supposed innocence. Where they got taken to, Mygo could only guess. He tried not to dwell on the spiked heads he'd seen upon his first visit to the camp.

He heard Vowt sniffle and turned to his companion, who was tied to his own post a few feet away. Both men sat on the ground and had been left alone for several hours as the festivities outside unfolded.

"Chin up, Vowt," he said. "No need to be distressed."

"We're about to d-d-die," Vowt so vividly pointed out.

"Sniffles won't stop the cycle of life and death, my friend. It's best to greet death with as much stoicism as one can muster."

"I don't know what that m-m-means."

In front of Mygo, the tent flaps parted to let Geshar and Yetu enter along with a few warriors. The pair regarded them with casual indifference. The brims of their eyes were inflamed with sunken red and black shades, and their eyelids drooped as if freshly opened from a deep sleep.

"Your trial begins shortly, beast hugger," said Yetu. "The tribe will determine your guilt."

"I don't suppose this will be a fair trial," Mygo mumbled. "Likely too much to ask of a crowd drugged to unfathomable levels."

A dark grin slid over Geshar's lips. "To the contrary; detruid makes it quite easy to see the truth of matters. Abisholo helps us know a person's true intentions."

"I think your celestial is less mirajin and more dokojin," said Mygo. "This falls on closed ears, but I advise you to stop listening to it."

Geshar bent over and placed her hands on her knees as she leaned in towards him. "I would be careful mentioning dokojin at this point. Your association with these flayer beasts already has you on trial with this crowd. Not to mention, you were carrying a twister wand on you. Best to keep your mouth shut."

"I'm not the one affiliated with a dokojin," Mygo said in a low voice. This earned him a large gob of spit from Geshar. It slid down his cheek, painting his face with her disgust.

She pushed off her hands to straighten and loomed over him. "You try to confound us by claiming we are the lost souls when it is you who partook in abominable aether. What Yetu described was one of the most sickening descriptions I've ever heard. You will be found guilty. Your aura needs the cleansing of Abisholo."

"I hope whoever oversees our judgement is less biased than you," Mygo grunted. He hissed when her hand struck the side of his face.

"Enough. Steady your auras. Your fate awaits." She gestured to the two warriors, who approached Mygo and Vowt to untie their bindings.

Once released from the posts, Mygo expected his wrists to be bound again and was shocked when this didn't occur. A small glimmer of hope arose in him at the oversight, and he chalked it up to the drugged state of the Vekaul. Instead, the warriors remembered only to place a gag in his mouth before leading him and Vowt outside the tent into the cold night.

The tribe of Vekaul swarmed amid the trees. A giant fire, with flames that roared nearly as high as the needled pineoaks that surrounded it, crackled with the crowd's manic shouts. The drums beat into his ears, and his heart raced in response. Wild abandon seized the crowd. Many danced with unhinged movements, while others swayed or laid on the ground shrieking at the top of their lungs. The concert of clashing noises only heightened his anxiety as he was led towards a platform erected near the fire.

Mygo dry heaved when the smell of burnt skin crowded his nostrils, but the warrior at his back shoved him onward and up the platform's steps. Around it, smoke rose from newly spiked heads, their flesh blackened and shriveled. Blood sizzled as it ran down the poles in globs. Black skin ink could still be made out on some of the faces. More of the Ikaul, then.

Once on the platform, Mygo saw that a bridge connected the platform to the fire. So. He and Vowt were destined to be burned alive. He thought he heard Vowt let out a soft wail, but it was hard to tell over the crowd and the fire. Or maybe it was himself that let out the sound. His chest sank in as he tried to breath, but the smoky air clogged his throat. He licked his lips and struggled to swallow, unable to dismiss the fresh imagery of the bloodied spikes and shriveled burnt heads. Soon, his and Vowt's heads could be joining them.

Movement out of the corner of his eye caught his attention, and he turned his neck to see Geshar and Yetu joining them on the platform to face the crowd. The appearance of its leaders drew the tribe's attention, though many continued to dance and chant even while cheering and pumping fists into the air.

Geshar raised her arms. "Listen, people of Vekaul. Justice reigns again this night, as it does every night amongst our tents. Abisholo brings judgement down upon those who corrupted our original tribes, and has tasked us with meting out this judgement upon those worthy of it. We witnessed the trials of the Ikaul tonight, and found them guilty of treason and malicious intent. Now, let us have our final trial of the night."

The crowd's frenzy grew with each sentence, and soon her words were drowned out by a single chant from the crowd.

"Blood! Blood! Blood!"

Geshar moved sideways, dropped one arm, and gestured with the other in the direction of Mygo and Vowt. Whatever she said never graced Mygo's ears. He couldn't imagine how anyone could possibly have made out the words over the fire's frenzy and the crowd's furor.

A figure appeared at the front of the platform. The man climbed up over the edge and stood. Geshar and Yetu turned to him, and Mygo noticed their surprise at his arrival. The newcomer waved his arms wildly overhead and bellowed for the crowd to silence. The chanting died down some as curiosity overwhelmed primal drives.

"I have found her! I have found the Tecalica!"

The crowd erupted again in cheers. Mygo saw his own confusion scrawled over the faces of Yetu and Geshar. One of the warriors who had accompanied Vowt and Mygo approached the man in a clear attempt to persuade him off the platform. But when he laid a hand on the man's arm to nudge him towards the steps, the man shrugged him off. When the warrior tried again, the man shoved him over the platform's edge. The crowd roared, fueled by the violence.

"Listen!" the strange man shouted. "She is here among us! I saw her wandering around. Her skin is marred and her hair nearly gone. Look around you. Find the deformed woman with red hair and bring her up here!"

Geshar and Yetu exchanged fretful glances. Yetu darted towards the man with a string of protests but stopped short when the man swiveled towards him in a fighting stance. While the two argued, the crowd seemed to undulate as everyone turned in circles to find this red-haired culprit. A moment later, shouts broke out from the back of the crowd, and a small group moved together towards the platform, pushing the alleged Tecalica through the jeering mob.

Mygo's heart fell when he saw the woman—the one Yetu called Delilee—being dragged onto the platform past a distressed Geshar, who grabbed for the woman but was pushed away by those corralling Delilee forward. The man who had made the wild claims shoved Yetu aside and addressed the crowd as he moved up beside Delilee.

"Behold! Red locks of hair. The only family that still boasts this tainted color is that of the Tecalica. Where has she gone, many wonder." His hand flew out, snatched the back of Delilee's head, and shook it. "She is here!"

The crowd erupted. Arms flailed with frantic energy and some clawed at their hair and faces.

"This is not the Tecalica!" Yetu shouted. "She is not who you think she is. Release her."

The man regarded Yetu with a look of disgust. "They protect her!" He pointed at Yetu. "They are traitors!"

The screaming pitched higher. The crowd pushed forward, some clambering onto the platform. Mygo tried to retreat, but the warrior at his back refused to give up his post.

Still gagged, Mygo could only protest in a throaty squawk.

"Quiet, traitor," the guard growled. Behind him, though, Vowt was in a running sprint. He bent, ramming the guard with his shoulder and knocking him over with the impact. Liberated from his captor, Mygo wasted no time. He rushed forward in the direction of Delilee. Some saw his course and drove out arms to stop him, but this did little to slow his momentum as he collided with Delilee and the few who'd managed to swarm her. He, and those in his path, tumbled over the front of the platform and crashed to the ground.

Mygo heard a crack, and pain seared through his shoulder. He shrieked through his gag. The reality of his circumstances fought against the instinct to surrender to the pain, and he struggled to his feet. Hands scrabbled for him from all sides and heaved him up. They groped at his face and clawed at his eyes. He thrashed his waist to twist his shoulders about. The hands kept at him. He stopped struggling instead and dropped all his weight. Hands slipped free, and he made it into a crouch, then tore headfirst like a bull through the sea of legs surrounding him, managing to knock over some of his assailants.

Someone dropped their knife and it landed on the ground before him. He dove for it and sprang back up, swinging it wildly. The crowd backed away in a circle around him, still blocking him in. Mygo swiped out, and a man fell back with blood gushing from his stomach. The surrounding circle widened as everyone else stumbled back out of the vicinity of Mygo's whirling blade.

He risked the briefest of glances to the platform in search of Vowt. It was only a second—too short to actually locate his friend because he couldn't give these people a moment to overtake him—but what he did glimpse weighted his chest. He looked away, wishing he couldn't hear the shrieks that accompanied the haunting scene: burly figures dragging Yetu across the bridge and towards the fire. In between his parries of attacks from the crazed individuals dashing at him with their own weapons, Mygo heard Yetu's screams grow and grow until a final screech detonated, signaling the man's gruesome fate. His dying screams burned away with his body, only to be replaced by Geshar's jeers as she held her ground somewhere on the bridge.

Mygo spotted Delilee in the crowd, forcing his ears to focus on her shrieks instead of Geshar's. The red-haired woman was lashing out at the sea of hands tugging and yanking at her. A short-lived moment of freedom permitted her to turn and begin to run only to be yanked back by unrelenting fingers that found her tunic and hair.

Mygo ripped the gag from his mouth, unleashed a fierce yell, and sprinted towards her. Fists and knives swung at him as he shoved his way to Delilee. By the time he came up beside her, he'd earned a web of cuts and slashes across his exposed limbs and face. Still the Vekaul attacked. A frenzied woman screeched as she charged at Delilee, long fingernails slashing. Mygo pivoted the woman away, hoping to avoid truly hurting her. But when she came at them again, accompanied by an equally crazed young man, Mygo gave up such noble etiquette. Blood ran freely from the two assailants, who fell to the ground with large gashes that evoked howls.

Mygo pressed Delilee behind him, backing them towards the pillars of the platform until they were underneath it. To his relief, the area beneath the structure was empty, and he was able to push Delilee towards the open forest behind it as those on their tail closed in on them.

"Run! Don't look back, and run!"

He didn't watch to make sure she listened. There was no time. A man had taken advantage of his inattentiveness, his axe already swinging down on him. Mygo rolled away, barely escaping the blade's powerful downswing, and threw his knife at the man's torso. It landed deep, and the man dropped his weapon to work at the knife, giving Mygo an opening to retrieve the axe. He flexed his arms as he adjusted to the weight of this new weapon. His next swing came down on a new attacker's head, their skull splitting like a melon.

Mygo yelled out for Vowt as he continued to fend off those who spotted him in his makeshift lair beneath the platform. He listened for his companion's resounding response, but none came. Instead, he heard Geshar screaming at her kin up above. From the sound of it, she was cornered on the bridge, but she must have had some sort of weapon for her to have lasted this long.

Out in front of the platform and amongst the trees, where the crowd had gathered for Geshar's speech, skirmishes had broken out. The people congregated in clusters from which victors emerged after frantic screams, running blood, and rolling heads. Those victorious invaded other clusters, overwhelming those attempting an offense until their blood joined the pools staining the ground.

No sign of Vowt. Mygo's heart fell. He couldn't stay here. The strongest from each cluster would soon band together. He couldn't be around when that happened. He waited a moment longer, brought his axe down on a few more manic assailants. Geshar's verbal challenges to her opponents became frenzied shouts, and a scuffle on the floorboards above Mygo told him Geshar was being forced far too close to the fire. A howl of sheer terror split from her and then morphed into one breathless screech that rivaled the roar of the fire.

His time was up. Mygo turned and ran towards the forest. A bright line of red caught his attention as he ran. He swore violently at the wild flames engulfing one of the trees near the bonfire. There'd be a forest fire now. His sprint would be not only to escape murder but also to reach somewhere impervious to the flames, and the only place he knew—his bunker—was miles away. Behind him, he heard the endless pounding of drums and new cries of victory.

Sahruum, you damn bastard, Vowt better be alive.

The few stragglers who followed him into the forest taunted him with crass threats and dirty comments. Their boots pounded behind him, and he had no option but to keep running. He couldn't shake the desire to track down Delilee or find Vowt, but neither was an option with these demented stalkers on his trail.

Mygo's mind kept flashing back to the fire-tipped tree back at the platform. It grew in his mind, the blaze spreading until everything in his mind's eye succumbed to fire. It'd be upon them quickly. There was no way that drug-induced crowd had the means to stop a forest fire, and more than likely, many of them would fall victim to the same fate they'd forced on Yetu and Geshar.

Tortured screams and burned skin.

Lost in these visages of ominous death, he didn't hear or see the ambush. One of his stalkers had sprinted ahead and cut him off; they sprang at him now from behind a tree. The pair fell and tumbled across the forest ground. New scrapes split Mygo's skin. He returned to his feet quickly but empty-handed. A growl sounded nearby, and he turned in time to catch the brute force of his assailant's head with his abdomen. All air left Mygo's lungs as the man rammed them both into a tree. Stars danced in his vision as his head met the trunk, and he almost didn't see the flash of something metal in time to duck down. The knife bit into the tree's bark as he stumbled away, hunched over.

He glanced around for the axe lost to him during the tumble, but the night's darkness veiled the weapon. With no more time to look, he faced his opponent again. The knife lashed at him in sloppy streaks. The rustle of underbrush behind him meant the man's kin had found them; one newcomer emerged with blade drawn. Even as Mygo dodged the uncoordinated strikes of two inebriated attackers, the clock in his head ticked away, counting down to when he'd see that unnatural light pressing against the darkness from the direction he'd fled—a smoldering orange and yellow crackling with a vengeance and choked with smoke.

Fire was coming.

A blade slid across his arm, and he yelped. The sting brought him out of his thoughts again. He needed to shake these two. They would burn in the fire if he could get away. Already, he thought he could feel the drafts of smoke drilling into his lungs.

A sharp whistle pricked his ear. One of the attackers flew back with odd propulsion and landed on the ground with a thump. The other stared down at the fallen man, as confounded by the outcome as Mygo. Another whistle, and the remaining attacker's head split in two. Blood spurt into the air before he sank to fall flat on his face.

Mygo breathed heavily and spun in a circle. The arrows had ceased, but he wondered if they'd struck true, or if some drunken tribe member had accidentally killed his pals here and was now trying to aim for a third time at Mygo. A head popped up from behind a fallen log.

"Psst! Mygo."

Relief flooded Mygo as he trotted over to Vowt. "What are you doing here? Why didn't you keep running?"

"I got tired. We're farther from their c-c-camp than you think."

Mygo halted when another figure rose up from behind the log, but sighed heavily at the sight of Delilee's petrified face.

"I was hiding and saw—saw—saw her," Vowt explained. "Took d-d-down one of her stalkers with this." Vowt held up the bow with a sense of pride that bubbled into his voice. "Saved your ass too."

"And I'm grateful," Mygo said. "But we need to go. This place is going to be on fire soon, and if we don't start now, we won't be able to outrun it."

"A fire?" Vowt mumbled. "From where?"

Mygo had already grabbed Delilee's hand and was gesturing to her as he led them into the forest. "We need to run. Do you understand? Fire." He saw confusion in her eyes, and she flinched away from his touch. He pointed to the slain men. "Danger. Run."

That got through to her. She eyed the men and nodded. He let go of her hand and walked backwards on his heels to watch and see if she'd comply. When she did, he glanced to Vowt and waved at his companion to follow.

"We don't have time to discuss. We're going to the bunker. Neither of us stops without saying something; we can't lose sight of each other. I need you to take the lead, and I'll bring up the rear to make sure no one gets left behind."

Vowt put aside his curiosity and darted into the forest without further exchange. Mygo pointed after him and told Delilee to follow. She eyed him one last time, sizing him up with uncertainty before running after Vowt.

Mygo sniffed the air once before dashing after them. He could smell it. The fire scoured the forest already. Not far now. He wondered how many of the Vekaul had fled before it was too late. Wondered how many had stayed behind to try and put out their clumsy mistake, only to be devoured in the flames of their fury. He wondered how many had simply danced and howled at the moon as the fire overtook them, too damn drugged to realize their time in the Terrestrial Realm drew nigh.

CHAPTER 43

The fire came for them in a wall of devouring rage. The forest trees gave way to it with loud pops and snaps. Devoid of most life, the trees didn't spit any creatures into flight like Mygo and his companions, but at one point, he thought he saw something large out of the corner of his eye—a shadow that moved and defied all other shadows. He dared not waste any precious time in a panic over the possibility that it was a flayer, but was nevertheless grateful when the bunker came within his sights soon after. At his back, the fire encroached. Their race ended here, and just barely did they make it into the bunker before the wall of flames struck.

"Shut the windows! Use the metal slats!"

Vowt followed his lead and ran to the openings that left them vulnerable to the fire. Heat radiated from the other side, and embers spiraled in as he forced one of the slats shut. Objects battered the roof, no doubt detached branches.

"We should go deeper. We might cook on this level." Sweat drenched his clothes, and the sealed entry points weren't letting the fire's heat dissipate. "Let's go into the duality chamber. There's better ventilation there."

Vowt grabbed at his arm. "It's m-m-messy down there. From . . . before."

Mygo hesitated. He pictured the guts and blood spoiling down below. The smell alone might overpower them. He swore under his breath. "We can at least stand in the stairway and close the door until what's left to burn out there burns."

Once crowded on the stairs, he sealed them behind the iron door, which groaned when the mechanics clicked into place, and shoved the latch to lock it. Darkness engulfed them, but it was the smell that assaulted, just as he'd feared. He heard Delilee gag and take a ragged breath in a paradoxical attempt at finding relief from the stench.

"It smells, Mygo," Vowt murmured, as if his companion wasn't inhaling the same horrible odor.

"We need to clean up the mess," Mygo grunted. But he still didn't move after saying this. He didn't want to go down there and see the source of the stench. He didn't want to see the macabre manifestation of his failure.

Vowt tugged at his sleeve. "Let's go, Mygo. She—she—she needs c-c-clean air."

Behind him, Delilee's labored breathing finally registered for Mygo. He couldn't see her, but her rapid breaths and sharp inhalations made it clear that she was suffering some sort of anxiety or asthma attack. It was this—the necessity to face his disgust and fears in order to help someone else—that gave him the resolve to blindly make his way down the steps and enter the chamber. Vowt followed him, but Delilee remained huddled on the stairs.

"We need light, Vowt. Find the candle. Then we turn on the ventilators."

He heard Vowt move towards where the cabinet stood, followed by the scuffle of cupboard drawers opening and something breakable smashing on the ground. Vowt muttered under his breath, and then came a match strike. A flame burst to life, which Vowt tilted towards a candle sitting on the cabinet's edge.

Mygo turned slowly, covering his mouth with his arm. He'd known what he'd see, but the black liquid and contortion of bones sent him into a dry-heaving fit. He turned and coughed, his stomach constricting. Only clear bile spilled from his lips, as there was no food to regurgitate.

"Find the s-s-switch for the—the—the ventilation," said Vowt.

Mygo stumbled over to the far side of the cabinet, where a panel of smeared glass ran flush with the wall. He threw back the glass panel and shoved his fingers towards the red knob. The switch flipped and a low groan emitted somewhere behind the wall. Overhead, one of the ceiling pipes shuddered as the noise leveled out to a dull hum.

It took some time for the air to clear up. The stench never left, but its heavy weight did lift. When it became somewhat bearable, Mygo confronted the mound waiting for him in the corner. The candle's feeble light elongated the shadows of the carcass's humanoid face, which added unnerving angles to its expression. Mygo couldn't settle on what emotion it held—horror, rage, agony. Maybe all three. The glassy eyes stared up unblinkingly at the ceiling, while the mouth gaped open in a silent wail.

"I can do it all if—if—if you need me to. I've c-c-cleaned it all up before . . . by myself."

Guilt washed over Mgyo, and not for the first time, he admired Vowt's stout reaction to the scenery. Sometimes this stoicism in his companion disturbed him—he pondered how anyone with a sane mind could handle this type of butchery—but at this moment, he was grateful that one of them could stomach it enough.

"No. Not this time." He turned to Vowt, noticed the metal shovel in one hand, and took it. Vowt turned to retrieve the mop stowed away in a corner near the stairs. He noticed Delilee at the same time Mygo did. She was cowering against the wall and avoiding looking further into the chamber. She'd seen the carnage.

Mygo cringed. She had no idea who he or Vowt were, and they'd led her from one form of violence to the aftermath of another. He could only imagine what deranged imaginings were haunting her. To Delilee, the two men probably appeared more akin to kidnappers than fellow survivors.

Vowt went up to Delilee and murmured something, then came back down the steps with the mop.

"Is she okay?" Mygo asked. "Did you tell her what it is we're cleaning up?"

Vowt shook his head. "She—she—she didn't speak. Didn't want me anywhere near her. I told her to c-c-close her eyes and not look—look—look over here anymore. That we'd be c-c-cleaning it up."

Mygo glanced back to Delilee. She buried her head in her arms and scrunched up into a ball on one of the steps. "They say she can't form new memories," he said. "If that holds, she won't remember this tomorrow."

"A blessing, perhaps."

Mygo nodded, though the sentiment soured in his mind. Her memory loss probably scared her, and it seemed a stretch to think of it as a blessing, even in this scenario. Still, he wished he could forget. Wished he could slink away into a corner, confused about it all, and let someone else deal with the mess.

He tipped the shovel down. His shoulder protested with a surge of pain that he tried to ignore as he raked the shovel along the ground. Squishing sounds followed as dark shapes tumbled into the shovel's embrace. Liquid slid across the metal, glistening in the meager candlelight. He forced himself not to focus on these details that would certainly lead to another dry heave. He pushed the shovel towards the opposite corner of the room to a chute in the wall. The tunnel shaft led to a furnace, where the waste of previous attempts had gone for incineration.

Where he'd now dump the gory remnants of his latest failure.

***

Hours later, Mygo slumped onto the lowest stair and groaned. His back ached, and the odor clung to his clothes and inside his nostrils. But it was finished. The carnage of his failure was gone, swept under the ground, never to see the light of day again. Euphoric relief had leapt through him when he'd pulled the lever for the incinerator, knowing the fires were burning away the scraps of evidence.

Yet even as he surveyed the cleaned room and basked in the lack of gore splattering the walls, the jarring memory of what had cluttered the floor crept back into his mind. He shut his eyes, hoping that would help.

It didn't.

"So, who—who—who is she?" Vowt sank down beside Mygo while watching the woman higher on the staircase. She hadn't moved, but the subtle rise and fall of her torso indicated that smoother breathing had graced her at some point. Perhaps sleep had as well.

"I don't know, really," Mygo answered. "But I don't think she belonged with the Vekaul. More like she belonged *to* them."

"I want to know her story," said Vowt, and he went to stand but Mygo's arm shot out to stop him.

"Her mind ails her. She can't remember anything."

Vowt sank back down. "Mind sick. Sounds like Jalice. And her hair is the s-s-same red . . ."

Mygo sighed. "A bit discouraging, eh? If it turns out to be her, seems like our efforts down here have been nothing more than gory, failed experiments."

Vowt scowled at him. "What do you mean f-f-failed?" He pulled something out of his pocket and held it up towards Mygo. "We don't need this anymore?"

Mygo straightened to better inspect Vowt's item. The candle over on the cabinet barely illuminated the spot where they were resting. But whatever Vowt held reflected what little bit of light touched its surface.

"What is that?"

"The vial. From before they took us."

Mygo stared at Vowt, not daring to jump to a hopeful conclusion. "What's in the vial?"

"The brain slime from the f-f-flayer. I grabbed it during your chants, just like we—we—we planned. Didn't I tell you?"

Mygo shook his head, staring at the vial in disbelief.

"We failed to s-s-save the flayer," Vowt elaborated as he handed the vial over. "But we g-g-got the fluid, and we know that—that—that my elixir worked on that flayer. It feared fire again. Since it works, all I have to d-d-do is recreate it with this extract from—from—from the flayer."

Mygo held it up, seeing the slightest hue of green in the dim rays of light. "I wish we could have saved the flayer—the man and the critter."

"Me too." Vowt fidgeted with his hands as a restless wave of excitement crept over him. "But do you think we can s-s-save him? The Sachem?"

"Depends on if you can make this work, my friend. We used up what we had. Call me gloom and doom, but it's always risky to claim success before securing it."

"I can make it work," Vowt stated, his head bobbing up and down. "Just like it worked this l-l-last time."

Mygo offered the vial back. "I don't know if it matters. If that's Jalice up there, is breaking our backs worth it to save a fellow who doesn't want saving?

We were doing this for her. If she can't even remember her own husband, maybe that voids our task. She won't care if the Sachem is redeemed if she doesn't even know she's married to him."

Vowt frowned. "No. We are doing this because it is the right thing to d-d-do."

The statement hit Mygo like an arrow and he flinched. Once again, shame filled him, and he gave his companion a firm nod. "Aye, I suppose we are. Then I guess we need to make this count."

"It *will* count," Vowt asserted. He slipped the vial back into his pocket and hummed a string of playful notes as he swayed side to side on the stair's wooden boards.

Mygo left it on that hopeful closing, but his mind, as it always did, drifted back into the abyss of darker ruminations. The world literally burned above them. A woman bearing too close a resemblance to Jalice was cowering nearby with a complete loss of memory. And the Vekaul had descended into drug-fueled genocide.

The noise of guts spilling across bone and the imagery of coiling innards drove into his vision, filling the space of the chamber. He didn't fight it. To deny this darkness brewing in his mind was to invite insanity. When darkness existed, ignoring it only let it expand to unfathomable depths. He let it spill into his thoughts, his emotions, his vision.

Perhaps he and Vowt could repeat their success with the creation of the elixir. Perhaps it would save one man from a life of enslavement and pain. But so many were already lost. Saving the Sachem seemed pointless and even wrong given the man's role in the death of so many.

The innards gushed with blood as they twisted and moved like a writhing nest of snakes or worms. They crawled towards him, and he let the nightmare encroach.

Maybe in the end the only thing left to do was survive. Run and try to escape this nightmare. Mygo let this seed of fantasy grow, and it succeeded in overwhelming the mirage of sentient entrails.

He could take Vowt and Delilee and flee with them. That was all that was left to do. Mygo let out a long sigh and closed his eyes. He pictured the sea, the sails of a small boat. He heard the cry of gulls overhead. In between these conjured hallucinations, plans started to connect and form.

Yes, I'll flee when it's safe to leave the bunker again. Let the Sachem keep his land. He'll burn right along with it in the end.

For now, Mygo would let Vowt hold on to the valiant goal of recreating the elixir—the chymist needed something to occupy his anxious mind. But when the time came, Mygo would take them away from these violent tribes.

He knew, deep down, that these lands already belonged to death and dokojin.

CHAPTER 44

The road to Vekuuv was quiet and cold.

Once Annilasia departed the Orphan Mountains, she kept to less traveled roads that bypassed the unwanted company of strangers. The chilled wind dried her skin and hollowed out her lungs. Even her well-fitted cloak—insulated with fur—and the temporary extractions of aether that she heated with sparks of rage couldn't keep her entirely comfortable. In moments when the wind swelled and whistled in the untucked portions of her tunic to evoke shudders, her mind wandered to her last exchange with Drifter. She replayed the entirety of it more than once during her journey west.

To her surprise, the silence around her added to her discomfort. For months now, she'd been burdened with the unfortunate company of malicious twisters whose every move dripped with narcissism and a hunger for power. The idea of getting back on the road, alone with only her own thoughts, was what had spurred her to learn what she could during her many days at the coven. Now that such a departure had arrived, satisfaction floundered under the pressure of her circumstances. A gnawing cavern continued to grow inside her with each passing day. It was as if the absence of Inzerious had left a vacancy that her mind and aura simply couldn't accommodate, and they were thus eroding away. She was glad to be rid of the parasite but wondered if she'd ever learn to live without it. Her mind seemed hollow without another voice arguing with her thoughts.

She tried not to think of what awaited her should she translate now, after all that. Surely the dokojin had not given up or fallen away to prey on some other unfortunate soul. Its vendetta was likely fueled all the more by her insurgence. If she translated into its Realm, Inzerious would be waiting for her, and this time it wouldn't be so diplomatic in its quest to conquer her. She imagined its appetite for control—its taste for vengeance—would override the logic of resuming its long-game tactics for hijacking her body. Hence forth, she would avoid translating if possible. How she would gather more aether or exist as a formidable twister without entering an aether Realm wasn't something she wished to dwell on.

A problem for another day.

The only distraction that pulled her attention away from such ruminations was the Sachem, but in ways she hadn't ever conceived. For the first time since she'd decided, so many years ago, to take down the Sachem, she now imagined for Hydrim a fate alternative to a gory demise.

Hydrim. She hadn't thought of the Sachem as still being Hydrim since the day he'd enslaved her tribe. She blamed the resurgence of this perspective on Drifter. Had the twister not spoken of Hydrim's possible salvation, she would never have given it a second thought.

Out of nowhere, Jalice's voice trickled into her thoughts, and Annilasia cringed. Before hearing the mentors talk about her, she hadn't thought about the Tecalica in months. It seemed that dwelling on Hydrim had freed memories of the red-haired woman, whose phantom voice pleaded with her to spare the Sachem. Annilasia wasn't sure if Jalice had ever actually asked her to do that in so many words. Jalice had never been convinced anything was truly wrong with her husband until after the events months ago at the Black House. In fact, now that Annilasia thought harder on it, the sentiment of salvation had originated with Elothel.

Recalling the mirajin sent another shudder through her, sustained by the howling wind. Best not to dwell on faem. Not when her own hypocrisy came to spit in her face every time she glanced down at her glimmering wand. Saved one mirajin only to abuse another.

The sadistic workings of her mind kept falling back on Hydrim's doom. She pictured in great detail his last moments—the way his skin would stretch impossibly thin, how his eyes would bulge from the pain and the need to burst under the combustible force mounting within. Blood would push out the eyeballs—would flow out of the mouth and nose and eye sockets in fountains as his skin split into tiny shreds.

The scene ended abruptly at that climax. She wouldn't let her mind imagine what sinister force lay at the source of that combustion, or how the destruction of Hydrim's body would unveil an entity far too similar to Inzerious. It disturbed her enough that she was even contemplating such violent details. She'd always blamed Inzerious for such images. With the dokojin gone, she could only blame her own depraved mind.

She welcomed the distraction that came upon arriving at the border, though the obstacle simply replaced one set of stressors for another. The giant wall towered in the sky like a mountain range lacking peaks and valleys. The forest ran straight up against it, thinning to a clearing only where the gate interrupted the otherwise unbroken construction of stone and metal.

Beyond it lay Vekuuv. A land she hadn't seen in over two decades.

Annilasia nudged her steed forward, not wishing to accept the nostalgia trying to surface or its many other accompanying emotions. Sentimentality would do nothing to help her. The challenge of the wall remained. A battalion patrolled the clearing preceding the gate. Warriors marched and trained; guards stood at their posts in rigid discipline. At least three hundred or so that she'd have to either evade, conquer, or circumvent. None of those options promised a favorable ending for her.

When she came within range of the scouts that watched the paths, a horn blast split through the air. The marching ceased, and the men scattered to retrieve their weapons like a colony of ants. Arrows were notched into bowstrings and aimed in her direction. Shield bearers formed a line in front of warriors who wielded swords and axes. Then came those on horse to meet her. They broke formation and navigated the dirt path to where it converged with the forest's edge where she waited.

"Proclaim your name and purpose here," a warrior called. His vibrant yellow paint denoted his leadership status in the group.

"I am a twister seeking to cross the border into Vekuuv."

The warriors eyed her, and one edged her horse closer to the leader to whisper something to him. The leader's eyes grew wide, and he said, "You're Annilasia. Traitor to the Sachem." The warriors around him brandished their weapons.

She sighed. "I'm also a twister and former tillishu." She cocked an eyebrow at them. "Do you really want to challenge me?"

The leader hesitated. "You're one twister against an entire battalion. You can't kill us all before we slay you."

"You really want to take that chance?" she asked.

The hesitation deepened. Doubt crept into his eyes, slid down the stern lines of his face. "We can't let you through. There's a price on your head."

"A price set by who? The Sachem? Lucky for you, I'm on my way to see him. I'll save you the trouble of having to try and take me down and simply surrender myself to him."

"Why would you do that?" he asked. "Why are you running to him instead of away?"

"My business is my own," she responded. "Now, are you going to make this difficult, or are you going to let me through?"

She let the tension build around that question. The decision weighed in his eyes, as one did in hers. If he insisted on taking her captive, she'd have to use force. Not with her own glass wand, of course. She couldn't waste the precious mirajin aether on these imbeciles. Instead, she'd use one of the additional wands she'd brought, reforged from the glass globes she'd used for the solar model. Her hand dove into her pocket to grasp it.

The leader straightened. "In the name of the Sachem, unifier of the—"

The glass wand swiped into view, and she created a ward around her horse to keep it oblivious to the chaos to unfold. She let out a deranged cry. The wand twitched to point at the ground, and a halo of invisible energy blasted from its tip. The earth shook with a thunderous crack. Shouting from the battalion buzzed over the earth's grumbles. Their cries escalated into wails as the ground caved in. A massive sinkhole swallowed the warriors lined against the wall, while the mounted forces fought to keep control over their panicked steeds.

The wails trailed off. The ground began to seal itself, breaking apart to fill the sudden gap. The closing chasm shifted towards the horsemen, and all but one fell into it with their steeds. The last remaining warrior, the leader who had addressed Annilasia, leapt from his horse, losing it to the canyon, and scrambled across what remained of steady ground. The edge crumbled further, the hole inching closer to him. He teetered, one foot hovering over the drop. A knife flashed in his hand, and he threw it at her.

She twisted, letting the weapon clatter to the ground. A broad stride of her horse brought her close to the man. His wide eyes, previously swelling with fury, flashed with panic. Before he could stop her, she threw out her leg to kick him in the chest. The strike deflated his lungs, stealing away the dignity of a scream as he fell into the pit at his back. Dirt and rock encased the man as Annilasia flourished the wand to seal the ground once more.

The land between her and the wall was devoid of life now. Every tree and warrior that had moments before blocked her path now lay several feet below ground. If they weren't already dead, they soon would be. Perhaps someday someone would dig up their remains. That is, if anyone ever figured out that they were there at all. For a moment, she wondered how much aetherwaste she had just created in the Apparition Realm. Such violence had surely spoiled any purity gracing this portion of the land. But she dismissed this line of thought, unwilling to feel any dismay over the consequences of her actions. These men, with their violent motivations, had already been corrupting the aether Realms merely by existing. Ending them might have added to the aetherwaste, but she had done a service to the land by doing so. Now it was free of Ikaul filth.

And as far as personal consequences for using aether, she failed to sense any. Except perhaps for the emptiness that continued to eat away at her. The ever-widening pit had certainly expanded with the attack. Perhaps that was why she was so numb over it all. A past version of herself might have been troubled by such apathy.

Annilasia lifted the ward from her steed, who'd remained calm throughout the ordeal. The animal trod forward, unaware of the hundreds of bodies buried beneath its hooves as it approached the gate. A last twitch of aether lifted the massive slab of grated metal. Vekuuv stretched out before her.

Home at last.

For a brief moment, she permitted nostalgia to rush over her. This was the land she'd grown up in. The land that fed and nourished her people. A few flashes of childhood memories played out in her mind, full of laughter and lush forests. The blissful rumination shattered as she breached the other side of the wall. She tugged on the reins of her horse to bring it to a stop. Her stomach churned as she fought off a nauseating despair.

The contrast between Ikaul at her back and what lay beyond the border wall crushed her. Where once luscious forests sprinkled the rolling hills, a desert stripped of all life stretched out before her. Where once streams of clean, refreshing water bubbled and weaved between the valleys, a stale and stagnant slush festered with bulbous mounds that popped with acidic spray. No life caught her eye, not even the stray raptor soaring in the sky in search of a decaying carcass. Her steed found the scene just as disturbing, refusing her commands to proceed through the desolated land. It wasn't until she set another ward of ignorance upon it that it finally started moving forward.

She convinced herself that the scenery would change eventually—that this ominous display was only to dissuade those who dared to cross the border. But as the miles stretched on, the desert persisted. She watched for signs of life, scanning the horizon and eyeing the creeks of sludge. When truth set in, she stopped her steed again, leaned sideways, and hurled what spittle and food tossed about in her stomach.

This land was gone. Her kin were nowhere to be seen.

She'd suspected as much over the years. Rumors had spread after the Sachem's Purge when the border wall had been erected. The Ikaul warriors had boasted of raging fires and a mass exodus from Vekuuv villages and tent flocks. According to these rumors, the Ikaul had invaded the land and driven the inhabitants towards the Vekuuv Temple in the Bokivti Mountains. As time passed, such rumors were rarely discussed, and she could only gather vague accounts of her kin being forced into labor to construct the Decayer device.

She'd never been able to confirm the rumors though. Those of her tribe who had been present in Ikaul territory had been sealed off from their homeland when the Sachem took control, never to return unless sentenced for a crime. Her time as a tillishu had never brought her here either. So, despite the rumors, despite the horrible tales her fellow tillishu told around campfires, she'd held on to the slim chance that her homeland and its people were surviving. Crippled, yes, but surviving. Desecrated, but still standing. Assaulted, but still alive.

What surrounded her now obliterated those fanciful hopes. She saw nothing but death and decay.

The slow ride through the forsaken land dispelled her previous urgency. Memories refused to be suppressed this time, and they flooded her vision as strange phantoms amid the decay. She remembered her friends, her kin, sunny days, and warm fires in Wither. She willed them to be there. Some semblance of life had to exist. It couldn't all be gone.

Fog veiled the Bokivti Mountains, and it was only when Annilasia was nearly on top of them that they revealed themselves. Their peaks, once snowcapped and misty, ascended into the sky naked and barren. The weather's unpredictable nature had shown no mercy—a cruel effect of the aetherwaste that the Sachem's reign had ushered in. She made her way down the familiar path that led through the valleys until she came to the Vekuuv Temple. Despite all she'd seen already, the reality was no less haunting.

The Temple and its surrounding structures lay in ruins. Silence burrowed into her ears as she surveyed the desecration. This place needed sound like a riverbed needed water. Voices should have carried in the wind, the bustle of the tribe rolling in the gusts. But the empty air whistled around her in a frail attempt to fill the quiet

Then she came to the pit. The stench of death knocked Annilasia over, and she only barely managed to stay conscious as she fell from her horse. Her hands and legs scraped on the earth, but the pain was nothing compared to the agony pressing against her chest. The stone grounds of the Temple plunged at a sharp decline into a lake of black ichor. Massive piles of bones jutted through the surface. In between these, skeletal remains floated like islands of decay. A wail clawed out of Annilasia's lungs and throat.

They were dead. Every last one of them.

She sobbed as she waited to be proven wrong. Long minutes passed. She wailed again, daring even an Ikaul warrior to happen across her and hear the primitive sounds escaping her.

But no one came.

She forced herself back onto her feet. Mounting her horse again proved difficult. Her muscles quivered and threatened to buckle, too ravaged by the despondency consuming her resolve. Her thoughts plunged into the pit of hopelessness that she'd succeeded in avoiding over the past two decades. She'd held on for so long, endured tragedy after tragedy, and resolved to slay the man who'd taken everything from her and her kin. But she saw nothing worth saving now. No land to redeem or retake from those who'd ravaged it. No people to rescue. No kin to cheer in applause that the tyrant was dead. She'd simply be slaying a man in revenge with a hollow victory to follow.

Metal grinding on metal caught her attention—the first sound since breaching the wall. She straightened and listened. The sound carried over the lake, and she looked over it to see giant silver arches peeking through the fog about a mile away. The odd structure was nestled against the side of the nearest mountain.

Those were new.

As she stared out at the lifeless terrain, hot tears revolting against the frigid wind, rage erupted to replace her grief. Perhaps far too roughly, she spurred her horse onward at a harsh sprint, reins gripped with clenched hands.

The death of her tribe changed nothing. If anything, it only solidified the need to slay the Sachem and keep the Decayer device from turning on. She ignored the poisoned lakes and deforested hills. She ignored the occasional carcasses of dead animals, forsaken even by the scavengers.

She wasn't going to stop the Sachem for applause or reward.

She was going to stop a tyrant from destroying the rest of the world in this same way.

CHAPTER 45

Time slipped by, failing to settle in Annilasia's mind as she rode closer. She knew the metal structure was the Sachem's doing and that he was close, but her disgust over the lake festered and monopolized her attention. She wondered how many of the skeletons were people she'd known. People whose names she'd once spoken, whose smiles she'd once prized. It wasn't until she arrived at the base of the structure that she escaped these dark musings. As she dismounted, her gaze trailed the height of the massive structure carved into the mountain.

A set of metal stairs led up to a giant platform over which two massive circular rings were spinning in suspended animation. One was slightly larger than the other, allowing it to rotate around the smaller ring. A gust of wind shot down across the mountainside as they twirled and, with each revolution, slowly gained momentum.

The Decayer device. She'd found it.

The wind created from the rings' propulsions struck Annilasia, slamming her head and hair back.

At that moment, she wanted to die. To simply fall to the ground and be wiped from the universe. She let out a wail, a sound becoming far too familiar to her, unsure why this new wave of despair was upon her. Just as these emotions began to dissipate, allowing her mind to stabilize, another gust swelled around her. Tears streaked from her eyes unbidden. She shrieked up at the sky. Her body trembled, and for a moment she thought it might be possible to be free of it—to tear herself from this miserable shell of flesh and bone, to let her emotions out of the cage of blood and mind trapping them.

A part of her fought against this, recognizing its assault to be some horrific effect of the Decayer. In the brief moment that came before the next gust of wind, she grasped at her lost sense of agency and forced herself up the metal stairs. Behind her, she heard her horse trumpet, and risked a quick glance back to see if it would stay put. She caught only the moment when the horse catapulted itself over the edge of the pit into the bone-infested lake.

She jerked away to face the stairs. If she watched the horse drown, she just might follow it. Something in the device's unnatural wind tempted her towards the same fate. She limped up the rest of the stairs, fighting every new gust that ripped her resolve to shreds. By the time she came onto the platform, the rings were spinning so fast that she couldn't hear her own pants of exhaustion. Sound bent, the whirring of the rings drowning out all other noise. The higher she climbed, the more the air vibrated. The hair on her arms and neck stood on end, then a shrill noise tried to overpower the whirl of the rings.

She wanted to jump off the edge. To soar through the air like a falcon if only for a moment before the ground split her apart. Anything would be better than the absolute despair that hooked its barbed talons into her.

Her eyes darted about in search of something to keep her mind off these morbid ideas. She grounded herself in her surroundings. The platform, incredibly large and spacious. A giant panel, the only equipment present, blinking with lights.

A lone figure standing at the platform's center.

Even with his back turned, Annilasia knew it to be the Sachem. He was looking up at something. She followed his gaze until she spotted two stars shining in the space inside the rings.

Not stars, she realized. Metal orbs.

The Stones of Elation.

It took a moment battling confusion for this discovery to set in amongst the horrific thoughts already crowding her mind. The presence of the Stones contradicted the emotions weighing on her. On every occasion during her childhood when she had been anywhere near the Stones, only peace had graced her. That's why the tribes had them—the Stones were meant to promote civility and harmony.

In a flash, it clicked. The Stones weren't failing. It was the Stones lacing each howling gust of wind with torturous emotions and suicidal ideations.

The Sachem had somehow altered their emissions.

Annilasia drew out her wand and took heavy steps forward. She summoned to mind the lake of skeletons, letting her fury grow to choke out the effects of the Decayer device. She wasn't going to cave to this monster's creation. The Decayer didn't own her mind. She forced herself to recall a host of tragedies, all of which she blamed on the Sachem.

Every execution she'd witnessed under the Sachem's command.

Every scream of the innocent as they'd suffered at his hands.

The events of the Purge.

The conspiracies and fear around the Delirium.

Fury charged through her veins, so much that her hands shook. She forced her right hand tight around the wand and pointed it at him. He didn't even know she was there. This would be easy. She pictured how his skin would melt away, how he might even manage to let out a howl of pain before his innards and flesh exploded with the aether she'd force through him.

He turned around, and his eyes fell upon her.

Time stopped. The anger sputtered inside her, and she froze.

The eyes staring back at her no longer held a hint of Hydrim. The familiar brown remained within, but another energy clouded the sunken eyes—an energy she'd seen before.

In Inzerious.

The energy crept over the space between them, a primordial malice that held within it too many deaths to fathom. She shuddered. He hardly looked human anymore or anything like his age. Taut skin stretched tightly over muscle and bone, morphing the once elegant skin ink across his chest and face into bruised splotches. His nails were long, permitting a layer of dirt to gather under them; the result was more of a claw than a human hand. When he sneered at her, a wall of blackened teeth parted to spill out black ichor.

Despite this sickly display and the way he hunched, he somehow towered over her. Perhaps this explained why the skin looked so warped. Something inside him was forcing unusual proportions on a body that couldn't sustain them. Ragged clothes, torn and smeared with dark stains, flexed across the body. The muscles and skin beneath bulged with odd tumors that throbbed with thick, purplish veins. As Annilasia watched, the tumors pulsated, pushing up against the skin in sync with each cycle of the twirling rings.

Annilasia's breath shook. This wasn't the Sachem that glared back at her. It was Dardajah, ready to break free.

"You're too late."

The words never slipped past Hydrim's lips. An all-encompassing malevolence snapped the words into existence, defying the deafening roar of the spinning metal rings. The voice slithered across her mind. She didn't recognize it as Hydrim's. This voice belonged to something far darker than a depraved man.

"The time of the dokojin is here."

Annilasia blinked. The trance of horror broke. She lifted her hand, snapped up her wrist, and let out a defiant shriek. Mirajin aether exploded from the tip of her glass wand. To her shock, colors twisted through the air and bounded toward the Sachem. She spent the briefest of moments marveling at the impossibility. The Terrestrial Realm didn't reveal aether in color. Only the aether Realms did, and that was while translated. Something had changed for them to show now.

The Sachem had done it. The Realms were melding.

She urged the aether forward with her fury and the need to end the Sachem. To end the horror and the violence that had plagued the tribes for decades. Anger and agony poured into the wand and spat out in the form of the plasmic energy.

Dardajah's claws flashed, and as the aether came within arm's reach of the dokojin, a dark void of a portal cracked open before it. The aether dove into it like dust into a tornado. The vortex swallowed every bit of the stream of energy before flashing out of existence again.

Dismay made her flounder, but Annilasia recovered quickly and swiftly cut off the flow of aether. The aether would mean nothing if Dardajah did that again. She'd spend it all, only to have some portal eat it up before it even touched the dokojin. Her chances at victory narrowed with each lost drop of the precious substance.

The vibrations around them escalated. The rings were spinning so fast now that they appeared only in brief flashes. Soon they'd be invisible to the eye. This truth registered dully as Annilasia unleashed on Dardajah a flurry of aether streaks—short bursts meant more to test her opponent than actually strike it. She needed to flesh out a weakness. The dokojin dodged these blasts with ease, loping around the platform with a crude agility incongruous to its inhuman proportions. As the vibrations around them increased in intensity, its skin roiled like waves in a stormy sea. Blood gushed from the body's orifices.

Annilasia froze mid-strike. Pained eyes full of blood met hers, and the Sachem's gashed lips moved. Though she couldn't hear the words spoken, as they were lost under the overpowering thrum of the twirling rings, she was able to read his lips.

"Help me."

Annilasia gaped. It happened far too quickly, that expression of desperation vanishing behind the malicious sneer of Dardajah. But she didn't doubt what she'd witnessed. Somehow, Hydrim was alive in there.

More blood gushed out of the tumors as they enlarged on the Sachem's body. Any moment now, they would burst. The Decayer edged ever closer to melding the Realms, and it would seal Hydrim's fate. His body would tear apart, just as she'd envisioned. Out of it would emerge a monster.

She couldn't shake the look of desperation and agony she'd glimpsed. It too closely mirrored how she'd felt all those months with Inzerious. Maybe Hydrim really was a victim. Maybe he deserved mercy. She didn't have time to think it over. The vibrations indicated an approach to the Decayer's completion.

Hydrim's plea echoed in her head. Then Drifter's voice replaced Hydrim's. *"Do you plan to rescue him?"*

A split decision gripped her. Annilasia repurposed the aether in the wand and pointed her weapon towards the Sachem. She drove her will into it one last time. The energy charged out of the wand's tip to latch onto the metamorphosing husk of Hydrim's body, and at the moment of collision, Annilasia yanked the wand back so as to tug the thread of aether like a lasso. Had it been any other moment during the device's cycle, the attempt would have failed. But she'd translated enough times to know this would be the only time this might work.

For they now existed in a state between translation. Not quite in the physical, not quite in an aether Realm. They were in both, and yet neither.

The aether recoiled, and the glob of morphing muscle and organs howled as it split into two distinct forms. Fluid followed the new form as it broke free of the original husk, slick on the nude body that flew onto the ground. She watched this newcomer slide some feet across the metallic panel flooring and grimaced at how the residual slime sizzled and melted the platform. Then she noticed the large umbilical-type cord that ran between the two forms. The new form looked up at her.

Hydrim, without any hint or trace of Dardajah in him now, gazed at Annilasia with a look of pure horror, seemingly unaffected by the acidic nature of the ichor that covered him. He looked like a shell of the man she'd seen over the years. Despite having the bones and structure of a bulky frame, he looked weak and timid. Too thin in the chest, with no tone of muscle. The slime that covered him only softened his features more, adding to the sickly appearance.

She looked away from him to the remaining figure that stood before her. Her heart skipped.

Dardajah loomed before her in all of its horrific glory. Just as Hydrim no longer reflected the dokojin, Dardajah no longer held any of Hydrim's likeness. Rather, an entity of immense magnitude evolved before her in the span of several painful heartbeats. Its stature blocked out the peak of the mountain at its back, and with the entity's metamorphosis, something thicker than the device's despair clogged the atmosphere.

The Decayer device's vibrations reached their apex, and with this, the muscles and skin of the dokojin solidified. Cartilage and an exoskeleton snapped into place with sharp crunches and cracks. Giant wings flew out behind it, curling and snapping at the ends under the pressure of the rings' wind and yet still spanning the width of the platform. A reptilian snout sprouted from its face and gnashed a set of razor-sharp teeth together. Its bulging, bloodshot eyes fixed on Annilasia. As it moved and flexed its newly birthed form, Annilasia noticed similarities to both insect and reptile, noting the thick exterior hide that pinched out into thorny points along its sternum and the leathery skin wrinkling across the flat of its stomach and its limbs.

Its gaze happened across Hydrim, and Dardajah bellowed down at the trembling man, who cowered back and shrieked in response.

Annilasia snapped her wrist. Very little of the mirajin aether remained. But she knew what purpose she intended for it. The last blaze of plasmic energy howled from the wand. A stream of colors drove into the cord connecting Hydrim to the dokojin. Much like the spray of sparks at the severance of her own lifechain, a fan of iridescent color shot up at the point of collision.

The wand quivered. A jagged line crawled across the glass seconds before it exploded, forcing out the last remnants of aether. The stream of energy surged into the umbilical cord, ending with a satisfying snap that whipped the two severed ends of the cord into the air. Black ichor poured out of both ends in slimy protest, eating away at the platform's tiles.

Annilasia's victory earned Hydrim a meager freedom, but she had no time to revel in her success. Dardajah was already charging, maw unhinged, massive teeth and leathery arms outstretched, ready to shred her into a mess of blood and innards.

She bent and dodged. Its massive claws caught on the hood of her cloak, sling-shooting her through the air towards Hydrim. The gunk from Hydrim's separation was slick beneath her as she landed, and she smelled burnt leather and wool even as her momentum nearly sent her off the edge of the platform. She managed to latch onto Hydrim's ankle to avoid a tumble over the side. As she scrambled to get her bearings, warmth blossomed over her gloved hands, the slime's acidic hunger working fast. She quickly let go of Hydrim's wet leg. His wide, terrified eyes met her own. His mouth moved, and she could make out the plea to take him away from the scene, but the pulses from the rings silenced his voice.

She looked past him and saw Dardajah's massive form charging at them. She jerked her head in the opposite direction and peered over the side of the platform. They were miles high, and the platform plunged down sharply.

A final look to Hydrim. Beyond him, Dardajah's maw drove down, ready to scoop them into its teeth. There was no time left to hesitate, and no more mirajin aether as a defense. Grabbing hold of Hydrim, well aware that she risked the acidic ichor eating through her clothes and skin, Annilasia rolled onto her back, lifted the man on top of her, and rolled them again. They tumbled off the edge. She caught one last look of Dardajah as it loomed over the side and roared down at them, though the noise didn't carry any more than Hydrim's voice had over the vibrations and the rings' wind.

Yet a voice in Annilasia's head made clear what was lost to the wind. A voice that squirmed inside the emptiness left behind by Inzerious but filling it with a malevolence far greater than her previous tenant.

"You escape a moment, Unworthy Bones. I will feast on you yet."

Scowling, Annilasia twirled to face the impending ground with Hydrim still clutching to her. The wind fought against her movements, but she managed to grasp the last spare wand she'd brought. It glimmered with aether, though not nearly as brightly as the one she'd wielded against Dardajah.

The ground shot up at them. She pointed the wand down and unleashed its aether with a fuel of confidence. She wasn't going to die. No matter what the horrible wind of the twirling rings rife with death and despair was telling her.

The aether slowed their descent, but not enough. Hydrim let out a yelp in the last seconds before impact. Annilasia heard the sharp snap of bones as an abrupt darkness stole her away into nothingness.

CHAPTER 46

The memories were getting harder to summon. Time failed to touch the sunless chamber.

Jalice couldn't keep up with the scenes of horror that were her current nightmare. It was as if her mind could only handle the current terror to which it was being subjected. Her identity had unraveled and now hung on by weak threads, often evaporating in the endless screams she unleashed. Sometimes that was more frightening than the circumstances. Whenever she lost her sense of self, she'd panic and forget whatever torture Spiracy was utilizing in that moment until she forced her mind to recall her name.

I'm Jalice. Tecalica of the Unified Tribes. Sister to Kerothan. Of the Vekuuv tribe.

But these words lost meaning too. She couldn't recall what constituted the Unified Tribes, or who Kerothan was—what he looked like, what he sounded like, what he meant to her. Still, she recited the names in those awful moments of amnesia.

Jalice. Tecalica. Kerothan. Vekuuv.

There were others with her. People who had no names and who wore the same frozen state of terror on their faces that she felt. They couldn't tell her why they were trapped. They had no families to speak of, nor any insight into how they'd arrived in the cavernous lair that had no exit. Of what little she recalled, she'd seen them tortured too. The nameless screams haunted her mind, even if she couldn't put faces to the agonizing sounds. She did remember running from a blue-speckled room at one point. Her fellow prisoners had run out like cattle let loose, only to dart in a hundred different directions when they'd entered the shadowy chamber.

The chamber with no way out.

Even the path back to the blue-speckled room had vanished within the void of infinite shadow. There was no light, and the walls of the room were always near but never able to be reached. She either ran when caught by a mimic, or huddled on the floor and recited her names.

Jalice. Tecalica. Kerothan. Vekuuv.

And in here, the hatched mimics roamed freely.

The *mimics*. One of the few things her mind actually refused to let go of, unlike her sense of identity or the past. The abominable creatures paraded around in translucent skin that shifted and morphed. Sometimes the prisoners skittering about turned out to be mimics themselves. She'd converse with them, and they'd nod with their eyes wide like any other terrified victim. But then they'd try to speak, giving away their true form. Mimics, she'd learned, could only speak what they'd already heard. And victims usually only screamed out pleas or obscenities in their presence. So, that was all they recited—screams and obscenities. That was when she'd fight to get away from them, only to have the mimic follow her and try to copy her frantic thrashing and her own unique cries for help.

There was never any escape. It only ended when Spiracy would intervene.

Spiracy. That was the other thing her mind couldn't erase, perhaps out of a deep need to know the darkest, most formidable danger that threatened her existence. The dokojin would appear out of nowhere, slipping from the shadows, trailed by the tendrils of her cloak. She'd smirk down at Jalice's discomfort and distress, her face muddied by spirals of dark and light hues that bled across her skin like ink blots in a puddle. The wraith would purr, and pet whatever mimic had most recently tormented Jalice, then send the creature off into the depths of the inescapable chamber.

"Come, Jalice," Spiracy cooed after one such episode. "I want to show you something."

As Spiracy took Jalice's hand and guided her through the darkness, hoots and clicks echoed above their heads. Jalice had learned not to look. The ceiling hid the creatures, but she didn't need to see them to know what they were. More mimics, hatching from hanging cocoons. More abominations that would soon find her and learn, like their kin, to replicate her screams and expressions of horror.

Jalice wanted to yank her hand out of the marble palm of the dokojin but dared not. Resisting might be worse than obeying. A tickle in her mind told her this was true, even though she couldn't recall any specific moment that proved it. She forced down a whimper as she stared at the spindly hand and nails that somehow still dwarfed her own. Her gaze ran up to the long, silky hair that swayed back and forth, shifting from dark to light. So beautiful that she wanted to reach out and touch it. Maybe Spiracy would show her mercy.

"Have you enjoyed your time in here with my pets?" Spiracy asked over her shoulder as they ascended a set of stairs onto a platform free of the natural cavern formations that riddled the rest of the lair.

Jalice lowered her head, unwilling to look back into that pristine face. She stilled when the dokojin halted and turned to face Jalice.

"You were so arrogant when you first arrived," Spiracy stated. "Tried so many times to distort my Realm with those pesky memories. Such strong aether. I wasn't sure how to combat it at first. But whatever skill you had has now diminished with the melting of your mind under the supervision of my spawn. Constant terror erases all things eventually. Bravery. Identity. Morality. It is the purest of all tests, and it erodes most things. Your unpredictable conjurings were no exception."

Spiracy moved aside to reveal a long slab of stone. On it lay a naked middle-aged man with a bronze tan and a closely shaven head. His eyes were stretched wide, yet he never blinked. Such a crazed expression of terror looked off-putting on a man muscled and framed for any physical challenge that might face him. Still, he remained motionless, doing nothing but staring up into the indeterminate light source that illuminated the slab.

"Do you know who this is?"

Jalice blushed and looked away. "Please don't hurt him."

"So, you don't recognize him?" Spiracy pressed. "He's my newest dreamer. The one that keeps this lair in existence. Some might say I owe him a debt for such a sacrifice. But he's nothing but a tool. A stair that buckles when I tread upon it as I rise up into a glorious destiny." She grinned down at the frozen man and ran her hands across his arm as if to soothe him. "There was once a time I was too weak in my infancy to speak. I had to use these conduits. At first I could only manage moans. It was strange to hear them coming out of another creature while waiting for my vocal cords to develop. Sometimes I like to make the dreamers talk like that still."

Spiracy let her mouth drop open as if to let out a cry or a scream or a wail. But nothing came out.

At least, nothing from her. The man on the table flinched, and his mouth hinged open. A shrill moan broke past his lips and broke the air. It escalated until he was shrieking at a disturbing pitch that caused Jalice to stumble back.

"Stop!" she shouted. "Don't hurt him!"

Spiracy closed her mouth, and the man fell quiet. His mouth closed in sync with the dokojin's. A deep yet lustrous chuckle bubbled out of the dokojin as she turned to Jalice.

"I like to see just how loud your kind can scream in here. That's the fun part of this Realm. It's not real. Not like the physical world. You can scream and scream until you feel like your lungs will give out. But they never do because you're not in a real body while here." She paused and tilted her head as she considered something. An amused grin leapt to her face. "I look forward to trying it out in the Terrestrial Realm though. It must be something to burst a set of lungs just from screaming."

"Stop!" Jalice cried.

Spiracy chuckled. "How about we take a look at what I do to those who've lost their purpose in here? Here's a hint! I find them a new purpose."

Out of the darkness there came a shriek of terror. Jalice twisted towards the sound. A new area of the cave a few yards off was suddenly illuminated. A malnourished scrawny man stumbled in place, swiveling around in an attempt to face every direction at once. A low grumble broke out, and Jalice glanced back at Spiracy to find that the dokojin's grin had grown, a ravenous desire tugging the lips unnaturally high into her cheeks.

The attack happened fast. One moment Spiracy was there at Jalice's side, suspended a few inches in the air. In a flash, her form had sailed the distance separating her from the distressed man, like a hawk striking an unsuspecting critter. Her victim had time enough to let out a pinched shriek, but it was cut off abruptly and replaced by far harsher sounds. The crunch of bones and the gurgle of liberated fluid echoed in the cavern. Jalice flinched, watching with wide eyes. It took a moment for her mind to catch up to what was occurring.

Spiracy was feeding.

Even with the dokojin's form blocking most of the carnage, she saw enough blood to know the man would not survive the encounter. In the dim lighting, she made out glimpses of the man's limbs twisting about as Spiracy handled him like a roasted hunk of meat meant to be stripped off the bone. When Spiracy turned to Jalice, blood smeared her chin and dripped from her mouth in thick globs.

Jalice's eyes flickered about, but she saw no sign of the man. Her gaze again met Spiracy's, and she resisted the innate desire to flee under the wraith's display of obvious pleasure. The dokojin sighed and shuddered, sending her cloak's tendrils flitting outward like a squid's tentacles.

"He was soon to die, you see," Spiracy said, her chest heaving with a sudden odd energy. "His aura would have tried to pass into the Apparition Realm while his physical body rotted away in your Temple. I make sure my little Skinflakes don't abandon us here. I recycle their auras." Suddenly her throat swelled, and she craned her neck forward as a gush of ichor spilled out in bucketfuls across the ground.

The liquid raced towards Jalice. She screamed, stepping back but unable to escape the thin layer of black slime that rushed at her feet and trickled past to spill down the steps behind her. Something wiggled between her toes, and she skittered back a few more steps while kicking her feet out to try and free them of Spiracy's regurgitated meal.

More movement under her feet. She teetered from one foot to the other, eyes scanning the ground. The slime writhed. She froze, focusing on the odd motion that seemed to be giving the very ground beneath her a sense of life.

"His aura has birthed new spawn. More of my pets for you to scream at."

Jalice inhaled sharply, swallowing a screech. It wasn't the ground that was alive. Tiny vermin, like enlarged tadpoles or veiny worms, slithered about in the ichor with zealous vigor. She counted dozens upon dozens, maybe even hundreds, in the depth of Spiracy's vomit. A shift in the mass occurred, and the worms suddenly began to jump and flop as if trying to take flight. And some of them did. They wiggled like worms on a hook, strung on some fisher's invisible line. As if encouraged by their kin, those still left on the ground writhed with a newfound need to be airborne, and each found a way to break free of the slime that had carried them out of Spiracy.

"Fly, my children," she heard Spiracy cry. "Make a home in the darkness above."

Jalice opened her mouth to shriek only to have one of the veiny maggots slip past her lips. Her cry choked off as she sputtered to spit it out, all the while being pummeled by dozens of its kind as they ascended towards the ceiling. She felt movement in her hair, and she scraped her hands through it, her fingers brushing across moist lumps that squirmed under her touch.

Jalice fell onto her backside, which gave her an unexpected escape from the mass of worms that were now mostly above her head. She stared in disgust at Spiracy's creations, cringing at the enthusiastic hoots above as the worms disappeared past the indeterminate light and into the shadowy depths of the ceiling.

Where the cocoons were.

She wondered if the worms would become the embryonic mimics she'd encountered. She envisioned the cocoons that would somehow overtake the worms as they grew until their matured forms hatched back out.

More mimics to torment her. Though her revulsion persisted, a fury shot through her, replacing the fear. She turned her eyes to Spiracy and squeezed out the cowardice that urged her to flee.

"This place isn't real," she said.

Spiracy turned her obsidian eyes onto Jalice. "What did you say?"

"You admitted that none of this is real. You might birth these monsters and blink us in and out of places inside this lair. But it isn't an actual place. Which means you might not be real either."

Spiracy's face, too smooth and perfect to permit wrinkles, tightened ever so slightly with irritation. "I assure you, Skinflake, I am very much real."

"Maybe none of this is," Jalice continued, waving her hands at the darkness that surrounded them. "Maybe not even me." She paused, summoning the courage to go on. "Which means anything is possible in this nightmare. Impossible things."

Spiracy bared her needle-thin teeth. "Isn't this something? The cowardly Tecalica, trying to be brave." She glided through the air over to Jalice, leering inches from her face. "You're nothing, little Skinflake. Your stupid memories cropped up enough times for me to know just how people feel about you. No one loves you."

Jalice forced herself rigid. She wouldn't tremble anymore in this dokojin's presence.

"Hydrim never did," Spiracy continued. "You only got a demented version of affection from that man, one that you cursed out of him. Kerothan was so disgusted with how you acted that he ran away, and he refuses to forgive you. Because of your stubbornness, your friends have either died or been pushed away. Who does that leave by your side, little Skinflake?"

Despite the truths behind them, Spiracy's words sparked a brief moment of clarity, and Jalice remembered the kindness of Elothel and Xiekaro. "I have friends," Jalice protested. "Not everyone hates me."

Spiracy's teeth parted to emit a breathless laugh. "But they do. They all hate you. You're a burden to them. Just as you are a burden to yourself. You squish yourself inside that flimsy fluidbag you call a body, and all the while your own aura is desperate to be free of it. Your own soul can't bear to stay inside the same husk that's trampled around the physical world and gotten so many killed. I can feel all of this, Tecalica. It is my skill to see the pitiful state of your kind."

The trembles set in, and Jalice couldn't stop them this time. She looked away from Spiracy, fighting off tears. Her dwindling sense of courage, however, didn't change the fact that her claim was right.

This place wasn't real.

She closed her eyes, ignoring the terror of how close Spiracy loomed. Her mind wrestled with the emptiness that had obliterated her memories and sense of time. There had to be something she could do. Spiracy feared her. That explained why the dokojin had diverted the conversation to Jalice's inadequacies. It explained why Spiracy was so desperate to unnerve her by showing off the man on the slab and consuming that unfortunate prisoner.

Vivid colors sprang into her mind: the forests that thrived in Vekuuv; the mountains covered in snow during Wither; a trail of children darting amongst the trees, laughing and hollering as they chased each other.

Her friends. Her family.

"What are you doing?" a voice hissed in her ear. "You pathetic, insignificant little Skinflake. You'll be nothing by the time I'm done with you. You won't remember your name, your existence. All you will know is an eternal death."

Jalice opened her eyes to brightness. The cavern around her burst with trees and foliage. Overhead, a blinding light splintered through the ceiling to bathe the leaves and flowers. A cold wind like that from Vekuuv's Bokivti Mountains swirled around her. Overhead, the cocoons rattled. The mimics that resided up there hooted and screeched, unsure what to make of the abrupt alteration to their nest. Jalice spotted her fellow prisoners darting about, hiding behind tree trunks as the mimics on the ground stood frozen in shock.

An enraged roar drummed the air behind her, but another surprise kept her from attending to the fear she'd have otherwise felt at the vengeful sound. A charged wave of vibrations instilled the space around them. Its arrival brought with it an instantaneous evolution to the cavernous chamber that was now filled with forestry. The colors around her shimmered, and a force like invisible hands yanked at her and stole her away from where she stood. In the span of an eyeblink, she was transported.

***

Jalice sat up with a harsh inhalation. The first thing she became immediately aware of was the mask over her mouth. Out of an instinctual panic, she yanked the constrictive piece off and threw it to the side.

She glanced around feverishly, wondering what had occurred. The imagery and details of moments earlier were vivid in her mind, and as she surveyed her surroundings, she found that the scenery remained somewhat the same. Woodland trees and underbrush created a paradoxical contrast to the metal walls that they splintered through, as if the two environments were in an immobile war for control. Unlike before, she now lay on the ground. Spiracy was nowhere to be found. Lining the metal-tiled ceiling above her were luminescent streaks that cast the room in a sickly yellow glow.

A timid hope grew. Perhaps she'd escaped Spiracy's lair. The room's familiarity tugged at her mind, and for a moment, she wondered if this was a place she knew. Out of the foliage, she could make out a set of walls surrounding her to form a small chamber. It didn't look like any dungeon she'd experienced while in Spiracy's captivity.

Her mind somersaulted as it tried to accommodate a rush of memories while retaining the nightmarish details of her time with Spiracy. She remembered Rejiett, the templite priestess, and the twisters who had shoved Jalice into a room. They'd given her some sort of tincture, but her recollection grew murky after that point.

What remained far too clear were the torments she'd suffered inside Spiracy's lair. Jalice's hands went to her hair as she searched it for worms, then she searched the floor. To her horror, a layer of slime coated the metal tiles beneath her, far too similar in texture and color to the substance that had spewed out of the wraith. No movement though. No worms squirming about.

There was a rustling, which grew steadily louder as its source approached. A figure emerged at a sprint through the doorway that Jalice had failed to notice previously, as it was veiled by a sea of branches. The pale robe indicative of templite status was recognizable even in the dim lighting, though the cloth retained very little of the unblemished quality it had once boasted. Black streaks formed chaotic patterns across the front; the wearer had obviously endured a panicked state, which was further denoted by the rips in various spots.

The newcomer spotted Jalice and rushed forward through more of the vegetation. Rejiett's glare became clear when she came to a halt a few feet away. Though a mask covered the lower half of the templite's face, Jalice could hear the snarl in her voice when addressed.

"Did you do this?" Rejiett demanded. "It should have been a clean meld. The Decayer is active, and Spiracy is here in our Realm now. But it's chaos because you conjured this absurd forest. The mimics are devouring my kin because we didn't have time to imprint on them, you stupid wench."

Jalice stared up at her, mouth agape and unsure what to make of the woman's babbling. When she didn't respond, Rejiett bent down and hauled Jalice up. She stumbled after the templite as she was dragged out of the room and into a larger chamber that spilled forth with even more woodland. Thick pineoaks plunged upward through the ceiling, while smaller species of trees, along with bushes and flowers, littered the space. She marveled at the display but became distracted by immense machinery that stood in stark contrast to the organic ecosystem. Rejiett froze a few yards into her stride as she, too, beheld the machines. It took Jalice only a second to recall that she'd seen these devices before, upon first arriving at the twister base: the exploding star frozen in time and the coffin with a backboard that glowed and into which dozens of wires snaked.

But she quickly noticed what had caused Rejiett to grow still. A group of figures gathered around the smaller machine—three men, two of whom looked fit for a skirmish and wielded swords with glowing blades. The older of them, a man with snow-white hair and a stern expression, spotted the women and grew rigid before lifting his sword defensively. Jalice recognized him as Cephus, and her mind quickly placed the other two men when their heads lifted up in response to his reaction. Kerothan stood at his side but was in no position to brandish his sword, which instead remained sheathed on his belt, as he was preoccupied with supporting the weight of a very frail-looking Ophim. Jalice cringed at the sight of numerous puncture wounds running down Ophim's arms and legs, and at the unhealthy, pasty complexion of his skin. Unlike his companions, he wore nothing but a loincloth and one of the twister's rubbery face masks; every inch of a body that had once boasted bulk and muscle was exposed and now showed the initial signs of atrophy.

Kerothan stared back at her, and she held her breath. None of this seemed real, and for a moment, she wondered if she was still in Spiracy's lair. This struck her as too surreal, a mirage summoned by the wraith to taunt Jalice. Were any of these figures even the individuals she recognized them to be? Or were they mimics, parading around in others' skins to play a cruel joke on Jalice?

A dark splotch obscured a miniscule portion of her vision, and her focus left Kerothan to study the writhing streak that was slowly ascending through the air.

A black worm. Perhaps this *was* a trick. Perhaps she hadn't escaped the lair at all.

She focused back on Kerothan, wondering if she could spot anything in his demeanor that might tag him as one of Spiracy's spawn. A heaviness drifted from his wide eyes, and his expression revealed his utter shock at her presence. Though he still exhibited elements of youthfulness, the wrinkles on his pale face and around his eyes betrayed his departure from early manhood, and years of struggle riddled his muscles and regulated the very way he held his weight.

The pain she saw in the way he beheld her, how the slightest hint of irritation entered his eyes upon seeing her, permitted a shallow hope to grow. Maybe he was indeed real. She had yet to encounter a mimic that could replicate the kind of genuine trauma that only life's unrelenting curses could inflict.

She decided to trust this conclusion, and a euphoric relief washed over her. Despite her lifetime of mistakes and her own cruelty towards him, her brother had decided to come for her. He'd crossed the canyon of hatred that she'd created between them. His arrival here, during her most dire state, elicited an odd comfort that in turn brought a single phrase to her lips.

"You came to save me."

A mere second passed, and yet she caught in his eyes a look of horrified guilt. It confused her, but she didn't get the chance to decipher it. The last thing Jalice saw was her brother, mouth agape and tears in his eyes. A great sadness filled Jalice then. She'd missed Kerothan's presence in her life all these years. So much time, lost.

What followed was peace, in as much that it meant an end to her suffering. The guilt she'd carried, the shame and penance, all vanished in the blink of an eye.

CHAPTER 47

"There's too many of them."

Kerothan peered down the long stretch of corridor that led to a doorless room. Yellow light spilled out from it, and dark silhouettes would periodically pass by inside the open entryway. He'd counted at least a dozen twisters, though it was too hard to tell how many were just the same individuals walking back and forth inside. Either way, it seemed there were far too many for him and Cephus to take on alone.

He looked over at his clanhead, who stood with his back against the opposite wall, Aruzz held tight against him. Cephus once again held a knife a few inches from the twister's neck, a temporary guarantee that Aruzz would keep quiet. There was no telling when the next twister would decide to enter the corridor, or from which direction. This particular passage offered a few offshoot rooms to which they might flee, but it was impossible to know where those led. The last thing they wanted was to get trapped.

"I don't think we have a choice," Cephus said in a low voice. "We didn't get much of a warning that we'd arrived at our destination." The clanhead glared at the back of the twister's head.

Aruzz, who, although he couldn't see Cephus, could hear the irritation in his voice, grinned with a look of malicious victory even as he wheezed between heavy breaths. "Time . . . to give me . . . a mask."

"No," Kerothan countered. "You didn't warn us about this. If we hadn't spotted them up ahead, you would have led us straight into a den of twisters."

"We keep our promises," said Cephus. He pushed the twister off him and put away the knife, then pried the mask off his lower face. Handing it over, he looked Aruzz in the eyes. "Take it and go back up to the Temple."

Kerothan gaped at him. "We're not letting him go."

"We can't take him in there," Cephus said, referring to the chamber ahead.

"And we can't afford to split our attention between him and the others."

Kerothan opened his mouth to protest but didn't get the chance to argue further. Aruzz darted between them before either could get a hold of him, and sprinted down towards the chamber filled with twisters, where he entered the yellowish glow and stopped inside the open entryway.

"Well, Dardajah's spit and shite . . ." Cephus mumbled.

Kerothan didn't wait for his clanhead. He sprinted after Aruzz, keeping his eyes locked on the twister's silhouette. The element of surprise was gone now. There was no point in trying to sneak in. Only thing left to do was make a grand entrance or retreat back down the corridor. The latter wasn't an option. Kerothan wasn't going to retreat—not when he knew that Ophim might very well lie somewhere in that sickly yellow light.

He leapt through the arched entryway and swung his sword. The blade cut through Aruzz's neck with a satisfying ease. He saw the barest amount of blood follow the sword's pass and the initial stage of combustion setting in around the twister's neck as his leap morphed into a somersault that transitioned into another attack upon the next unsuspecting twister in his path. Kerothan's sword flashed out, appearing like a trail of blue light as it sliced through the air. Before it made contact, the twister's glass wand released a stream of invisible aether at him. Had it not been for the absorption properties of his sword's blade, the energy would have torn him apart. Kerothan noted just how brightly his blade glowed, and knew that it might very well be the last aether the blade could afford to contain. The blade cleaved off the twister's arm that wielded the wand. A torrent of blood gushed from the wound, and the twister released the beginnings of a scream that ceased when the rest of his body exploded in a mess of blood, innards, and shattered bone.

More decoration to join the crust of blood already filming Kerothan's armor.

The air around Kerothan buzzed with electric vibrations. Aether soared at him, and he expected at any moment to go up in the same type of carnage that he'd bestowed on his enemies. He kept moving, making himself a difficult target, even for twisters. He managed to glimpse the Fence Post—a giant flower of odd cylinders sprouting from a round core—at the back end of the room, as well as a smaller contraption at its base.

Cephus charged into the room, yelling as he brought his blade down on another twister. His victim attempted to spring back, aided by a propulsive lift of aether, but the flight came too late. The blue blade ripped through cloth and skin. A shrill cry emitted before cutting off sharply as the twister exploded. The force of the eruption drove upward in the direction the twister had leapt, spraying the far wall.

Kerothan had been in the room only a moment and already knew this wouldn't end well for him and Cephus. It didn't matter how nimble or lucky he got. There were too many twisters—all of whom wore the unnerving rubbery masks—just as he had calculated in the corridor. Eventually, a sliver of aether would brush against him and Cephus, sending their insides coiling and curling in reaction to the foreign energy. They would be dead in less than a few breaths, and he hadn't even located Ophim.

Just as this realization set in, an intense vibrational shift occurred. The hairs on the back of his neck straightened up as an overwhelming dread set in. He dropped his sword to his side and let out an agonized groan at the unexpected emotional toll. He wanted to die. Let the aether take him. All that mattered was the embrace of nothingness. Yet this sentiment didn't last long, as the metallic nature of the room altered so quickly that it shook him out of the depressive trance. He remained still, absorbing the barrage of new elements crowding around him.

Where once had been a barren room, aside from the machines and the cluster of twisters, trees and foliage now existed. The sickly lights that had illuminated the room were gone, replaced with far dimmer lighting from some unseeable area overhead. A cold wind rushed in around him. It came with the strangest of nostalgic energies that ushered in an unbeckoned array of memories from his childhood. As odd as the setting was, it reminded him of home. He surveyed the scene, unsure what to make of its abrupt appearance. Perhaps it was a twister spell—some sort of mirage meant to hide the twisters away while they escaped from him and Cephus.

Whatever the purpose, it had worked in his favor. Just as he could no longer see any of the twisters who had littered the other corners of the room, he was no longer in their line of attack. Clasping this opportunity, he leapt past the trees, his boots thudding on the metallic ground of the chamber now broken by roots and topped with loose rocks.

He came to an abrupt halt when a chorus of hoots and clicks echoed from above. His gaze lifted to follow the noise, only to find that the ceiling was far higher than before, rising into shadows that veiled whatever was producing the unsettling sounds. Scuffling joined the chorus, and he was reminded of a grimalkin's claws scraping against a tree trunk. Something—or some*things*— were skimming down the walls to the ground. The darkness that dominated the room made it difficult to make out, but he thought he glimpsed a few shadows dive downward, like bats streaking through the twilight sky to pursue prey.

His heart pounded in his chest as he resumed his frantic sprint, unsure of where exactly he was running. Just as he decided that his intent was to find Cephus, he burst into the area that hosted the Fence Post and the smaller machine. He approached these slowly, marveling at the plethora of yellow twinkling lights and rubbery wires that trailed off the baseboard at the back of the smaller device. At the bottom of the baseboard, a coffin-like container wheezed out compressed air via an array of pumps and vials that were attached to its lid. Something pale and organic caught his eye at the head of this contraption. His heart stopped. A cold panic gripped him. A breath later, he leapt forward towards the coffin and crouched down to peer into the face that peeked out of its rubbery encasement.

Ophim didn't open his eyes. Not even when Kerothan shouted at him to wake. The machine continued to churn, refusing to give up its victim. Kerothan straightened and ran down the length of the coffin. The knobs and levers that he found offered no clue as to their function, but adrenaline kept him from considering the implications of a wrong decision. He cranked whatever levers his hands could find and shoved his fingers across random knobs, fueled by the groans and whistles the machine emitted with his efforts. The air compressions ceased, and the pumps slowed until they finally grew still.

He couldn't pry the shell off Ophim fast enough. A sucking sound almost made him pause—perhaps it had been rash to free Ophim without pondering the potential risks of doing so—but relief flooded him when the coffin's lid unlatched and shot upward at his earnest tugs. His heart sank at the sight of numerous red tubes that hung down from the inside of the lid and looped like the tentacles of a bloodthirsty kykaleech into various areas of Ophim's body. He hesitated to touch these, and instead ran back to the head of the coffin to see if Ophim had woken. To his dismay, his fellow clannite still had not stirred. Kerothan placed his hands on Ophim's shoulders to raise him up, only to discover a thick metallic wire dangling from the back of the man's head.

A new panic jarred Kerothan's sense of urgency. He had no idea what to make of the wire or the red tubes that connected Ophim to the lid of the machine. For all he knew, he might very well have harmed his fellow clannite by hitting all those levers and lifting the lid. His hands trembled as he traced the wire up to the base of Ophim's skull. He slowly tugged on it, praying that the action would free his beloved from whatever prison kept him in a coma. A slight give in the wire's greedy attachment on Ophim gave Kerothan pause until he realized the item was meant to be twisted off. He followed the motion, hearing a conclusive *thwip* as the wire came loose. An empty socket of metal remained in Ophim's head from where the wire had detached.

He cradled Ophim against his chest. Cold, clammy skin compelled him to let go, but Kerothan tamped down the instinct. His right hand trembled as it approached the mouthpiece that muzzled the lower portion of Ophim's face, and he yanked at the tube that ran from the mask to the machine. The mouthpiece snapped off, and he flung it away before running both hands through Ophim's hair, whispering over and over again to his would-be lebond.

"Wake up. Don't leave me here alone. Wake up."

The whispering escalated to shouting, but he didn't care. If the urgency of his voice could break the curse over Ophim, then he would scream until he perished. He'd do whatever it took to bring Ophim back. He'd slay every last twister, drive out every evil the world ever hosted. Anything to see Ophim's golden brown eyes and his infectious smile once more. Tears ran down his cheeks when Ophim's eyes fluttered open, shrouded in confusion and relief, to gaze up at him.

Kerothan's mind whirled with too many conflicting commands. He ripped off his mask, knowing that Ophim would need it. He couldn't let his beloved succumb to whatever poisons tainted the air. To the deep abyss with whether Kerothan instead inhaled it. Nothing so sinister would ever again curse Ophim's life, not if Kerothan had anything to do with it.

But in the second before he placed the mask on Ophim, another instinct stilled his arm. Kerothan didn't hesitate, didn't care what might happen after this next moment. All that mattered was now, and he followed his impulse to its conclusion. He lowered his head and brought Ophim into a kiss. Part of him panicked then, expecting Ophim to immediately pull back, to protest and deem such an action inappropriate given the circumstances. He always had before. He would now.

But Ophim kissed him back.

An eternity beckoned in this moment between them. If Kerothan could have stayed in it, he would have. Still, nothing would take him away from Ophim ever again. This he vowed in the press of his lips against Ophim's. This he vowed in the touch of his fingers that gingerly held his beloved. Kerothan's very essence was now solely the earnest drive to protect.

Only the voice of Cephus could break this moment.

"Where is Jalice?"

Their lips parted, and Ophim gazed back at Kerothan for a mere second before shifting to look past him at Cephus. Kerothan saw a fearful embarrassment mark Ophim's face, and he turned to look at his clanhead. Cephus stood over them with a grave expression, but if anything in the kiss had irritated him, he didn't show it.

"We need to leave," Ophim croaked, his voice scratchy and weak. "Now."

"Where is the Tecalica?" Cephus asked again, this time more firmly.

Ophim shook his head in pained dismay. "I don't know, lebond."

"Let's get you up," Kerothan said, voice cracking from the emotions swirling within him: fear of their vulnerability to the twisters and affection from the

first tender exchange he'd shared with Ophim in too long. He straightened
up to stand, ripping the many tubes free of Ophim's body. Ophim, who had
always before muffled his pain behind his massive exterior, now let out harsh
whimpers during this rushed process that made Kerothan cringe. He tried
to avert his eyes from the numerous puncture wounds lining Ophim's body,
each pouring with blood, and hauled him out of the coffin. The other man
groaned as he clumsily staggered out of the contraption, and would have fallen
had Kerothan not shifted all of his weight to support him. Kerothan slowly
pivoted to turn them towards where he and Cephus had entered. With the
introduction of the forest, he could no longer see the passage, but it had to
be no more than a couple dozen strides away.

"Get us masks," Kerothan said to Cephus as he placed his own on Ophim.

Cephus searched the floor, but if one of the twisters' masks lay amid the
foliage, he was blind to it. "There's no time to search. We'll make do with the one."

Before they could proceed forward, Cephus raised his sword as two
figures burst out of the foliage to their right. Kerothan's heart stuttered as
he recognized Rejiett and Jalice, both unmasked. The priestess had Jalice
gripped by the wrist, and a gut deduction told him that Jalice wasn't traveling
with Rejiett willingly. His sister looked confused and terrified, her hair and
clothes disheveled to an unusual degree for the Tecalica. An instinctual
protectiveness towards her coursed through him before he smothered it. He
still had no proof Jalice wasn't in league with the twisters, no matter how
distressed she currently appeared.

Rejiett had halted upon spotting the clannite warriors. Jalice stood behind
her, a spark of hope dancing in her ocean blue eyes at seeing her brother.

"You came to save me," she said.

Guilt washed through him. He hadn't thought twice about Jalice, at
least not until Cephus had brought her up. He'd come for Ophim, and only
Ophim. Now Jalice stood before him, shivering and frightened yet touched
that Kerothan had come to her rescue.

Her relief did not last. Behind her, a metal wall and the trees burst into
shrapnel as a large mass drove through them. Kerothan turned his face to

avoid the debris, holding fast to Ophim as tree branches and bark scraped them in their wild trajectory through the air. When he looked up, a tree trunk lay collapsed across the ground. Metal tiles littered its branches, speckled and smeared with dark red fluid.

Above it, a wraith hovered in the air, clad in elegant white sheets that trailed around it as if submerged underwater. Its silky hair did the same, swimming around it like subdued snakes while simultaneously shifting color between a dull white and muted black. Teeth as sharp as the needle in his pocket appeared when its lips spread apart to sneer down at him and the others. Its obsidian eyes held no distinction between sclera and iris—just a film of sheer shadow and enmity that surpassed what he'd seen in any twister. Dangling in its open jaws like a limp doll, Jalice's body discharged waterfalls of blood that splattered the fallen tree and metal tiles below. The wraith unhinged its jaw to release its kill, and Jalice plunged downward to meet one of the fallen tree's branches.

Kerothan flinched at the sound of his sister's body driving into the bark—of flesh parting and bones cracking. He stared at her skewered corpse.

This isn't real. It's just a dream. A nightmare. A mirage, just like the forest that has appeared out of nowhere.

A growl from the wraith tore his gaze off Jalice's mangled body, and he blanched at the blood trickling from its mouth. Jalice's blood. His sister's blood. The wraith's eyes, bottomless and empty of anything resembling mercy or compassion, fixed on Kerothan as its tongue trailed between the razor teeth to lick at the globs trickling off its porcelain skin. A voice glided through the air towards him with a serene beauty that defied the gore and havoc the wraith had committed.

"So, this is what it means to have a shell. This is the taste of real blood."

CHAPTER 48

Kerothan stood there staring up at the wraith as time marched by. Cephus was yelling at him, but the words weren't registering. All he could hear was Jalice's last words to him.

"You came to save me."

Too many emotions tumbled inside him. He was vaguely aware of how these very same emotions seemed to be breaking away from him as threads of electrifying light. Those that brushed against the blade of his sheathed sword sent a charged glow through the glass, and the fingers that gripped at the hilt tingled with these pulsations. But all of this came as a distant realization, and even when Cephus took Ophim out of Kerothan's arms, he could not muster a response. All he could do was stare up at the abomination that hovered high above them, unsure if the carnage he'd beheld could be understood as truth and reality.

He wanted to look back to Jalice, but only for confirmation that her corpse was indeed skewered on a tree branch. That she was indeed dead. But another part of him refused. Perhaps if he didn't look, then it would remain untrue. Perhaps, like the forest, this was all a trick of the twisters. He didn't have to accept it as real.

The ear-piercing shriek decided for him. He jerked his head to behold his sister. Blood lathered the branch impaling her, its tip splintering out of her chest like a mountain rising from the earth. Her arms and legs hung out limply, her head hugging one shoulder at an odd angle.

But whereas her body proclaimed the absolution of death, her mouth gaped open to permit a horrific sound that seemed unnatural to the lungs of any human. Her lips stretched far too wide, and Kerothan wondered if their edges might crack and split under the siege of the shriek. He watched her eyes, convinced that they would snap open, but they never did.

Instead, the squelch of flesh catching on bark temporarily interrupted her screech as her body lifted upward and off the branch in a spectral flight. Kerothan held his breath, unable to move or speak or cry out as he watched Jalice's body float towards what could only be the dokojin Aruzz had called Spiracy. The wraith grinned at the performance with a knowing look that told Kerothan that what would follow would haunt him until his own death.

Spiracy lifted a hand up in front of her face, curled it into a fist. A lone finger sprang up to create the universal symbol for quiet. Kerothan should not have been able to hear the sound that graced the wraith's parted lips. Not from this distance. Nevertheless, he heard the coarse exhalation of air as it grated through the rows of teeth.

"Shhh . . ."

Jalice's shriek broke off abruptly. Kerothan exhaled in relief, hopeful that whatever horrific curse the wraith had cast over her was gone. He wasn't prepared when Jalice exploded in a spray of red particles, wasn't prepared to witness his sister meet a second death that obliterated her broken body. Kerothan cried out, his eyes darting between every miniscule remnant of his sister as the blood-colored dust floated down into the treetops.

He had time enough to choke on another lungful of air, time enough to look at the wraith and notice how it now traced the journey of Cephus and Ophim as they made their way to the chamber's exit—a look that warned him of its intention to attack. Adrenaline surged through him, shattering the trance of paralyzing shock. If only he could have known of the danger in time to save his sister. If only he hadn't been so selfish. But he wouldn't let the same happen again.

Especially not to Ophim.

As the wraith arched back to propel itself down at his clanhead and fellow clannite, Kerothan let out a cry of rage and unsheathed his sword, slicing the blade forward in an upward arc. He had no idea what would happen. He'd never tried such a tactic, but the vaguest inkling of a truth and the odd vibrations in the air drove his instincts. In the back of his mind, a conversation replayed in a sequence that defied the current passage of time.

The conversation had occurred over the breadth of minutes but now split into segments that flashed through him at once.

Rejiett had explained the glass wands. Had explained how wielding aether was a matter of convincing the mind of that ability. The idea didn't seem so abstract now. In this moment, as the overwhelming guilt over his sister's death and the rage for the attacking wraith charged through his veins and scourged his mind, it seemed only natural to push those emotions into the aether at his fingertips. The energy was there, waiting inside his blade to be unleashed at his behest.

The blade came to a skyward point, and he funneled his guilt and rage through the glass. The aether unleashed, splintering the air with a stream of energy. The room lit with a rain of vibrant colors that illuminated the trees, the metal walls, and the odd cocoons that infested the ceiling.

The wraith didn't expect the attack. It howled as much from shock as from agony when the aether collided with it and sent it sailing backwards. Kerothan didn't cease his command over the aether until the wraith had tumbled far enough to strike the farthest wall of the chamber. He watched it crash downward out of sight beneath the treetops, and only then did he bring his sword down and relax his muscles. The blade no longer glowed, absent of any aether, and the room had returned to the dim, shadowy veil of before.

A bittersweetness washed over him. The aether attack had taken something from him. In a cathartic release, the energy had harvested his emotional onslaught and journeyed it away, leaving him both relieved and upset. Grief bubbled up where rage had once resided. He had no control over the tears that ran down his cheeks, and had it not been for Cephus shouting his name, he would have collapsed there and then onto the ground to sob.

"Kerothan, Ophim needs you."

Those words buoyed his strength and pushed down his bereavement, if only for a time. He gripped his sword and sprinted towards his clannites—but halted as he beheld the blood-lathered branch that had so briefly hosted his sister's corpse.

Kerothan inhaled sharply, his breath fluttering through his nostrils as he struggled to keep his composure. A barrage of memories teetering between pleasant and torturous flooded him. He recalled every moment of their childhood, every shared laugh. He couldn't stop, either, the wave of other recollections, such as her betrayal that had nearly cost him his life, or every moment of pain that had followed as a result of her naivete.

All of it, leading to this. Him standing under a mountain of his own guilt, and not even a body to mark her departure from his life.

Before absolute despair could drown him, he took flight and scrambled over the fallen tree trunk and past the haunted branch. He didn't look back. His sprint took him through the patches of forest that had grown through the metal tiles and rocky walls. Cephus waited for him in the opening that led into the corridor, with Ophim propped limply against the moss-covered tile wall.

"You run ahead and clear a path for us if need be," said Cephus.

Kerothan nodded, but before he moved past them into the corridor, a chorus of hoots sounded from beyond the foliage that surrounded them. Other sounds filtered through, ones that had gone unheeded as he'd interacted with the wraith. Now, all he could hear were the human screams that slithered through the trees and the ecstatic clicks and hoots that he attributed to something inhuman. "What's happening in there?" he asked. "What's making all that noise?"

"We don't have time to discuss that," Cephus urged. "Get us out of here, clannite."

Kerothan darted into the corridor. He glanced back periodically to ensure the other two still followed. When he reached the end of the corridor and came out into the massive space at its other end, he halted. Panic reared up in him. He had no idea where to go, and a sea of darkness stretched out before him. Cephus and Ophim hobbled up behind him a moment later, and he still hadn't figured out their route.

"We have a problem," he told his clanhead. "I have no idea how to get us back to the lift. Aruzz took us in such a roundabout way . . ."

"Dying stars," Cephus swore. "Those things are going to catch up if we don't keep moving."

A sound like bone scraping on metal came from the other end of the corridor. They all turned to see a crude silhouette standing in the chamber they'd just left. A shiver ran down Kerothan's spine. The foliage in the other chamber blocked most of the yellow light, permitting him only the barest of details. Though standing on two legs, the figure looked anything but human. Its arms were too long, and one of its shoulders was set too high above its head. A guttural shriek blasted as the figure broke into a mad dash towards them.

"Direction no longer matters," Cephus exclaimed. "Just run!"

Kerothan let his companions pass and postured himself defensively in the corridor's opening. He clenched the hilt of his sword as the shadowy figure crashed down the length of the passage. It didn't run like a human either, and that unnerved him more than any twister ever had. He knew how to fight an aethertwister. He had no idea what to expect from whatever now charged at him.

The creature breached the passage and leapt at him with animalistic strength. He dodged the attack, though he felt the slimy touch of his attacker as it managed to slip its hands across his forearm. He let out a sound of disgust and flailed his arm to liberate some of the fluid before returning both hands to his weapon. The creature was already circling him, and he tried to glimpse it better in the faint light that bled from the corridor.

It was human, and yet it wasn't. He could make out the shape of a head, but its translucent skin and lack of features struck him as embryonic in nature. Whatever it was that now stalked him, it surely wasn't a twister or human of any sort.

As if to taunt him for this conclusion, the creature croaked out a voice that nearly disarmed him.

"You came to save me."

The words were interjected with gurgles, a crude and choppy mimic of their original utterance, and yet Kerothan could swear it was Jalice's voice. He flinched when the creature said it again. And again.

"You came to save me. You came to save me!"

Kerothan screamed in defiance, willing the words to stop. Perhaps encouraged by how disquieted he now was, the creature chose this moment to pounce. He was ready though. He drove his sword upward in a pinnacle strike that skewered the creature mid-leap. The collision brought him down with its descent, but unlike him, the creature remained motionless on the ground afterwards. He searched its face for a moment, willing it reveal how it had spoken with Jalice's voice, but only a mangled, half-formed deformity stared back at him. More hoots sounded at the far end of the corridor. Kerothan didn't turn to look after he ripped his sword free of the creature. He leapt off in the direction he'd seen Cephus dart, hoping to glimpse the glowing sword of his clanhead somewhere in the shadows. The light from the corridor didn't reach far.

He caught the barest hint of light peeking from around a pile of abandoned scrap metal. To his relief, Cephus crouched behind it with sword in hand. Ophim was on the ground, his back against a giant contraption that could only belong to a bygone era.

"You're right, we need to move," Kerothan said between heavy breaths. "There's more of those things coming." He didn't mention what the creature had said. Or the voice it had somehow spoken with.

"We still don't know a way out," said Cephus. A cough struck him suddenly, and he sputtered into the sleeve of his shirt. He raised his head to Kerothan, a look of concern in his eyes at the unexpected symptom. "Ophim is too delirious right now to offer much help either."

"But there's a chance he might know of a streamlined path," Kerothan pointed out. "Maybe we hide away until he's recovered."

"Recovered how?" Cephus stated, his voice coming out in a wheeze as if something were caught in his throat. "We have no healer supplies, and he's got multiple puncture wounds on top of the ones from the kykaleech. He won't survive down here."

"He only needs to be lucid enough to tell us the way out," said Kerothan. "What other choice do we have?"

Cephus looked back at him, mirroring the same dismay that Kerothan felt. He cleared his throat before saying, "We hide. But one of us needs to scout the area in hope that we can find a way out. It's not just Ophim who won't survive forever down here. We have no food, no water. We have only one mask to share amongst the three of us. We're on a timetable that is not in our favor."

Kerothan understood the dire nature of their circumstances, and he wasn't going to argue further. Cephus was right. They had mere days to survive down here in these desolate ruins, and if he was interpreting the abrupt onset of coughs plaguing Cephus correctly, it wouldn't be long before the poisonous air made permanent residence in their lungs. But it didn't make sense for all three of them to wander around and get lost while being hunted.

"We find a safe place out of range of those creatures, and away from that wraith," said Kerothan, even as he hoped the sinister specter wouldn't recover from his attack. It had taken quite a hit from his blade's aether. Maybe he'd slain the dokojin. But he knew better than to count on it. "As soon as we pick a spot, I'll do the first exploration."

Cephus nodded and was quiet for a second, hesitating over his next words. "Your sister . . ."

The guilt and shame returned. "Was any of that real back there? Why are there dokojin amongst us? Maybe this is all a trick . . ."

Cephus's answer came out rushed and jilted, as if he didn't want to speak the words leaving his lips. "I don't think this is a trick. I saw the twisters fall prey to those creatures back there. They're real. And if they're real, then I think that means the wraith is too."

His words ended there, but there was an unspoken implication that followed. If the wraith was real, then so was Jalice's death. Kerothan swallowed and suppressed the swarm of emotions that bumbled about in his chest and constricted his throat. "This isn't the time to grieve. In due time."

"In due time," Cephus repeated, bestowing upon him a look of pity mixed with admiration. His face lit up suddenly. "If the wraith is here in our Realm, what must that mean about the mirajin in the Temple? Perhaps they have returned with an answer as to how to stop this disaster of dokojin we now face. If we can get to the surface, we can warn everyone else and have the mirajin dispel the wraith and those creatures."

As the three moved again to find a safer place to hide away, Kerothan couldn't shake the emotions that had resurfaced with the reminder of Jalice's death. The scene replayed in his mind again and again.

He'd recall her hope and relief upon seeing him only for the wraith to come crashing in to ensnare her in its jaws. He'd replay her descent through the air until she landed, skewered on the tree branch. Here, his mind would snag, fixated by the mess of snapped bones and torn flesh, unwilling for a moment to progress to what had occurred next. Then, as if compelled by a twisted sense of duty to see the memory to its end, the imagery would lurch on to show Jalice's ascent, her body's macabre answer to Spiracy's silent call before finally combusting at the mere whisper of the wraith.

If only he'd thought to save her. Maybe then, Jalice's hope at seeing him might have been justified. If he'd looked for her first instead of Ophim . . . If he'd cared even a little to search for her . . .

"You came to save me."

Those words would haunt him until his dying breath, whether that would be in a few days down here in this forsaken place or years from now. He'd gotten what he'd wished for.

The Tecalica was dead.

EPILOGUE

Pain greeted Annilasia before sight or sound seeped through, searing numerous areas of her body. She moaned as a burning rolled through her leg, and she clutched at it, then moved her hands to her chest where another stark pain flared. A shushing sound responded to her noises, and then a hushed voice.

"Quiet, or they'll hear."

She peered through slit eyes, wincing. Hydrim's grime-covered face hovered over her. Even with the layer of dried ichor, she could make out the curves of skin ink swirling across his face. He glanced up from her and looked toward a faint light that bathed his features. She followed his gaze to find the mouth of the cave they were apparently in several yards away.

"Where in the bleak abyss are we?" she asked between clenched teeth.

Hydrim grimaced and waved his hands at her. The same black film that was smeared over his face also covered his arms and bare chest, adding a darker layer to his brown skin. He lowered his voice to a whisper. "Stop talking. We're hidden. Too many."

"What are we hiding from?" she demanded. Another ripple of fire coursed through her leg, and she hissed.

The sound made Hydrim cringe. "Quiet. Or we die. Or, actually, we get gobbled up here, and then there." An unsettling, distant look leapt across his face and a wild smile lit up his lips. "Dokojin eat twice now!"

Her hand shot out and she gripped his wrist. "Answer my questions, or I'm going to force you into noises you couldn't dream of making."

Hydrim crouched down beside her while still watching the cave's entrance, looking like a malnourished critter frightful of the predators outside. "Machine is on now. The Realms are united. The dokojin run amongst us." The same wild smile returned, and he let out a few wheezy, hoarse chuckles. He paused, and his lips moved, but no sound came at first. He finally added, "The dokojin. Can't hide now. Maybe for a bit." His eyes flickered towards the cave entrance. "Maybe just a little while. Then they chase. And then we try to run." He shook his head, grinning like a child who thought their joke too funny to finish. "We try—" The smile suddenly vanished; his eyes swirled with a new thought, and then he looked to Annilasia with a suppressed excitement. "Have you seen my Jalice? I keep looking for her. Where is my Jalice?"

The way he said it, with delusion underlying each word, made Annilasia's every hair stand on end. She didn't respond, instead retracing his babbling words to see if she could find any clue as to what was happening. *Jalice. Dokojin. Run amongst us.* She stiffened. The dokojin were in the Terrestrial Realm. No one was safe now, not even the Eastern tribes. Only desolation waited for them all. She ran her hands across her clothes. "Where's my cloak? And where in Sahruum's ass is my wand?"

"Sticky acid on your cloak. Had to take it off of you."

Annilasia glowered at him, then recalled what had preceded their fall from the platform: she had grabbed hold of Hydrim and earned an acidic ichor bath. She grabbed at him again now, finding that the dried crust of ichor covering him no longer ate at her gloves. "Where in the deep abyss is my wand?"

A look of unease settled on Hydrim's face. Annilasia stared up at him, finally realizing how intent he was being at looking everywhere but at her. She craned her neck and spotted the wand behind him on a flat piece of stone, the light from outside bouncing off its elegant surface. "Give it to me," she barked. "Unless you want to take on a dokojin by yourself with no help? At least one of us should be armed, and I don't think you know how to wield a wand."

Hydrim hesitated but crumbled under her harsh glare. He turned and went to retrieve the weapon. Annilasia noticed his nude state and made a point not to look down past his waist. She cringed at the organic husk plastered to his back and the flimsy cord that protruded from its center to dangle down between his legs. She let out a noise of revulsion. "Why haven't you removed that?"

Hydrim swiveled around to face her, wand in hand, and looked to her in confusion. Realization dawned, and his face went from confused to surprised to vivid embarrassment. Self-disgust wrinkled his expression, and he avoided her eyes when he extended the wand out to her.

"It's stuck to me," he said in a shamed, whimpering tone. "I can't … it's too …"

Annilasia snatched the wand from his hand, wanting to waste no time in ridding herself of the pain in her leg. There was hardly any aether left, and she wondered if perhaps she'd be better off saving it for a possible dokojin attack. But she wouldn't be much use if she couldn't walk.

She pointed the tip of the wand down at her leg and funneled a surge of irritation through the glass. She wasn't at all surprised when Hydrim let out a shriek and tumbled over right as the pain left her, gripping his own leg in the same place hers had been injured.

"What did you do to me?"

Annilasia stood and wobbled a bit when her limp remained. Old wounds were harder to banish than newer ones, and it seemed the limp was here to stay. At least her leg wasn't broken anywhere though. She gestured at Hydrim to get his attention.

"Your turn to be quiet."

"What did you do?" he whimpered again. "How did you—"

"Better for the prisoner to be wounded rather than the captor," she stated. She gazed towards the light pouring in from the outside world. "Now, you said there were hundreds of them?"

Between sharp gasps and whimpers, he managed to speak, sounding like a whiney child who'd been disciplined with harsh strikes. "You didn't have to do that. I wasn't going to hurt you."

"I can't promise the same to you, obviously." She glanced at his leg and sneered. "You didn't expect me to stay incapacitated, did you?"

He glared up at her. "Where is my Jalice? She's kind to me. I need to see her …"

Nausea rolled through her at the raw display of obsession gripping him. She again refused to acknowledge his pestering inquiries and asked, "Where exactly are we?"

"Cave. Under the Decayer. Had to drag you in here after our tumble."

"So, we're inside the Bokivti Mountains," she clarified. "Does that mean you saw dokojin near the ruins?"

He nodded, face still quivering from the pain she'd bestowed upon him. His eyes grew wide as he recounted what he'd seen. "The land is crawling with them. Dardajah . . ." He trailed off at the mention of his previous master. "It spoke to them. So much shrieking . . ."

Annilasia slumped against a nearby rock jutting from the ground. "Dying stars, I would be stranded with the damn Sachem with an army of dokojin surrounding us." She spat on the ground, then noticed he was shivering in his nakedness.

He blushed under her scrutiny and drew his legs in, wincing at the pain from the wound she'd transferred to him. His teeth chattered between speaking, and he huddled in even more before asking, in his irritating whine, "Why did you save me?"

Annilasia arched an eyebrow. "You obviously don't know me very well anymore. Too busy enslaving and slaughtering innocent people to pay attention to childhood friends."

Hydrim's expression fell, and tears welled in his eyes. "That wasn't me. You have to believe—"

She cut him off. "Stop. If you value your comfort, or what little you have as a pathetic wounded imbecile, then you'll stop speaking. I'm the wrong person to complain to." She crouched to his eye level and reveled in how he craned his face away in a poor attempt to escape her. His eyes remained fixed on her despite his obvious fear.

"I'll tell you why I saved your miserable excuse for existence," she said. "I couldn't defeat your parasitic friend up there. Wasted too much aether on my own problems. So, I did the next best thing. I dragged you out so I could squeeze out every last secret you have so that I can win next time." She raised a finger and wiggled it back and forth. "And don't mistake prudence for mercy. As soon as I'm done with you—and you'll know exactly when that is—I'm going to make you pay, very slowly, for every crime you committed as the Sachem. If you're lucky, you might actually die at some point in that process." She straightened back up to loom over him. He lowered his eyes, hid his face in his arms, and sobbed.

"I want Jalice," he wailed. "Where is my Jalice?"

Annilasia's stomach clenched in disgust. Her lips curled into a snarl, and she kicked him in the side. This elicited a sharp yelp, and he stopped his wails for the Tecalica. "Yes, that's enough of that," she growled. "Let's talk about something else, shall we? Hydrim, friend of the dokojin, what can you tell me about Dardajah?"

But even as he answered, her attention was stolen by a whisper that spiraled from the depths of the cave, slinking through the stalagmites and crevices until it burrowed into her ears like a leech taking root in skin. Her hand shot out to silence Hydrim, who obeyed with an instant silence. She stared into the darkness that led deeper into the mountain.

"Did you hear that?"

"Hear what?" he asked timidly, sounding unsure of what exactly Annilasia expected of him.

She strained to listen in the silence, and when long seconds stretched on without interruption, she wondered if she'd imagined the sound—or rather, the word spoken at her. A name that she'd hoped to never hear again. Just as she was about to turn back to Hydrim and resume her interrogation, the slithering whisper came at her again, and she had to force herself not to tremble. In that moment, Annilasia understood her personal nightmare wasn't gone. Her victory back at the coven had been nothing but a farce, a temporary reprieve from a parasite that would never let her escape until she was crushed into an oblivious state of nonexistence. Careful avoidance of translation would not save her now. The Sachem—or rather, Dardajah—had made sure of that. Her adversary was here, in her Realm.

A voice, a howl, a dungeon of terrorized souls clamoring to speak as one, bled out of the tunnel's abyss.

"Bloodspill . . ."

If you enjoyed this book, please consider leaving a review
on Goodreads and/or wherever you placed the order. Reviews help readers
find new reads and they help authors reach new readers.
By leaving a review, you help spread the word!

ACKNOWLEDGMENTS

Writing this story didn't come as easy as I anticipated it would. The global events of 2020 made it difficult to tap into the creative flow that writers and artists pursue, and I know that I wasn't alone in that struggle. A sequel also comes with its own set of insecurities that I had never experienced before. Needless to say, it wasn't a smooth process, and I can honestly say that if it weren't for the individuals I'm about to list, I probably would have pushed this off for a while.

First, I want to express my gratitude to my partner, David. He endured my daily worries and put up with my unfounded stresses. Anytime I mentioned giving up, he'd either roll his eyes at my temporary cowardice or calmly state that giving up simply wasn't an option. Were it not for his patience and his willingness to put up with my writerly woes, this story would never have been finished. Not only was he a pillar of encouragement during the writing of this novel, but he also provided a sense of security during this last year of turmoil.

To my readers, I want to express my deepest gratitude for your loyalty and enthusiasm. Since the launch of my first book, I've received generous reviews, social media posts and tags, and even fan art. You have no idea how much those mean to me, and how they helped me on the many days when I struggled with imposter syndrome or felt like giving up. Without you, this timid author would be writing only for himself without the courage to share his work with the world.

Next, I want to thank those who helped with the process of turning this story into an actual product for others to enjoy:

Thank you to my beta readers, who read the unpolished draft of this story pre-editing, and helped validate the elements of this story that worked well, while also providing feedback and critiques that addressed confusing portions or pesky inconsistencies. Beta readers add that extra layer of feedback that help a story morph into the product that the public can better enjoy in its final form.

Samantha Zaboski, thank you again for diving into this dark world I've created and polishing it. If it weren't for editors like you, authors would be giving readers only the crude frame of a story complicated by typos, poor grammar, and incoherent storylines. I am grateful for the magic you perform on these books and for agreeing to work on this series with me.

Thanks to the talented cover designers, George Cotronis and Natasha MacKenzie. George imbued the e-book covers with a mix of abstract fantasy and sci-fi that certainly fits the style of the story, and Natasha created print covers that I could place on my bookshelves with a sense of pride. Both of you applied my notes and critiques flawlessly, and I appreciate your patience with me in my quest to have the best covers possible.

Thank you to Paul Palmer-Edwards for agreeing to create the interior files for this series. Although covers are what draw a reader in, it's the story inside that keeps them, and as such, I appreciate the meticulous layout you provided to frame my story.

Finally, I want to thank Daniël Hasenbos for creating the map of this story's world. You took the crude sketches I provided and turned them into the glorious masterpiece that appears at the front of this novel. My readers will no doubt appreciate having that map as I drag the characters from one location to the next.

In closing, I say thanks once more to those listed above and to those whom I have overlooked. Each of you has influenced the words that make up this story. Without you, there would be no book titled *The Spawn of Spiracy*.

ABOUT THE AUTHOR

Enthralled by the magic that written stories contain, Jesse Nolan Bailey has always wanted to be an author. With his debut fantasy series, *A DISASTER OF DOKOJIN*, released to the masses, he can now feel validated in his growing sense of imposter syndrome. He lives in Durham, North Carolina, where he has embraced the equally-gratifying lifework of hosting a trio of spoiled cats and two mini-aussies.

Author website: jessenolanbailey.com

Twitter: @jesseNbailey

Email: jessenolanbailey@gmail.com

THE ATROCITIES OF ANNILASIA

COMING WINTER 2022

The Sachem has turned on the Decayer Device. Mimics and dokojin infest the land, bringing chaos and blood.

Many flee to safer lands, but Kerothan can no longer run from his past. Spiracy alone poses too great of a threat to ignore. He resolves to find a way to contain the evil unleashed, but doing so will force him into questionable allegiances and risky plans.

Elsewhere, Annilasia tracks down the Nekazrin Deck. With the power imbued in these aether cards, she believes herself powerful enough to face any threat. Yet with each desperate attempt to eradicate the dokojin, Annilasia evolves further into the very wickedness she seeks to conquer.

As the lands fall victim to the dokojin, it is only a matter of time until nothing is left but waste and destruction...

...unless someone can stop them.

CPSIA information can be obtained
at www.ICGtesting.com
Printed in the USA
LVHW011055051121
702532LV00019B/1400